CHILDREN OF DARKNESS

DANIELLE THOMAS

CHILDREN OF DARKNESS

MACMILLAN
LONDON

First published 1992 by
MACMILLAN LONDON LIMITED
a division of Pan Macmillan Publishers Limited
Cavaye Place London SW10 9PG
and Basingstoke

Associated companies in Auckland, Budapest, Dublin,
Gaborone, Harare, Hong Kong, Kampala, Kuala Lumpur,
Lagos, Madras, Manzini, Melbourne, Mexico City, Nairobi,
New York, Singapore, Sydney, Tokyo and Windhoek
Reprinted 1992
ISBN 0-333-56555-X

A CIP catalogue record for this book is available from
the British Library

Typeset by Pan Macmillan Production Limited
Printed by Mackays of Chatham plc, Chatham, Kent

For my husband Wilbur Smith
who has filled my life with love and laughter
and
for my parents Jim Thomas and Bess Clack
with love

PROLOGUE

T HE blue police badges painted on the doors proclaimed
the authority of the daffodil-yellow van which bullied
its way down the Blue Route freeway and through
the tightly packed lanes of home-going traffic. 'Get off the
white line,' Stan le Roux roared at the driver of a green Mini
hugging the centre of the road. 'You're not doing a drunken
driver's test.'

Richard cringed as his red-haired sergeant mouthed obscenities at the commuters, who gave way reluctantly to the police
car as it forged ahead to where the bunched-up cars had
become inextricably tangled. An old fish-tailed car, its grey
body leprous with rust, was welded to a scarlet Ferrari which
it had smeared against the metal guard railings.

The cold north-westerly winds which rage over this southern
tip of Africa had crowded the clouds, dark with rain, up
against the mountains guarding the vineyards of Constantia.
The bruised clouds broke and icy rain blinded the burly
sergeant and his driver as they slithered towards the scene
of the accident.

Richard Dalton hung well back. He watched Stan squeeze
his massive frame into the front of the rusted vehicle to examine
the black driver draped over the wheel. He shuddered as Stan
lifted the dark head and studied the face, gingerly touching the
torn flesh studded with glass. Dismissing the dead body with a
shrug, Stan picked up a grey leather Filofax lying on the seat
beside the well-dressed young man. He eased an envelope from
the back pocket of the book, stamping it red with his bloody
fingerprints.

His forehead folded into deep creases as he studied the
name on the envelope. It was his own. 'Damn,' he whispered.
'Another one.'

The letters were neatly cut from magazines and pasted on
to the paper. It looked identical to the missive he had received

1

a few weeks previously, which had taxed and frustrated the finest brains in the police force and the CID.

He looked at the dead man, noting the tight curls cut close to the scalp, the well-formed features and high intelligent forehead, marred only by a jagged scar above one ear. Shaking his head he pocketed the notebook. The enigma would have to wait.

He wiped the blood from his hands on the grey paintwork, beckoned to the shivering youngster and splashed his way to the Ferrari.

Reluctantly Richard followed him and climbed on to the red bonnet. Impaled into the leather seat by the steering column was a short, muscular man. He cradled the dark head of a young boy on his shoulder. The child's eyes were closed and he seemed merely to be asleep.

The officer eased his broad shoulders through the shattered windscreen and tried to move the sturdy little body away from the man, but the child was wedged firmly behind the crumpled dashboard. Instinctively the man's fingers tightened on the boy's head. For a moment he opened his eyes and pain like branding irons smoked the blue of his eyes and they glazed. Slowly his head sank and his bloodless lips touched the child's curls.

Grunting, Stan beckoned his driver. Richard, wishing desperately that they could wait until the ambulances arrived, crawled acrosss the slippery bonnet to join him. 'We shouldn't move them,' cautioned Richard as Stan tugged the man's body from behind the wheel.

'Guy's dead. We have to get the kid out,' wheezed Stan, pushing the man through the windscreen. 'Here, take him.'

Gingerly Richard cushioned the body in his arms and placed a shaking hand beneath the flaxen hair to support the lolling head. His fingers sank deep into warm tissue. He doubled up over the body, gagging, the man cocooned in his arms. The wind whipped tendrils of yellow saliva from Richard's mouth and cobwebbed the front of his tunic.

Stan's eyes glinted and narrowed as he looked at his driver huddled miserably in the mud. He turned his attention back to the child. With the man's body no longer blocking the seat he was able to slide the boy from behind the dashboard and lift him through the windscreen. Tenderly he stroked the child's dark curls, wondering why the little face with a mole high on the cheek seemed familiar. He crooned softly to the boy as he clambered down from the sports car.

As he ran for shelter to the police van, he heard, sweet as angels' trumpets, the sirens of approaching ambulances.

CHAPTER

1

TONI BALSER shivered involuntarily as she stepped out of the steaming bath. She had revelled in the hot perfumed water, lying motionless until the tips of her fingers were wrinkled and white. Dead man's fingers, they had called them at the boarding school where she spent most of her childhood.

Reaching for a fluffy white towel, she scrubbed at her legs and stomach, steamed to the bright pink of a freshly boiled prawn. Silently she bemoaned the extra inches, a testimony to the large quantities of avocado pear sandwiches, luscious green and yellow flesh nestling between thick slabs of buttered bread, and the endless selection of chocolate bars which she had started consuming before the birth of her son Timothy three years ago. Peering at herself through the swirls of steam which misted the mirror, she decided that a strict diet was no longer merely desirable but necessary.

The blurred image reflected in the glass would have gladdened the heart and eye of Renoir. She was voluptuous, her skin smooth and glowing, usually tanned to a honey-brown, was now a winter's pale ivory and olive. Her breasts were firm and large enough to fill a man's hand comfortably, her rounded hips and thighs made a mockery of the painfully thin unisex figures which were the mode. Tendrils of shoulder-length dark hair – she had pinned the rest on top of her head – clung damply to the long graceful neck, and her slender wrists and ankles would have been the envy of many a Victorian lady, in that era when exposed flesh was at a premium and a well-turned ankle was an important asset.

Toni tugged at the curls irritably, trying to smooth them

4

down, but they bounced back from between the tortoise-shell teeth of the comb and danced about her face. Leaning forward, she cleaned part of the mirror with a corner of the towel and her face came into focus with startling clarity. She studied it carefully for a few moments, searching for any wrinkles which would signpost the end of her twenties, before reaching for the bottle of body lotion.

Her eyes, bluer than robins' eggs, were much too large, she thought, and she endured them as a stigma. Her school years had resounded to cries of 'Why are your eyes so big, Grandmama?', 'All the better to see you with', followed by peals of cruel, childish laughter. It had surprised her once she left school that people, men particularly, considered her eyes to be one of her most attractive features.

'I may in time forget you, but your eyes, never. They haunt me.' One of her boyfriends at university had said that, and she had hugged the words to herself. He had been an inventive young man, her classical scholar. He had called her *ma petite coquette*, explaining that the small black mole high on her cheekbone was a sign of a lady who enjoyed flirting but wished to have no serious relationship. Toni smiled, massaging cream into her thighs as these thoughts drifted like wisps of smoke across her mind. The mirror clouded with steam again, obscuring her high cheekbones and laughing mouth.

Carefully she flicked at a blob of cream on the silk thicket covering her plump pudenda. Unable to remove it, she rubbed it into her warm flesh, the rhythmic movement awakening prickles of desire. Guiltily she wiped the lotion off her fingers on the towel, her Irish grandmother's words coming back to haunt her. 'If you touch yourself there, or if you let anyone else touch you, you'll go mad and they'll lock you up in a cage just like the monkey at the tennis club, and everyone will laugh at you.'

The caged monkey had terrified her as it responded to her early overtures of friendship and gifts of fruit by hurling itself against the bars screeching maniacally, its large saliva-flecked teeth bared and its eyes hard with hatred. For years she had walked past the sad, maddened animal with averted eyes. Grandma's warning had rooted itself firmly in her young mind, and kept all fingers away.

5

Tossing the damp towel into the linen basket, Toni pulled a woollen nightdress over her head as she ran lightly from the warmth of the bathroom to the large chrome and black-leather bed which dominated the glass-walled bedroom. She burrowed beneath the white blankets, suffering the cold sheets stoically, and lay motionless.

Outside, the winter wind shrieked and whooped like a daredevil skier as it schussed down from the heights of Devil's Peak and wedeled arrogantly through the forests of pine which carpeted the mountain slopes. Missing a few turns, it threw up clouds of leaves and twigs as it raced past the houses at the foot of the mountain, knocking off roof tiles and flattening fences, bleeding off speed slightly to herringbone up the side of Wynberg Hill before its final raging run across the vineyards of Constantia.

Toni curled up tightly and listened to the rampaging wind. As the heat of her body gradually warmed the clammy sheets she wriggled her toes gingerly and tucked another pillow under her head. The untidy tower of books on her bedside table tottered precariously as she selected one from the bottom. Books were her refuge and her painkillers, helping her to endure the many nights and weekends she spent alone in the modern glass and chrome house. They effaced the mental pictures of her handsome husband Serge, wining and dining the slim blonde beauties who surrounded him like the links on the gold identity bracelet he wore, badges of his success as a business tycoon. The advertising agencies, the large import–export companies he had set up to break international sanctions against his country, and the secret exporting of illegal ivory and rhino horn were all very profitable. They allowed him complete freedom from office hours and time to devote to the young women who came to the cities searching for love and marriage and, failing to find either, finally accepted the fleeting warmth of copulation.

Her slender fingers riffled through the pages and soon she was lost in the world of words.

Her concentration was broken by the clamour of the telephone which could no longer be ignored. Impatiently she leaned across the table to lift the phone, the book sliding from her knees to lie spreadeagled on the pale birchwood

6

floor. 'Damn. Who can this be at nearly eleven o'clock at night?' she muttered as she hung over the edge of the bed, the blood rushing to her head, the book just out of reach of her fingers.

'Hello,' she snapped.

'Hello, my honey,' answered a deep voice, the European accent giving a foreign lilt to the words. 'Why does my sweet one sound so angry? Is it because I'm not at home? Believe me, my hon, I would love to be in our bed, and have you in my arms, but I had a business meeting which only ended late and . . .'

Toni listened as Serge's warm voice soothed, caressed and lied to her, and she longed for the early years in their marriage when she had been able to trust and believe him. She had idolised her charming husband, and still tried hard to rationalise his deceit, hoping that they could recapture the love and closeness they had once enjoyed. She knew that in his strange way he still loved her and Timothy.

'Toni?' Serge queried. 'Toni, why don't you answer me? What are you doing?'

Biting back a sharp retort, Toni breathed deeply. 'I've dropped my book on the floor and am trying to pick it up, Serge. Where are you?'

'So, tonight you are not typing one of your articles for the newspapers. You are with your books, your many children, I think.' His laughter rang loudly over the phone. 'Well, put your children to bed and dress in something beautiful. We'll be up at the house in about fifteen minutes.'

During the six years they had been married, Toni had learned great self-control; she had learned to answer silently, giving herself the satisfaction of venting her feelings without bearing the consequences. Charming as Serge was, it took only a few ill-chosen words to cause him to fly into one of his terrifying rages, which were followed by an even more soul-destroying period of silence. This was the most fiendish form of mental torture, perfected by a master craftsman. After four to five days of complete silence with all attempts at conversation ignored and all overtures greeted with silent scorn, even the strongest would beg for forgiveness, and the innocent plead guilty.

7

'Who's coming up? Where are you? Do you know it's eleven o'clock?' Toni asked quietly.

'Yes, yes, now don't be difficult.' Serge's voice, no longer placatory, was momentarily drowned by raucous shouts and laughter in the background. 'We're all at the Congo man's place, but we can't have drinks here. He's locked the house keys and his car key in the car, and he's been taken to hospital.'

'What's locking his keys in the car got to do with his being taken to hospital?' asked Toni, exasperation hardening her words. The Congo man was a large, muscular ex-mercenary who had fought in most of the bloody wars on the African continent and was discovering that a soldier without a war was like an eagle in a duckpond: incongruous and miserable. He earned his beers at the local pub by allowing the weak, the weary and the wicked, who seemed to make up the bulk of the clientele, to smash their fists into his stomach and stub out cigarettes on his arms. The drinks won by these antics were beginning to soften the outlines of a once rock-hard body, and the formerly feared soldier was becoming a figure of fun. Toni sensed a hidden pride and gentleness in the man. She liked and pitied him.

'He put his fist through the car window and cut an artery,' explained Serge, 'but he'll be up at our place later. See you soon, honey. Get that fat maid of yours out of bed and tell her to make a fire in the sitting room. It's freezing out here.'

Toni stared at the cream telephone, and her knuckles were white as she slammed it down. 'Damn him, damn him, damn him. I'm damned if I'll wake Izuba to make a fire at this time of night.' She swung her legs out of bed, her flesh pimpling in the cold. 'Something beautiful, indeed,' she snorted.

She picked up the creased black jersey slacks and roll-neck sweater which she had discarded before her bath. Pulling on the crumpled clothes and wriggling her bare toes into black ballet slippers, she padded outside to the woodpile and swore as she stumbled over a log in the dark.

'Damn you, Serge Balser,' she muttered as she rubbed her knee. 'You and your women and your drunken friends.' She staggered back to the sitting room and each log thrown into the fireplace was her husband.

The wood was damp and her reddened eyes were still smarting as the first of the cars thundered up the long gravel driveway, wheels spinning and hooters blaring. Dusting pieces of oak bark and flecks of sawdust from her black sweater, she went to open the front door.

Within minutes, the sitting room was filled with colour and movement, the patterns changing constantly as some of Serge's guests threw fresh oak logs on to the fire, and others reeled in, laden with crates of beer and huge gallon jars of red and white wine. A few sat on the floor and sorted through the CDs, flooding the room with rock music. Toni, a forced smile on her face, moved through the crowd greeting friends, acquaintances and strangers. Serge collected people. Silence and solitude bored him. He was a creature of the modern age. He enjoyed the discordant wailing of rock singers, the gyrations of sweat-drenched bodies, their flesh dyed carmine, emerald and violet by epileptic discothèque lights, and the conversation of inebriated friends in bars fetid with cigarette smoke.

'Hey, folks, we're to witness another strong man act tonight, yes?' The grating, guttural voice of Hans Wold, Serge's closest friend and confidant, rang out across the room. 'Serge's going to show our tough Congo man how to open a glass door. I think he too wants to have a needle in his bum and a bandaged arm, yes?' He roared with drunken laughter and pointed at the enormous glass sliding doors which separated the lounge from the tiled patio.

Toni disliked Hans Wold, and when he was drunk her distaste increased. Everything about him annoyed her. His resemblance to Hitler, the lank hair flopping across his forehead. His calculating small, grey eyes and thin-lipped mouth. The way he ended most sentences with the word 'yes?' His gloating glances at her when he and Serge had spent the night carousing. His treatment of the women Serge found for him, bedding them and describing the fornication in minute detail to anyone who would listen. He repulsed her. His touch reminded her of a jellyfish which she had once trodden on, the broken translucent fragments squelching and sucking into the wet sand.

Yet her husband and Hans had been close friends since their

9

university days. Hans was the perfect sycophant, lavish with praise and slavish in devotion. Serge had enticed him away from a lucrative job with a leading design studio in Salzburg to head his top advertising company in the Cape.

The only thing which impressed Toni about Hans was his knowledge of music. It must have been a wrench for him to leave the city where all great musicians and orchestras congregate, and she fervently wished that he had remained there. She tolerated him only to please Serge.

She sighed and looked across the sitting room to where Hans was pointing. Serge, standing outside, his blond hair wet and plastered to his scalp, his square jaw firmly set, was pitting the strength of his short muscular body against the wooden doorframes in a vain attempt to slide them open. Behind him, laughing, stood a tall slim man, seemingly oblivious of the driving wind and rain, his face lost in the shadows.

'Tell him the doors are jammed because of the rain, Boots,' Toni shouted at the corpulent man standing in front of the huge glass sheet, warm in the comfort of the room, miming encouragement to Serge. 'They'll have to go around to the front door. It's open.'

Boots nodded in reply, drained his can of beer, and bellowed Toni's instructions through the crack between the doors. The wind was buffeting the walls of glass alarmingly, and the leaping flames in the fireplace were reflected in wavering washes of yellow and gold, causing the figures outside to tremble and dance.

Irritable and bored at the prospect of yet another drunken party, Toni did not at first hear what the wispy blonde, eyelashes fluttering and protruding front teeth causing a permanent pout, was saying.

'Isn't it him, Toni? Hey, Toni, are you listening? It's him, isn't it?' queried Baby Botha, the vapid wife of Boots, who, bloated belly straining the buttons of his mauve shirt, had picked up a fresh beer and was belching his way to the front door to greet the two men.

'Who?' asked Toni wearily, seating herself on the edge of the grey marble-topped coffee table. 'Who is who?'

'That man out there with Serge. I'm sure it's Nicholas Houghton,' she lisped in her breathless, little girl's voice.

'You know who I mean – that sexy guy who's always on telly and writes about saving animals and birds, and pollution and funny things like that. He has the cutest bum. I never listen to what he says. I just watch him.' For once Baby had caught and held Toni's attention.

Nicholas Houghton. The name electrified her. A few months ago whilst Serge was on one of his many business trips overseas she had taken her son Timothy to celebrate his third birthday with her father in Botswana. James Joseph Swayne adored his only grandchild but was becoming increasingly reluctant to leave his thatched cottage on the banks of the Okavango river. After four decades spent battling in the political arena and striding along the corridors of power in the magnificent but sad country which lies at the foot of the great continent of Africa, he had found his Eden.

It was here, one sun-baked midday when only the cicadas broke the hot silence with their monotonous drone, that Toni had first found and opened the slim red volume entitled WHY? by Nicholas Houghton. She knew that his name was a household word in Africa for his work on wildlife and conservation, and she now read on the dust jacket that he had an honours degree in entomology, headed some of the most important committees on conservation and wildlife management, and was a roving consultant to a giant chemical conglomerate. He seemed to hold down a dozen important jobs in the interests of ecology.

Whilst doing research for her newspaper and magazine articles she had heard that he spearheaded forays into delicate government preserves and secret business transactions with scant regard for consequences to himself. He was called a madman by the people whose egos he had bruised and whose schemes he had nullified, but he was idolised by those concerned with the preservation of the planet.

She also knew that he was paid handsomely by television producers and newspaper editors, as his appearances and articles were always controversial, but she had been unaware that he wrote poetry.

His poems of love ached with a deep underlying sadness, reflecting her broken dreams and deteriorating relationship with Serge, and as she read them tears ran down her cheeks

11

and plopped on to her dusty khaki shirt. She had found a man who sang her silent songs, and when she returned to the Cape the red book was in her suitcase.

'It must be him, Toni,' Baby Botha continued, shaking Toni's arm, her long silver fingernails digging into the black wool. 'He was on telly last week. They called him a firebrand crusader. I remembered those words, they sounded so clever, a crusader for ecology. He was talking about those big black buck in Angola. He said that the Cubans, and the dummies who run the government, are shooting them to feed the soldiers and if they weren't stopped the buck would become extinct.'

'Giant black sable,' Toni said, moving her arm away from Baby's plucking fingers.

Baby twirled her fine blonde hair around her finger hoping that Toni wasn't going to spoil the evening by making her concentrate on animals, pollution or politics. 'You know so much about animals and things, Toni,' she gushed. 'It must be all the years you have worked for the newspapers.' Then, fearful that Toni was about to describe the sable, she quickly changed the subject.

'Gee, he was so good-looking on TV,' she said. 'I think he's dreamy, even if he says weird things like all sprays must be taken off the market. Imagine not having any hairspray. That's crazy. Anyway, he could still put his shoes under my bed any . . . ' She broke off in breathless confusion as Serge approached them, the dark stranger in tow.

'Toni, honey.' Serge bent down unsteadily to embrace her. 'I see we didn't give you enough time to change,' he said, eyeing the black slacks and sweater disdainfully, 'and I've been boasting to Nicholas about my beautiful wife.'

'With very good reason, Serge,' said Nicholas Houghton, his voice warm and deep as a Zambezi pool. He stepped forward and took Toni's hand in his. 'I am enchanted to meet you, Mrs Balser. It is, indeed, a pleasure to meet the lady who writes with such feeling about Africa and its people.'

Toni glowed with pleasure. She had not expected one so elevated in the wildlife hierarchy to have read her articles. He had the aura of strength and authority which encircles successful men and she smiled as she looked up into his eyes, the green and grey blended like the early morning mists. His

12

heavy horn-rimmed glasses could not hide the sparkle as he studied her, and his lips which brushed her hand lightly were full and beautifully shaped.

Serge bristled at the attention being paid to his wife. He disliked the public acclaim Toni was receiving. The quiet, shy young girl he had married had blossomed into a competent reporter whose liberal stance on politics and conservation differed vastly from his own. Her articles on ivory poaching were fuelling public outrage and endangering his clandestine operations.

'Toni will do,' he said brusquely. 'She's a good wife, but she should stop grubbing around the back streets looking for stories. It's not a job for a mother.' He patted her on the head.

Toni fumed silently, keeping her expression neutral. 'You, Serge Balser, know that I hate assignments which take me away from Timothy, and you also know that he loves staying with Helen and is damn well looked after.'

'Come,' said Serge, turning away from Toni. 'Let's find you a drink. I'm soaked on the outside and dry on the inside. Aha, that's a good one, hey?' He slapped Nicholas on the back and led him away to where a group of men were paying homage to a diminishing stack of beer cans.

'Wow, he's even better looking than he was on telly,' babbled Baby, fluffing up her blonde curls. 'I love men who have those long creases down their cheeks when they smile and black eyebrows which almost meet. Don't you, Toni?'

'You just love men, Baby,' answered Toni, watching the two figures walk away. Nicholas was a good head and shoulders taller than Serge and he walked with the easy loose-limbed stride of an outdoors man.

'Did you see the size of his shoes, Toni?' whispered Baby. 'You know what they say about guys with big feet – they're also supposed to have huge . . . '

'Why don't you go and talk to Boots? Look who's with him,' said Toni, cutting Baby short. It was a masterly stroke. Baby's eyes widened as she recognised the hulking Springbok rugby player. In a country which had forsaken the Commonwealth, thus depriving the people of a time share in the British royal family, the public lavished most of their attention and adoration on the rugby fraternity.

13

'I'll join them,' lisped Baby as she stood up, tugging at her sweater. The white angora wool barely restrained her swelling breasts, the silver and pink sequinned butterflies embroidered on the front quivered and bounced as she teetered away on her high-heeled shoes, and her buttocks beneath the tightly stretched pale rose slacks jiggled like two mounds of pink blancmange. Toni watched her leave with a sigh of relief.

Serge invited the Bothas to all of his parties and Toni found them as acceptable as a large dose of castor oil. They epitomised the narrow-minded, self-righteous, small section of the population whom she regularly crucified in her columns. People whose forebears had left Holland to settle in the Cape over three hundred years earlier, and whose Calvinistic traits were still much in evidence. Members of their Calvinistic church had governed the country for almost half a century, and they still believed sincerely that God had meant different races to live separately. The mesmeric oratory of the leader of the new conservative right wing party and his policy of returning to racial discrimination attracted them strongly, even though it was a policy which could be likened to the use of flint implements in an age of microchips and lasers.

Toni spent most of her working days arguing with these people about politics and politicians. They felt betrayed by the government their fathers had helped to put into power. It had gone soft. All the good old laws which gave preferential treatment to their kind had been abolished. Toni knew that they were afraid because the government was negotiating with the blacks. Soon there would be a black president and they would share power. Their government was dealing with former terrorists in the African National Congress. The fact that early presidents-general of the ANC were clergymen, lawyers and teachers, and the government's reassurances that these were men committed to peaceful reform meant nothing to them. Toni's explanations that in the future men would be judged not by their colour but by their capabilities, and that mass education would do away with insensate political violence only added to their confusion.

Boots Botha and Serge had been drinking buddies for years. Serge enjoyed the coarse humour of the barrel-bellied ex-rugby forward and had offered him a job in one of his companies.

14

Boots had soon proved his worth, knowing instinctively which palms would close over silver and which eyes could be blinded to false cargo certificates. There was less pilfering in the warehouses under his control as his famous boot still swung out, savagely bruising many a black backside.

When Serge queried the complaints from his staff, Boots strongly defended his methods of persuasion. When Serge examined the profit and loss accounts for the company under Boots' crude control, the healthy figures in black stifled any further enquiries into the methods he used, and their friendship strengthened.

'I've brought you a whisky. I noticed that your glass was empty.' The deep voice startled Toni. She had been watching Baby and Boots and had not noticed Nicholas settling down cross-legged on the silk Qom at her feet.

'Why, thank you. That was most thoughtful of you, Mr Houghton,' she said.

'Nick. Please call me Nick,' he replied, handing her the tumbler. He raised his glass and inclined it gently towards her. She noticed his nails were clean and clipped short, and his hands were slender yet strong. 'Always study a man's hands,' her old granny had cautioned. 'They're a dead giveaway. Dirty torn nails show a mean and dirty mind.'

'To you,' he smiled, and suddenly Toni felt happy, light-hearted and young.

'Thank you.' She sipped her drink and smiled back at him.

The noise in the lounge had increased to a deafening roar. The bodies twisting to the hard pounding beat of the music and backlit by the flames in the large open fireplace writhed like creatures in an inferno. Nicholas and Toni were oblivious to the uproar. With the instant rapport of old friends with shared interests they flitted from subject to subject, happily exploring each other's minds and worlds. Nicholas had just returned to the Cape with an overseas television team from war-torn Angola, and Toni was eager to learn if they had seen any Giant black sable.

'No,' he replied. 'I spoke to one of the last game scouts to leave the reserve and he says that the Giant black has been wiped out.'

'Oh, no,' whispered Toni, and as she closed her eyes a picture of the giant antelope, as she had last seen him, filled her vision. His skin a burnished black satin, his great horns sweeping in a breathtaking curve to touch his back, his huge liquid eyes anxiously watching his females and young as they cantered for cover in response to his snorts.

'So it's true,' she said. 'Those wonderful reserves are now mass cemeteries.'

'Yes,' he answered quietly. 'It's been a massacre of animals sanctioned by the government. A massacre by army machine-guns.'

'The short-sighted idiots,' muttered Toni.

'Armies march on their bellies, Toni,' reasoned Nick. 'The country's economy has collapsed, chaos rules, and hungry men see no sense in preserving animals when there are no tourists paying to look at them or hunters paying for trophies.'

'You're right,' said Toni bitterly. 'It's the story of Africa. The wildlife which makes our continent unique has to die so that men can play power politics.' She sighed. 'Can nothing be done to save this wonderful country, Nick?'

He stretched up and put his hand gently over hers, then quickly withdrew it. 'We've thousands of people like you, Toni, people who have a deep love for the country, its people and wildlife, and that's where hope lies.'

'Hope?' she echoed. 'Africa nowadays seems only to listen to the voice of the gun, not to reason. It frightens me.'

Nicholas deftly turned the conversation away from the rape of the country and soon had Toni laughing. To their delight, they discovered that their grandparents had been early pioneers in Northern Rhodesia, when that wild, magnificent country was holding out her hand to the young and hardy, enticing them with enormous salaries to work on the newly opened copper mines. Adventurers poured in and legends were born. Names of the famous and infamous were known to both of them.

'I always feel very privileged to have been born in Northern Rhodesia,' said Nick, 'living on a farm deep in the bush collecting birds' eggs, hunting rabbits and guineafowl with the black kids, our closest neighbours over thirty miles away. It was a magical childhood.'

16

Toni studied Nicholas as he talked. She delighted in the way his mouth curled at one side just before he laughed, in the creases which deepened around his eyes when he smiled, in his dark hair, the first stray, grey hairs highlighted in the firelight. He was a very attractive man.

'Which town has the honour of claiming you as its son?' teased Toni, a dimple deepening in her cheek.

Nick laughed. 'I was born in the swinging town of M'huba and my birth brought instant fame to the one dusty street, local general dealer's store and police station which made up the metropolis.'

'I don't believe it,' said Toni, her dark curls glowing in the soft light. 'I was born in M'huba as well. My grandmother always said that if a child survived the first five years of its life in M'huba, it would overcome anything, and eventually would have to be cemented into its grave to convince it that it had died.'

Nick chuckled. 'Let's drink a toast to two M'huba babies.' They lifted their glasses and smiled at each other. Nick looked at Toni over the rim of his glass, elated that he had allowed Serge to persuade him to join the party. He had met Serge at Congo's house. One of the Congo man's nefarious friends had brought a letter for him from a priest in an isolated mission station in the Central African Republic. The old priest had finally decided to sell him his collection of Cincindellinae, tiger beetles. Nick had been trying to obtain some for years to add to his own enormous Coleoptera collection. Excited, he had raced to Congo's house, arriving just as the ambulance drove the injured man to hospital. Assured that Congo man would be at Serge's party, he had accepted the invitation, determined to have the letter that night. Entranced with Toni, he had noticed neither the Congo man's arrival nor Serge's friends studying them.

'I've never seen Toni pay so much attention to anyone,' burped Boots, as he filled Serge's glass. 'I'd go and break it up if I was you. He's a ladykiller, that one. I can smell randy guys a mile off.'

Serge had noticed and disliked the two dark heads close together, but was not going to give Boots the satisfaction of

17

appearing uneasy about his wife's obvious interest in Nicholas Houghton.

'I don't have to worry about Toni,' snorted Serge. 'I could leave her alone with a naked rugby team and the guys would be safe. She knows where her bread's buttered.'

'Aha,' said Boots, snapping the ring on a fresh can of beer, 'Even the best of wives can use the apple of Eve, and Toni's a good looker. Careful, Serge, careful.'

Serge happily indulged his appetite for beautiful women, but he was jealous and possessive of Toni. Watching her lift her face to Nick's as she laughed in response to something he had said, Serge felt the first burrowings of the fat white slugs of doubt.

Suddenly a shower of sparks cascaded across the room like yellow streamers at a New Year's Eve celebration and Toni scrambled to her feet, dusting herself frantically. She was not quick enough to prevent the hot cinders scorching the wool of her sweater.

'Toni!' exclaimed Nick, his wine spilling on to the silk carpet as he leapt to his feet and put his arm around her, shielding her from further sparks. 'Toni, are you all right?' he asked anxiously.

'Yes, thank you,' she answered ruefully. 'A few burns in my sweater, but it's an old one.' She looked across at the splattering log in the fireplace, and merriment faceted her sapphire eyes.

Hans Wold had thrown the log on to the fire, heedless of the shower of sparks and hot cinders it sprayed across the room, and he was being berated by a woman who was angrily examining the scorch marks on her silk blouse. He cowered before her, surreptitiously wiping the oak dust from his hands.

The group around him melted away, unwilling to witness his humiliation, but Baby and the men lounging around the table laden with drinks in the corner of the room roared with malicious laughter. Looking across at the fireplace, Baby's eyes narrowed thoughtfully as she caught sight of Toni, pressed into the crook of Nick's arm, his dark head bent low over hers. Her lower lip crept away behind her front teeth and she lost interest in the woman yelling at Hans as she studied them.

'She sounds like my wife,' said Nick, listening to the tiny woman verbally whipping Hans.

'Your wife?' whispered Toni. His words ripped apart the fragile web of happiness which had enclosed her.

'Yes,' answered Nick quietly. 'This woman's outburst is a spluttering squib compared to Jade's explosions.' He smiled ruefully. 'Fortunately I travel a great deal and miss most of her temper tantrums. And depressions,' he added.

Toni glanced away. For a sweet while, only they had existed, but Nicholas had a wife and she had Serge. Toni looked quickly around the room. Serge was seated on a cream velvet sofa, deep in conversation with a fashionably thin blonde, her bleached hair a profiterole of curls piled precariously on top of her head, her pointed breasts a few inches away from his chest, her lips kept moist and inviting by her small pink tongue.

He's running true to form, she thought dispiritedly. He'll probably find an excuse to drive her home. Always the perfect gentleman, my husband. Why can't he just love me the way he used to, and stop proving how irresistible he is to other women?

Nick felt the sudden tension in her body and let his arm fall from her shoulders. The tableau on the sofa was momentarily blocked by the magnificent body of a tall imposing woman who, tears streaming down her face, had broken away from the small group standing in front of the CD player. She had the face of a madonna, framed in tumbling waves of hair the flaming red of a setting African sun. Her perfect features had been marred only when her irises, the cool grey of twilight, had been painted. A streak of green had been smeared across one of them, drawing attention away from the glory of her hair and focusing it on her eyes. She was a striking woman. She and Toni had been friends since they were students at university and the friendship had deepened over the years.

Hans Wold, eager to break away from his tormentor, flung out his arm to stop her. 'Now, now, Helen. I'm still here,' he said, his thin greasy hair streaking his forehead.

'You swine,' she sobbed. 'You cold-blooded little swine. How could you tell them?' She ran out of the room, closely followed by a well-built young man, brown eyes cold, his lips pinched and his craggy face white with anger.

19

'Leave her, Clive. She'll get over it,' slurred Hans. The young man swung round and faced him.

'There'll be time for you later,' he hissed. 'I'll make sure of that.' He shouldered his way through the dancing couples and ran after Helen.

'Hans,' demanded Toni, 'what have you done to Helen?'

'Nothing that Clive Markham hasn't done,' smirked Hans as he smoothed his hands suggestively down the front of his pants. 'Clive needed friends to tell him that his beer has had the froth skimmed off by someone else, yes?'

Toni curled her lips in disgust. 'The beast,' she said, turning towards Nick. 'He's a vicious little man.'

'I wonder what attracted her to Hans,' pondered Nick, watching as Hans lewdly described something to the men around him, his hands making obscene gestures.

'Nothing,' said Toni. 'Her mother had just died, and she was lonely and unhappy. Sensing her weakness, he offered comfort.' Toni bit her lip as she watched Hans. 'They say he's tireless, keeps going for hours,' she said bitterly, twirling her empty glass. 'Not the only thing he keeps going for hours. He's a master at the art of monologue.'

As Hans left the fireplace and strutted past them Nick studied his close-set grey eyes, scar-line mouth and tiny curled ears. He turned and looked at Toni. Her eyes were troubled and the colour had changed to that of an angry sea; her square jaw was set and her slender fingers nervously tapped the glass in her hand. He felt a sudden overwhelming tenderness towards her, an uncontrollable urge to hold and comfort her.

'Come, Toni, come and dance with me,' he said. She moved into the warm circle of his arms, felt the soft tweed of his jacket against her cheek and inhaled the aroma of whisky mingled with the clean sharp tang of his aftershave lotion. She moved easily to his rhythm as they danced to the haunting strains of 'Lara's Theme'. Leaning lightly against him, she felt herself relax and the tension melt away.

'Some where, my love,' he sang the words of the theme music in a warm deep voice, resting his cheek softly against her forehead. 'You'll come to me out of the long ago, warm as the wind, soft as the kiss of snow.'

Her silky curls tickled his nose and mouth. She smelt clean

and fresh like a bunch of wildflowers picked after a shower of rain. He moved his hand to the back of her neck, stroking the soft skin. His arms tightened around her, he could feel her strong thighs moving against his and suddenly he wanted her, wanted her desperately. The ache of longing knotted in his belly, and drove into his groin, hardening him. He moved his body away from hers slightly, but his fingers tightened and pressed deeply into her flesh. Sensing the change, Toni lifted her face from his shoulder and looked up at him. She saw the shadows of seriousness replace the laughter in his eyes, and his breath was warm on her face and the smell of him tightened her breathing. She squeezed her eyes tightly closed, trying to turn those few seconds into an eternity. But he merely brushed her curls with his lips and held her head close to his chest, whispering into her hair. She heard only fragments, as the words were muffled by the beating of his heart loud in her ears.

> *. . . and that Hafiz came or Omar to imprison the aroma*
> *In some half-remembered measure which has rhythmed me to you.*

The words were beautiful but she did not recognise them.

> *. . . for I have felt the burden of a passion vague and virgin,*
> *Which you quicken to remembrance of a former life we knew . . .*

His voice was broken and husky as they swayed gently to the plaintive strains of the music.

'What is that poem, Nick?' whispered Toni, her face still pressed to his chest, afraid to move and break the spell. 'It's so lovely.'

Gently he lifted her chin and studied her face. 'An old poem, written by someone who had discovered his love and his soulmate,' he answered, his fingers lightly caressing her cheek. Reluctantly he dropped his hand from her face and held her away from him. 'Toni.' His voice cracked. 'I must leave now. I find that I'm jealous. Jealous of someone I hardly know and who isn't mine, and it's an emotion I dislike.'

'No,' Toni exclaimed involuntarily, reaching up to embrace him, to enfold and keep him with her.

'I can't stay here, holding you in my arms knowing that you belong to someone else.' His eyes searched her face as if memorising every plane and contour. 'You're so lovely, Toni. Meeting you has been very special.' His voice was low. 'Goodbye, little kitten.' He kissed her hand lightly, resting a finger on the tip of her nose, then turned and strode quickly from the sitting room. She wanted to cry out, to run after him, but instead she dug her long fingernails into the palms of her hands until they throbbed and ached. She watched as the headlights of his car flickered across the rain-splattered glass walls of the sitting room and then vanished, leaving only the wind-torn darkness outside.

Her mind accepted his reasoning, but her body rebelled against it. Their attraction for each other had been deep and instantaneous and she cried out silently at the unfairness of losing what she had only just discovered. She knew that they were committed to their separate ways. They had been brought up to observe the morals and rules of society, but she yearned to retain the joy they had shared. Like a child who refuses to believe that Father Christmas is but another adult deception, so Toni refused to accept that their meeting had merely been one of life's bonbons. Lost in unhappiness, she did not notice Baby, her large breasts joggling importantly as she moved towards her.

'You're looking as miserable as a wet cat, Toni. What's wrong?' asked Baby, swaying slightly on her high-heeled silver shoes. 'Is it because the famous Nicholas Houghton has left you and the party?' She grinned knowingly and took a sip of wine, leaving a waxy pink smear on the glass.

'Don't you ever think of anything else, Baby?' asked Toni bitterly as she piled up empty glasses on a tray and started walking towards the kitchen, away from the taunting voice.

'Sometimes,' answered Baby, her protruding front teeth sucking eagerly at her lower lip. 'But I know men. Love 'em and leave 'em is the big boy's motto, and me oh my, he's a real big one that Nick Houghton.' She laughed vulgarly, her fingers worrying the silver charms jingling on her bracelet. 'I bet he's warmed more beds than you've had hot baths.'

Toni did not deign to answer and worked her way towards the kitchen, picking up tumblers and ashtrays overflowing with crushed cigarette butts, a mark of defiance by Serge's friends who believed that they had divine protection against lung cancer. The sound of crunching glass alerted her and she walked quickly in the direction of the noise. Her eyes widened in dismay and her face flushed with anger.

'Are you mad?' she shouted. 'Put that down immediately.'

Placing the tray on the carpet, she ran to where the Congo man, almost senseless from the combination of wine and the local anaesthetic he had received, was slowly and methodically chewing up one of her prized crystal goblets. Seated on the steps leading down to the kitchen was an admiring group, watching him in awe. Gazing at her near-sightedly, he lifted the glass daintily and bit another piece out of it, crunching it as contentedly as a Jersey cow chewing the cud.

'You madman!' shrieked Toni, lunging towards him and snatching away the remains of the glass. 'Spit that out!' He stared at her adoringly, a grin on his blood-speckled lips. 'Spit it out now.' She pinched his ear lobe viciously and held the half-eaten glass up to his mouth. He dribbled the shards of slimy red crystal into it.

'Now take a mouthful of wine, rinse your mouth and spit the rest of the splinters out,' she commanded. He obeyed her as obediently as a loving child and held her hand tightly as she crouched beside him making him rinse his mouth repeatedly until she was certain it was clean. Choosing one of the more sober-looking men in the gathering, she put the Congo man into his care with firm instructions to drive him home and not to return until he had seen him tucked into bed, under the ministrations of his wife.

Shaking with barely suppressed anger and shock, Toni added the broken goblet to her tray and walked in silence past the crestfallen crowd. Pushing open the heavy kitchen door with her hip she swung into the room, almost colliding with Serge who was talking to a stranger dressed in skintight blue denims and a purple checked woollen shirt, the buttons open to his navel. His hairless chest was pallid in the harsh electric light.

'Ah, Toni,' said Serge, his tongue thickened with drink, curling carefully around the words. 'Our friend has had a small accident. Tell the maid to come and clean it up.'

'Izuba is asleep, Serge. It's now three thirty,' said Toni, forcing herself to be calm and reasonable.

23

'I don't care what bloody time it is. My friend needs help,' he snarled. 'Tell her to get her fat arse in here and clean this mess.'

'Serge,' reasoned Toni, 'Izuba has worked late almost every night this month to earn money to pay for her brothers' new clothes and I can't ask her to come in at this time of the morning.'

Serge, furious at having his authority undermined in front of his friends, dug his fingers deep into Toni's shoulder and spun her towards the back door.

'I pay that cow's wages and she'll do as I say and so will you,' he hissed. 'Bloody new clothes! They can buy their own clothes and then maybe your precious maid will be able to keep awake and work when I need her.'

Stung by the unfairness of his attack on Izuba and humiliated by his physical attack on her in front of strangers, Toni dispensed with caution.

'You understand nothing about the Xhosa people or their customs,' she said, 'or you'd know that the family are responsible for replacing all of the boys' belongings when they return from their circumcision school. Izuba has not been working overtime for fun. She's had to make extra money and deserves one night of rest.'

'Customs,' spluttered Serge, mindless of the young man sliding away from them pressed against the tiled wall. 'If they want to work and be part of our society, then they'd better forget their mad witchcraft and customs. There's no place for it. I'll not have such nonsense in my home.' He dropped the cigarette smouldering between his fingers on to the tiled floor. 'Tell her to get here and clean the floor as well. It's filthy,' he sneered. 'Or keep on protecting your beloved maid and clean it yourself.' He hiccuped and laughed, then walked away from her, slamming the door behind him.

Toni breathed deeply, trying to deaden the pounding in her ears, and turned to the young stranger.

'Oh, Mrs Balser,' he stammered, 'I tried to get him to the back door but he couldn't make it.' He swallowed nervously and fingered the stubby hairs on his unshaven chin, 'I'm . . . I'm sorry.' He gestured timidly towards the stainless steel sink at the far end of the narrow gleaming white kitchen.

24

Bent over the sink stacked high with plates and glasses was a bald-headed man, his shoulders heaving convulsively and a fine sheen of sweat coating his freckled pink scalp. Toni's stomach muscles contracted as she neared the sink. The sickly sweet smell of vomit hung heavy in the air.

'Pour a bucket of cold water over him,' she said icily, fighting back the bitter taste of bile forcing its way up to her throat and threatening to flood her mouth. 'I want every piece of crockery washed, and immediately, or I'll rub his face in it, and my maid will not come in to help.'

'Yes, ma'am,' stuttered the youth as he picked up the yellow plastic bucket which was behind the door.

Toni strode past the stinking sink, flung open the back door and stepped outside. She gulped in great draughts of the cold fresh air, and the wind whipped past her, deodorising the kitchen. She hugged herself and shivered, relieved to be alone but alarmed by her angry reaction to the consumption of her crystal goblet and to the scene in the kitchen. These quarrels with Serge were becoming more frequent. She knew that he would not forget the argument, and she would have to pay for her temerity. She had foolishly ignited his anger and an explosion would surely follow.

Blinding white headlights cut a swathe across the red and purple bougainvillaea which spilled down the gravel bank behind the kitchen. Toni looked up at the dark car, its outlines blurred in the rain.

'Nick,' she whispered. 'It's you. You've come back.' She ran lightly to the car, smiling happily, a hairnet of raindrops covering her head.

'Oh, Toni,' said Clive Markham as he unfolded his large frame from the car and ran for shelter beneath the overhang of the roof, 'I'm so glad to see you out here. I need your help.'

It wasn't Nicholas. The flush of adrenalin faded, leaving her sick with disappointment. She licked her lips and swallowed hard.

'What's happened, Clive? Is it Helen?' she asked, the picture of the shattered woman, her Titian hair swinging wildly around her shoulders as she ran from Hans, still vivid in her mind.

'No, it's not,' he answered, his voice cold at the mention of her name.

25

'Clive,' said Toni, putting her hand on his arm and looking up at his set, angry face, 'Helen's a wonderful woman and she loves you.'

He squeezed her hand but ignored her defence of her friend. 'It's the barmaid from the pub. She had too much to drink here and on her way home she drove her car into the ditch outside the British Embassy.'

'Not again,' said Toni shortly. 'That's the third time this month that she's had to be towed home.' Toni had scant sympathy for the woman who ran the local pub. If gossip was to be believed the woman was insatiable and the pub's regulars spent many happy hours proving the rumour to be true.

'I've left Helen with her,' Clive continued. 'She's trying to stop her singing "Eskimo Nell".'

'I doubt whether the Ambassador would approve of that bawdy song at four o'clock in the morning,' giggled Toni. 'You go back to them and try to keep her quiet, and I'll ask Serge and any of his friends who can still stand to come and help you.'

'Thanks, Toni, you're a love,' answered Clive gratefully, giving her a quick kiss on her cold cheek. He ran back to his car, his shoes and trousers splashed with red mud.

There was a general exodus from the sitting room when they heard of Clive's predicament. Baby Botha, her sense of virtuousness and outrage reinforced by too many glasses of red wine, led the way, and Toni paled to think of the scene which would shortly be enacted outside the ambassadorial residence.

In the middle of the sitting room were left a beery bevy of men who had long since given up the effort to stand, and were sprawled in a circle on the carpet around a portable radio listening to a recording of a rugby match.

The commentator's voice, harsh with excitement, rose to a squeaky crescendo and rasped Toni's senses. She had an almost neurotic dislike of rugby, and felt that Sir Thomas Elyot's description of its precursor in the sixteenth century as 'nothying but beastely fury and extreme violence' described the game perfectly four hundred years later.

Boots called to her as she bent over the sofa plumping up cushions and dusting away the dandruff of cigarette ash.

'Toni, have you any more of these?' he asked, licking some

of the crumbs from his lips. 'They say that this was the last packet, but they're all notorious liars.' He held up an empty biscuit packet, his hairy hands crumpling the picture of a gurgling toddler on the front. Toni glanced from the laughing face of the baby to Boots' lips, greasy with saliva and studded with soggy biscuit crumbs.

This evening, her emotions, like old well-worn elastic on a boy's catapult, had been repeatedly stretched to their limit, and now, seeing these drunks dipping the last of Timothy's buttermilk rusks into their beer and slurping up the custardy mess, the finely stretched strands gave way.

'Get out,' she screamed, her voice, an ice-water douche, shaking them out of their alcoholic stupor. 'Get out of my home. You disgust me. Now. Immediately. Get out, out!' The men stared at her stupefied, their mouths slack with disbelief. Serge's tame obedient wife had become a shrieking virago. Boots opened his mouth to protest, but when he saw the revulsion blazing in Toni's eyes, he stumbled to his feet and led the way unsteadily out of the room.

'Dames,' he spat as the front door slammed behind them. 'Only good for two things and I'm not so sure about the second.'

* * *

The grey, swirling cloak of mist was lined with the yellow silk of dawn when Serge's mud-splattered red Ferrari toiled up the driveway. Toni, her eyes kohled with fatigue, opened the door. Her weary smile faded and she swallowed her words of enquiry as he roughly pushed her out of his way and slammed the door behind him.

'So,' he hissed as he tore off his wet coat and threw it in a heap on the floor, 'so my wife has to play Miss Bloody High and Mighty. My friends aren't good enough for you. They're not allowed in my house.' He stumbled over the words, almost incoherent with rage. 'They're thrown out of my house, *my* house, do you hear? Do you understand, this is my bloody house and you're only here because I allow you to stay.' His voice shook with anger and blue veins swelled and throbbed in his temples.

'Please don't shout, Serge. I only— '

'Don't shout! Don't you tell me what to do. Don't try to dictate to me the way you did to my friends.' He loomed over her, his pale blue eyes wide and maddened with fury and shook his finger in her face, the nail scratching the side of her mouth.

'Let me tell you something.' Serge pushed his face close to hers. She ached to wipe away the fine spittle which latticed her skin, but she remained motionless. 'In my house a guest is *the* most important person. You'll entertain them and be polite and charming, just as you were to Mr Bloody Hotshot Houghton – you could fawn and simper over him all right, couldn't you? My friends'll stay until they want to leave, and don't you ever forget that, you sanctimonious little bitch.' His lips were rimmed with white and his eyes bulged as he glared at her.

Hands shaking with anger, he took a crumpled packet of cigarettes from his pocket and tapped it against his hand. He took one letting the others spray out and fall at Toni's feet. She bent down to pick them up and he lashed out with his foot, kicking her hands away.

'Don't touch them!' he shouted, grinding the cigarettes underfoot, the tobacco flakes filtering into the rich pile of the carpet. 'Don't ever touch anything that belongs to me. Ever.' Shakily he lit the cigarette and inhaled deeply.

'Please, Serge. You'll wake Tim,' begged Toni.

'You don't give a damn about him when you're researching stories to get your name in the papers. Then he's dumped with your friend, but now I must whisper.'

'That's not fair and you know it,' cut in Toni angrily. 'He's left with Helen as little as possible. Don't you tell me that I don't care about my son!'

'Wake Timothy!' he continued. 'Nowadays, it's only your bloody son, your bloody, bloody books and that spoilt bloody maid who get your attention. And she'd better be on duty in future when I need her,' he continued, 'or she'll find herself back in the township without a job and with no help for her kids' schooling and clothes.'

Toni struggled to control her anger. She curled her toes in her soft black shoes until they ached. She longed to remind him that the help Izuba and her family received was not from him, but from the articles she sold, yet she knew that when he was spinning in the mad vortex of drink and rage it was wiser to remain mute. She swallowed hard, drowning her words of resentment as she listened to his taunts in silence.

'You can't even put on decent clothes for my friends,' he said derisively. 'Look at yourself. I'm disgusted with you. Not only can't you dress decently, you can't even behave decently. Who the hell do you think you are?'

She stared into his eyes, hard as heads of nails, and she trembled. His words battered at her defences, wounded her pride, and tore down her self-confidence. Assault wave after assault wave washed over her until, bruised and wearied, she crumpled. Once again she apologised, willing to humble herself to end the tirade.

'Serge, I'm sorry,' she said quietly, not allowing her resentment to surface. She clenched her hands to stop them from trembling, the white bone of her knuckles almost bursting from the skin. He had metamorphosed into a malevolent stranger, his eyes glazed with truculence, his face bloodless in anger and his words as sharp as the knives wielded by Somali women, artists at slowly skinning their victims alive.

'Sorry, sorry,' he sneered. He splashed brandy into a tumbler and drained it. Toni edged past him and began walking down the long passage leading to the bedrooms, willing herself to remain calm and not run. She knew that in these drunken confrontations the longer she faced him, the worse his mood became.

'Oh, God,' she breathed, 'don't let him follow me, please, dear God, please.'

'That's right, run away,' he taunted thickly. 'You can't even stay and listen, you bitching weakling.' He watched her for a moment, her head held high and back ramrod stiff within the straitjacket of tension and anger. Picking up the bottle of brandy, he started to follow her, hesitated, shrugged, and walked back into the sitting room.

The fire had died down to the flicker of a few smouldering sticks and the windows, reflecting the cold light of breaking day, shook spasmodically as the wind whipped past them. Sinking into the leather armchair, Serge closed his eyes.

Toni eased open the door of Timothy's room. The plastic Donald Duck, his orange beak split in an eternal grin, swung on its hook, scraping the white paint on the wall. She stepped quietly into her son's bedroom and as the warmth enfolded her and the familiar smell of a small boy's body comforted her, she closed the door and turned the key in the lock, shutting out for a short while the hatred and the violence.

Timothy whimpered in his sleep, stretched out like a sky-diver under the blankets. She stood quietly, willing him not to waken, and as he settled down her shoulders slumped and she slid to the floor, hugging her legs tightly to her body, her chin resting on her knees.

'Why, oh God, why?' she whispered, as her body shook to the music of silent sobs. But tonight she found no warmth or comfort in her prayers and her God seemed far away.

She had too much pride to discuss Serge with her friends, even with Helen, who was closer to her than a sister. She longed to go to Izuba's room and find comfort in her homespun philosophies, but that would be a sign of weakness. To live with Serge she had to be strong.

Nor could she ever burden her father with her problems. He had not been in favour of the marriage and had compared Serge Balser to a zirconia, desirable and sparkling on the surface, but of little real value. 'I'd be uneasy doing business with him, Toni,' the astute old man had remarked. 'There's something behind that smile that chills me.' Toni, deeply in love and deaf to all criticism, had tweaked the white tufts of hair above his ears, kissed him on the forehead and laughed.

'You're an old grouse who doesn't want to lose his daughter. You know that I've a special love for you and nothing will ever change that, so smile and be happy for me.'

Her father had smiled for her, but the trepidation remained.

Timothy sighed and flung out an arm, knocking his fluffy toy kitten on to the floor. The brass bell tinkled and he whimpered in unison, then grunted and was quiet.

Toni lifted her head and her swollen eyes were soft with love as she looked at the little boy. He was the reason she was still with Serge. She quailed at the thought of her son being used as a weapon of war between two adults who had parted and were determined to destroy each other. She had grown up in a home with a hated stepfather and did not want a step-parent to blight her son's childhood.

Timothy's birth had been meant to herald a new beginning. Serge, his manhood assured by the appearance of a son, would once again be the exciting, wonderful man she had married and loved so passionately. He would become a doting father and a loving husband. His stable of long-legged blondes would be put into retirement, his extended overseas business trips would be curtailed, and drunken parties with strangers fouling her home would become a thing of the past. Her longing for a child fulfilled, she would float on clouds of happiness. She would be a perfect wife, a perfect mother and would run a perfect home for her perfect family.

Toni had long since realised that perfection is seldom attained. She dropped her head heavily on to her folded arms and the faint ticking of her wristwatch became a round white clock on the wall at the foot of a bed, in a clinically cold room, ticking away long hours in the labour ward. Hours when her body was ripped and torn with pain, as doctors and nurses tried to dislodge her son from his warm and comfortable waterbed in the womb.

Those dreams of a perfect future with a perfect husband and child, dreams bright as rainbow-splashed soap bubbles urged her to accept the agony.

Time was measured only by a brief respite, a few precious minutes between spasms. Her breathing was rapid and shallow and the child would not be cajoled. The nurses murmured anxiously, the doctor ordered the operating theatre prepared, and plans were made to cut the baby from her exhausted body, but the knife had not been necessary. Her longed-for son had been born but nothing had changed.

Toni remained huddled on the floor, cold and shivering, too steeped in misery to wrap a blanket around herself, and as she listened to Timothy's soft breathing she cried silently over shattered hopes and dead dreams, until the throaty cooing of the plump pigeons in the oak trees outside the nursery window and the lightening of the wet grey sky awakened Timothy.

'Mum, Mum,' he mumbled sleepily, kicking off his blankets and holding out his arms to her. Stiffly Toni stood up and bent over his bed, marvelling that this little boy was hers.

31

She delighted in his porcelain-clear skin, smooth and soft as brushed velvet, in his long dark eyelashes framing large toffee-coloured eyes, the pinprick of a mole on his cheek a miniature replica of her own, in the dimples when he smiled. She adored him, this most precious of all gifts. She kissed him lightly, first on the tip of his nose then on each eyelid, a ritual they never tired of, and he squealed happily. She lifted him up and inhaled the warm smell of his body – it was like burying one's nose in the soft fur of a kitten. Her arms tightened around him and her heart ached.

'Mummy's wet,' said Timothy as he patted her cheek.

Toni hastily brushed away the traces of tears with the back of her hand. 'Yes, my love, it's raining outside. The sky is crying for the sun to come back.'

'Let me see, Mum,' demanded Timothy stretching his hands towards the curtains. She swung the warm, wriggling body on to her hip, and together they stood at the window watching the raindrops splash into the muddy puddles. Pigeons, their feathers ruffled and fanned out, pecked disconsolately at the saturated earth.

CHAPTER

2

S ERGE BALSER forced his half-smoked cigarette through
the pile of butts heaped in the ashtray, and ground it out
irritably on the glass base. The polished surface of the
bedside table was pitted with black scars, bearing eloquent testimony to Dana's annoying habit of standing lighted cigarettes
upright on any available surface, and leaving them to burn into
the wood or plastic while she preened in front of the mirror.

Lying on the rumpled bed watching her apply layer after
layer of colour to her eyelids in her pretty but vacuous face,
he wondered what thoughts, if any, passed through her mind.
Glancing at the triple mirrors on the dressing table, he noticed
with distaste the glass smeared with fingerprints where she had
adjusted the mirrors to facilitate a more minute inspection of
her features.

Her hairbrush was matted with thick blonde hair, and the
formidable array of cosmetic jars offering eternal youth and
beauty were standing uncovered, their expensive contents
filming over and drying out. Another prick of annoyance was
added to the pincushion of his dissatisfaction.

Perhaps Hans is right, he thought as he looked at her
rumpled apricot petticoat lying across the dressing table
stool. Perhaps one should just have them and leave them.
Leave before they have time to enmesh one in their spider's
webs of warm wet bodies and devouring mouths. He could
use Hans's apartment for his amorous assignations as he had
in the past. It overlooked the four beaches of Clifton, famous
for the voluptuous long-limbed brown bodies which chequered
the sparkling white sand, women young and eager to taste the
delights offered by the owners of the luxurious apartments,

33

glass-walled buildings which stood shoulder to shoulder on the steep rocky hillside as if jealously guarding their harvest of golden girls. He smiled as he thought of some of the wild parties they had enjoyed in that beachfront duplex where wine and willing women flowed freely.

Serge's upbringing and training by Swiss parents had imbued him with a desire for order and cleanliness in others. Dana's personal untidiness and slovenly habits had not upset him at the beginning of the affair, when he had considered her but another mistress, not a permanent part of his life. Her uninhibited and wild abandon during lovemaking had excited him and like a heroin addict he had kept returning to the woman who so skilfully administered his fix. Now their affair, constantly spiced with the erotic variations of her fertile mind, had lasted for two years and was gaining the permanence of a marriage.

Yes, Hans was correct. Women are here only for man's pleasure. He would speak to Hans in the morning and start phasing out his relationship with Dana.

'Say, that's a shame,' drawled Dana, returning to the bed and running her pointed fingernails down his flank. She lifted the heavy damp hair away from the nape of her neck. 'Fancy Toni paying so much attention to him in your home, and in front of all your friends.'

'Yes,' snapped Serge, irate at Dana who was worrying at the story of Toni and Nicholas like a terrier tormenting a cornered rat.

He had told her the story because his wounded pride needed soothing. Wives were supposed to remain unobtrusively in the background tending to their husband's every whim and need, not nestle in the arms of handsome men. He had expected to be soothed and petted, but the thought of the perfect wife Toni stepping out of line titillated Dana, and she licked the details like a lollipop, anxious to make it last as long as possible.

Dana, the tall, enviably slim woman lying beside him still sweaty from their recent lovemaking, was a slick product, packaged and exported by America. The Kennedy administration had started this overseas trade, sending their young and idealistic to offer help and spread the message of the great American way of life to all the under-privileged and newly emergent nations of the globe. These guillible youngsters poured into Africa in droves, flooding the market. Their immodest dress – cut-off blue denim shorts and clinging T-shirts – dismayed the black women; their indiscriminate lovemaking delighted the young rural blacks, with whom it soon became a status symbol to have bedded an American girl; their ideas of equality between the sexes angered the black men, whose cultural heritage gave black women no status and privileges at all; their grandiose schemes, which could work only in a highly technological society, not in one where the majority could neither read nor write and where tribal loyalties took precedence over any government, upset the white colonials.

Dana had meandered down through Tanzania, Zambia and Botswana helping to spread the credo of Coca-Cola and chewing gum to the outlying reaches of the dark continent. She loved Africa. The relaxed way of life, warm hospitality and easy friendliness enchanted her, and she finally found her niche in Cape Town, a city tiptoeing into the turbulent meeting place of the great Indian and Atlantic oceans. The unpolluted seas, clean white beaches, hot golden days and easy living all appealed to her. She was still able to indulge her missionary zeal by moving amongst the homeless in the squatter camps which cradled the city like a new moon, a more sophisticated audience than those she had played to in the outlying villages of central Africa.

'Gee, I know it makes you angry, Bunny,' said Dana placatingly, 'but she doesn't usually do that sort of thing, does she?' She walked her fingers up and down his side, her nails tattooing a rhythm of pain. 'You often say that you don't worry about her finding out about us because she's always busy at home, especially now that she has the child.' She ran her moist fleshy tongue up his neck, her breathing heavy in his ear. Serge pulled away from her under the pretence of lighting another cigarette. 'I've seen his picture in the newspapers, he's quite a famous guy, that Nicholas Houghton, good-looking too, but a bit serious. Is he serious, Bunny?' she said in a throaty voice, running her finger down the crease of his buttocks as he bent over to shield the flame of his lighter.

'When are you going to stop calling me Bunny?' said Serge irritably. 'You know I don't like the silly name.'

Dana laughed. 'You're just like a rabbit, always ready. It suits you.' She flattened herself across the bed and nipped his rounded buttock with her strong, white teeth.

Serge winced and dropped his lighter.

'It's probably Houghton's interest in conservation that attracted Toni to him,' Dana mused, releasing Serge's buttock. 'She writes about the poaching of ivory and the desecration of wildlife in her newspaper articles, doesn't she? Actually her columns are quite good.'

Dana rambled on and failed to see the look of annoyance which flushed Serge's face. His pale eyebrows drew together and the fine lips which she had delighted in running her tongue over a few minutes before tightened into a straight line.

'Funny, isn't it, Bunny – you think you know someone so well and then they go and fall for the proverbial tall, dark and handsome heartbreaker.'

'She didn't fall for him, Dana. She merely danced with him,' retorted Serge, drawing draughts of smoke deep into his lungs.

'Danced and spent all night talking to him, Bunny, all night,' reminded Dana.

Abruptly Serge swung out of bed. He had to leave the flat. It was becoming claustrophobic and Dana's words were beating on his brain like drumsticks wielded by a mad drummer. He had never indulged himself by having a tantrum in front of Dana; he saved those rages to use on people who were bound to him by family or business ties. With her, as with his other mistresses and people he wished to impress, the ranting Mr Hyde vanished and the likeable, suave Dr Jekyll emerged. This was in danger of changing, and he bit back the angry words as he strode across the room to where they had thrown their clothes as they laughingly undressed each other, the sparkling wine they had enjoyed with their lunch making them giggle like schoolchildren.

'What are you doing?' wailed Dana sitting up, her large breasts swinging.

'Dressing, Dana, dressing,' answered Serge, the muscles in his legs contracted as he nestled his genitalia into the snug sling of his underpants.

'But we were going to our Chinese restaurant tonight,'

moaned Dana. 'It's her, isn't it? You're going back home because of her.' Dana plucked nervously at the frill on the blue pillowslip. 'You never used to worry about the time, you always said that she'd wait, but now you're scared, some other bull is circling your corral.' She watched him pull his trousers up over his taut buttocks and zip up the front, the expensive cloth resting lightly on his strong thighs. 'Oh, Bunny, don't go,' she pleaded. 'It doesn't mean anything. He probably does this all the time. It's part of being famous like the movie stars, they're always kissing and cuddling and hopping in and out of every one's beds. It means as little as going to the toilet to them, and I'm sure he's the same,' reasoned Dana. 'Come over here, Bunny, please,' she pleaded holding out her arms to him.

Serge buckled his belt and forced himself to smile and walk over to sit on the edge of the bed. Looking at the fine blonde hairs which were starting to line her upper lip, his resolve to talk to Hans about the use of his flat hardened.

Suddenly, sensing the coldness and anger in him, she leaned towards him and cradled his face in her strong hands and drew his head down to hers. As his breath quickened she ran her hands skilfully over him, easing off his shirt and trousers, her fingers changing his rage into fierce desire. Drawing the hairy hardness of his body down on to hers she smiled contentedly. Later she lay stroking his hair wet with perspiration, as he blew softly on her nipples and watched them pucker. Looking down at his fair head resting on her breasts, she sighed happily. Once again Serge was hers.

* * *

Serge was feeling good. He whistled as they locked the door of Dana's flat and ran up the stairs to the roof where he had parked his Ferrari. It was an excellent place to park the distinctive red car as the chances of Toni or any of her friends seeing it were minimal. Toni. He grinned when he thought of the expression on her face when she had seen and remarked on the Yale key on his keyring.

Laughingly, he had explained that it was the key to his mistress's flat, knowing that she would never believe that he would blatantly carry it with his car keys. This was a favourite theory of his, and one which he expounded at length to his cronies in the cosy confines of their local pub. 'Always tell them the truth. They never believe it.' It never failed. He believed that she trusted him completely, and that was how it should be. Wives should love their husbands unreservedly, leaving the husbands to pursue their private pleasures in peace.

The Chinese waiter bobbed greetings as he seated Serge and Dana at their favourite table overlooking the sea.

'Oh,' breathed Dana, 'the sea's all silver.' She put her hand over Serge's. 'The ships' lights look like fireflies caught in a moonbeam.'

He smiled at her, his earlier irritation forgotten. She might be untidy but she was an attractive companion and he enjoyed the attention she commanded when they entered a restaurant.

'To you.' He lifted his glass.

'To us,' she answered and ran her tongue around her lips.

'This smells good,' said Serge as the waiter heaped dishes laden with sweet and sour pork, mounds of fried rice and great black Chinese mushrooms on to their table.

'Oh, yes,' he said as he munched the black mushrooms contentedly, 'these blacks are good.' Then, looking across the table at Dana, he smiled impishly. 'But not as good as your blacks in the townships. According to you they're all perfect.'

She saw no humour in his weak joke. Her mood changed; her lips tightened and she became defensive, adopting what he called a liberal drawing room stance. Born in Europe, Serge found it difficult to understand the black conception of Western democracy; to him it seemed as if the newly independent countries of Africa had merely adopted a sophisticated form of tribal dominance.

'You are talking like a racist again,' she said. 'As long as you're wealthy and comfortable, you couldn't care about those living in plastic and tin shacks. You don't give a damn about the humiliation and degradation they've suffered. You think that all you have to do now is say sorry about the past, and everything will be perfect.'

'Right,' said Serge, angered by her sudden animosity. 'One can't change the past, but one can sure as hell learn from it.' He kept his voice low and gripped her wrist across the table. 'You and your kind are building up expectations in the young, the majority of whom are semi-literate and believe you. You tell them that all they need is the vote to give them fine homes and cars. They anticipate a golden future and are dissatisfied and become violent when the expected glories are not immediately available. You, by trying to be kind, are being unbelievably cruel.'

'I'm being cruel,' she said stabbing at a mushroom with her fork. 'In my squatter camps there are thousands of people who for decades have known only bigotry and could see only a future of darkness for their children. If I can bring hope to a few of them I will, and don't you dare call me cruel.'

Serge leaned towards her, his face close to hers, his light blue eyes serious. 'Oh, Dana, your naïvety appals me. You understand so little.'

'Well,' interjected Dana, 'you'd better get used to my so called naïvety, Bunny, because our child is going to be brought up with my principles, not yours.'

Serge's face froze, expressionless as a granite sphinx. He stared at her, noting how the candlelight turned her bleached hair to spun gold, how the strapless white dress accentuated her figure and how her glossy lips had just opened and closed over words which could ruin his life. Only a pulse throbbing in his temple gave any sign that he had heard. Dana stared back at him, two figures turned to silent stone.

No, she screamed silently, it was not meant to be like this. It was going to be so wonderful, the most wonderful moment of my life. Why did I allow myself to get into this argument?

She pressed her hands flat on her stomach and beseeched him wordlessly to understand. She had planned the evening so carefully, the new dress, the wonderful Chinese meal. Finally, walking along the beach, the sand painted silver in the moonlight, she would tell him that she was to be the mother of his child, an exquisite blonde daughter. She had played this scene so often since she had received the positive result of the pregnancy test, and each time Serge had greeted her news by enfolding her in his strong arms and telling her that he loved her, and that they would start a new and wonderful life together as man and wife.

'Serge,' she whispered, 'Bunny, please say something.'

39

Ignoring her, he summoned the waiter. 'Bring the bill, please. The lady's not feeling well.'

'I am very sorry, sir. Perhaps a pot of jasmine tea would be good? I'll— '

'The bill,' snapped Serge. 'Now!' Looking at Serge's impassive face and compressed lips, the little Chinese waiter bobbed away, leaving a trail of apologies behind him.

Serge had not spoken on the way home, and Dana leaned against her front door and watched the red tail-lights of his car blend and fade into the stream of traffic. His parting words hung in the heavy sea spray and swirled around her.

'There can be no child. I'll contact you tomorrow.'

* * *

The stars were paling by the time Serge gunned his sports car down the road winding along the foot of the flat-topped mountain which loomed majestically over the city, wedged in by the thundering oceans on either side.

Serge was oblivious of the mountain, known by astronomers in this modern Age of Aquarius to be one of the great magnetic points of the planet Earth. He had spent hours seated in the dark car digesting Dana's unpalatable news and had finally reached a decision. He would deal with the matter the following day. His thoughts now raced ahead of the car and concentrated on his home, nestling in a peninsula which is one of the largest and most magnificent wildflower gardens in the world.

Serge Balser was a proud man. People bested by him in business referred to him as cynical and exploitative, discarded mistresses as manipulative and faithless, and his wife, knew him to be a charming hedonist and feared his deviant behaviour. He was extremely proud of his possessions, his magnificent home on the slopes of Table Mountain, and of the woman who ran it. He had chosen well; Toni was a good wife and he loved her. He did not love the numerous women he bedded, so he did not consider the liaisons to be infidelities.

He flicked the ash from his cigarette and drummed his fingertips on the leather-covered steering wheel, beating time to the music from the car's stereo. Toni suited him perfectly.

She was always at home when he arrived, always had dinner prepared for him, and sat at the table, even if it was three o'clock in the morning. Saved him a fortune by planning the garden, and doing the interior decorating of the house herself. He could have afforded the best in advisors, but enjoyed making her economise. Thrift was a virtue to be practised by others.

She never complained, though she was inclined to be a little unreasonable about the lipstick stains on his shirts. He had to invent a series of drunk women who stumbled over him in bars, smearing his shirt while he was attempting to help them. She entertained his friends well, whether she liked them or not.

He stopped drumming his fingers, remembering the scene a week ago when Toni had screamed at his friends and thrown them out of his house. It was the first time she had ever behaved in this manner. He had not spoken to her since and her pale face and pleading glances had been cool, soothing ointments to his scratched pride.

She was a good mother, perhaps a little too firm and methodical, but good; she was doing a wonderful job of raising his son. He did not see very much of him, but that was fine – small children should be seen occasionally and not heard. He tossed his cigarette out of the window and the wind twirled it away in glowing circles.

He was proud of having fathered a son but it was time that she gave him a daughter. He had always wanted a daughter, a pretty blonde girl to show off to his friends and to spoil. He wondered why she had not fallen pregnant; he had been certain after Timothy's birth she would conceive easily. A thorough inspection of her cupboard drawers and the medicine chest in the bathroom had revealed no trace of contraceptive pills and she had assured him that she had not had an intra-uterine device fitted. He shuddered when he thought of the two years before Tim's birth. Years when his life was ruled by thermometers, phone calls which had him rushing home to copulate at prescribed times, temperature charts, and visits to the hospital. He had no wish to repeat that performance.

Changing gears smoothly, he pulled away as the traffic lights changed to green and turned off the main road into the avenue lined with oaks, now sporting only a few tattered leaves, which wound towards his house.

Timothy had finally been conceived on holiday. His pulse quickened as he thought of those Tahitian island girls who had given themselves to him so freely, sleek as otters as they swam and cavorted in the crystal-clear waters, their waist-length black hair curling around their naked bodies like drifting seaweed. Toni had relaxed in the islands. Maybe that was what she needed now – another holiday and then a daughter.

Pressing his foot hard on the accelerator, Serge screeched up the driveway. He would mention the holiday to Toni now, and they could start working towards his daughter immediately. She was always compliant after one of his silent periods, ready to meet any of his desires and permit any of his excesses.

His blood raced as he slammed the door of the Ferrari and let himself into the silent house.

CHAPTER

3

THE whisky gleamed like liquid amber in the crystal tumblers. Taking one of the glasses Nicholas Houghton filled it with apple juice. The pale green liquid swirled as it blended with the golden whisky.

'It's a sin to do this to good whisky, Jade,' he said as he crossed the room and handed the drink to his wife, who was still seated at the baize-covered bridge table which had been set up beneath the mullioned windows overlooking the rose garden. The fat buds on the bushes were still tightly closed, giving no hint of the breathtaking display of perfumed colour which would soon unfold. 'The Scots would have you in the stocks for abusing their "water of life".'

Jade crossed her legs, the fashionably short black skirt rucking up over her freckled white thighs. Her breasts were pushed high by the tightly wired bra, creasing and folding the flesh into the cleavage. Her green and black spotted silk blouse was unbuttoned to the bra line, and as she moved to pick up the glass the silk slid away uncovering her breasts. Taking a puff of the thin black cigarillo, she left it hanging loosely in the corner of her mouth, knowing well that her habit of talking with a cigarette between her lips infuriated him.

'You're only paying for it, darling, not drinking it, so shut up,' she answered, slurring the words slightly. She had lost at cards consistently all afternoon and, as usual, losing had put her into a foul mood. She gulped a mouthful of her drink and glared at him belligerently from behind a cloud of smoke.

She was still irritated over the last hand of bridge they had played; winning the final rubber had been well within their grasp but Nicholas had thrown it away. She had made a forcing call and he had failed to respond, leaving her in the wrong suit. Nicholas was an excellent bridge partner but his mind had not been on the game and she was furious at having lost two rubbers to inferior players.

Studying her as he moved away from the card table, he wondered what had happened to the witty fun-living divorcee he had married. He had been a university graduate with a Ph.D. in entomology, about to embark on an important job with one of the major chemical companies when he met her. He had been impressed by the advertising executive who used with flair the glib and amusing throwaway remarks which were the hallmark of her trade. The laughing woman with a quirky sense of humour offered an easy camaraderie as well as expertise in bed and he was fascinated by her.

'You're looking particularly beautiful and sexy this evening, my sweet,' he said, as he bent over and held a lighted match to the hissing gas in the fireplace. The small flames tasted the artificial coals and he saw once again leaping flames hungrily consuming oak logs in another fireplace, the warm light flickering across a glossy head of curls, and huge blue eyes filled with happiness as they gazed up at him, the mouth dancing with laughter.

The sharp pain of naked flame scorching his flesh snapped him out of his reverie and he hurriedly flicked out the match. Sucking his finger he folded himself into the chair beside the fireplace.

'Your legs look very good in that short skirt,' he continued. Nick had discovered over the years that constant references to his wife's obvious and well-displayed charms mollified her and usually averted one of her neurotic screaming rages, during which words and household utensils were hurled at him with equal abandon.

Raising an eyebrow at him and curling her upper lip, her sharp pink tongue licking at the corners of her large mouth, Jade turned to the man slumped in the other armchair.

'Boots, darling, let's dance, let's make sweet music together. Put on something slow, something we hardly have to move to.'

Nick sighed and wished that he had never encountered Boots and Baby Botha at Serge Balser's party. Boots had

44

followed up the meeting with a phone call claiming friendship and reminding Nick that they had been at university
together.

Nick had been hard pressed to remember Boots, and to
cover his embarrassment had invited them to his home to
play bridge, an addiction of Jade's. She, like many bridge
players, was fanatical about winning. Twice that afternoon
he had infuriated her. Once he had overtrumped a trick she
had already won, and then he had failed to respond to her
forcing call. The game had dragged on interminably, and the
soft wash of afternoon sunshine had given way to long grey
shadows before they had stopped playing.

Nick had hoped that after this final whisky the Bothas
would leave, but Jade was being a prima donna, the diva of
the afternoon's performance. He recognised the signs of an
impending tantrum and he feared that the night would prove to
be as endless as the afternoon, a long opera of human frailties.
Nick prayed that it would not be a major performance.

In his haste to comply with Jade's invitation Boots splashed
whisky down the front of his pink shirt and on to his grey-
flecked trousers. Jade leaned across and flicked away the
droplets, her fingers lingering as she brushed the pleated front
of his trousers.

'You're clumsy, Boots, but it won't stain,' she said, smiling
up at him seductively. 'Here, help me up and we'll choose the
music together.'

Breathing heavily, he took her hand and pulled her to him.
Putting her arm around his waist, she sneered maliciously at
Nick as she swayed past, then turned to whisper throatily into
Boots' ear. The words painted his neck crimson and oiled his
eyes with expectation.

Nick watched them walk past and sighed. 'Here, Baby,' he
said, bending across Boots' wife and taking away the empty
glass she had been tapping on her knee, 'let me refresh it
for you.'

'Thank you, Nick,' she lisped, her little girl voice rasping his
nerves like a knife sawing a plate, 'but I don't think I'll have
another. We should be leaving. We've been here all afternoon
and it's late.' She looked at her husband, now dancing with
Jade. His shirt clung to his back in large sweaty patches and

his face rested as close to Jade's breasts as he could manage without dancing on tiptoe, as Jade, almost as tall as Nick, towered over him.

'Boots,' she called, 'Bootie, don't you think we should be going home now?'

He broke away from Jade, the air cooling the front of his shirt where he had been plastered to her body.

'I'm dancing, Baby,' he snapped, the salty beads of perspiration burning his eyes now that he had opened them. 'Can't you see that I'm dancing? Why don't you dance with my old friend Nick? That'll take your mind off your watch.' He laughed coarsely and moved back to suction himself against Jade.

'Nicholas dance?' jeered Jade. 'He falls over his own feet. Two steps and he starts talking and forgets to dance. He loves hearing himself talk, of course. A real little know-all, aren't you, dearest?' Having their attention, she ran her fingers down Boots' spine causing his buttocks to wobble spasmodically. 'Dance, that's a good one.' She laughed maliciously, pressing her thighs against Boots. His forehead immediately broke out in a new wet rash.

'Oh, Jade,' said Baby breathlessly, fluffing up the blonde curls over her forehead, 'Nick dances beautifully. I've seen him, he's super.'

Jade's long scarlet fingernails dug into Boots' back, her eyes narrowed and Nick saw the familiar gleam of madness filter through.

'Come on, Baby, you're talking nonsense,' laughed Nick. 'Of course you haven't seen me dance. As Jade says, I am useless on a dance floor. Tell her you're only joking.'

'Oh, no, I'm not,' said Baby righteously, failing to pick up the signals Nick was frantically sending. 'You were dancing with Toni and you were fabulous. I watched you. You were dreamy.' Baby sighed. She had spent the entire afternoon trying to elicit some attention from Nick. He had been polite but impervious to her charms. Perhaps he would dance with her if she defended him now.

'You danced with her for ages, Nick. The two of you looked so super. I love dancing,' she said wistfully, willing him to put his arms around her and dance the way he had with Toni. She looked across at him hopefully and was surprised to see him staring at Jade, ignoring her completely.

'Ah yes,' said Jade smiling sweetly at Baby, 'yes, of course. Toni. Tell me, Baby dear, which Toni is this? We know a few Tonis.'

Eager to respond to this display of sweetness, the first kind words Jade had thrown in her direction all afternoon, Baby babbled enthusiastically.

'Toni Balser, you know, Serge's wife. He's the good-looking Swiss guy, wealthy too. They have a super home up on the hill.' Urged on by Jade's smiles and nods, Baby painted the story of the evening at the Balsers' home in lurid detail. Believing that she was ingratiating herself with Nick she fantasised about his dance with Toni, making it seem as if the whole party had watched in awe and fascination as they whirled and twirled to unending strains of romantic music.

'I see,' said Jade at the end of the recital. 'I wish I'd been there.' Her lips tightened as she looked at Nick. 'And my dearest was a regular Fred Astaire.' Untangling herself from Boots she walked across to the bridge table, picked up her glass and drained it. 'Another smoky apple for me, dearest,' she ordered and held out her glass to Nick, her eyes glittering like facets in the crystal.

'Jade, my sweet, do you think that's wise?' he cautioned as he stood up.

'Just do it,' she hissed and, crooking her finger at Boots, she patted the seat of the chair beside her. He lumbered across like a well-trained puppy. 'Baby,' she cooed, 'come and sit here with me. I just love listening to you. You describe things so well. In fact I could smell the semen and hear the heavy panting.'

Nick's shoulders drooped wearily. It was starting again.

Basking in the unexpected praise, Baby tugged at the sides of her flowered gypsy skirt, tightened the wide elastic belt nipping her waist and seated herself carefully opposite Jade.

'You two play poker, don't you?' Jade queried, her wide mouth embracing them in a conspiratorial grin. They nodded in unison. 'Good, because I'm dealing for a hand of strip poker.' She riffled the cards, swiftly dealing to four places.

'Count me out,' said Nick, placing her drink on the table.

'Oh, dearest, Baby is dying to see your cute twinkletoes and those gliding thighs, and who knows, if she looks very closely she may see your excuse for manhood. You can't possibly disappoint her.' Jade looked up at him spitefully. 'Sit, dearest, and be the perfect host,' she snapped.

Studying her, Nick recognised that an outburst was very close. He acquiesced, hoping to stave off the explosion.

Baby wriggled in anticipation and licked her lips, setting them in a lascivious pout. She knew men were fascinated by her enormous breasts and hoped that Nick would have the opportunity of admiring them. Boots swallowed repeatedly, noisily, his throat dry with excitement at the thought of Jade's white body, the splotched freckles enhancing its purity, uncovered for his delectation.

The three crouched over their cards. Nick played cautiously and looked at the growing pile of clothes and jewellery with distaste.

'Fours,' called Jade.

'Four kings,' croaked Boots hoarsely. 'I have kings. I beat your queens, Jade.' He bounced on his chair in excitement, and his naked torso jiggled like curdled milk. 'Strip. Bra off,' he exhorted, his voice squeaking in excitement. 'Strip!'

Jade, conscious of being in the spotlight, languidly fiddled with the clip of her lacy bra.

'Boots, darling, you'll have to help me. I can't undo it,' she said, turning her back towards him and smiling viciously at Nick. His hands sweating and clumsy with haste, Boots finally unclipped the scrap of lace and released the breasts he had been nuzzling on the dance floor. Jade, still gloating at Nick's discomfiture, did not see the look of dismay on Boots' face as the objects of his desire, released from their wired cages, flopped and hung loose.

Baby bit her lip in anger. It wasn't fair. She had much better boobs. If that was all Nick had to admire then she could not fail to stun him with hers. She prayed that the next hand would allow her to forfeit both her blouse and her bra. The little gremlin who listens to prayers like this, and delights in the situations caused by granting them, was on duty. She turned to face Nick as they swung free, the large brown nipples pointed and hard. The breasts, white as polished marble delicately veined with blue, rested on the green-baize table top and seemed to dominate the room. Smiling happily Baby preened, thrusting out her chest.

Nick glanced up idly and returned his gaze to the cards in his hand. The size of her breasts had caught his attention but had aroused no erotic desires. He was delighted by women with small, firm breasts, breasts barely large enough to cover with his hand.

'That's right. Look away guiltily,' snarled Jade, livid with anger at the interest which had been shown in Baby's boobs. 'We all know you want to wallow in them. Go on. Baby won't mind if you fondle them. She has spent the whole afternoon making cow's eyes at you and thrusting them under your nose, but you weren't even man enough to notice.'

Spittle gathered at the corners of her mouth and, like an enraged snake, she withheld none of her venom.

Boots and Baby, white-faced and instantly sober under the stinging lashes of her tongue, were dressing with frenzied haste, too embarrassed to look at Nick who bent and swayed under the torrent of abuse, like a reed to the force of dirty flood waters.

'That's right,' screamed Jade. 'You cause all the trouble, flaunting your cow udders, and then you run away. Go on, you middle-class bores. Out.'

'Now, Jade,' Boots was foolish enough to remonstrate. 'The Good Book says that there is a time and a place for everything, and this is not— '

His words were cut short as she lashed out at him.

'You and your Good Book make me sick,' she hissed. 'You mealy-mouthed hypocrite. You paw and pant all over me and then quote the Bible. Out, you fat pig. You and your simpering wife. Out!'

'No woman talks to me like that,' boiled Boots. 'You apologise, you— '

Jade lunged forward, the glass still in her hand. It cut his lip as it clicked on his teeth. The attack was so swift and unexpected that he stood stupefied, watching the blood drip down his shirt.

'Boots, come,' shrieked Baby hysterically, 'please come,' and she ran to the front door.

A string of abuse followed them out of the house, the words stinging like wasps.

The smell of burning rubber drifted into the room, as Boots reversed down the driveway.

'Congratulations, Jade,' said Nick as the roar of the Bothas' car faded in the distance. 'You've done it again.'

In reply she smashed the other three glasses against the wall behind his head, the liquor staining the dragged wallpaper with ugly Rorschach blotches. Her face was contorted with anger, the freckles standing out like livid weals. Lacking further ammunition, she turned to the heavy decanters on the polished sideboard. Swiftly Nick crossed the floor and held her arms, restraining her from destroying the beautiful antique containers.

She writhed and kicked at his ankles, the sharp heels of her shoes cutting thin crescents of blood on his shins. Sinking her teeth into his arm, she swore when the thick tweed refused to tear and she was unable to draw blood.

'Bastard!' she screamed hysterically. 'You lusting bastard! I hate you, do you understand? I detest you. The smell of you, the look of you and the feel of you. I hate you.' She gathered a gob of saliva in her mouth and, bringing her face close to his, she spat at him. The trails of spit ran down his nose and cheek, paused at his lips and dribbled off his chin.

His mouth ringed with white lines of fury, Nick propelled her up the oak staircase to the bedroom. Thrusting her thrashing body into the room, he locked the door and retreated downstairs to the accompaniment of hysterical screams and the sickening sound of pictures and cosmetics being smashed against the door.

The flames had sucked the coals to a gleaming crimson and Nick held his hands over them. The heat stilled the tremors and warmed his body, cold with shock and disgust. As he relaxed, kneading his fingers over the flames, images of the Jade he had loved clicked over like a slide show. The future had seemed so secure and certain when they were on honeymoon in Xian. He once again saw Jade holding her sides and shrieking with laughter as he tried to balance and fold his long legs into the intricate exercise patterns of t'ai chi.

Jade, a blue Mao cap enamelled with red and white stars and doves of peace perched jauntily on her bronze hair, smiling at him as she bargained for patchwork jackets. Jade stroking the silkiness of a jade bracelet, the translucent green shimmering like the reflection of a lotus bud in a water furrow. Jade, feeding him tiny dumplings from teetering piles of bamboo baskets, demanding a kiss between each offering. Jade in a million poses, laughing and loving during the day and passionate and demanding at night.

It had been a time of delight before the serpent with fangs of jealousy and eyes of the deranged had entered their Eden. She had been the woman of his dreams, the future mother of his children. The woman he adored, that was his Jade in China. Not the Jade he now saw, the religious taker of pills to ensure that no child would thwart her career. Not the vindictive, demented creature upstairs.

Gradually Nicholas became aware of the silence. The house was still. Walking upstairs carefully to avoid the steps which creaked, he slowly opened the bedroom door.

Jade lay sprawled across the bed like a discarded rag doll, her smudged mascara streaking large toy eyelashes on her cheeks, her smeared lipstick painting a red downturned mouth across her face. She gave a mama-doll groan as Nick lifted her legs on to the bed and looked around for a blanket to cover her. The pillows and blue satin eiderdown had been thrown out of the windows and the blankets had been submerged in a bath full of water. He found a fleecy dressing gown and draped it over her legs.

Drawing the heavy silk curtains he switched on the reading lamp, flooding her desk with a soft orange glow, and tiptoed over the carpet of broken glass to the door.

Leaving the door open so that he could hear if she called during the night, he rested his head on the jamb. 'Where did it all go wrong, Jade?' he whispered, looking at his wife as she whimpered and grunted in her sleep. 'What happened to our dreams and our love?'

He studied her and shuddered as he realised that this was all his future held. Tomorrow she would awaken contrite, protesting her love and making wild promises, which once accepted would be instantly forgotten. She would tearfully plead and entreat, needing the physical act of lovemaking to ensure his forgiveness and her continued hold over him.

It nauseated Nick. He was incapable of holding and loving her after these scenes, and he knew that until he had performed his duty the cajoling would continue with the risk of her entering into another mad rage.

Jade had played Nick skilfully over the years. She was a master fisherman. The bait was her insatiable appetite for sex in all its many forms and variations. The strike was leading him to the altar blinded and palpitating with lust. The reeling-in she extended deliciously, allowing him to take line and run, to leave on one of his trips into the wilds of Zambia or the Central African Republic, to head a research team into the Okavango swamps to ascertain the effects of the deadly DDT, or to star in television films on wildlife and conservation; but on his return he paid in full for his brief spell of freedom. She was insanely jealous of Nick's success and by belittling him she tried to denigrate his achievements.

He had spent hours with her in psychiatrists' rooms. Hours baring his soul and innermost thoughts to the cold, clinical inspection of strangers. Hours spent at home where she twisted the psychiatrists' findings to suit her own wishes, and blamed him for her outbursts and her neurotic rages. Blamed him for his success and his fame, blamed him for his long absences from home, blamed him for living. When he could no longer accept the humiliation and degradation, he leapt and thrashed. She realised that the hook was in danger of being thrown and she was on the brink of losing him. Then she would ease off on the ratchet and wait for the waters to become calm, allowing him to swim easily for a while.

She would gentle him in bed, soothing him with tearful apologies and wonderful promises; and for years he had believed her, desperately wanting to recapture their early romance. But any world acclaim awarded to him or a television interview lauding his work was met with an immediate tightening of the drag and the line was remorselessly reeled in. Long years of not knowing when the waters would become calm, or how long the deep blue serenity would last before her winds of temper whipped it up into vicious slapping waves had wearied Nick, and he longed for the frayed nylon line binding him to her to snap. He prayed for his freedom, yet still felt a reluctant responsibility for this maddened, obsessed fisherman, his wife.

Nick turned away from his wife snoring softly on the bed, crossed the passage and walked into his study. Running his hand over the pitted leather surface of the desk he found a page of writing paper and picked up his old blue fountain pen, the one he had used to write his Ph.D.

Dear Toni,
I've missed you. I tried not to see or contact you, but I've failed . . .

CHAPTER

4

T HE large tawny ridgeback pricked up its ears, the hairs along its spine stiff as porcupine quills. Stones flew from beneath its huge paws as it scrambled down from the top of the gravel bank where it had been lying in a patch of pale spring sunshine and pounded down the long driveway. The dog flashed past the rows of oak trees which were tentatively unfurling a few tender leaves to test the weather, the bed of hydrangeas beneath them showing no sign of the magnificent blue carpet they would unroll in summer, and reached the beginning of the driveway just as the gleaming white sports car swung in.

'Down, Chops,' shouted Toni, but the ridgeback was not to be dissuaded; he knew from experience that if he made the motions of jumping up at the pristine white door of the car it would open and he would be allowed into the back seat. Toni had tried desperately to deny Chops this daily ride up the driveway, but had discovered to her chagrin that if she stopped the car to remonstrate, he covered her with sloppy licks to show how much he loved and had missed her, and if she accelerated, he challenged the car to a race and was in danger of falling under the wheels as his body brushed the paintwork.

'All right, you old tiger, jump in,' said Toni, resignedly holding the door open. Chops settled down thankfully on the back seat, shedding a fine coating of red and yellow dust on the cream leather; as the car gathered speed he hung his head out of the window, gulping and snarling furiously as the wind flattened his ears and snatched at his tongue, wringing the saliva from it in a fine spray. In the front seat Timothy shouted with excitement, frantically trying to undo his seat belt and join his beloved Chops.

Often, when alerted by a sudden silence in the house, Toni would run outside to look for Timothy. She would find him stretched out on Chops' back, his soft cheek pressed against the golden brown one, the two of them sleeping contentedly in the sun. When he was younger Timothy would spend hours trying to twist the dog's slippery tongue out of his mouth or turn the silky ears inside out, using the tips as a teething ring, chewing the hairy skin happily. Chops would bear all these indignities patiently, until little hands or needle-sharp teeth inflicted real pain. Then he would rumble and stand, shaking Timothy off, like a housewife shaking a doormat, and lope away to find refuge on the high bank overlooking the bougainvillaea-covered garage.

Screeching to a stop outside the kitchen, slamming the car door closed with her hip, Toni, her arms laden with parcels, called to Izuba Mapei, her maid. Izuba, the name given by the Xhosas to the large-breasted proud Rameron pigeon, was a Xhosa woman of imposing proportions. Her girth was much admired by the males of her tribe, her skin was a polished bitter-chocolate, and when she smiled her teeth were whiter than the crisp starched collar and cuffs of her bright green overall. She waddled majestically into the kitchen.

With a screech Timothy abandoned Chops and hurled himself at Izuba. 'Zuba, Zuba,' he called as she enfolded him in her generous arms, 'I'm so thirsty.' Izuba, in common with all members of her Xhosa tribe, revered cattle and children, both being considered signs of wealth and success. She had four children of her own and considered Timothy her fifth. She smiled at Toni as she stroked his dark head.

'Be calm, my little Intakumba, my little flea,' she soothed. 'Your lunch and fruit juice are ready. Come.' She turned to lead Timothy away to have his face and hands scrubbed and Toni thankfully tumbled the packets on to the gleaming steel sink.

'Were there any messages for me?' called Toni quickly before they left the kitchen, and Izuba turned back, fumbling in the pocket of her white lace-trimmed apron.

'Aai, Ungumtukathixo,' she answered using the name her family had given Toni. 'Child of God' they called her, for she

55

loved and cared for all of them. 'Thank you for asking me. I am becoming forgetful.' She clucked irritably as she pulled an envelope from her pocket. 'I have a letter for you, and it must be a most important letter as the man made me bury it deep in my pocket. He made me swear on the memory of Tshawe, who was the beginning of our Xhosa royal family, the ama Tshawe, that I would give the letter only to you. He is a man who speaks our tongue and knows of our roots, yet it troubled him greatly to give me the letter, he thought that I would be foolish as a young girl and lose it. Me, a mother of four children, and both a sister and mother to my young twin brothers. Me, lose a letter of such importance.' Her chest swelled with indignation as she smoothed the crumpled envelope and handed it to Toni.

'What did he look like, this mysterious man?' questioned Toni, as she studied the writing.

Izuba saw again the tall man's eyes, blue as the skies and green as the hills in her homeland, commanding her attention as he handed her the letter. 'This letter must go only to Mrs Balser as it has news of great importance, but news which is for her eyes only.' 'It will be as you say. The words written down will not see the light of the sun until Miss Toni releases them,' she had answered, hiding the envelope in her pocket.

Izuba had enjoyed talking to him; he knew her homeland and her village well and spoke with feeling of the people. Izuba was sure that he was a white sangoma, for like their witchdoctors he knew of the insects and the medicines obtained from them. She had enjoyed talking to him in her native tongue and respected his command of the clicks which make it such a difficult language for Europeans to master. Time had passed quickly and she watched the big blue car drive away with regret.

'He was a man with a car, a beautiful blue car. A car as large as the heavens,' answered Izuba. Size was her tribe's sign of beauty and she scorned the small sports cars driven by Serge and Toni. 'But he was not like his car. He was too thin. He looked strong like a spear, but not a good broad stabbing spear. If he drank *amasi*, and filled his belly with *umbona*, then our soured milk and good maize porridge would make him big and beautiful like his car,' she theorised. 'His eyes died like the sun does when dark thunderclouds pass before it, when

56

he heard that you were not here, Miss Toni,' she continued, hoisting Timothy on to her broad hip and cuddling him against her soft bosom.

'Oh, Izuba!' laughed Toni. 'Let me read the note and find out who this creature is who so impressed you.' She never tired of listening to Izuba talk. Her sweet, lyrical descriptions were more common to the Zulu than the Xhosa, a legacy perhaps from the days when the Xhosa people had settled in Zululand, after migrating from north-east Africa. The good peaceful days before they were scattered in tribal warfare, choosing to flee, rather than endure slavery and suffer the annual winter raids by the powerful Zulu armies. The Xhosa fled to the East Cape colony where they in turn ousted the gentle San, commonly known as the Bushmen, and the small, yellow-skinned Khoi, or Hottentots as they were called by the Europeans, because of the sharp, clicking sounds in their language. Those little people who chose to remain were absorbed into the Xhosa tribes, and gave to the Xhosa language the rhythmic clicks which Timothy had no difficulty in repeating when Izuba spoke to him in her mother tongue, but which confused Toni, and had Izuba screeching with laughter at her mistakes.

The paper crinkled as Toni unfolded the note and the words seared her. 'I've missed you. I tried not to see or contact you, but I've failed. I had to see you.' The words blurred. Toni caught her breath and sucked in hard, her heart pounding joyously. The letter was from Nick. She had pressed every word of their meeting between the pages of her mind. Quickly she skimmed through the letter.

'I'll be working in Kirstenbosch Gardens next week studying the reports on the effect of the last mountain fire on the insect life. I'd love you to join me in the afternoon when I'll be doing field work on the mountain. Do say you'll come Toni. I'll wait for you at 2 p.m. on Monday at the Skeleton Gorge footpath . . . '

Nick, her heart sang, Nicholas needs to see me.

'It is good news, Ungumtukathixo?' asked Izuba, watching Toni carefully.

'Good, oh yes, Izuba, the best news,' answered Toni delightedly. She flung her arms around Izuba and Timothy, and buried her face in her son's dark curls, trying to hide some of her joy

57

from the large Xhosa woman. Izuba had been well endowed with the natural intelligence and intuition common to her tribe and Toni did not want too much importance placed on the man with the blue car large as the heavens who had left the letter.

She blew softly on the back of Timothy's neck, ruffling the downy tendrils of hair and making him shriek with glee. 'More, Mummy, more,' he pleaded, 'more elephant kisses.'

Toni blew again and hugged him tightly to her, wondering how a little boy this perfect could have come from her body. 'You're my beautiful, beautiful boy,' she told him.

'Beautiful Mummy,' he laughed, swinging away from Izuba and putting his arms around her neck.

'Oh, my sweetie. I adore you,' sang Toni as she whirled round and round the kitchen, her son in her arms. Putting Timothy down she inhaled deeply regaining her breath.

Yes, she rationalised to herself, I'll meet Nick. I love walking on the mountain and I may learn enough from him to do an article on the devastation caused by bush fires.

Izuba watched her white family. It was a long, long time since she had seen her Child of God so happy.

Many years ago when she was one of the women who cleaned the students' rooms at the big university on the mountain and had met Miss Toni, the young student had laughed and smiled all the time. She had left her job at the university to look after the girl from Northern Rhodesia, first in the small flat in the students' suburb of Rosebank and later when they moved to this big glass house with Mr Serge. Miss Toni had been happy then – her eyes danced with joy and she sang all day; but later she grew quiet, and often in the mornings her eyes were as red and swollen as if burned by the sticky sap of the milk bush. Now she laughed with true happiness only when she held her man-child in her arms.

Izuba grieved for her as she knew it needed a good man to keep a woman singing, and Mr Serge treated Miss Toni not with the respect of a chief wife, but as a much lesser wife. It was not good, and it made Izuba angry to see this young woman she had grown to love, suffer and become silent as the aged. In her tribe when a bad husband shamed a woman, there were many blood sisters to turn to for comfort and all in the tribe were sisters, but Miss Toni had been the only proof of her father's manhood and had no sisters to strengthen her. Izuba, barely old enough to be Toni's mother, had taken on the role of protector and she was fiercely possessive of her charge.

This letter had made her Ungumtukathixo dance again and her eyes were shining like sun-spangled water. She silently blessed the thin man who had brought the letter.

When she was told that she could leave early to spend the weekend at home with her family, she realised that the letter was indeed very big news. She locked the door of her cottage facing the kitchen courtyard and sailed regally down the driveway.

* * *

There was not a whisper of a breeze. The raging south-easterly winds, powerful offshoots from the anti-cyclones which circle the southern hemisphere, had died down. These mighty winds, keen and fresh, travel across five thousand kilometres of watery waste before they hit the mountains of the Peninsula, where they scour it, dispersing pollution and pests.

The Cape Peninsula lay sweltering in the heat and the Capetonians prayed for the reappearance of the wind they usually cursed.

The wooden hut baked in the late noonday sun and the oily smell of cars' exhaust fumes wafted heavily into the botanical gardens. Toni unbuttoned the top of her red shirt and fanned her face with her cotton hat as she stepped on to the verandah of the ticket office.

The attendant lay sprawled in a chair with his head thrown back, snoring softly. She coughed loudly and grinned as the man swung his legs down from the counter and scrambled to his feet.

'Sorry, miss. Afternoon, miss,' he said as he buttoned his pale blue shirt and dabbed at the perspiration trickling down his neck.

'Good afternoon,' said Toni, showing him her membership card.

'It's a hot day for walking,' he cautioned, glancing at the white card.

'Stinking hot,' agreed Toni, 'but I'm going to climb up Skeleton and it'll be much cooler in the gorge.'

'Maybe,' he grunted, 'maybe.'

As Toni turned on to the gravel path leading up to the towering rampart of Nursery Buttress, he settled back into his chair and closed his eyes.

The traffic noise faded as Toni walked deeper into the gardens and the oppressive stillness was broken only by the shrill chittering of sunbirds as they angled for position over the choicest proteas. The mountains shimmered in the heat haze and seemed far away; in the valley a beige cloud of pollution hung in the dense air.

'Wind,' said Toni, breathing deeply as the path rose steeply. 'Wind to clear the air again.' But the sun burnt down from a cloudless, searing blue sky.

She glanced at her watch. It was almost two o'clock and Nick would be waiting. Her stomach clenched at the thought of what she was doing but she hurried on. She buried her feelings of guilt quickly and with determination. Izuba would be putting Tim down for his nap now and she would be home before he woke. Serge was in one of his moods and was not talking to her. He had been irritable and distracted since the party, and had lashed out at her when she had asked if he was having problems at work. As deep shade and tall trees heralded the entrance to the gorge Toni's footsteps quickened and her thoughts centred on the man she was to meet.

'Toni,' Nick's deep voice rang out from the shadows and he moved into the sunlight to greet her. 'You've come. How wonderful.' He took her hands in his and pressed them gently.

She looked up into his smiling eyes, now shaded more green than blue, and suddenly she was as light-hearted as a child, eager to explore the mountain and be close to him.

They climbed steadily through the trees, the thick mat of fallen leaves deadening their footsteps. Nick stopped frequently to examine plants and insects. He excited her interest with detailed descriptions of the flora and fauna and then reduced her to helpless giggles with stories of expeditions he had undertaken in Africa. They soon intersected the contour path and left the stream trickling down Skeleton Gorge behind them.

60

'Not much further,' said Nick as he stretched out his hand to help her down a steep bank. 'We're almost at the place where the last fire blackened the mountain.'

Toni gazed about her. The houses on the slopes of Wynberg Hill in the valley were small as matchboxes. She breathed in the cooler air gratefully. It seemed to be fresher high up on the mountain.

'It's hard to believe that this slope was heat-scarred and covered with ash,' she said looking at the dark green and grey Proteacae shrubs and grasses.

'Right,' he answered, peering into a Waboom shrub, the pale lemon flowers bobbing above his head. 'It's fire-climax vegetation, and a good fire every twelve years or so does it the world of good. But these fires are happening too frequently and the seeds have no time to mature.' Suddenly he froze. 'Come and look,' he whispered.

Toni tiptoed up behind him. 'It's beautiful,' she breathed, leaning over his shoulder and watching a tiny butterfly fanning her dark red wings on the oblong head of a white bud.

'It's the Protea Scarlet,' explained Nick, backing away from the bush. 'She's one of the insects we're worried about. They only exist in proteas, as the larvae feed on the buds. Once their habitat is destroyed they'll join the long queue for extinction.'

'Nick,' said Toni, studying the black-bordered wings slowly opening and closing in the heat, 'would you mind if I used this butterfly? I want to make the public aware of the dangers of picnic fires and live cigarette ends thrown carelessly about.'

'Mind?' said Nick smiling down at her. 'I'd be delighted. We need all the help we can get. Write your article. Use the little Protea Scarlet to stop the fires, Toni.'

He brushed twigs and leaves from a granite rock. 'Sit down and rest for a few minutes before we go back. There are hundreds of stories on this mountain, Toni. If you join me for a few afternoons each week, I'll give you enough material for dozens of articles.'

All thoughts of Serge had vanished. Being with Nick was right and Toni felt good. Her cheeks dimpled. 'Done,' she said. 'You have a willing listener for the next few weeks.'

Nick smiled and stretched out on the grass beside her, and the red butterfly dipped swiftly past them and settled on another protea.

* * *

They hurried down the dark alleyway, two shapeless figures muffled in light coats. Even though the night was hot and airless the collars were pulled up, concealing the lower half of their faces. The semi-detached houses lining the alley had at one time been painted in fresh pastels, pinks, yellows and pale greens, but the crisp colours had faded and mildew clung to the walls. The street gangs boasting colourful names like The Red Hot Lovers, The Dragons and Tough Tsotsie's, had added to the sordidness by covering the walls with mindless graffiti, political and lavatorial.

The couple kept to the shadows, avoiding the pools of light cast by the Victorian streetlamps. There were no eyes to peer at them from the darkness, as in this poor residential area only the gangs roamed the streets after dark, and locked doors and closed windows barricaded the residents from their violence.

The area bordering the banks of the Liesbeek river and overshadowed by Devil's Peak, the towering rock flanking Table Mountain, had been very rich agricultural land studded with fine old farmhouses until the new railroad turned the rural community into a bustling suburb. When the large businesses expanded and outgrew the available land, they dragged the workforce out on to the sandy and windswept Cape Flats, and these little villages were left like ageing spinsters, their beauty faded and their usefulness ended, easy prey for the marauding groups of youngsters.

Startled by a scuffling noise behind him, Serge tightened his grip on Dana's arm. She shivered and pressed herself closer to him.

'The old bitch had better do the job tonight,' he muttered, his uneasiness making him tug Dana's arm angrily.

He hurried on. This was his third visit and he was determined that he would not be turned away. It had taken weeks to make contact with the old hag and arrange a meeting. The first time, the dark green door with the paint peeling off in streamers had been opened a fraction, and a disembodied voice had quavered, 'Go away, go now, it's not safe.' They had run back to where they had parked the car, their hearts pounding, expecting to feel the stern hand of the law on their hunched shoulders.

The second visit was little better. 'Don't park near the house. It's not a good night. Come again on Friday at nine o'clock,' and the green door had slammed shut.

Serge slid back the cotton cuff of his shirt, tailored by one of London's best shirtmakers, and looked at his watch. The roman numerals gleamed greenly in the dull light. Exactly nine o'clock. He rapped sharply, aiming a kick at a marmalade cat the size of a well-fed terrier which had started chewing the leather toe of his Italian loafers. It snarled and dug its claws into his ankle, enabling it to suck the leather unhindered. Serge swore with pain but stood still, not wishing to provoke the cat to further excesses. The door swung open suddenly and they were blinded by the light. A naked bulb hung from a ceiling, festooned with flypapers, peppered with black flies. The cat released Serge's foot and streaked into the house, intent on reaching the kitchen and foraging before it was thrown out.

A pot-pourri of odours assailed their nostrils as the door closed behind them. The hot spicy scent of curry mingled with the harsh tang of cheap tobacco. Dana wrinkled her nose and stood behind Serge.

'Have you brought the money?' demanded the old woman, her thick frizzy hair held down with luminescent clips of orange and green.

'Here,' said Serge curtly and handed her a wad of red notes. Licking her forefinger, she counted the notes carefully, folding each one and tucking it away in some secret place beneath her worn but clean smock.

The transaction completed, the woman, hands on her hips, studied Dana and Serge, seemingly oblivious to the cacophony in the next room. A baby, its piercing wails rising and falling as rhythmically as the tide, was competing with the popular song 'Lady in Red', played at maximum volume; a radio announcer monotonously reciting the market prices for vegetables was coming a poor third in the dissonance.

The wailing drilled into Serge's skull like jackhammers, but he knew there would be no respite as he needed this old midwife and her skills and the game would be played according to her rules. She grunted and pointed at a chrome-legged chair, the back broken out, standing against a wall in the passage.

'You sit here and wait,' she ordered Serge, 'and you come with me,' she said, leading Dana to a door plastered with pictures of pop stars. Dana turned and smiled tearfully at Serge, willing him to call a halt to the awful proceeding, to stop the sacrifice, to take her back to their flat and love and protect her, but the High Priest was immovable, the Priestess had been paid and the rites were to be performed.

Serge Balser let out a sigh of relief as the door closed, causing the rock stars to shiver and shake for a few seconds as though performing for him, an audience of one.

'Thank goodness,' he breathed, 'this whole damn mess will soon be over.' He shuddered as he studied his surroundings but consoled himself with the knowledge that the old woman was a good midwife. The nurse who had given him the address had assured him that she was efficient. He rested the back of his head against the beige wall, its paint crinkled like old custard, and closed his eyes.

The past two months had been a nightmare, starting the evening that he and Dana had spent at the Chinese restaurant on the beachfront. Serge shifted his head trying to find a more comfortable spot on the stippled wall in the passageway. He lit another cigarette, the smoke helping to mask the sour odours of poverty. Yes, he thought, the last few weeks had been soul-destroying, weeks when Dana had raged until she was incoherent, cried until she collapsed into exhausted sleep, and pleaded for marriage, walking across the floor on her knees to fall at his feet like a penitent at Lourdes.

Finally, she had accepted that she would not become the second Mrs Balser, and the thought of bearing and bringing up his child without the security and comfort of marriage had dismayed her. The promise of a quick abortion followed by a prolonged overseas holiday had mollified her.

Only when Serge started making enquiries about a doctor or a midwife to perform the operation did he realise what he was up against. In a country which had been gripped in the merciless fist of Calvinism for so long there were no doctors who dared to help. He soon discovered that those brave souls who had performed abortions in the past had been struck off the medical register, ruining their futures and negating the seven years of intensive training which they had undergone, a high price to pay for a small act of charity. Most of the doctors he approached agreed to help if a miscarriage occurred and, seeing his desperation, warned him against using a back-street midwife. They had all spent time wresting back from death young bodies haemorrhaging and ravaged by the dehydrating fires of high temperatures and septicaemia. All caused by old midwives operating in unhygienic rooms, using unsterilised instruments, but filling a void, heeding frightened and desperate appeals for help. Serge had formed a sneaking respect for these furtive angels of mercy who operated in dingy tenement houses, terrified of being discovered and going to jail.

In a planet already facing destruction due to overpopulation and pollution, they were reviled. They were punished for helping to ease the burden in the overcrowded houses of refuge for unwanted children, for lessening the sickening numbers of battered babies, all unwanted and unloved products of man's short-sighted laws. These laws had finally brought Serge and Dana to this house.

'That's it, take off your coat and panties and lie down,' said the old lady, pointing to a red and blue striped sofa, the armrests and back faded and threadbare.

Stepping carefully over a white enamel pail and a plastic basin of soapy water, the shavings of blue and white soap lying motionless as drowned maggots on the surface, Dana lay down gingerly.

'Right, lift your knees,' ordered the crone, her wiry grey hair brushing Dana's face as she bent over her. Dana held her breath, trying not to notice the hot smell of garlic on the old woman's breath. She stared fixedly at the sparkling stones set in the orange and green plastic hairclips, willing herself to concentrate on the twinkling colours, not on what the woman was about to do.

'Relax,' ordered the midwife and Dana gasped as hard, experienced fingers opened and entered her and probed deep inside. 'How long since you saw your last period?' asked the woman as she withdrew her fingers and wiped them on a paper towel.

'Eight weeks, I think,' lied Dana, relieved to be free of the questing fingers.

'No,' said the old lady shaking out a cloth and carefully covering the contents of the basin. 'No, you're at least twelve. It's too late, it's not good, not good at all,' and she shook her head.

'Oh, please,' cried Dana. 'You must, you must do it for me. You said you would, please.' She caught the old brown hand and held it to her cheek. 'I'll pay you more, please.'

'It's dangerous when you are so far gone,' she answered. 'I don't do any at ten weeks. You need a hospital. I'll tell him out there.' She walked out to find Serge.

Sitting up, Dana dropped her head into her hands, the nails pitting her scalp. She was trembling and bit her lip to stop herself from crying. Pay her, Serge, pay her anything she wants, she urged silently. Now that she had accepted the fact that Serge would not marry her, she was sick with terror at the thought of not being able to have the abortion. The creaking of the door alerted her and, dropping her hands, she looked up to see the old woman tucking a handful of notes under her smock as she walked towards her.

Wiping her mouth with the back of her hand, the midwife muttered, 'I still don't like it. Lie down, put your legs up. Wide apart,' she pulled at Dana's knees, stretching them wider. 'Come,' she said, 'don't be afraid.'

Dana blinked, blinded by scalding tears of humiliation and fear, and spread her thighs.

The trickling and splashing noises in the basin stopped and Dana held her breath. With a sickening lurch the world went black and turned upside-down. A searing pain tore into her body but she couldn't scream – a calloused hand was clamped down tightly over her mouth.

'Lie still,' the woman's voice echoed through the waves of pain. 'Once more and that should do it.'

Again she thrashed. This time her head was thrust over the edge of the couch and held above the bucket. She was released when only a dribble of slime was left dripping from her trembling mouth.

'Up you get. It's all over,' said the old midwife, wiping Dana's face tenderly with a wet cloth. 'The pains should start towards morning.' She put her arm around Dana's shoulders and led her to the door.

Serge jumped up, knocking over the chair. 'What in the hell have you done to her?' he shouted, shocked at Dana's pale face and lustreless eyes. She staggered across to him, hunched over and shivering. He wiped away the tears and held her to him, fear and pity making him shake.

'It's you who did this to her,' answered the old woman angrily. 'You men are all the same. You have your fun then when your girlfriends' roses don't show you come running to me, and I have to get you out of trouble.' She glared at Serge. 'I don't do it for you. I do nothing for men. You're all rotten. I only help the poor girls.' She stroked Dana's blonde head. 'It'll all be over soon. Look after yourself, little one.'

She grabbed Serge's shoulder and with surprising strength propelled him down the passageway to the front door. 'Now go quickly, leave here and remember I've never seen you. I will not go to jail for you.' She opened the latch on the front door. 'Whatever happens, don't come near me ever again.'

The orange cat slunk into the passage and wound itself around her legs, looking up at her adoringly, and purred its song of love loudly.

The following fourteen hours were peopled with all the demons of hell. Dana's heart-rending cries for help and pleas to end the pain, as the abortionist's art was brought to fruition and the unwanted foetus was slowly dislodged from her womb, tore at his soul, but he was too mindful of his position and reputation to summon help.

In an area where screams were commonplace, hers passed unnoticed. The western coastline with its sun-bleached mountains and pristine beaches had attracted people who enjoyed the dubious joys of city life, the ready access to mind-bending drugs and the unending round of parties. In this setting, Dana's cries were acceptable, shrugged off merely as someone having a bad trip on heroin, or some sexual perversity being carried to extremes.

But to Serge, worse than her agony was the blood, incarnadine blood, spreading and flowing everywhere. His nostrils were clogged with the ferrous smell and his head pounded with the song played incessantly at the abortionist's home, 'Lady in Red'. Dana, his lady in red, lay on the bed, the wadded towels staining crimson, and the used ones on the floor darkening to purple.

A tide which he was powerless to stop, her life oozing away whilst he struggled ineffectually to help. When the dull hum of traffic increased to a roar as it thundered along the coastal highway, signalling the end of the day and the commencement of the night's frivolities, he realised that surgical help was necessary. This was not going to be a quick, quiet abortion and he would have to accept the risk of being recognised by someone at the hospital.

The glossy white doors of the operating theatre swung open and the gynaecologist strode through, hitching up his green cotton trousers, the theatre gown flapping around his calves. His eyes were cold and his voice clipped with dislike.

'You're lucky, you're very lucky, Mr Jones. Another few hours and we'd have lost her, she'd have bled to death. You would have had a lot to explain, a back-street abortionist when she was ten weeks pregnant, and failure to bring her in immediately the bleeding started.' He studied Serge carefully, noting the deep rings of fatigue cradling his eyes and the trembling nicotine-stained fingers holding the cigarette.

'I strongly advise you against repeating this performance, Mr Jones. We'll be keeping her in hospital for a few days and she'll need care and attention when she leaves. It's been a harrowing experience for her. Good day.'

He spun on his heel and disappeared in a flurry of green. Serge lifted his cigarette, filled his lungs to capacity and exhaled slowly as he walked down the long white-tiled passage to the window at the end. Pressing his forehead to the cold pane of glass, he gazed out at the lights of the city spread at his feet like a paisley shawl sparkling with diamanté and sequins. The doctor's cold words resounded in his ears and chilled him. He had been powerless to refute them.

He drew away from the soothing coolness of the window-pane and turned to stub his cigarette out in the gritty sand of a nearby ashtray. Looking down at his hand he shuddered. His fingernails were caked with dried blood. Never, he thought, never again, as he pulled a used matchstick from the sand and scraped the slivers of dried blood from under his nails.

Tomorrow he would send Dana a bowl of the satiny pink roses she loved, and when she was well he would end their relationship. He walked out of the hospital into the velvet night, his mind racing as he chose and discarded stories to explain his two-day absence to Toni. The thought of her finding out about Dana and the abortion made the hair prickle on the back of his neck.

He had no wish to jeopardise his home life, as a well-run home and a good-looking wife and son were necessary props to the suave and well-polished image which he presented to the business world.

* * *

Beads of perspiration were rolling slowly down Izuba's broad nose, spotting her red cotton blouse, part of the uniform of her Zionist church sect. She elbowed her way down Station Road to join one of the ever-lengthening queues at the bus terminal. Izuba was happy. She straightened her starched white cap and tucked the plastic bags under her arm. She had finally saved enough money for her brothers' clothes and she was spending the weekend with her family. Queues of black and coloured domestic workers jostled, fighting for position in the line, eager to spend the weekend at home with their families. The air buzzed with noise and the distinctive Xhosa tongue, clicking like castanets, rose above the general uproar.

She forced her way through the crowds thronging the pavements and spilling over into the street, the bright colours of their clothes blending and separating as they moved. There was an air of festivity in the narrow side streets leading to the bus terminals and the stations. It was the end of the month and a Saturday morning; the workers were flooding into the tiny stores, spending their salaries on meat and groceries, and putting down deposits to secure the clothes displayed so temptingly.

It was the ideal hunting ground for pickpockets darting through crowds as swiftly as trout raiding salmon nests. Well aware of the danger, Izuba tucked her bag firmly under her fleshy arm and hugged her parcels tightly to her chest.

'Here, Mama, good shoes, cheaper than factory prices,' shouted a vendor standing in front of a window displaying rows of rainbow-coloured shoes.

'No, no, Mama, don't buy his shoes, they're only painted plastic,' cajoled a wiry gnome of a man, his gums gleaming in a toothless grin. 'Look at my *ilaphu*, cloth specially from the Transkei, Mama.'

He fluttered a length of navy-blue and red cloth in front of Izuba and, like the waving tail plumes of the sugar bird, it immediately caught her attention. Izuba paused. In common with many Xhosa matrons who had been born in the homeland *kraals* but had forsaken the traditional way of life to follow their husbands to the large cities, she preferred the cotton material with traditional patterns to the new synthetics; but she had just paid the final deposit on clothes for her twin brothers at the men's outfitting store and did not have sufficient money to put a 'lay-by' on the material. Regretfully she handed the length of *ilaphu* back to the trader.

'Perhaps next week,' she said softly. 'I may have money for it next week.' Izuba smiled at him, her wonderful warm face-splitting smile, and his ancient hormones stirred. Few were immune to the radiance of her smile.

'I'll keep this cloth for you, Mama. Without a lay-by,' he added.

'Thank you,' said Izuba happily, 'you are a good man.' She forged ahead to join the queue at the end of the street.

Izuba smiled. The little trader was keeping her *ilaphu*, and she had the parcels containing the orange and green sports jackets and brown trousers for her young brothers, Justice and Wisdom, who would be returning home in a few weeks' time from their *khwetha*, or circumcision school.

She was going to work overtime the following week to pay for new grey suede shoes for them. When their initiation period ended they would have no clothes, as the hut built for the initiation plus all their ritual clothing and utensils would be burned, representing a complete break with the past and their acceptance into the tribe as men. It was with great pride that the family was at last able to buy new outfits for the boys. The twins were almost eighteen years of age and their circumcision had been postponed to allow them to complete their schooling – education the twins were determined to obtain, despite savage rioting, the burning of schools and intimidation by illiterate street louts. The family was proud that the boys had chosen to be circumcised and schooled in the secrets and history of the tribe, for many youngsters had forsaken the old traditions and were groping blindly in the new darkness now empty of familiar and honoured guidelines.

She also had a large bag of pink and white marshmallows for her children and her old mother, who had reluctantly left her village in the Transkei for the first time to visit the big city.

Thinking of her brothers, boys whom Izuba had cared for since they were skinny six-year-olds and had left her mother's village to attend school in the city, and lost in daydreams of the great feast they would have to welcome their return, she did not notice the crowd opening up before her like slices of ham peeling away from a carving knife. The two youths dressed in tight, studded jeans, dark green aviator glasses perched low on their noses and baseball caps jammed back-to-front on their heads, came racing up the street, the short knife gripped in the leader's hand still flecked with blood.

He collided with Izuba, his head barrelling into her stomach, the razor-sharp blade opening a river of rich red blood down her arm; as she folded and collapsed like a spineshot black buffalo, her parcels spun into the gutter, the white plastic bags tearing. The new jackets, finally in her possession after months of saving, soaked up the dirty puddles of water left by the spring rain. The boys vanished into the crowd. No one tried to stop them so cowed had they all become by the wanton reign of terror conducted by the children.

Izuba lay on the pavement, stunned and gasping for breath until high-pitched ululating, black women wailing for their dead, brought her to her senses. A distraught screaming mob had formed at the bus terminus and Izuba shivered as the menacing roars of outrage and anger bellowed up the street. The wizened man who had begged Izuba to buy his blue material gathered her parcels and wrung the muddy water from the jackets, whilst strong willing hands hoisted her to her feet and led her to a nearby pharmacy to ask for help.

'Children!' exclaimed the pharmacist as he probed gently

71

into the cut on Izuba's arm. 'Every Saturday people are brought in here who have been robbed, stabbed, slashed or beaten up, and always it has been by children.' He held the bleeding edges of the cut wide apart and squeezed a thick yellow squiggle of Betadine into the raw flesh before taping it tightly closed.

'There are always *tsotsies* in the crowds on Saturdays. Was it one of the coloured gangs?' he asked, standing back to admire his handiwork.

'No,' said Izuba wincing as he smoothed down the tape, 'they were not of mixed blood, they were of my people. The children of my tribe now form packs and hunt their own kind. Aai,' said Izuba bearing the pain stoically, 'they behave as if bitten by dogs with madness in their eyes and thick foam in their mouths. They no longer listen to their parents or the old ones of the tribes. They burn down their schools, leaving in ashes the ladders of learning which they need to climb before they can sit with the men who make the laws.' She relaxed a little as the pharmacist wove the gauze bandage around her arm. 'Children are our sticks to lean on when we are old and our dreams for the future, but many of ours have become crazed.'

The grey-haired man tied a neat bow in the bandage and squeezed her broad shoulder. 'Mama, there have always been children who turn their parents' heads white, but there are also those who gladden their old age,' he comforted.

The pharmacist had formed a great liking and respect for most of the black men and women who were his customers and he enjoyed speaking to them of illnesses both physical and political. He had warmed instantly to the large black woman whose arm he was bandaging. She used words like a brush to paint vivid pictures and she was what he considered to be 'one of the good old ones'.

Izuba unfolded herself from the chair and stood up, feeling suddenly weak and shaky. 'You have been kind and I thank you.' She smiled at the pharmacist, a small sad smile. 'You are right, all of the children are not bad. Some shout and it is but the angry wailing of a hungry baby, but others have felt the teeth of the mad dog and what they cry is evil.'

She walked out leaning on the arm of the little trader, who had offered to walk with her to the dry cleaner's where the sports jackets would be returned to their pristine state.

The threatening roar of the tightly packed mob at the end of the road subsided to a low growl, the throbbing centre calmed and the crowd melted into a fluid organism as people started drifting away from the red-haired officer who had appeared in the centre. With waving arms and thundering voice he was directing the metamorphosis of the crowd. Stan le Roux was an officer who found it impossible to sit behind a desk. No call was too unimportant for him to attend to personally. His ginger hair flamed at scenes of burglaries, riots, rapes and school fetes.

Most of the police force in the southern suburbs were very much in awe of Stan. He had been decorated for bravery four times, was incorruptible and the possessor of a fiery temper which matched the red hair now thinning and carefully combed over his sun-splotched scalp. His superiors turned a blind eye to his activities, happy in the knowledge that they had a legend who was feared by criminals, respected by a diverse population and loved by young children.

'Have you called up an ambulance?' he roared at the young police driver wrestling his way through the crowd, the stale stench of sweat and the sour smell of anger pressing down on him like a face mask.

'Sir,' affirmed Richard Dalton.

'Then come and help me with these poor dead sods,' said Stan, digging in his ear, tufted as heavily as that of a bat-eared fox, and studying the flakes of wax which he had dislodged. 'Cover them and let's get the place back to normal.'

'Yes, Stan, sir,' said the young man, his pinched face dwarfed by the blue police cap. His face was ashen and the wispy moustache, grown in the hope of making him look mature and masculine, was startlingly black against the pallor of his skin. Richard Dalton seemed much too frail and delicate to be a policeman. He had recently been transferred to the Wynstaat Police Station where the men had piped his entry into the locker room with low wolf-whistles and called him Marilyn, a sneering tribute to his sweeping eyelashes and violet-blue eyes.

Tugging at his luxuriant ginger moustache, Stan studied the youngster as he gingerly bent over the bloodied corpses.

Strange bloody cops the colleges are turning out, he thought. They've all the answers to all the problems, can quote the political jargon of all the bloody parties and sound more like politicians than the ones we have in Parliament. Makes me feel an idiot when he sounds off on one of his theories. These damn alphabetical names give me indigestion.

He watched as Richard tried to steady one of the heads which lolled loosely every time he touched the body.

Theories are all very well, Stan ruminated, but this is where people bleed and die. Here on the streets is where it counts. It's all very well to understand the tribal customs and loyalties, but this is where real cops not bloody eggheads are needed. Balls, it takes balls to do a cop's work in the street. Just as well I have the poor little sod with me, he decided. I'll toughen him up.

The sheet of black plastic was narrow and as Richard moved the two bodies closer together, the shrill keening began again, prickling the skin on Stan's forearms and running cold fingers along his spine.

'No, no, Mama,' he said softly, bending over the old crone, her face a rutted country road of wrinkles, the tears flowing over the corrugations like a river over rocky rapids. He gently patted the frail bony shoulders and lifted her to her feet, turning her away from her two daughters, sprawled on a rich crimson carpet of blood.

The elder daughter had her arm flung across the body of her sister, protecting in death that which she had been unable to shield in life.

'Aai,' she sobbed, 'my daughters, oh, my daughters. I am lost.'

'Richard,' bellowed Stan, cradling the bent black body in the crook of his arm, 'come here and put her into the car. As soon as the damn ambulance arrives we'll take her home. Be gentle with her,' he admonished.

Richard Dalton jerked the plastic over the girls' heads, their sightless eyes staring up in terror, and went to lead their mother to the car. Throwing back her head, her mouth open, a few blackened teeth pockmarking the gums like burnt tree stumps, she wailed to the heavens and drew down ancestral curses on the black-jeaned hyenas who had stabbed both her

74

daughters and fled with their purses bulging with their month's salaries.

He settled the old lady in the car and, closing the door softly on her, stared at his fingerprints, bright red on the yellow paintwork. He gulped nervously and fear washed his mouth with bile.

'Blood and AIDS. A death sentence final and irrevocable.' The training lecture, and the cold clinical voice of the Professor of Virology, pebble glasses glinting in the light of the naked bulb in the lecture room, came back to haunt him.

'AIDS is a devastating disease, gentlemen, caused by an entirely new virus named HIV. A virus which outstrips science, a unique virus, a terrifying virus, for not only does it avail itself of the apparatus of cells in the body for its own use, it also has the Machiavellian ability to reverse the ordinary flow of genetic information.'

Richard remembered the lecture clearly. Every chilling word was stamped on his mind. He scrubbed at the crimson prints, leaving an orange smudge on the car. He then spat on a corner of his handkerchief and carefully wiped the blood from his fingers. He could see the Professor's cold eyes peering at them over the top of his glasses.

'Science must pioneer a new area of medicine and, until it has succeeded, AIDS will spread and consume relentlessly. It is a killer which will terrorise us for a long time.'

Richard studied each finger in turn, fearful of finding any lacerations which would allow the blood into his body; then, stuffing the stained white handkerchief deep into the pocket of his trousers, he returned to where Stan was giving colourful vent to his feelings. Stan's world was black and white, he allowed no grey areas of compromise. Laws were made to be kept and law-breakers deserved to be punished.

'We'll put the plain-clothes guys on to finding these bastards. Murdering little sods,' muttered Stan as Richard joined him. 'The papers call it political unrest. Political unrest, bloody hell, to stab women and rob them of their wages, to hold up and loot delivery vans, smash shop windows and pinch radios and videos; all acceptable political protests according to the fool newspapers.' He spat in disgust. 'Any idiot can see that these kids are using the unrest as an excuse for stealing.'

Stan paused in his tirade to wave a group of young school-girls away from the plastic-covered bodies. 'Forcibly seducing kids no older than these girls,' he continued, glaring at the passers-by, daring them to stand and stare. 'Babies for the Revolution, they call it – free bloody sex, that's what it is. Little bastards believe that laws don't apply to them.'

Stan had a lifetime of street experience to his credit and Richard listened attentively. He did not agree with all Stan said, but he had much to learn from this irascible officer.

When Izuba, the shallow cut on her arm swathed in white bandages and oozing orange Betadine, climbed on to the lumbering bus, all that remained of the tragedy was a mound of white sand blotting up the blood.

* * *

The mighty north-westerly winds which reach up and claw viciously at the rocky Cape Peninsula during the dreary months of winter had turned away and were whipping up the seas of the southern ocean when suddenly, exhibiting all the capriciousness of a spoilt child, they swung in from the Atlantic, once again to batter the rocky finger of land and smother the jagged peaks of the Twelve Apostles in dirty sheets of grey cloud. They dragged the soiled sheets across the flat top of Table Mountain and pulled them over Devil's Peak, letting them lie in a crumpled heap in the valley.

They showed no compassion for the flowered petticoats which the Cape had shaken out for spring. Oak leaves soft as lettuce hearts were ripped from the branches and the gold and white daisies carpeting the hillsides were torn and bruised. They beat up the waves in Chapman's Bay into peaks of white cream and then rolled the balls of spume along the seemingly endless stretch of white beach.

Toni slammed and locked the door of her sleek sports car and braced herself against the wind as she struggled to zip up her powder-blue anorak. Thrusting her hands deep into the pockets she turned and ran lightly down the gravelled path leading from the small parking area to the beach.

Seated on a granite boulder, his open denim jacket flying like a pennant from his shoulders, was a tall, dark-haired man. He was staring out to sea, heedless of the wind or the stinging sand blowing into his face.

Toni stopped at the end of the alleyway, well-sheltered by wind-resistant Port Jackson bushes, and studied the man.

In spite of her determination to control her emotions, her heart sang as she looked at Nicholas Houghton. The afternoons she had spent with Nick climbing the mountains or walking in the botanical gardens had become very important to her. Toni relived their conversations before she closed her eyes at night. She awoke in the mornings eagerly looking forward to the afternoons.

She found him a sympathetic and intelligent listener. Talking to him about her love for Timothy and her longing to see more of her father had been easy. They had formed a close companionship and she was able to discuss her strained relationship with Serge. Nick's advice was reasoned, not condemnatory, and she accepted it happily.

Leaving the protection of the alleyway, she walked across the sand and over the twisted and dried kelp to Nick. The wind muffled her footsteps.

'A penny for them, Nick,' she said, and was convulsed with laughter at his startled reaction.

The wind had tangled her curls and blushed her cheeks, and her eyes mirrored the soft blue of her jacket. Holding her hands in his, Nick knew that he wanted and had to win this woman.

'Only a penny?' he grinned.

'Tell me what they are and I may pay more,' she teased.

'All right,' agreed Nick sliding down from the rock. 'I was thinking what a lovely woman you are and how lucky I am to have you with me in the afternoons.'

Toni glanced away and the colour in her cheeks deepened. 'I love being with you, Nick,' she answered. 'Now let's find wet sand to walk on before my face is sandpapered in this wind. Race you,' she shouted and, slipping off her canvas shoes, she ran into the wind and down to the breaking waves. Nick caught up with her as she stood wriggling her toes in the foam.

'Come on, Twinkletoes,' he said. 'Let's walk.' He stretched

out his arm and took and enfolded her hand in his. 'You'd better give me your hand or you'll be blown away in this wind.'

They walked close together, leaning towards each other to prevent their words being lost on the wind.

'Oh, look, Nick,' said Toni, pointing to a dozen ruffled sanderlings battling, heads down, into the wind behind a receding wave; as they scuttled back up the beach out of reach of the next breaking wave the wind upended them, lifting their pale grey tails and ploughing their short beaks into the sand.

'A most undignified position,' agreed Nick, 'especially for a bird with such incredible powers of flight.'

'They migrate from Siberia and the Arctic, don't they?'

'Right. They ringed one on the west coast and it was recovered in Russia almost thirteen thousand kilometres away.'

'You really are a storehouse of knowledge, Nick,' she said.

'Most of it useless,' he mocked. 'Come on, I'll race you to the *Kakapo*.' He set out for the rusted ship beached high on the sand.

Toni struggled through the soft sand, gritting her teeth against the wind-whipped grains which lashed her legs. She panted with relief as she reached the wreck, its corroded ribs thrusting through the sand like gnarled fingers.

'Nick?' she called. The wind echoed his name across the dunes. 'Nick, where are you?'

A muffled answer came from the great cankered boiler standing clear of the sand-smothered steamer.

'Come,' he shouted. 'It's windfree inside.'

Toni giggled as she rounded the huge steam boiler and saw Nick stretched out on the sand inside.

'We'll have to thank the old navigator who mistook his bearings and put the *Kakapo* up here, instead of doubling the Cape,' laughed Nick. 'Here, I'll give you a hand. Brace your foot on the side and I'll pull you up.'

Toni flew through the round opening like a popping champagne cork and they lay in a tangled heap, helpless with laughter.

Suddenly Nick sat up and leaned over her, smoothing the soft curls away from her face. His mouth softened as he lowered his lips to hers. In that fleeting moment she knew him, the feel and taste of his mouth, the warm musky smell of his breath. It was so familiar; she had always known him. Their lips parted tenderly, unwillingly, like kittens being weaned.

Toni's heart raced and she held her breath as he traced the outlines of her face with his lips. Then, taking off his glasses and placing them on the sand above their heads, he drew her close to him. The spicy smell of musk was strong as he covered her mouth and Toni closed her eyes, pressing herself against his hardness, giving herself to his demanding mouth and questing fingers.

Her anorak lay like a soft blue cloud beneath her and her cotton shirt was now open to the waist. Nick held her nipple in his mouth, tugging at it gently as he unzipped her jeans and eased them from her hips. Toni lifted herself to him as his lips moved to her navel, lost in the heat of desire, wanting only to feel his hands and mouth. She moaned her need softly, wanting to melt into him, to be one with him.

Suddenly she felt cold damp sand beneath her warm buttocks. It electrified her and shocked her back to reality.

'Nick,' she pleaded. 'No, please. I can't. I mustn't.'

Nick froze and the wind drummed hollowly in the rusted boiler. A kelp gull mewed plaintively as it battled to fly into the wind. He breathed deeply, struggling to restrain himself, as he gently snapped the elastic of her panties around her waist and zipped her jeans. Leaving her blouse open he cupped his hand over one of her breasts and drew her head down on to his shoulder as he stretched out beside her.

'I'm sorry, Nick,' she whispered, burying her face in the rough weave of his shirt. 'I'm so sorry.'

'It's all right, little kitten,' he answered, his breathing now disciplined. 'It's all right,' and he stroked the tendrils of hair curling in her neck.

'I'm so embarrassed, Nick,' she continued in a small voice. 'It's just that I've never done anything like this before. I'm still married and— ' She paused. 'Even though I no longer love Serge, I am his wife.'

The silence deepened as Nick waited for her to continue. 'I wanted you then, Nick, more than I've wanted anything else, but . . . Please understand.'

'I do understand, Toni,' he said. 'We're both married and I believe that we've truly tried to make a success of our relationships.' He brushed his lips lightly over her forehead. 'Jade and I no longer have a marriage. These past few weeks have shown me how much more life has to offer and I know now that I can't and won't continue to live with her. Serge— ' He paused. 'Serge is so short-sighted. He has a rare gem and is discarding it for tawdry baubles. You deserve much better, my little one.'

Nestling her head in the crook of his arm, he leaned down and kissed each rosy nipple, then buttoned her blouse.

'Nick,' said Toni as he sank back on the sand beside her, 'thank you for not being angry.'

'I couldn't be angry with you,' he answered. 'I— ' He swallowed the words. 'Toni, I'll be flying up to Zululand in a few weeks' time to do a documentary on a proposed pleasure resort which a business consortium wants to build in the wetlands. I'll have the weekend free and I'd love to show you a wonderful little hideaway deep in the hills of Zululand. Will you join me?' He lifted her face to his. 'It'd be good to have a few days together, away from our daily routine. We could ride and fish and get to know each other. Please come.'

Toni looked deep into his eyes and smiled. He still wanted to be with her. Her rejection had not changed his feelings. 'Thank you, Nick,' she answered. 'Your invitation sounds wonderful.' She bit her lip and frowned. 'Timothy could spend the weekend with Helen and Serge'll be overseas with Hans. They're thinking of opening up a new branch for one of the export companies and Hans is to design logos, so my family will be no problem.' She put her hand over his and stroked his fingers. 'Spending a weekend with you is a form of commitment, Nick, and I need to think about it.'

'Of course,' he answered. 'But remember the power of positive thinking.'

'I will,' said Toni, a dimple creasing her cheek, 'and I'll take into consideration the fact that there are no rusty boilers in Zululand.'

'Right,' laughed Nick. 'But he warned, I may find a substitute.'

An immature gull ruffled its mottled brown and grey feathers and squawked disconsolately as Nick and Toni approached. He hopped a few steps, hoping that he wouldn't have to test the force of the wind, before he compromised and skimmed low over the sand and out of their way.

His wails, shrill and clear, answered their laughter which drifted over him as he waddled back to the breakers.

* * *

It was a public holiday, and Izuba was looking forward to spending a few days with her family. But as she climbed down from the bus and walked along the strangely silent and deserted streets of Shonalanga, the township sprawled on the Cape Flats only fifteen minutes' drive from the city and about a half an hour's drive from Toni's home, Izuba felt the first tingles of superstitious dread prickle her scalp. Even though she was a Christian and belonged to the Zionist church – a massive organisation incorporating millions of blacks – she still clung to her tribal superstitions. She was happy that her church wisely allowed her to have traditional beliefs, and she easily associated her ancestors with Christian saints, though, unlike the Trinity, spirits she believed in could still possess people.

Her Zionist sect wore bright crimson cotton blouses with starched white collars and cuffs belted over black skirts, and crisp white caps, and they stood out in a crowd like red Christmas crackers on a mahogany table. The music and colourful uniforms helped to continue the rituals and religious practices which her people had enjoyed in tribal life and had lost when they flooded to the cities.

Izuba shivered as she walked slowly along the pavement, and she whispered to herself, 'The *umkholwane* is working his evil.' The hornbill, a bird not found in the Cape, was nevertheless an ill omen in her village in the Transkei. 'He came to me in my sleep last night and his visits always bring news of misfortune and death.'

The puddles in the potholed road were undisturbed by small bare feet splashing through them. The shrieks of children spinning old bicycle wheels down the street, or racing their cars and aircraft painstakingly crafted from old wire coat-hangers, with the appropriate hooting and zooming sounds, were absent. A brooding stillness hung over the streets. Rounding the corner, Izuba bumped into a huddled group of women.

'Mama, we greet you,' said one of the younger women, looking at Izuba with awe. She respectfully ignored the bandaged arm. Izuba was held in high regard in the area, as not only did she own her own house, an extremely rare occurrence among Xhosa women who were traditionally regarded as inferior by the men, but she had a son at university and a daughter about to go to college, a tremendous status symbol in a country where for decades university education had been denied to blacks.

Izuba was also consulted by the women on government policies, as it was well known that her 'Madam' worked for the newspapers and that Izuba was wise in the strange ways of the law. Over the years she had acquired from Toni a good working knowledge of the history and laws of the country, as well as of the evils of pollution and the abuse of wildlife.

'You were indeed fortunate that your children were not in the street today. The sun shone on your head, mama.' She hugged her bulging stomach and rocked slowly as she spoke.

'What's happened?' queried Izuba, lines of anxiety creasing her placid face.

The story was a familiar one. The opening of small businesses by the blacks had led to an epidemic of minibuses. They covered the roads of the peninsula like white spots lining the throat of a diphtheria patient and, like wayward bacteria, they flouted laws and regulations, bringing chaos to the already congested freeways. Their profit lay in taking loads of passengers from the city to the outlying townships in as short a time as possible.

In order to do this they flung their overcrowded vans into the lanes of traffic, leaving a river of wild-eyed trembling motorists in their wake. They roared towards the townships, practising the suicidal changing of lanes and tight turns which their heroes performed nightly on television. Once they entered the townships they reached the peak of their performance, executing feats with the vans which should have terrified the manufacturers, and had the stunned designers rushing back to their drawing-boards.

Most of them had forged driving licences, another small business with tremendous growth potential, and the cap and jacket of power and authority which they wore when seated behind a steering wheel turned the young drivers into certifiable maniacs.

One of the potential death vans, driven by a man still saving money to buy a forged licence from the local printer, had spun into a road near Izuba's house, and the toddler, his huge eyes as soft as the velvety centre of a pansy, had been unable to scramble away from the puddle in which he was floating matchsticks.

'Mama, it was her last-born. A son. After bearing eight daughters she paid much money to the *Igqira* for good medicine to make a son,' continued the young woman. She broke into a body-racking fit of coughing, and an old woman, her sweaters of acid green and violet a vivid splash of colour in the sombre group, continued with the story.

'The witchdoctor was very powerful, and a son with an *umthondo*, which would father many good children, was born.' She licked her cracked lips and swallowed painfully. 'A son who, when they picked up his body in the road, was soft in their hands, like a dark red plum which falls to the pavement and is squashed by many feet.'

Izuba shuddered, thinking of her own small daughter safe at home, visualising the tiny body smeared on the road.

'I'll visit her home to add my sorrow to hers,' she said, moving away from the group, 'but first I must see my children, and know that they are safe.'

Izuba paused and turned back. 'The driver?' she queried. 'What of the driver?'

Silence fell over the group.

'Why do you not speak, my sisters?' she asked.

'Mama,' answered the young woman who had spoken first, 'he is in the big hospital but I do not think that he will live.' She shook her head, her eyes downcast, grooving a line in the soil with the toe of her shoe. Patiently Izuba waited. 'The people, when they saw the crushed body of the boy, were maddened. The police had to fire the gun with gas that burns the lungs and makes water run from the eyes to turn them away before they could pick up the driver.'

The young woman paused, twirling her finger in her nostril, an involuntary sign of discomfort and uncertainty. She said, 'I think he will join his ancestors tonight.'

Izuba accepted the story solemnly. 'Thank you, my sisters.'

She shivered. *Umkholwane*, that bird of evil omen, had brought death and would bring further misfortune, as the day had not yet died. Izuba whispered a quick prayer to her ancestors and a short plea to Umdali, God, as she left the huddle of women.

'Umdali, watch over my children when I am away, at Miss Toni. Keep them as you kept your son.' Then, remembering that Umdali had allowed his son to hang on a cross of wood and be mocked, she quickly changed her plea. 'Keep them and do not allow anyone to harm them.' Mindful of how busy Umdali was and how many prayers he had to deal with, she gave him a quick inventory of the Mapei children. She did not want the great Umdali to become confused and protect the wrong family.

'There is Storchman, my eldest boy, Umdali. He has just started at the big university. He is lucky. Then there is Beauty. Guard her well, Umdali, as she nears the end of her schooling, for she is a good daughter and respects the ancestors and tribal ways.' Izuba paused and rested the heavy parcels on the ground. 'Do not take your ear from me, Umdali, for there are still two to protect. Joshua, my youngest son, a boy who finds all things easy and has many friends, and my little one, Soze, my last-born.' Satisfied that her children were well placed in the queue for Umdali's attention and that her ancestors would look after their own, she swung the bags over her forearm, the white plastic biting deeply into the pliant flesh.

Ancestor worship was very important to Izuba and to her tribal people. Like them, she did not believe that death was the end of life. She believed that spirits continue to live and play a part in the daily lives of the living.

Her ancestors were expected to explain fate, and protect the living. They in turn expected the family to follow the traditions of the tribe. Should the family fail to do this the ancestors become enraged. They have to be appeased, witchdoctors consulted, and offerings made.

Izuba walked quickly to her home, and even though the

flapping wings of the *umkholwane* had darkened her spirit, she could not resist the glow of contentment which warmed her whenever she saw the solid red-brick building.

Miss Toni had insisted that the house was registered in her name in case her husband Abraham took a second wife, as those Xhosas who could afford it still took two. In her Xhosa society, where traditionally on marriage the woman is owned by the man and has only the utensils in her hut to call her own, this house made her feet break into the shuffling rhythm of one of the ceremonial dances of thanksgiving whenever she walked up the path to the front door.

The small house was usually overflowing with people, as Izuba, her husband and four children shared it with her twin brothers, Justice and Wisdom, and her older brother with his wife and their three children.

Today only Soze, her baby daughter, came tumbling down the steps to greet her. She had been born a little over two years previously when Izuba had thought her juices had dried and she could no longer present her husband with another baby. In order to confuse the malevolent spirits, who may think that a child born after a long period of barrenness is valued, they had given her an unattractive name. She was called Soze, meaning 'the one who is of no account and is to die'.

Dropping her parcels Izuba scooped up her baby awkwardly. Her eyes huge with happiness to see her mother, Soze shyly touched the white bandage on Izuba's arm before twining her chubby fingers around the necklace of silver and blue beads.

'Uma, I greet you,' Izuba called to her mother as she walked into the house, but only the silence of a darkened home answered her.

'Beauty,' she called and waited for her elder daughter to reply. 'She must be working late at school,' she said to Soze. 'You have a clever sister, my little Soze, and if you work as hard as she does, you too will be able to train to be a nurse or even a schoolteacher.'

'And Josh?' added Soze, wanting her brother included in the praise. Izuba's heavily lashed eyes, brown as maple sugar, softened as she thought of Joshua, a lanky youngster on the threshold of his teens.

'And Josh,' she agreed. 'He will be a very important man one day and you and I will be so proud of him.' Once again she called for Beauty. 'Where is everyone?' she muttered. 'Where is grandmother?' She opened the curtains, allowing the spring sunshine to flood into the room. 'Where is Umakhulu?' Izuba asked her daughter.

'There,' pointed Soze fearfully. Opening the bedroom door, Izuba ran in and fell at the feet of the huddled figure seated on the edge of the bed. Her mother's frail body was shaken with sobs and she wailed in a thin cracked voice.

'What has befallen us, Uma? Why do you grieve?' Izuba asked, stroking the skeletal hand, its fingers knotted like the roots of the ginseng plant.

'Aiee, daughter, we are disgraced. Our ancestors will bring down their wrath on our and our children's heads.' The old lady rocked back and forth, her thin lips quivering as she spoke. 'What shame. The name of Mapei will be spread in the streets like dog dirt.'

Izuba waited patiently until the paroxysm of sobbing had stopped and slowly the story unfolded. During the darkest hours of the night, when no one ventures outside for fear of meeting the evil spirits or the reeking hunchbacked hyena, Izuba's twin brothers had entered the house, their bodies ghostly white beneath the coating of powdered sandstone, and covered from head to foot in the grey and red striped blankets of their initiation school.

Justice and Wisdom had not returned to the Transkei to undergo their initiation into the tribe as men, but had chosen to be circumcised near the township. The Xhosa tribe considered any male regardless of his age to be a mere boy until he had experienced the rites of initiation, and no proud Xhosa girl would condescend to marry an uncircumcised male.

The rites performed near the cities lasted only a few weeks instead of months, and the boys were no longer subjected to unmerciful beatings as they were taught the secrets of manhood and tribal laws; but the actual slicing of the foreskin still had to be borne without the dulling aid of anaesthetics.

The isolated hut in which they had to live naked during the period of instruction, their bodies painted white to protect their identities and save them from the machinations of evil spirits, was hidden deep in the thickets which covered the sandy flats.

The boys foraged through the thickets for food, killing anything they could find and stealing when desperate. Stealing was acceptable, but being caught in the act was not. A blanket was the only covering they were allowed when away from the hut and, as the rites were carried out during the winter or early spring, it afforded little protection against the howling gales and stinging rain.

The twins had just suffered the agonising age-old rites of circumcision. The old man, who had been very carefully chosen, as he was in a position to practise witchcraft on the young boys, sliced through their tender flesh. They sat on a skin *kaross* with their legs spread wide, gritting their teeth until the veins in their necks corded and their eyes bulged wildly. The operation over, they had crept away bowed over with pain and secretly buried the tiny piece of amputated skin. Justice, the elder and stronger twin, had been fortunate and had found an ants' nest where the bleeding piece of flesh was quickly consumed, and he was free from the fear of anyone finding it and using it for witchcraft. Wisdom, a gentle, delicate boy who idolised his brother, had searched for hours before finding a safe grave for his slice of skin. He knew that the ancestors favoured Justice, and was now resigned to following in the footsteps of his beloved brother.

Their *kunkuta*, or guardian, had left them alone whilst he led the doctor through the maze of green bushes back to the road leading to the township, and they were lying on the floor of their beehive-shaped hut lost in misery. They would be denied water for two days and their mouths were already dried and their tongues fat and furry. Their mutilated penises ached as if formic acid was eating into the raw flesh, and the medicinal dressing of green leaves did little to alleviate the throbbing pain.

They had their eyes tightly closed, trying to deaden the pounding in their skulls, when the hut's flimsy door was torn open and a gang of *tsotsies*, lawless youths from the nearby township, had dragged them, struggling desperately, outside into the cold drizzle. These taunting children, young enough to believe in their own immortality and inflamed by revolutionary rhetoric, exulted in their newly found power over parental and tribal authority, and were trampling centuries of laws and customs underfoot.

They relit the dying fire and, whilst waiting for the coals to heat, they amused themselves by mocking the two young initiates for submitting to the age-old rituals of the tribe.

Finally, the coals glowed to their satisfaction, and the leafy dressings, now glued to the twins' penises with dried blood, were ripped off and replaced by sizzling coals. The coals sunk into the soft pink flesh, charring the edges of the skin black. The twins' agonised screams and pleas for help drifted unheard across the rain-soaked bushes, and were swallowed up and lost in the dense fog.

Izuba's mother collapsed, and was able to continue with the story only after Izuba had held a mug of home-brewed beer, thick, foaming and full of vitamins, to her lips. Izuba, horrified and aching to comfort her brothers whom she loved, gently stroked the old woman's head. She longed for earlier times when this and other anti-social behaviour would have led to the offenders being banished from the tribe to spend weeks alone in a remote place with the elders, either emerging from the rehabilitation ready to accept the laws and customs of their tribe, or remaining in the wilderness, a pile of bleached river stones marking their graves.

'Izuba, my child, your brothers when they were able to stand dragged themselves here for help. They were desperate and came even though they know they are forbidden to be near a woman until the white is washed from their bodies, and their hut burnt at the end of the initiation. Aiee,' she wailed softly, 'the *tsotsies* even took my sons' necklaces made with the tail hairs of the sacred cow from our village. Necklaces made with strong magic to protect them. What is to become of them? My sons, my sons, my last-born. What are we to do?'

She opened her tear-filled, rheumy eyes and looked helplessly at Izuba, her eldest daughter and the strongest of her children. Cowering in the doorway, her finger in her mouth and her huge dark eyes fixed on her grandmother, Soze's mouth turned down at the corners, her eyes filled with tears and her childish wails mingled with the old woman's cries.

Izuba ascertained that her mother had dressed her brothers'

wounds with the white man's medicine which she kept locked in the cupboard, and not one of the traditional salves, and that no one had seen them arrive or leave. The children had been asleep in the bedroom curled around each other like puppies in a basket and had not awakened. She then set out to soothe her aged mother's fears and convince her that, because the twins had been attacked by a *tsotsi* gang, the ancestors would sympathise and forgive the boys for having sought help from a woman. It was difficult to convince the old lady, as she knew that if a woman approached the initiates or went near their huts, she risked being put to death. Izuba's aged mother believed that, as she had seen the boys, this would be her fate.

Rocking Soze in her arms, the little tear-streaked face gazing up at her trustingly, Izuba spoke softly and persuasively, citing dozens of instances where tribal customs had had to give way or be changed in the cultural melting-pot of the city.

'Uma, tomorrow I will go to your sister who accepted the call of the shades. She listened to the ancestors and became a witchdoctor and we will offer a good goat to appease our ancestors. If Justice and Wisdom finish their initiation safely and become men in the eyes of the tribe, we will know that the spirits have forgiven them.'

Comforted by these words, the old woman allowed herself to be led from the bedroom and seated on the front step of the house. The watery sun warmed her arthritic limbs and her sunken cheeks blew in and out, like a worn pair of bellows, as she contentedly sucked a pink marshmallow.

It was late that night when Abraham, Izuba's husband, returned. Three of her four children were in bed.

Izuba's oldest boy, Storchman, usually came home when the younger ones were asleep. Izuba was certain that it was a girlfriend and not the library which kept him late on campus, but he merely laughed when she questioned him.

Abraham, a grey-haired, dignified man, had a good job. He was the chauffeur for the director of a large construction company in the Cape. His boss, who had been born on a farm in the Transkei, had grown up tending cattle, setting traps for birds and hunting small animals with the Xhosa herd boys. He understood Xhosa customs and spoke the language

89

fluently. This was unusual in the Cape where few white people spoke Xhosa. Most were proficient in English and Afrikaans and relied on the blacks to communicate in either of these two official languages. The long trips they took together were made pleasant for Abraham by being able to discuss politics and the day's happenings with his boss in his native tongue.

'My wife,' he sighed as he mopped up the remains of the pungent dried-fish stew on his plate with a ball of maize porridge, 'it has been a long and hard trip. I drove over one and a half thousand kilometres and I am as weary as an old ox who can no longer leave the *kraal* to graze.'

He stood up from the table and stretched, his joints cracking like squibs in his huge frame. Izuba clucked in sympathy. She was not able to visualise one and a half thousand kilometres, but knew that it was an enormous distance.

He flung his clothes in a heap on the chair and like a falling oak collapsed on to the bed.

'My wife,' he said, 'come and lie beside me. It is good to have a bed to sleep on.' He patted the side of the bed and Izuba went to him.

Abraham's body ached and his eyelids were heavy, and the story which Izuba whispered to him as she lay cradling her aching arm did not allow his body the rest it needed. He did not wish to hear the softly spoken words, but knew that as head of the house he would have to pronounce judgement.

'Izuba, my wife. There is much trouble in the land, the Nguni people are breeding black jackals who prowl in the darkness, preying off their own kind, breaking sacred laws and defying the dreadful wrath of our ancestors.'

He grunted and turned over, facing her. Placing his lips close to her ear, he whispered. 'In the matter of Justice and Wisdom, you did well. We will kill a goat for the ancestors and the boys will complete their *khwetha* and become men.' Before his eyes closed and his breathing deepened, he muttered softly. 'My wife, all is changing.'

'Changing, my husband, yes,' thought Izuba, and a wave of fear washed over her. 'We, too, my beloved Abraham, we are changing. Tonight, once again, the white of your eyes is stained brown, brown as the waters which become the colour of coffee when they wash over the dark stones in the mountain streams.'

She stroked the tight curls of black and grey scattered across his chin.

'It is the white man's brandy you have drunk. You have visited the *shebeen* and bought the brown hell water from those women who would see a man die if it put money in their grasping hands. That brandy weakens you and you will crawl on your knees and become weak as a girl, to have more. You become like a woman who has the *thikoloshe*.'

At the thought of this hairy little dwarf who carries his enormous penis slung over his shoulder and as a woman's familiar is frighteningly evil, Izuba hung her head over the edge of the bed, checking the wooden legs to make sure that they were raised on bricks, keeping the bed out of the *thikoloshe*'s reach so that he could neither rape her nor cause her to be frigid to her husband.

Satisfied that she was safe, she nestled up against Abraham. Stifling a sob, Izuba put her plump arm around him. 'Oh, my husband, may our ancestors and Umdali save you from the fire curse of brandy.'

She buried her face in his throat, and found comfort in the soft pulse, like a kitten lulled by the beating of its mother's heart.

* * *

The sacrificial animal chosen by Abraham was a favourite among the southern Nguni people, for not only are goats cheaper than cattle, but their sharp, drawn-out death cries are said to please the ancestors.

Izuba's house overflowed with family and friends. Beer was brewed, the coolness of beer being a great attraction for the ancestors who love cool things, and the witchdoctor, the *Igqirakazi*, an aunt of Izuba's family, was there to officiate.

She was most impressive in her swinging white-braided skirt, her right forearm bound up in white beads to guard against evil spirits, her cap of animal skin bobbing on her head and her *sjambok* made from hippo hide clasped firmly in her left hand. Her medicine bag was tied to her body as was her intricately beaded tobacco bag into which was tucked her long-stemmed beaded pipe, an essential part of the adult Xhosa's dress.

They all squeezed into the front room and watched in fascination as the witchdoctor twirled her three-pronged spirit stick in the medicine brewed especially for the goat. There was a roar of applause when the white foam bubbled up and spilled over on to the floor, the thick foam a sure sign that she was a good witchdoctor.

The male goat was untethered from the wooden gatepost and dragged into the house by Abraham and Storchman, with Joshua pushing from behind. Its head was forced down into the foaming liquid and it drank.

'See,' shouted Izuba's mother, 'the goat has drunk. Our ancestors are pleased with our choice. Look at how strong he stands. He will not bring bad luck to my sons by kneeling. He is a good goat.'

Izuba chuckled softly at her mother's joy.

Joshua ran into the room with a spadeful of hot coals and Storchman sprinkled sweet-smelling herbs over them.

The men tugged the goat's head into the fragrant smoke. Its white beard swung wildly as it tried to back away but he was made to inhale.

Abraham passed a green twig of the fragrant herb under the goat's tail and across its back, and the heavy animal was swung upside-down. The men struggled to keep the powerful creature on its back while Abraham raised the short blunt spear they used for all ceremonial occasions and stabbed down into its chest. The old goat's hide was tough, and the spear did not penetrate. It bleated and struggled to escape. Abraham, sweating profusely with the effort, pockmarked its chest with shallow cuts before the old blade finally sank deep into the flesh. With a sigh of relief he twisted the blade and the goat screamed piteously. The family smiled, for this goat was singing beautifully for the ancestors.

Izuba's family believed strongly in the power of sacrifice, and they sat impassively watching the goat convulse as the steel ground into its chest.

Its neat black hooves beat a final tattoo in the air and the tormented animal lay still. Abraham set about butchering it. Izuba handed round the beer, and soon there was much laughter and lively chatter.

The mouthwatering aroma of boiling meat wafted into the room from the kitchen and alerted the witchdoctor. She swiftly ended her whistling conversation with the ancestors and announced that they were happy with the sacrifice and would watch over and protect the twins.

This news was greeted with praise for the Great Spirits, and the family applied themselves to the serious task of feasting.

CHAPTER

5

T HE rays of the setting sun stretched up high from behind the darkening hills and touched the clouds, drifting as softly as fluff teased from a powder puff, and they glowed peach and gold.

The powerful chords of the 'Eroica' symphony echoed in the valleys and hung in the dust thrown up by the blue Mercedes as it wound its way through the maze of Zululand hills. Little herd boys, their polished black skins dulled by the thick coating of dust, scampered to chase the goats and cattle away from the road as the car approached.

The music thundered to a crescendo, and as the final notes throbbed into silence Nick glanced at Toni. The light from the gleaming clouds had gilded her tanned skin and tipped her thick eyelashes with gold. Her eyes were closed and a small smile lifted the corners of her mouth.

'Wake up, Toni, we're almost there,' he said, and she opened her eyes.

'I wasn't asleep,' she answered, running her fingers through her curls and lifting them from the nape of her neck. 'I was listening to the music.'

'Yes,' he teased, 'and keeping time with kitten-like snores.'

'Oh, Nick. I don't, I never snore,' she said.

'I hope not, or else I'm in for a sleepless weekend,' he answered as he lifted her fingers to his lips. Toni watched his mouth, and as he kissed each finger a tremor of excitement ran through her. Soon they would be alone. She had refused to think about the night ahead, either on the flight to Zululand in the company jet which Nick was using, or on the long drive in the hired Mercedes, from the private landing strip to the lodge.

94

She thrilled at the thought of being with Nick, but the enormity of her action still worried her. She had left Timothy with Helen for the weekend. He loved being part of Helen's pre-school crèche and she was happy leaving him in the hands of a child therapist. But her sparkling eyes and air of barely suppressed gaiety when she took Timothy to the farm had made Helen ask who had issued the invitation. She had evaded the question and it made her feel guilty.

Nick lowered her hand on to his knee and covered it with his own.

'You'll see the lodge as we crest the next hill,' he said. 'There, there it is.'

Toni gasped with delight as they drove down to the wooden bridge. The apricot luminosity of the sky had softened and blended the colours and created a silkscreen of the holiday retreat.

Thatched chalets were scatterd along the banks of a mountain stream and the crystal-clear waters were the colours of drowned rainbows.

The high forest behind the chalets was a wonderland of tall trees festooned with trailing green-grey beards of lichen, and thick knotted ropes of wild grape vines and climbing saffron. Toni identified the giant black ironwoods shouldering aside the sneezewoods and the red and white alders, as they battled to rise above the dark shade canopy. She recognised most of the smaller trees, the sweetly perfumed keurboom with its lilac blossoms, and the bright red and orange of the tree fuchsia which splashed colour across the dappled forest floor.

She smiled as she realised that she had three days, three glorious days to spend in this place of hills, folding and unfolding until they merged and were lost in the misty blue of the skies.

'Oh, Nick,' she breathed, 'it's beautiful.'

He squeezed her hand. 'I knew you'd love it as much as I do,' he answered. 'I wanted to share it with you. This is going to be a very special weekend.' He braked the Mercedes, leaned across and brushed her lips lightly before turning off the ignition.

Yes, thought Toni, smiling at him as he walked around the car to open her door. Very, very special, Nick.

The porter, immaculate in white jacket and trousers, cupped his hands to receive his tip from Nick, clapped twice to show his thanks and padded softly out of the two-bedroomed chalet.

Toni turned to Nick and though she smiled, her eyes reflected her uncertainty.

Easy, Houghton, Nick warned himself. Rush things and you'll lose her. Take care.

'Right, Toni,' he said, bending to pick up her suitcase. 'Would you like to use this bedroom as your dressing-room? I'm sure that you'll want to wash and change for dinner.' He put his arm lightly around her shoulders and led her into a room bright with flowered chintz and polished yellowwood furniture.

'The scenery on the drive is spectacular,' he continued, 'but one pays for it with the dust.' He gave her a quick hug, swung her case on to a painted luggage rack and left.

'Thank you, Nick,' Toni whispered.

What you need is a long cold shower, Nicholas, he decided, and not only to wash away the dust. He looked at the closed door of Toni's room and walked slowly across the sitting room to the adjoining bedroom.

* * *

Nick had just crossed his long legs and settled down on the teak bench outside the chalet preparing himself for a long wait when the click of heels alerted him. He jumped up and opened the door.

'Toni,' he breathed, 'you look wonderful.' The short black linen dress clung to her curves and accentuated her shapely legs, and the high-heeled sandals added a provocative swing to her walk. Chunky gold earrings matched the choker around her slender throat and the blue of her eyes was intensified by violet and grey eyeshadow.

He was accustomed to seeing Toni wind-blown and devoid of make-up on their mountain hikes and was stunned and delighted with the beautiful woman who stood before him holding out her hand. 'Thank you,' she answered, enjoying his obvious admiration.

The hollow beating of a cow-hide drum filled the room.

'Oh, good,' said Toni. 'Dinner. I'm starved.' She tucked her hand into Nick's.

Nick smiled at her, proud to have this lovely woman on his arm and relieved that the anxiety he had detected in her earlier had vanished. Toni was relaxed and happy and his spirits sang as they walked through the gardens to the lodge.

They laughed and teased each other over dinner, and the waiters smiled as they served them, enjoying their happiness. Nick regaled Toni with libellous stories about film crews he had worked with, and she described the frightening and funny episodes she had experienced whilst researching her articles.

It was late when they opened the door to their chalet, and the great harvest moon hung low in the heavens.

'Look,' giggled Toni. 'More champagne.' Nestling in a bed of ice in a silver bucket on the low glass-topped table was a dark green bottle.

'Well, well,' said Nick, holding a damask napkin beneath the wet bottle, 'a Bollinger. We certainly can't waste this.' He popped the cork.

'Nick,' said Toni, 'look at *your* bed.' She pointed through the open door at the huge brass bed piled high with lace cushions. 'I've always wanted to have a four-poster bed.' She ran into the room and bounced on the crocheted counterpane. She leaned back against the cushions and stretched out her hand for the glass of champagne Nick was holding.

'You may have the four-poster,' he laughed, 'but there's a catch. I come with it.'

Toni sipped her drink looking up at him over the rim of the glass, and her eyes were suddenly serious. 'That's no catch,' she said. 'That's an added attraction.'

Nicholas studied the woman framed by the soft lace pillows. Her curls had escaped from the gold clasp which held them sleeked off her face and lay tousled across her forehead. Her dress had slid up high on her thighs when she kicked off her shoes to jump on the bed, and the glow of the bedside lamp shimmered on her stockinged legs. He caught his breath and leaning across the bed he took her glass and placed it on the bedside table, spilling a little on to the hand-embroidered cloth.

He smoothed the curls away from her face and lovingly

97

ran his thumb across the heavy lids of her eyes, and traced her finely arched eyebrows with his fingertips. His breathing deepened, yet he hesitated, not wanting to lose her by moving too fast. Sensing his indecision, she lifted her arms and, cupping his face, she drew his lips down to hers. Nick tasted the desire and eagerness in her mouth and knew that the woman he wanted so fiercely was his.

Carefully he unclipped her earrings and choker and slipped his hand under her back, sliding down the zipper of her dress. Again he ran his tongue lightly over her lips, probing and tasting her, and then pulled away and sat up.

'You're so beautiful, Kitten, so very lovely,' he said, running his fingers over the smooth bare skin above her stockings. He unclipped the silk from her black suspender-belt and ran his lips down her legs as he peeled off the stockings, delighting in the texture and smell of her skin.

His lips pressed for a moment against the black scrap of lace between her legs before he stripped it away. Toni instinctively covered herself with her hands, but he gently eased them away.

'Let me look at you, Kitten,' he murmured. 'You're a lovely woman. Let me touch you.' Toni quivered as his tongue found and caressed her and soon she pressed herself up to him in her need.

'Nick,' she whispered.

He moved up to cover her and they looked deep into each other's eyes as their breathing quickened.

'You're mine, Kitten,' he said huskily as their bodies started to move in the timeless rhythm of love. 'Mine.'

'Yes, Nick,' she answered, and her voice trembled as she gave herself completely to the man pressing down over her.

The pearly moonlight filtered through the lace curtains moving gently in the night breeze and painted fanciful shapes and figures on the light wood of the ceiling, transforming it into a monochrome Sistine Chapel.

Nick and Toni lay, staring up, as had Michelangelo when he painted the magnificent ceiling in the Vatican. They were entranced with the black, grey and silver painting above them and lay quietly gazing at the moving patterns. A corner of the ivory curtain lazily flicked at a bowl of roses, scattering the heavily scented red petals.

Two white-faced wood owls, well camouflaged against a tree trunk, chanted their syncopated duet to the stars and the wind wafted the call into the bedroom, a feathery choir for the moonlit chapel.

Toni stretched voluptuously, tearing her eyes away from the shadow paintings on the ceiling above her, the thin cotton sheet clinging to her body. She turned to the man lying beside her.

'Do you remember the *Kakapo*, Nick?' she murmured, smoothing down the luxuriant hair on his chest, making a silky pad on which to rest her cheek. She looked up at him, his face soft and blurred in the frosted light.

'I do. In fact I remember it very well,' he answered sleepily.

'I still feel embarrassed when I think of how I pushed you away. I must have been crazy,' she said softly. 'I've never known such joy and excitement in making love. You've made me feel so very desirable.' She kissed the dark brown nipple on his chest gently.

A spasm of tenderness shook him, so sudden and so poignant that he had to swallow before he could speak again.

'Come here,' he said, sliding her body up so that her head rested on the lace-edged pillow beside his. His fingers traced the lace patterns transferred on her silky skin by the curtained moonlight.

'I love you, my kitten,' he said. Toni lifted her head. 'No,' he said, 'don't say anything. Not now.' He kissed her gently and closed his eyes.

The melting ice clinked in the ice bucket standing beside the brass bed as the cubes slid down the sides of the empty champagne bottle. Toni's eyelids drooped, heavy with sleep, but she forced them open, determined not to miss a moment of precious time spent with Nick in this idyllic retreat in the quilted hills of Zululand.

The three days passed as swiftly as a whirlwind which spins everything into its surging vortex then vanishes, leaving only a soft veil of dust hanging lightly in the air.

They wandered through the short days in a trance of happiness, planning their activities over breakfast seated on the flagged patio overlooking the river. They watched the bulbuls at their morning's ablutions, their soft yellow feathers fluffed out under their tails as they shook and splashed in the cold water, and they placed bets on the fishing success of the kingfishers.

They dripped wildflower honey on to their homemade bran muffins, and ate omelettes flavoured with freshly picked herbs from the kitchen garden, revelling in the peace and beauty around them.

They returned to the lodge at midday flushed and laughing after galloping over the grassy hills on sure-footed horses, each hilltop unfolding a vista more breathtaking than the last.

Lingering over their coffee at night, they watched Venus, the evening star, peering through a chink in the curtains of the heavens, studying the earthly audience before allowing the glittering cast to come on stage.

Nick had pointed out the stars, telling her the names given to them by the Bantu tribes.

'There is *U-cel izapolo*, the one who asks for a little milk from the teat,' Nick said, pointing out the evening star to Toni.

She had looked up at the sky, sucking melted chocolate from her fingers, having eaten the last of the homemade champagne truffles.

'Why, Nick? Why do they call Venus that?' she enquired.

'Because it's the star which appears in the evening when they milk the cows. Unlike the Xhosa, the south Sotho tribe call it *Sefalabohoho*, or crust scrapings, because that's all that is left in the pot for anyone who arrives for supper after the evening star has risen.'

Toni laughed and questioned him about other picturesque names given to the stars and planets.

They scanned the heavens lazily, then walked slowly to their chalet, breathing in the clear night air perfumed with the sweet smell of jasmine and gardenias which bordered the pathway, the crunching gravel beneath their feet silencing the frogs who were building up to a croaking crescendo in their nightly talent contest.

Their bedroom had become a university for their love, and they were insatiable students eagerly exploring each other's bodies and minds, resenting the few hours of sleep which interrupted their research.

She blossomed and grew under his hard body and gentle fingers, always craving more, until they moved as one, each sensing the other's need and waiting until their bodies exploded in a trembling, throbbing unison.

Each hour they spent together made the thought of returning to their respective lives more unacceptable, and they clung like limpets to each other.

On the day of their departure they took a picnic lunch and followed the river into the forest. It was a hard climb up into the hills and when they arrived at the small rocky rapids, the birthplace of the large body of water which raced and whirled past the lodge, they were hot and tired.

Toni kicked off her soft shoes and walked carefully over the slippery stones until she reached a large polished rock around which the water bubbled and churned. She pulled up her skirt and bent down to scoop up the cold water, her long, smooth thighs exposed. The invitation had proved irresistible and Nick was now seated on the grassy bank in the sun, drying his trousers.

'I'm so pleased we stopped here. This is a lovely place for a rest,' said Toni, unpacking the picnic lunch.

'A rest?' grinned Nick, fingering his sodden trousers. 'I've a frozen bum and a pair of very wet trousers.'

'I noticed that you had some difficulty balancing with your trousers around your ankles,' she teased.

'It was your fault, wench. I was sorely tempted,' he explained, 'and once again, I fell prey to temptation.'

'Hallelujah for a sinner,' laughed Toni and leaned across to kiss him. His eyes darkened as he pulled her down over him. Cupping her face in his long tapered fingers, he looked up into her eyes a few inches away from his own.

'Toni, I love you and I want you. I no longer want to share you. I know that you worry about taking Timothy away from Serge, but I'll love your son and look after him.' His voice broke. 'I want to have you with me always. I want to wake up beside you and fall asleep with your lovely bottom tucked up against me.' He stroked her cheek. 'I'm proud of you, I love you and I want the world to know.

101

I need you, my kitten. I want to grow old with you beside me.'

Toni held her breath, afraid to speak and break the magic of his words. How she had longed to hear them.

'This weekend has made me realise how rich and full life is with you, and I shudder at the thought of living without you. I have watched you bath, cream your face, have listened to your soft breathing while you sleep, and watched you awaken in the morning, your head buried under the pillow, only your nose and mouth visible.' He brushed her lips gently with his own. 'You have become very precious to me, my kitten, too precious to lose.'

Slowly the tears welled into Toni's eyes and she buried her face in his shoulder. Much as she wanted to, she could not tell him that she would leave Serge. She needed time to plan what would be best for her child and time to build up courage to face Serge. Nick held her in his arms.

What I sought to what you are love,
was a starlight to a star love.

Softly he recited the poem she loved, gently stroking her hair and calming her. The sun beat down on them and the smell of rich red earth and crushed grass was strong in their nostrils.

Their idyll had ended and Nick decided to return to Cape Town with Toni on a commercial flight. The Boeing roared up into the night sky, the acceleration pressing them back into their seats, and the craft creaked and cracked as it accepted the strain of thrusting one hundred and sixty tons of weight up to cruising altitude.

The winds buffeted it as it forced its way up to the calm air found at high altitude, and the landing gear groaned as it was tucked away into the sleek white belly.

As the lights of the airport faded below them Toni reached across the seat for the comfort of Nick's hand and held it tightly, feeling the rim of her gold wedding ring cutting into her flesh. The aircraft, a fragile flying insect, droned through the night.

CHAPTER

6

A PIERCING whistle alerted the passengers and warned late-comers and stragglers that one of the methodically lined-up trains was about to leave the station.

Toni was seated in her white sports car parked against the kerb, and she glanced up at the crush of people clogging the pedestrian walkway high above the road. They exhibited all the aggression of rats trapped in an overcrowded cage, using suitcases and elbows to force their way across the bridge and down to the station. She looked at her watch and patted the hand lying clenched on the seat beside her. The delicate fingers restlessly kneaded a sodden handkerchief. She would have just enough time to complete the interview with Izuba's daughter before the girl left Cape Town with her grandmother.

'Don't worry, Beauty,' she said. 'We still have twenty minutes before the train leaves. Izuba will have found a seat for your grandmother. This won't take long.'

She pressed the rewind button on the tape-recorder and checked that the tape was running freely. Her voice, sounding high and tinny, filled the car and she listened intently, making certain that she had left out no important facts.

A few years ago our children in the townships were caught up in the euphoria of public violence. They smashed up classroom furniture, burned down schools, disregarded parental authority and challenged police authority. Their schooling was interrupted. When the schools were rebuilt and re-opened, the desire to work had dimmed. The absolute power and heady freedom which the children

103

had experienced was a worm which had entered their entrails and is still gnawing at them relentlessly.

We had educated them only to a level of dissatisfaction. So that now the gradual process of blacks and whites drawing closer to each other across the quicksands of brutal wars, cultural differences and mistrust, is too slow for them. Like children gathered around a Christmas tree, they are eager to be given and to open the presents immediately.

Beauty wiped her eyes with her handkerchief, and fresh teardrops again beaded her lashes. She sat patiently waiting for the recording to end.

Thousands of these youngsters embraced Marxist ideology and called themselves Comrades. Desperate to be accepted and to partake in the riches of the country, not mature enough to understand or accept the laborious process of negotiating a new system of government, and still distrusting the new face of the powers they had learned to hate, they held meetings with other children. They planned to steal guns and make fire bombs. They spoke of owning fine white houses and businesses and driving smart cars.

They planned to recruit young girls into their cause by making them pregnant and the cry 'A baby for the Revolution' was born.

Toni, satisfied, punched the button cutting off her own voice.

'Beauty, you have already told me how you met the leader of the young Comrades. Would you now tell me about the meetings you attended?'

Beauty closed her swollen eyes and saw again her lover, a tall powerful youth of eighteen. He was well versed in the slogans of war and hatred, and like so many members of his tribe was a natural and compelling speaker. She had fallen under his spell.

The soft whirr and squeak of the tape-recorder became for her the mesmeric words of her Comrade lover, and when she described the tin shack used for the meetings she repeated his words faithfully, almost in a trance.

'Our parents do not understand the modern world. They know only the tribal laws and customs. This is our time and we must take it. We must show them the way.'

Beauty swallowed and continued.

'They say they'll share the government with us. They lie. They say they'll share the money from *i'goli*, the great gold fields. They lie. They lie because they fear the might and anger of the black man. There is only one way.' Beauty saw his eyes glitter, and the candlelight casting dancing shadows over the faces of the youngsters crammed into the dark back room of the shack. 'Only one way. Kill them and take power.'

She heard again his words as they throbbed in the utter stillness. 'This land is ours, not to share but to own. We will own everything, everything in this land. All the groups with letters for names are weak. They talk like old women around the cooking fire and their strength drains away in words. They believe that we are but children. We, my brothers, are strong and will take the land. All will be ours.'

Beauty remembered how she had joined in the frenzied applause and shouting. Hysterical with the vision of a new and wonderful life, she had eagerly lain on the dirty sacking, spreading her thighs as he humped over her.

Toni, afraid to break the flow of words, kept silent. The tribal peoples' gift of total recall still amazed her.

Beauty opened her eyes. She respected Miss Toni and always mentally excluded her when her lover derided the elders and the whites. She knew that she could not tell Miss Toni of the meeting when, lying on the mat curled up beside the Comrade leader, she had told him about Miss Toni and her vision of a new country.

'You, Nomhle,' he had screamed, 'are you too one of the whites' fools?' He had jumped up and straddled her body, standing over her like a colossus as she lay trembling, looking up at him. His genitalia hung heavy between his thighs and the muscles in his shoulders bulged as he clenched his fists on his hips.

'Are you a traitor to our cause?' His eyes blazed. 'Do you believe that the whites have won just because the soldiers have stopped the riots and the Boer Government has put chairs around the table for the blacks to sit and talk?'

He kicked her thigh, his foot like rough sandpaper scraping and scratching her tender skin. He looked down at her quivering body in disgust. They should never have allowed women to join in the meetings.

In their tribes, meetings and fighting were men's work, but the bearded ones from overseas, who came in the night to instruct them, said that women must be included. The youngsters had obeyed them, because the strangers were showing them how to break down the whites and throw out the government.

'You fool!' he shouted. 'Have you listened to nothing in the meetings? Have you not heard of the houses which are built on wooden legs, and of the little brown beetle which crawls into the wood and eats away quietly inside, until one day the strong wooden legs crumble and the huge house smashes down?'

He kicked at her thigh again. She pressed her legs tightly together, trying to evade the pounding foot, and bit her lip to stop from crying out loud. Centuries of tradition had taught her complete subservience to men and she lay terrified, hypnotised by his anger.

'We are those beetles, thousands and thousands of beetles, and we are eating away quietly and soon the whole white system will smash down and we will own everything. The power will be ours.' His eyes flashed and the strength of his vision flooded into his loins, hardening him. Looking down at the soft black body beneath him, he smiled. A hard, cruel smile. Slowly he lowered himself over her, his thighs spread wide as he squatted, his manhood pulsing violently.

She had learnt her lesson well that night, and had avoided any further mention of help or advice received from Miss Toni, whom she loved and looked upon as a member of her family. She had wiped the blood carefully from between her aching thighs and swollen vagina before creeping home.

'Oh, Miss Toni,' she sobbed. 'I have shamed my family and now I will never go to college and wear the white and maroon uniform of a sister in the hospital.' She blew her nose. 'I have broken my mother's pride and I have to go far away from her. I have to go to our *kraal* to have the baby.'

106

Toni put her arm around Izuba's daughter and patted her softly, trying to lessen her unhappiness. 'You'll come back, Beauty,' she crooned. 'When the baby is born you'll come home to your mother.'

'My mother says that I am her eldest daughter, who made her heart sing and her feet light. She says that I have become like one of the filthy ones from the *shebeen*. I am like a dog vomiting up food it has eaten. I have thrown away everything they gave me.'

Beauty hiccuped and Toni stroked her cheek.

'I cried for my mother to beat me when I saw the pain in her eyes. I cannot heal the hurt I have caused her.'

A final whistle from the train echoed shrilly in the car.

'Izuba will always love you, Beauty. You're her daughter,' comforted Toni. She switched off the recorder and they ran into the station.

Through a mist of tears Izuba watched Beauty climb into one of the floating carriages and she tightened her grip on Soze's hand. The little fingers curled trustingly around hers, and the little girl peered fearfully from behind her mother's voluminous, brightly flowered skirt, staring at the noisy machine which had swallowed her beloved grandmother and Nomhle, her sister.

Tears ran unheeded down Izuba's cheeks. No longer would she return home to find her mother telling the children colourful tales of their ancestors, no longer would her lovely child Beauty come running to greet her and brew a pot of tea to refresh her after her journey. It would be a year before she could save enough money to take the children and visit her mother and Beauty in the Transkei. She would not be present for the birth of Beauty's baby and even though her daughter had shamed her, her love for the beautiful girl was deep and unbroken.

Izuba wanted her mother, that gentle aged woman, close to her. She realised it was necessary for her people to accept both the powerful Western culture and keep their own traditional beliefs to survive in a country where strange European middle-class values had been imposed on them. She needed the wisdom of her mother's years to help her accept the strange and changing society she lived in. Her heart ached for the

107

loss of her mother and daughter, and she was oblivious of the crowds jostling her as they hurried back to work.

Toni stood watching her, then she put her hand on Izuba's arm.

'Don't cry, Izuba,' she said softly, shaking out a handkerchief and handing it to her to wipe her eyes. 'Nomhle will be happy with your mother. She'll learn to live the traditional life of the Xhosa woman. Think, her son will join the boys and learn to track and kill rabbits and guineafowl. He'll swim in the rivers and learn about your Nature Spirits, the River People. They'll be so happy in the beauty of your ancestral lands, Izuba.'

Comforted by Toni's words, Izuba dabbed at her face. 'They will be true Xhosas, not the hyena offal who live in the cities and prey on their own people,' she answered Toni as she tucked the wet handkerchief into her pocket.

Together they watched the train slither out of the station, sinuous as a grass snake. As its tail pulled away from the covered platform it picked up speed, the carriages creaking and swaying on the burnished silver rails. The hooter shrieked a farewell to the Mother City and hailed the Transkei, the land across the Kei river which belonged to the Xhosa people.

There was much laughing and joviality in the packed coaches, filled with city workers returning to their wives and families in their homeland villages.

In a system where a man can have as many wives as he is able to afford, and the abduction of young girls for marriage is considered legal, many of the men were hard pressed to support both city and homeland families, and it was usually the homeland wives who suffered and had to rely on the tribe for support.

Izuba's mother sat on the hard wooden bench watching the trees and houses blending and blurring as the train rattled past. She was pleased she had ended her sojourn in the big city. Her feet rested on a blue plastic case which Izuba had bought and which held her dearest possessions, a new red blanket, a metal teapot and packets of tea, a large brightly coloured tin of biscuits which she would display proudly in her hut and packets of seeds. Her toothless gums worried at a sticky brown toffee. She had a handful in the pocket of her knitted green jacket; they would help pass the long day and night she would spend sitting on the bench before the train reached its destination.

She was happy to be returning to tribal life. Her youngest daughter and her five grandchildren would be waiting to greet her, the earthen floor of her hut would be swept, and fresh water would be standing inside the door. As the sun grew pale and weak she would tell the women stories of the city while they stirred the fluffy white maize meal over the smoking coals. She would shock the women with tales of the city children's disregard for laws and customs as they boiled the bitter, green *umsobosobo* plant to eat with the porridge.

The old woman loved her family in the city dearly, but the air smelt stale and strange, the streets were never still, the cars and people hummed and buzzed, like maddened Matabele ants, and the tribal laws of the white man bewildered her. The political violence and jargon used by the youngsters alarmed her. She came from a nation whose history was written in the blood of tribal wars. That she understood. She knew that men fought for their tribe, that their loyalty was with their tribe and the individual was unimportant – it was the lineage that mattered; but she did not understand the men who listened to people from overseas and who had the ANC, SWAPO, PAC and UDF as their tribal names.

The old lady shuddered, buttoning her cardigan with trembling fingers. Beauty, sitting beside her, wiped the tears from her cheeks with the back of her hand and leaned across to help with the remaining buttons.

'Thank you, Nomhle, Beauty,' she said and offered the girl a toffee.

She looked at the girl's lovely oval face, the brown eyes clear and trusting, the glowing skin the colour of milky coffee, the hair gelled into a frizzy halo very much the fashion among the young girls in the towns.

It is bad that Beauty has to return with me to the *kraal*, she thought. She would have fetched a good bride price for Abraham and Izuba. The family could have gained many good cattle for Nomhle. The old rheumy eyes slid over the girl's swelling bosom and rested on her stomach, the bulge already apparent, spreading the folds of her turquoise pleated skirt.

Abraham and the men from the young Comrade's family

would have to decide on a price to be paid for the support of the 'revolution baby' which Beauty was carrying and would give birth to on the dusty floor of a secluded hut in the village. She wondered which midwives would be chosen. They would be women well past menopause, so no hint of ritual impurity could interfere with the birth process and harm the child.

She knew that Beauty's baby would be welcomed into the tribe as children were fundamentally important to her Nguni people. She smiled at Beauty. It would be good to have another baby in her family.

Lulled by the rocking of the train, Beauty thought of how she would miss Izuba, her huge dignified mother. She had destroyed Izuba's pride and dashed her hopes, and she ached for the pain she had caused the mother she loved so dearly. She knew she would also miss the dark hours spent in the shack with her lover, miss the meetings which made the blood race in her veins and her breath quicken and her heart pound, like the frightened hare chased by dogs.

The train whistled a long mournful wail as it slipped easily as a mole into the dark tunnel piercing the green and purple mountain ranges which isolate the Peninsula from the interior.

Wails of consternation broke out in the carriage as the train swayed deep into the velvet darkness. Beauty found and held the old woman's hand tightly, her eyes wide, her ears filled with shrieks from the initiates to train travel and loud admonitions from the ones who knew that this black belly of the mountain would soon open into the sunlight. They sat swaying in the dark, a plump young hand and a wrinkled old claw joined firmly together, as the train twisted and turned on its tortuous journey to their homeland.

* * *

The typist's hands flew over the electric keyboard and her thin fingers darted at the keys with the lightning speed of a chameleon's streaking tongue. The dark green earphones were clamped over her carefully permed hair. Only a few strands had escaped the blue rinse and showed up startling white in the ocean of mauve waves.

At precisely nine thirty a buzzer sounded on her desk.

She flipped up the silver watch pinned to the bodice of her black dress and, satisfied that it was indeed nine thirty, she stood and opened the heavy oak door leading into an inner wood-panelled room.

'Mr Cunningham will see you now,' she said, beckoning imperiously to the young woman seated on one of the chairs.

'Thank you,' said Toni, smoothing down her short grey skirt and straightening the large shoulder pads in her blue and grey checked jacket. Shoulders held rigidly back, she followed the tightly corseted secretary into the office of the editor of the *Cape Daily*.

'When you're nervous or unsure of yourself, lift up your chin and walk proudly.' Her father had given her this advice when she was a skinny teenager, unhappy at home, hating her stepfather and about to enter the confusing world of womanhood.

She entered Cunningham's office with a smile masking her inner turmoil.

'Good morning. Do sit down, Mrs Balser.'

Toni seated herself in the heavily carved wooden chair and wondered whether the rumours that Cunningham dyed his hair were true. He had the good looks of a film star, though time had lined the perfect skin and softened the clean-cut jawline.

He had held his prestigious position for almost three decades and many an unwary reporter had found that behind the good looks and gentle blue eyes lay a razor-sharp mind, an iron will and an intolerance for anything which fell short of his standards of professionalism.

Many cocksure reporters had walked into that office only to slink out, their ears smarting and the ethics of professional reporting deeply engraved on their minds.

Toni forced herself to sit passively, legs pressed lightly together, her hands resting in her lap. She watched quietly as he flicked through a pile of papers on the desk in front of him.

He selected one, tilted back his wingback chair, the leather armrests worn shiny with age, and studied the paper.

'Mrs Balser, you have been writing articles for my paper for many years.'

'Yes,' answered Toni.

He raised his eyes for a moment and studied her, then returned to his perusal of the paper in his hand.

'This article you did entitled "Children, have a baby for the Revolution" – where did you do your research? Are the facts substantiated?'

Toni took a deep breath to still the tremor in her voice. 'I visited all the hospitals in the area and spoke to the young girls who had just given birth as well as the nursing staff and the matrons. There's been a definite increase in girls, in some cases very young girls, coming in to have babies. As you know, our African girls mature early and a twelve-year-old could pass for eighteen. Some refused to talk to me, they considered me the white enemy, but others were proud of the part they were playing in furthering the aims of the revolution and boasted of the army of black babies they were spawning. They truly believe that by increasing the black population, they're ensuring that their people will have a say in the running of the country. They're desperate and this candy stick held out by the Comrades is being eagerly accepted.'

Cunningham sat watching her as she spoke, making no move to interrupt or question her.

'I spoke to parents in the townships,' she continued. 'Some supported the idea of an endless black tidal wave sweeping across the land. But many disliked the interruption in the child's schooling and were opposed to their daughters being taken and impregnated without the traditional payment of *lobola*, for as you know, Mr Cunningham, the payment of the bride price not only compensates the family for the loss of their daughter, but it ensures that her new husband treats her well. If she's unhappy she can return to her father and the young man forfeits the cattle, or nowadays, the money which he paid for her.'

Toni paused and, receiving no response, she continued with her explanation. 'The girl in the article whom I called Patience is based on my Xhosa maid's daughter, Beauty. Izuba, her mother, is a wonderful woman.

'Beauty is just sixteen, a lovely girl. She was top of her class at school and was looking forward to entering a nursing college. When the mass intimidation of schoolchildren began, Beauty was accosted by a young group of Comrades on her way home from school. They ripped her books into tiny pieces and made her chew and swallow some of the pages. They then began punching and kicking her, accusing her of being a sell-out, a government lackey and a Boer-lover. The torment was stopped by the arrival of the leader of the group. He scattered his Comrade friends and led the shivering girl home, earning her gratitude. Soon Beauty was secretly attending Comrades' meetings at night, attracted not by the violent slogans, but by the young mesmeric leader. The inevitable happened, she fell pregnant, her schooling and hopes of becoming a nurse were abandoned and she has returned to the Transkei to have her baby. She is there now. A girl-child who had a baby for the revolution.'

The room was quiet but for the tapping of the editor's well-manicured nails on the paper. Toni surreptitiously wiped her damp palms on her skirt and shifted uneasily in the baronial chair.

'Good, Mrs Balser,' he said.

He riffled through the white pages with the expertise of a blackjack dealer shuffling cards and selected a page. 'I've your latest article here, the authenticity of which has been queried by a sub-editor. Would you like to skim through it to refresh your memory?'

Toni accepted the article headed 'Children of Darkness' and silently read the opening paragraphs.

In the book *The Reality of Magic* by Abbé Simmonet, it is written that the whole race of Cain proved inherently evil. Cain turned away from God and sought help from Satan and the fallen angels, and they corrupted the race by betraying the secrets of God, and imparting dark knowledge. We are the children of Cain.

The great flood came to drown the land and wipe out the witchcraft and diabolism practised by the children of Cain, but Ham, one of Noah's three sons, survived the terrible flood and revived the evil, black science. The mysteries he practised and spread were even more dark and dangerous than the primitive satanism and sorcery practised by Cain and his followers, and Ham's sons, initiated by their father into the grotesque secrets,

113

separated into various tribes and from his son Cush, father of the Ethiopians, came all African witchcraft, and all the secret cults of all the black tribes.

The young black Comrades are the sons of Cush. Witchcraft did not suddenly burst upon us; it developed in the long process of time. It has always been with us. The mob which surrounded the home of the mother of five in Shonalanga screaming that she was a witch and demanding her death by fire were as inflamed and blinded by superstition as the chanting crowds who surrounded the lovely young maid from Orléans, centuries ago. Fears and superstitions do not excuse— '

The editor coughed and Toni stopped reading and looked up. Quickly she forestalled the question. 'I obtained the facts for that article from the two policemen who were first called in to deal with the situation and from the lady accused of witchcraft.'

'She spoke to you?' queried Cunningham.

'Oh, yes,' answered Toni. 'She was shocked and afraid but also very angry.'

'How long after the incident did you talk to her?'

'I spoke to her the same evening,' said Toni, and seeing the query in his eyes she quickly explained. 'Helen, a friend of mine who is trying to open a crèche in Shonalanga, was in the area and followed one of the police cars. A young rookie told her what had happened before his superior ordered her away from the scene.'

'You believed her? You believed her story?'

'Certainly,' answered Toni. 'Witchcraft, herbalism, ancestors and spirits are closely yoked to psychiatry, modern medicine, psychologists, and churches, and together they pull the unwieldy wagon of black Africa through the gulleys of tribalism and the swamps and quicksands of Western civilisation.' Realising that her speech was becoming flowery and emotional, she took a deep breath and forced herself to be impassive.

'Her story is true. The young Comrades who accused her of witchcraft were probably spurred on by men envious of her new home, but the two hundred chanting youths who threw

114

rocks and stones at her house, shattering the windows, were convinced that she was a witch and had raised the dead bodies of their friends.

'Mr Cunningham,' she pleaded, 'I spoke to the two men who had to face the enraged mob alone. One of them was Stan le Roux, an honourable man, and an unsung hero in the townships. He is seen in the middle of almost every situation of unrest.'

Toni's face flushed and her eyes sparkled as she defended her informants.

'The children listen to him, Mr Cunningham. The Nguni tribes respect fearlessness and strength, and Stan le Roux has these traits in abundance, plus a large dash of compassion and pity for the plight of deprived people.'

The editor, his fingers steepled, elbows resting on the desk, motioned to her to continue.

She studied Cunningham's impassive face for a moment and then went on.

'A few years ago a survey was carried out in Soweto. They estimated the black population of that complex bordering the gold fields to be a million, and it was found that three-quarters of the people believed implicitly in witchcraft, and some of them are fifth-generation city people.'

'Mrs Balser,' the editor interjected, 'I wish you to read the closing paragraph of your article for me.' He leaned his head against the back of his chair and closed his eyes.

Toni swallowed apprehensively. 'If the men who are jetting around the world in luxury, shouting loudly for powerful nations to continue sanctions and bring further hardships on the suffering black man; if they would shout as loudly for the wealthy nations to pour money into the country for black education, then our children could emerge from the darkness and use knowledge and learning to combat tribal fears and ignorance and cries of "Burn the evil witch" would be silenced.'

Cunningham leaned across the desk and took the page away from Toni. 'Your work over the last two years has shown great depth and compassion. People seem to have replaced animals and environmental disasters as your top priority.'

Toni opened her mouth to speak but he continued quickly.

115

'Your political persuasions seem to swing from the far right to the far left depending on which subject you are addressing. You seem to have no sacred cows. Everyone is given the Toni Balser treatment.'

Toni licked her lips nervously. He had obviously arranged this meeting to tell her that they no longer wished to publish her articles. Disappointment washed over her and chilled her like a sudden shower of rain. She had been proud of her articles; they had been so well researched and she had written them with such feeling.

Cunningham continued talking, and with an effort she pulled her thoughts away from the cold douche of rejection and listened.

'Therefore, Mrs Balser, in the light of the letters I've received from members of the government and various churches and societies, I'd like you to consider writing a weekly column for the *Daily*.'

Toni stared at him. He had liked her articles; so had groups ranging across the spectrum of politics and they wanted her to write for them. She wanted to dance on the red leather top of his desk, she wanted to fold her arms around him and hug him hard, she wanted to scream out her joy, open the sash window overlooking the cobbled square and shout out the wonderful news to the stallholders, jugglers and dancers who warmed the grey square with colour and laughter.

Instead she dug her fingernails deep into the palms of her hands and said quietly, 'Thank you, Mr Cunningham.'

'You will of course have your own byline and photograph, and you'll receive a handsome retainer. You'll have the use of one of the paper's secretaries and a photographer, plus an allowance for any travel expenses connected with your articles.'

Watching her face brighten and her eyes sparkle, a rare wave of affection for an employee entered the editor's austere world of work and business ethics. He ordered a tray of tea and his secretary bustled away, every step registering stern disapproval. It was most unlike him to enjoy a social cup of tea at the start of a busy morning, and she did not wish to encourage such behaviour.

'Now,' said Cunningham when the tea had been poured and

116

they were crunching biscuits, 'tell me a little about yourself.' She soon had him chuckling over incidents in her childhood in the wilds of Zambia.

To his surprise he found himself talking of things he had kept locked away in the dusty attic of his mind. When his secretary could no longer contain her impatience and knocked on the door, he realised why Toni's articles were so good. She was a listener. She had no need to pry; people wanted to talk to her, to share their hopes and fears. Taking her hand in his to say goodbye, he was pleased that she was on a retainer to his paper.

She walked out of his office, her feet barely touching the carpet. She had used work as an antidote for her loneliness at night. Alone in her quiet house she had poured out her findings on thick white notepads, and the cure had been recognition. She was part of the conglomerate which would cement this country, cracked and crumbling like a derelict cottage, into an indestructible concrete tower reinforced with steel rods of understanding and compassion.

The old wino sitting with his back against the warm brown bricks of the newspaper building held up a tin to Toni as she tripped down the granite steps and his face broke into a delighted grin as he heard the crinkle of paper pushed into the old syrup container. 'No, miss,' he replied to her query, 'I won't buy wine, I'll buy bread. God bless you, miss.'

He buried the note quickly beneath his patched jacket. He would be able to buy a hot-dog made of the local spiced sausage, and there would be enough for a litre of 'sweet', the sugary golden wine he loved. He settled back happily against the wall, his blotched face turned up to the sun, and watched as the smiling lady walked quickly to a nearby phone booth and closed the door. He saw her dial and drop a silver coin into the slot and he smiled as he saw her laugh.

'Nick,' she said, 'I just had to phone you. I'm so happy. I have the most wonderful news. I— '

'Kitten,' he laughed, 'slow down or I won't understand a word you're saying.'

Toni took a deep breath, exhaled and said, 'I've just been given my own column on the *Daily* and all the extras which go with it.'

'Magnificent,' he answered. 'Congratulations, Toni, you deserve it. Your work is excellent and you'd be a credit to any newspaper.'

'May I take that as a completely unbiased opinion?' she asked impishly.

'You may,' he said tenderly, 'and consider yourself well kissed and hugged and . . . '

The old wino saw the pretty lady blush scarlet, speak for a few minutes, then replace the receiver. She stood indecisively, tapping her polished nails on the grey metal phone box. Then she pushed open the door and swung out of the booth. Catching the door before it closed, she stepped back inside and slowly dialled a number.

'Mr Balser, please,' she said, and waited. She glanced at the old wino propped up against the wall of the *Daily* offices and wondered what he would do with the money she had given him.

'Balser, yes,' snapped Serge, and her fingers tightened on the receiver.

'Serge, I do hope that I'm not disturbing you,' she apologised, 'as this can wait until tonight. It's not that important.'

'My honey,' he soothed, 'it's a pleasure to have a call from you. You phone the office so seldom. Tell me, what has happened?'

Toni gulped. 'Mr Cunningham at the *Daily* has offered me a weekly column of my own.'

'Yes,' said Serge, his voice suddenly cold. 'And?'

'And I have accepted it.'

Tension twanged between them like tightly tuned guitar strings.

'I consider the offer to be an acknowledgement of my work and an honour, Serge.'

'An honour?' he said. 'It's an honour to be a good wife and mother. It's no honour to rake up dirt and write about it.'

Toni closed her eyes. It was starting again.

'Journalism is an esteemed profession, Serge,' she reasoned.

'Esteemed only by the muck-rakers and glory-seekers who are in that business,' he answered caustically, 'and you, my dear wife, seem to enjoy grovelling with them.'

'Once again you're being unfair,' she retaliated. 'Why can't

118

you just congratulate me and enjoy my success? Why must you always be derisive?'

'Congratulate you?' he sneered. 'That'll come when you stay home and work at having a family instead of writing liberal muck.' His voice rose and fell over the telephone and the anger in Toni drained away and was replaced by steely determination.

'Serge,' she broke in, 'Serge, I'm not prepared to argue over the phone. I merely asked you to share my happiness. I'm sorry you can't. Goodbye.' She held the phone for a while longer, listening to the tirade. Then dejectedly she put it down and dialled another number.

'I'll do it,' she whispered whilst she waited for Nick to answer the call. 'I'm damned if I'll live like this. I'll go with Nick to the meeting with his lawyer. I'll see his friend David Anstey and take counsel.'

* * *

The massive brass lion's head trapped the burning rays of the sun, and the ring in the animal's mouth was hot and heavy in Nick's hand. He glanced up for a moment at the moulding above the huge teak doors, enjoying the craftsmanship in the old Cape-Dutch building. He let the knocker drop. Almost immediately he heard footsteps clacking across a tiled floor in response to the summons.

Nick looked at Toni standing beside him, lifted her hand to his lips and smiled at her reassuringly. 'Don't worry, my love. It'll all work out well.'

Toni shivered and stood closer to him. Now that he had made the decision to divorce Jade and she had decided to consult David Anstey, his lawyer, she was afraid.

She was worried about the pain and anger Nick's decision would cause others and the lives it would affect. Nick, a public figure, would have his reputation sullied. The tabloids would gloat over the scandal and his friends would be drawn into the drama. He would have to deal with the indignity of private detectives, as Jade had told him during many of their soul-destroying fights that she would never let him go.

She was apprehensive of the decision she would soon have

119

to make about her future. Timothy, her son, now a sturdy little four-year-old: how would he react to leaving his home and Chops, his beloved dog? Izuba, whom Tim adored – would she come with them, singing her haunting lullabies to Timothy at night and scolding and loving him in Xhosa by day? Thinking of Serge's reaction terrified her and she refused to contemplate it.

Toni smiled back at Nick, a small worried smile, and her blue eyes, darkened by anxiety to a deep violet, searched his face, imprinting each line on her mind, while her fingers stroked the fine dark hair on the back of his hand, lovingly committing the feel to memory. After this meeting it would probably be a long and unhappy period of waiting before his divorce was finalised. Nick squeezed her hand as the doors opened and a uniformed janitor waited to lead them to David Anstey's office.

David had been a close friend of Nick's for many years. He was the senior partner in the firm, and commanded enormous respect from colleagues and opponents alike. Many a matron paid for unwanted counsel merely to have half an hour alone with the powerful and elegant lawyer. He accepted the adulation with equanimity.

He scrutinised Toni as she walked into his office with Nick. He liked her firm handshake and her steady gaze. By the end of the meeting he was her friend and admirer. He listened to Nick intently, taking notes and saying very little. Then he sat back in his chair and grinned. 'Your decision is one I applaud, Nick. I wish you'd made it a long time ago.

'Now, Mrs Balser,' he said, swinging his chair around to face Toni, 'let's discuss your problem.'

Half an hour later he pressed the bell and ordered tea. Toni's honesty about her position, her fear of Serge's rage and possessiveness, and her anxiety about taking Timothy away from his home and father impressed David Anstey. He outlined the divorce proceedings in clear hard lines, making her aware of all the ugliness which surfaces when love rots and putrefies into hate.

'Think about it carefully, Mrs Balser,' he continued. 'Do nothing until you are certain that your present position is intolerable.' Then he smiled at her warmly. 'Remember that I'm here to help and advise you. You only have to lift the phone.'

'Thank you,' said Toni as she relaxed in the armchair, dropping the stiff, upright position she had kept throughout the interview. 'I appreciate that.' Nick smiled as he watched David bustle around the desk to pour a cup of fragrant peppermint tea for Toni. Later he watched David, his silver head inclined, listen to Toni as she revamped his diet.

'Coffee is aggravating your migraines. You must cut it out immediately,' she said. 'And no sneaking the odd cup when you are feeling better, Mr Anstey.'

David smiled, leaned across and refilled her cup, the clear smell of peppermint filling the room. 'Please call me David and if I may, I'd like to call you Toni.'

She smiled at him. 'I'd like that, David. Thank you.' A red light flashed on his desk console and David pressed the button.

'Yes, I'm in conference.' He listened intently for a few moments. 'All right, bring the papers to me and I'll check them quickly.' He released the button. 'Would you mind if one of my young clerks comes in for a few minutes? He has to appear in court in half an hour, and I need some information which he has been researching.'

'Not at all,' said Nick as the door opened and in walked a tall, well-dressed young Xhosa.

His dark suit was well chosen and the discreetly striped grey and navy tie perfectly knotted. He held himself upright and walked with assurance to David's desk. His skin glowed with health, and his black curls, cut close to his head, were parted on one side by an old scar.

'Justice,' called Toni, her voice high with pleasure. The young man spun to face her.

'Miss Toni,' he answered. 'Good morning. I am very happy to see you.'

'I'm so pleased to see you here, Justice,' she said. 'Izuba tells me that you enjoy working for Anstey and Lyle.'

David cut in proudly. 'Justice is my protégé. He is articled to us.' He smiled at Justice. 'He is an asset to our firm.'

'Thank you, sir,' said Justice, placing the papers on the desk in front of David. 'It is an honour and a privilege to work for your firm.' His English was stilted and formal, the African tongue giving the language an extraneous cadence.

121

'Your sister must be very proud of you,' said Toni. 'I know that I am. I'll enjoy telling her that I've seen you here when I return home.' She smiled at him and noticed how his dark eyes washed over Nick, assessing him and filing the knowledge behind a mask of indifference.

'I'm sorry to have interrupted your work with Justice,' apologised Toni, looking at David, 'but he is my maid's brother and I haven't seen him or Wisdom, his twin, for ages.'

Justice dropped his gaze on to the papers in his hand. He could not look at this woman, for she would read his eyes.

David grinned his acceptance of her apology, happy that she knew and liked Justice.

'Excuse us for a few minutes while we attend to this matter,' said David and two heads bent over the papers.

Toni studied Justice as he talked, his long fingers pointing out paragraphs to David.

Listening to the soft murmur of voices, a small frown crept between her eyebrows. There was a watchfulness about Justice which she had not noticed before. He had always been a carefree, laughing child, but the grown man had veiled his eyes, masking his thoughts, and it made her uneasy. She resolved to talk to Izuba about Justice at the first opportunity. She would warn her about the danger of her brother falling prey to the glib talkers who were scouting the townships for intelligent men who could be used to recruit others to their particular political party. Izuba should warn the twins, so that they would be on guard and resist the blandishments offered by the agitators.

Justice nodded and gathered up the papers. 'Thank you, Mr Anstey,' he said. 'It was very good to see you again, Miss Toni, and I will give my brother Wisdom your good wishes.'

Bending slightly towards Nick, his eyes hooded, he murmured, 'Good day, sir.'

Nick looked at the young man and smiled. He was pleased that he had found a job for Izuba's son in David's firm. Toni had been right, the boy deserved a chance.

'Goodbye,' answered Nick. 'It's really heart-warming to meet a young man who is ready to grasp the opportunities which are being offered to him today. I wish you much success.'

'Thank you.' The smile stretched Justice's lips but was not echoed in his eyes.

'I'm sorry for the interruption,' apologised David when they were alone, 'but he's showing such an extraordinary grasp of the principles of law and is so hard-working that I enjoy helping him personally whenever it's possible.'

'Well, I'm pleased to have met Justice and I'm sure that you'll be very proud of him one day,' said Nick.

'I've no doubt of that. Now let's return to our problems,' said David, uncapping his pen and pulling a clean sheet of paper towards him. 'I need a few more details about Jade.'

The meeting scheduled for an hour extended until lunchtime.

'Nick,' said David, looking at his wristwatch, 'I'm sure that you and Toni have things you'd like to discuss. Please use my office and we'll meet again at the end of the week.'

He stopped beside Toni and held her hand in both of his. 'It's been a pleasure meeting you, Toni, and I hope that I'm going to see a great deal more of you and Nick in the future.'

'I'd love that,' she answered.

Nick and Toni watched David Anstey walk away. 'He's a good friend,' said Nick, closing the door of David's office. 'Now, my girl, come here, and promise me that you'll not have the effect on my other male friends that you've had on David.'

They remained in David's office for almost an hour discussing their future plans. When he grandfather clock chimed two o'clock Toni started.

'I promised Helen that I'd fetch Timothy before three, and if I'm late he'll drive all the fowls neurotic, upending them in his hunt for eggs.'

Nick laughed and enfolded her in his arms. 'This is the beginning, Toni. Soon the ugliness will be over and we'll be together. Believe that and be strong, my love.' He bent down and kissed her tenderly. 'I love you, my kitten.'

Tears filled Toni's eyes and she bit her lip to prevent them from spilling over as she quickly walked away from him. He turned back into the office. Waiting for Toni to decide on her future was going to be worse than he expected, and he hated watching her return to Serge.

David,

Toni and I thank you for your advice. Please expedite my plans. Hire the best detectives available. I'll keep in touch.

Nick

He placed the note on David's blotter. Please God let this go according to plan, he thought.

CHAPTER

7

T HE parking areas were free of the kamikaze minibuses and there were long queues waiting impatiently for the first wave to return from the townships. Izuba had refused Toni's offer of a lift home to Shonalanga as she wanted to be alone to nurse the loss of her mother and Beauty. She and Soze climbed up the catwalk and crossed from the station to the square in front of the City Hall.

Here on the square stood the lumbering buses, belching black fumes as the engines warmed up.

They found one going to Shonalanga and paid the fare, pushing the money through the grille. It was dark when they arrived home as the bus stopped frequently to collect and deposit passengers.

A group of young boys lounged at the bus stop, tormenting a stray dog. The animal's thin ribs were outlined starkly through its matted hair, its scabbed and torn ears hung down dejectedly and it looked at the boys beseechingly, a world of hopelessness in its dark eyes, begging for a scrap of food or a kind word, but a well-aimed kick landing in its sunken belly was all it received.

Izuba clutched her large bag firmly under her arm and, holding Soze tightly by the hand, hurried past them. These youngsters had for years used 'the fight for freedom' as an excuse for their lawlessness, and now preyed on the workers, staking out the railway stations and bus stops demanding money, wielding razor-sharp knives with deadly effect when their demands were denied. Their eyes rested on Izuba's bag and then on her formidable girth. A silent decision was made and they turned to study the other passengers.

125

Izuba walked quickly down the dimly lit streets. Fear twisted her stomach and her breath came in short, sharp pants. Sensing her mother's uneasiness, Soze pressed close to her side.

Rounding a corner near her home, Izuba looked up. She breathed a sigh of relief and her footsteps slowed. Coming towards them was a group of men armed with knobkerries, the long carved sticks with a heavy wooden knob at the end designed to crack a man's skull.

'We are happy to see you,' said Izuba, greeting the men.

The group waited for a man, his scalp capped in tight curls, to answer. The smell of strong cheap tobacco and a thick haze of smoke hung over them like a black umbrella.

'We see you, and tonight all is well,' replied the leader puffing at a pipe. 'Have you seen any of the lawless ones on the streets?' he asked.

'Yes,' said Izuba. 'At the bus shelter there are five *tsotsies*, lying in wait to take and eat what others have earned.'

The men in the group exchanged glances and tightened their grips on the knobkerries.

'We thank you,' they said, and walked purposefully towards the shelter.

'*Hambani kakuhle*, go well, goodbye,' called Izuba.

The leader of the group nodded his thanks, spoke sharply, and the men split up. There were no youngsters in this body. They were all strong middle-aged men, the equivalent of the elders of the tribe, men who sat in judgement and meted out punishment in the villages.

Here in the city, they were appalled by the behaviour of the youngsters. They had concluded that the drawn-out Western system of justice, the arrest, detention, trial and prison sentence, was not going to stamp out the insurrection and predation, so they had revived tribal justice.

Wrong-doers were tracked down, questioned, warned about the behaviour expected from them in the future and were then beaten senseless, their bodies left lying on the ground as a warning to others.

Their actions were understood and accepted by the black community. They had lived with this form of justice for centuries.

Opening the creaking gate, Izuba could faintly hear hoarse shouts and thuds, and she smiled in the darkness. The elders were protecting her and her family. Her smile faded as she opened the door and walked into the front room. The electric light had been switched off, and the bearded men seated around the table were ones she instinctively feared and distrusted.

They had come to her home many times before, always at night, and spoken in low voices to her brothers. Now the laws had been changed and they could speak openly of their plans and policies, but these men still preferred the darkness.

The flickering of the oil lamp which had been placed in the centre of the blue plastic tablecloth deepened their eye sockets, so that they looked up at her from black sightless pits.

Seated at the table with the two bearded ones were Justice and Wisdom. They had become strangers to her since their circumcision. They were now considered men by the tribe, but instead of looking for good Xhosa girls to take as wives and beget children, they spent all their time meeting with these men who spoke of frightening things.

Both boys had good jobs. Wisdom, a quiet, gentle boy who followed blindly in his brother's footsteps, believing implicitly in everything he did and said, worked in a bottle store and was entrusted with checking the tills, a responsible job at which he excelled. His boss, a genial man in his fifties, liked the quiet, shy young black man and when they had been working late would take him home to Shonalanga in his car, saving him the long trip by bus. The bottle-store owner's wife, Mrs Kahn, a plump, friendly woman with two sons of her own at university, brought Wisdom clothes raided from her sons' wardrobes and watched over him with motherly concern as she sat in her glass-fronted office in the store. She found her house empty without her sons, and relentlessly poured cough syrup down Wisdom's throat at the first sign of a cold and brought cakes and biscuits to supplement his lunch. She had found a surrogate son.

The birth of twin boys, Wisdom and Justice, had been considered a good omen by the tribe. The boys would be lucky and would possess special powers. They were expected to share each other's experiences, and the two euphorbia trees planted outside their mother's hut when they were born to protect them from witchcraft were also the barometers of their future. Should the trees flourish, then the boys would continue to be strong and healthy, but should one of the trees sicken and die, then the twin whose tree it was would also die.

Justice had joined Wisdom at the bottle store but the work soon palled. His mind was aflame, he wanted to be where the laws were made. He wanted to understand how the government worked. Izuba, his sister, delighted that he wanted to better himself and learn more, asked Miss Toni for help. Toni had appealed to Nick, knowing that he liked her large Xhosa lady. Nick had spoken to his lawyer, David Anstey.

Justice put down his glass, brimming with brandy, as Izuba closed the door. Izuba looked at Wisdom with pity. His head was bowed over his glass, and the whites of his eyes were muddied with liquor. He was easily led and dominated by Justice. Alcohol affected him badly. Soon he would run from the room, his stomach contracting violently as it rejected the strong spirits. Straddling a chrome chair at the end of the table, his arms crossed on the back and his chin resting on his hands, was Storchman, her eldest son.

Izuba's eyes narrowed and her wide nostrils flared as she saw the empty glass in front of him. Storchman was a tall, attractive young man of twenty with the same dark coffee-coloured skin as his sister Beauty. He was a student of social studies at the Cape University and a source of great pride to Izuba.

He studied hard and was doing well. Izuba did not wish to see him seated with these vultures. They sat up high and in safety, watching while the dust whirled and the killing was done beneath them. Then they moved in to take over and to gorge on the bloody remains, cawing and squawking obscenely over the carcass, leaving the bones stripped white and clean. She wished Storchman would leave the table and not have his fine mind and ears polluted by the filth they spoke, but this was not the time. She could not shame him in front of strangers. Izuba bent down to put Soze on the floor, her face hidden from the men around the table as she composed herself.

Soze, released from her mother's tight grasp, ran shrieking with joy to a figure Izuba had not noticed. He sat quietly on a chair in the deep shadows cast by the lamp.

'Josh, Josh,' she called as she scrambled on to his lap.

'Joshua.' Izuba froze. Her youngest son, a baby of fifteen, sitting with these men, hearing their words of evil. Her self-control broke. 'Joshua, what are you doing listening to men's talk?' she scolded. 'You have your work to do for school tomorrow.'

The bearded men stared at Joshua and Izuba felt the tension in the room. Something was happening that she did not understand. Her flesh crawled and it seemed to her that the inky arched wings of a giant hornbill flapped slowly over the men's heads, and its enormous yellow beak, like a great hooked nose, pointed menacingly at her son, at Joshua.

He sat with his baby sister on his lap, gently curling and uncurling the delicate fingers of her hand, his face expressionless. The silence stretched interminably. Suddenly Justice stood up, his chair crashing loudly as it tumbled over on to the cement floor.

Everyone looked at him, but still no one spoke. 'My sister,' he said, his words slurring slightly, 'Joshua has the right to sit with these men and listen to men's talk.'

Izuba glanced at her brother and then looked back at Joshua. 'Why, Joshua?' she asked. 'Why would you, a child, not yet ready for *khwetha*, sit with these men?'

Joshua looked up at his mother, his eyes blank, his lips tightly closed, the frequent blinking of his eyes being the only sign of his agitation.

One of the bearded men answered her. 'He sits with us because he is one of us.' The words oozed out from lips hedged in by a wiry black beard.

Izuba heard the words but refused to believe them. The bitter taste of betrayal filled her mouth, and their faces were demonic in the shadows. She stared at Joshua, willing his beloved face to come into focus. She could not look at the bearded one, for if she did she would sink her teeth into those thick, red lips and tear them from his face, and she would rip that lying tongue from his mouth.

Slowly her body stopped trembling and from the mists of anger Joshua's face took form. Izuba looked at the thin black body sitting stiff and upright on the chair, the large brown eyes cast down, studying his baby sister's hand. He was a child desperately trying to prove to the men that he was a worthy conscript, and that as such he was untouched by his mother's anguish.

Her heart ached. 'Iboni,' she pleaded, her voice harsh with anguish. 'Iboni, tell me why, explain to me, your mother.'

Joshua looked up at her quickly. She hardly ever called him *Iboni*. It was a name she had given him when he was a young child. Grasshopper, she had called him.

'Uma, my mother,' Joshua said, and started to rise.

'Comrade Joshua is one of our members,' the bearded one spoke again.

The words electrified Joshua. He straightened in his chair as if a wooden ruler had been thrust between his shoulder blades and he fixed his gaze on the smaller of the two bearded men. He was the older of the two. His eyes were set deep into the wrinkles of his face, and his heard, mangy as a stray cat, camouflaged his chin with patches of grey and black. The legs of his chair grated across the cement as he scraped it back and swung around to face Izuba.

'Your son has been a member of the Comrades for four years,' he said, tapping his fingers on the table. 'They are not children but men, still willing to fight and die if necessary, for the glorious aims and ideals of the ANC. You, Izuba Mapei, can be proud that your son is a Comrade.' He tilted his chair back, studying her whilst he sucked at his teeth.

Izuba turned on him like an enraged porcupine ready to ram her sharp quills of hate and despair into his belly.

'Proud?' she hissed. 'Proud to have my son a murderer? Proud to have my son march in front of the rallies so that if the police open fire it is my son who will be shot? Proud to have my son used by you strangers who were schooled over the sea, who worship the red flag with the curved panga which cuts the hammer? Proud to have my son fight to put you in power? You who do not love Africa or your African brothers, you who love only power and are using my people to get it for you!'

Izuba loomed over him, the angry words scalding like steam.

Soze, hearing her mother's voice raised in anger, screwed

up her face and wailed thinly. She scrambled down from Joshua's lap and ran to Izuba, folding her arms around her leg, and burying her face in the folds of her mother's skirt.

'You don't care that they are children. You are like the oxpecker birds who peck at a sore on the buffalo's back and will not let it heal because they eat the blood. You want power and the gold from this land, and you peck at it with your bombs and knives and will not let my country heal. You *ngusatana wenyoka*, devil snakes!'

Storchman put his arms around his mother, afraid of what he saw in the dark eyes of the two strangers. Afraid for her.

'Come, mother,' he said, dragging her away towards the kitchen. 'Come, let us eat and let the men talk.'

Izuba swung Soze on to her broad hip. 'May all the spirits of hell live in your souls and may your shades never return. You *zizinja*, dogs, who have taken my son from me,' she screamed at them as Storchman closed the kitchen door behind them. The bearded ones did not speak with the voice of moderation now used by many of the ANC but with the anger of the PAC, the group who Miss Toni had explained were wooing away the violent ones from the ANC. They wanted not equal rights but sole rights, not participation but domination.

She mistrusted the bearded ones and was certain that they were wizards who pose as human beings and bring sorrow to all. She knew that they were casting evil omens on Justice and Wisdom.

The boys had become suspicious and discontented, and Izuba longed to comfort them, to swing them on to her broad back and dance with them, hearing them gurgle with joy as they had done when they were children. She leaned over the cold stove, shaking with silent sobs. These strangers had robbed her of a daughter and now of a son.

The two bearded men stared at the closed kitchen door in silence. They were highly intelligent men, well trained in Russia and Cuba and totally committed to the Communist cause. Even though it had crumbled in Europe they were determined that it would work in Africa. They were preaching to people who had nothing, and therefore had nothing to lose. The strangers were part of a vast network of agents, working hard trying to persuade the blacks that the ANC was powerful enough to become the new Government. They had to keep morale high and the revolutionary groups strong.

Many of the young Comrades had lost faith when the promised freedom with its fine houses and cars for all failed to materialise immediately, and had turned their talents for evading the law into peddling Mandrax and stolen cars. They no longer obeyed the ANC, and were roaming the townships terrorising the inhabitants.

The men had met Joshua and Wisdom through Storchman, when they addressed a meeting of students at the university. Storchman had been one of the young men who questioned them, and seizing the opportunity they had invited themselves to his house to talk to him and recruit other members of his family.

Stretching across the table for the bottle of brandy, his bushy black beard flowing over his khaki shirtfront, the younger of the two men filled the glasses.

'We have work to do,' he said. 'Men's work. Important work that women do not understand.' He pushed a glass, half filled with the powerful brown liquid, across the table to Joshua.

'Drink, Comrade,'he commanded. 'You're fighting for the new system. We will win, for we have the glorious Mother State, Russia, backing us.' Even as he spoke, shadows of doubt like tiny black tadpoles darted across his mind. The Russia he knew had changed, and support for his party had dwindled.

Joshua swallowed the fiery liquid; the heat scorched his throat and stomach and the fumes blocked his nostrils and made his eyes water. He did not like the taste. It was like the medicine Izuba forced down his throat when his stomach ached. But he smacked his lips loudly and thumped the glass down on the table.

The younger stranger sipped his drink slowly. He had worked with these people in Africa for years but they were still alien to him. Most of the ANC members were Xhosa and he mistrusted them. He firmly believed that, given the choice between the wonderful doctrines of Lenin or their tribe, they would not hesitate to discard the Communist credo.

The older man was outlining plans for future attacks on black men who held positions of trust and prestige in the civil service and Izuba's twin brothers and Joshua, her youngest, were listening intently. The man talked persuasively, hitting the table frequently to emphasise a point, making the glasses jump and the plastic roses in the green glass bowl tremble.

He was high in the ranks of the *Umkhonto we Sizwe*, the spear of the nation, the military wing of the ANC. He believed that the way to power was by violence not protest marches, and scorned the section of the ANC who had entered into negotiations with the Boer Government.

The younger agent looked at the piece of paper which the speaker had placed on the table. It was a list, a long list naming the black moderates; men who were prepared to meet the government ministers and work out a system of power sharing, men who abhorred the senseless violence which was tearing their country apart, men who had a deep love for the land and the people.

'These men are traitors. They are dangerous.' The older man stabbed at the paper with his finger. 'They would lead you astray, they would make you believe that the whites will share power. The idiots must die and it must be known that the ANC has struck. They must be mutilated and their houses burnt, their cars burnt . . . ' He swallowed a mouthful of brandy and looked at Joshua thoughtfully. 'You, Joshua. You know about the Shonalanga burning. You were there. Remember?'

Joshua, his head swimming and his eyes heavy, stared at the crescent-shaped flame in the oil lamp. He had been much younger then, a mere child. A member of a gang of Comrades who waited outside the old Zionist church on a Sunday morning.

The leaders sat patiently on the outside rim of a worn black rubber tyre which flattened under their weight.

Eventually the old church organ wheezed asthmatically and was silent and the voices raised in praise to their creator faded. The congregation emerged from the dim interior, blinking myopically in the harsh sunlight. They fluttered in front of the church like butterflies, the women gay in floral prints and the men smiling and dignified.

A tremor like a breeze, giving no hint of the gale to follow, ran through the children and suddenly, swift as a hunting pack, they swarmed up the path and charged into the church-goers. Joshua was amongst the leaders as they reached their chosen victim. She was a young woman, and Joshua had no idea of her offence – other than that she had been branded a sell-out by the gang leaders. She was talking to the priest, her large brown eyes soft and trusting, her unpainted mouth turned up in a gentle smile, as Beauty's lover knocked her off her feet, tearing her pale blue blouse, exposing a threadbare white cotton bra. The young woman held up her slender arms to the priest and screamed in terror, begging the congregation for help, but they were not brave enough to remonstrate with these maddened youngsters. They huddled in a group on the church steps.

The pack of children fell on the young woman. They dragged her down the pathway by her legs, her pale blue skirt rucked above her waist, her screams rising and falling as her head thumped on the sharp gravel.

At the bottom of the path the knot of children tightened and swayed around the defenceless woman.

Joshua was elbowed aside as the leaders lifted the heavy tyre and dropped it around their victim's slender neck. He wrinkled his nose at the acrid stench of petrol as they struggled to hold the woman and fill the tyre. The leader struck a match. Their voices were high and hoarse with the lust for blood. A column of fire split the group and they scattered in its path. The flames licked at the blue tatters of material which hung from the spinning body.

The flaming petrol spilled from the rubber tyre and the tongues ate deeply into her flesh.

Smoke curled around her, screening the startling white of her eyes as they rolled back in her head.

The melting rubber bonded to her skin and melted it away.

The children watched entranced, eyes glazed and mouths slack with excitement.

Gradually her movements slowed and she writhed and convulsed on the sand, no longer able to scream and unable to die. Demented with killing lust, the children pranced insanely around the body, parodying her silent mouthings and convulsions.

Finally the spasms stopped and the naked body lay twisted in the ash, her eyes staring up at the sky. The congregation, silent with horror, slunk away. The priest, his white-capped head bowed low, stumbled into the church, too numb to repeat the words of the Lord he loved. 'Forgive them for they know not what they do.'

For many nights after the young woman had been necklaced Joshua had been unable to sleep. The rich smell of burning flesh suffocated him.

He shuddered and turned his attention back to the men.

The older man had refilled his glass. He had an extraordinary tolerance of alcohol and the younger agent had learned not to attempt to match him.

'Let's drink to our great and just cause.'

Watching Joshua closely, he scratched his matted beard. What we need is another show on TV, he thought silently. The Shonalanga necklacing had excellent results.

A local television company had filmed the charred body, hoping that the population would be so revolted that the support for the terrorist organisations and their commitment to violence would end. It was a misguided decision.

Terrorists and television need each other. Without television, terrorism becomes like the hypothetical philosopher's tree. It falls in the forest but, as no one hears it, it does not exist.

The film resulted in thousands of moderates paying lip service and the threat 'You will be burned' brought virgins to the cadres' beds, and added hundreds of people to the daily riots and demonstrations.

The bearded stranger nodded. Another spectacular would have to be arranged. He lifted his glass.

The men around the table drank with him. 'Let us drink to freedom for all men.' The glasses were raised again. Joshua merely wet his lips, as the walls of the room would not stay still and the flowers on the table were swaying. He clenched his teeth together, willing himself to remain upright.

'Let us drink to the death of all traitors.'

The men obeyed. The brandy spread its hot tentacles in Wisdom's stomach, a stomach recently emptied and tender, and the heavy fumes filled his aching head. He dropped the glass, rested his head on the back of the chair and closed his eyes, lost to the bearded one's inflammatory talk.

135

The older man ran his fingers through his mottled beard and pushed his chair away from the table, leaving the younger man to continue with the indoctrination.

Patience, he thought as he studied the faces opposite him, that is what Tambo, our leader, said when he returned from his study tour of Vietnam. But will our young followers be patient?

He leaned forward and placed a new bottle on the table. It would be a long night.

The first pearly streaks were backlighting the Hottentots Holland mountains when the door of Izuba's house opened and the two bearded ones slipped out. They glanced quickly up and down the street, deserted but for a cowering dog, its tail tucked between its legs and curled tightly against its belly, who was nosing in the gutters.

'Habits die hard,' said one. 'It's strange not to have to hide.'

His companion smiled and they climbed into the blue car parked at the kerb, the battered chrome fenders and hand-sprayed body making it indistinguishable from the others scattered along the street. The older one lit a cigarette and squinted at the younger one through the thin cloud of smoke. They grinned at each other, well satisfied with the night's work.

CHAPTER

8

THE brindled cat listened intently to the sound of approaching footsteps, then lazily rolled over on to its back, inviting the woman hurrying up the brick pathway to scratch its silky belly.

'No, fat cat,' admonished Toni. 'I don't have time to play with you today.'

The cat looked up at her, its huge green eyes soft with longing, and it mewed piteously. 'If that was meant to break my heart, it worked,' she muttered as she bent down and ran her fingers through its shiny coat.

'That's it,' she said, giving its stomach a final tickle before she ran up to the entrance of the small apartment block.

Toni walked up the wooden stairs lightly, counting them under her breath. She stopped on number nineteen and carefully stepped over the next one, glancing at the door on her right. She breathed a sigh of relief. It remained closed. The old lady had not heard a creaking stair. Toni grinned. 'Foxed you today,' she whispered as she reached the landing.

Nick had wanted to rent a sumptuous apartment for their trysts but she had resisted his wish. Her grandmother had brought her up on both beautiful and hair-raising tales of the wee people, fairies, will-o'-the-wisps and hobgoblins. She was superstitious, and secretly believed that the demons of ill luck would ignore a simple apartment and leave them in peace, but that it would be tempting fate to move to a luxurious place. The apartment was utilitarian and had little in its favour except proximity to where they lived, but the place, with its plain wooden furniture, was very dear to her. She often visited it when Nick was away on his many research projects, drawing strength from the rooms where she had found so much love. It helped her to weather Serge's mercurial moods. She knew that soon she would have to make a decision about leaving Serge, but she would not think about it today.

She was in a fever of impatience, eager to see what Nick had prepared for their Christmas celebration, and she jabbed hard at the door-buzzer.

'Welcome to Christmas in November,' Nick said as he opened the door to her ring. He wore a blue and white striped butcher's apron over his cream slacks and wielded a blockman's knife in one hand and a partially dismembered roast turkey in the other.

'Now close your eyes,' he commanded, 'and don't open them until I say so.' Happily Toni allowed herself to be spun in a circle and then led into the bedroom. The rich scent of roses weighted on the air and Toni gasped as she opened her eyes. Nick had transformed the little bedroom into a garden of flowers.

The drawers of the wooden dressing-table in the bedroom were crammed with huge red roses. An enormous white china jug of long-stemmed buds stood on the painted chair beside the bed and the golden wicker chest at the foot of the bed was not large enough to contain the armfuls of roses he had thrust into it.

'Oh, Nick,' she breathed as she turned to him, 'it's exquisite.'

Nick smiled, happy that his bower of roses had pleased her. 'Perhaps after lunch a certain lady could be persuaded to . . . ' He ran his finger over his mouth, a habit Toni found endearing and one which usually preceded some earthy remark. ' . . . slip into something comfortable, preferably nothing, and have a little rest.'

Toni grinned. 'This lady could probably be persuaded to have that rest before lunch,' she teased.

'Close your eyes again,' said Nick, 'quickly, before I succumb to temptation, and follow me.' He took her hand and pulled her into the tiny kitchen.

The stove top and counters housed a breathtaking display of pink and white proteas, tall lily-like purple and orange watsonias, great bunches of mauve and red ericas and stunning yellow and blue strelitzias.

'This is wonderful. The flowers,' said Toni, 'they're indescribably beautiful. You've turned the kitchen into a wildflower garden. It'll be like having a picnic in Namaqualand in spring.' She laughed, looking at the table covered with the most incredible assortment of delicacies. 'We'll need the constitution of ostriches to digest this mixture.'

Nick laughed and handed her a slim glass of champagne. 'To my love,' he toasted. 'May this be the first of many Christmases for us.'

'Yes,' she smiled, 'many, many more.'

Nick seated Toni at the wooden table and heaped caviare on a warm blini.

'This is heaven,' grinned Toni as she cut the blini, 'absolute heaven.' She licked the globular eggs and melted butter from her lips.

'Open up,' she said as she layered slices of smoked salmon and strongly flavoured snoek between black pumpernickel. 'Open your mouth wider.'

'Toni,' pleaded Nick, trying to swallow the offering before she fed him another, 'you're really testing my liver's capacity for abuse.'

'A man who has eaten crocodile tail and snake can handle this,' she countered, and popped a sliver of turkey breast topped with stuffed olives into his mouth.

One of the olives rolled down the front of her blouse. Quickly Nick put the half-eaten piece of turkey down on his plate.

'We can't have that,' he said. He carefully unbuttoned and removed her blouse. Gazing with delight at her firm round breasts, he slid down the zipper of her slacks. 'You'll probably mess these as well,' he added. 'We'd better put them out of harm's way.'

Toni giggled and sipped her champagne. 'Sauce for the goose is sauce for the gander,' she said as she stripped him, except for his blue and white apron, which he insisted a chef would not be without.

Nick then discovered that hard pink nipples topped with caviare both looked and tasted good, and he set to with a will to try other foods in place of the caviare. The kitchen echoed with shrieks and laughter as Nick tried to prove that Bollinger could be drunk from a more interesting receptacle than a fluted champagne glass, and as they lost interest in the food and concentrated on each other, the wooden legs of the old kitchen chair creaked and cracked with the regular beat of a metronome.

'What a magnificent Christmas this is. I'll never forget the flowers or the food or the loving,' said Toni, curled up in Nick's lap on the chair. 'It's all been so wonderful, Nick. We just seem to fit together so very well.'

'Indeed,' interjected Nick, 'it is a merry fit. Come, Kitten,' he said, lifting Toni easily in his arms and carrying her to the bedroom. 'It's time for the after-lunch rest I offered you.'

'Rest?' said Toni quizzically.

'Well, to begin with,' he answered and tumbled her on to the bed.

'Nick,' she said softly, 'do you remember the first time we made love?'

'The first,' he answered. 'That must be all of one thousand two hundred and seventeen times ago.' He smiled as he looked down at her, her dark curls tangling with the hair on his chest, her eyes huge and luminous in the room with its drawn curtains.

'Yes, my kitten, I do remember,' he whispered.

He still called her Kitten, the name he had used at their first meeting, as her enormous eyes slanting slightly upwards, soft and gentle in repose, could change instantly, mirroring her soul, like the felines he so enjoyed studying on his field trips. She also moved with the unconscious lithe gracefulness of the cat family, and he never tired of watching her.

'You look so innocent and helpless without glasses,' she whispered, 'that it's hard to believe you can be so wicked.'

Nick chuckled lasciviously. 'Innocent I am, but you tempt me and I become weak.'

He pinched her bottom gently, and like a feline she turned on him. He covered his armpits, knowing that she would mete out punishment by tickling him until he gasped for mercy.

'No, Toni, no,' he laughed as she threw back the covers and straddled him, searching for his ear. 'No, not my ears, Kitten,' he pleaded, as her questing tongue found his ear and

140

probed deep into the recesses. He pleaded in vain for mercy. 'Please stop. I'll never pinch your bottom again,' he gasped.

'Never,' she demanded, her breath warm and musky in his nostrils.

'Never,' he agreed, and as she relaxed he spun her over and pinioned her spreadeagled beneath him. Sliding his hands under her buttocks, he nipped her silky skin between his thumbs and forefingers.

'You promised!' squealed Toni, outraged. 'You promised!'

'But I had my fingers crossed.' Toni thrashed under him, trying to work her arms free, but as he lifted her buttocks and opened her gently, she stopped struggling and pressed herself to him eager and trembling.

'That', said Nick, his breathing still fast and ragged, 'is to repay a certain young lady who I recall chased me around our apartment not so long ago, threatening to use a long-clawed crayfish to pinch my bottom.'

Toni laughed as she wiped Nick's wet forehead with the back of her hand. She lifted herself up, leaning on her elbow, her nipples brushing his chest lightly, and kissed him gently on his lips. 'I love you too, Nicholas Houghton,' she said as she settled kisses light as drifting feathers on his face before turning over and snuggling against him.

'Enough to live with me?' whispered Nick. Her damp buttocks were curled into his loins and he held her close to him. He kissed her softly below the ear. 'Enough to start a new life together?' he asked and held his breath waiting for her to answer.

'Yes,' she said, and her voice trembled in the heavy, perfumed air. 'Yes, Nicholas. I'll live with you.'

CHAPTER

9

'DURBAN tower, this is Zulu Sierra Kilo Delta Tango at ten thousand feet. Out.'

'KDT, Durban, you are cleared to descend to five thousand feet. Call again at six.' The voice over the radio was metallic, distorted by the interference of an approaching thunderstorm. The pilot of the sleek red and white Beechcraft Baron which was streaking towards Louis Botha airport watched the tumbled cumulus clouds apprehensively.

Let's hope they don't have planes stacked up like waffles, he thought as he pulled the headset's microphone up to his mouth to request landing instructions.

'KDT, you're cleared to descend to fifteen hundred feet,' squawked the voice. 'Join right-hand downwind to land on twenty-three.' The pilot settled the headset firmly on his head and strained to hear the instructions. 'Wind is two hundred and thirty at ten knots. Call on base and on final. You're number one.'

'KDT,' said the pilot in confirmation. He narrowed his eyes against the glare and set the plane to descend at five hundred feet a minute. 'Thank goodness,' he breathed, 'I'll be down before the storm breaks.'

The city of Durban lay beneath him, nestling in the emerald green vegetation like a shimmering opal, reflecting the aquamarine rivers rushing to empty themselves into the warm Indian Ocean, and the bottle and lime green of the coastal forests and the sugar-cane fields.

The silvery-grey landing strip shimmered in the noonday sun and the Beechcraft bucketed and yawed as it rode the air thermals.

Holding her over the centre line the ground seemed to speed by much faster than the ninety knots shown on the speed indicator. The pilot cut the throttle and raised the nose slightly. This was the one part of flying Serge did not enjoy. He found it difficult to relax when coming in to land.

'Bitch,' he muttered as the wheels hit the ground hard and bounced the aircraft back into the air. He increased the power slightly, corrected the floating and the second time she settled firmly on the centre line. With a sigh of relief he touched the brakes as the speed decreased, and turned off the runway at the first intersection. Taxiing her into the parking bay, he turned off the landing lights. He automatically checked that the magneto and master switches were off and climbed stiffly from the plane.

The torrid heat pressed down on him like a wet blanket and his shirt clung to his back in dark patches. Serge did not enjoy the high humidity in this sub-tropical holiday resort. He much preferred the hot, dry summers in the Cape, but the fecundity of the vegetation bursting from the rich red soil, and the riotous display of bright purple, crimson and yellow tropical flowers excited him. His senses delighted in the pungent smell of moist earth and the langorous perfumes of the tropical flowers.

Shading his eyes with his hand, he squinted at the round-shouldered Indian in khaki overalls who came hurrying across the apron to the plane.

'Morning, Sam,' he called. 'The keys are on the seat.'

'Morning, sir. Welcome back,' said Sam with a smile, his teeth startling white and even in his dark face. 'How long will you be with us this time?'

'I'm not sure,' answered Serge with a small frown. 'No more than a few days, I hope.'

'Okay, sir. I'll have her refuelled and ready,' said Sam, swinging himself up into the seat. 'Enjoy your stay, Mr Balser,' he called down from the open door as Serge turned to leave.

'Enjoy this, Sam?' queried Serge. 'It's a damn sauna bath, and a greasy one at that.' He wiped the beads of sweat from his forehead with a damp handkerchief and picked up his overnight case, the linked Gs sparkling in the sun. Swinging his blazer over his shoulder he paused, and turned back to the plane.

'Sam,' he called out, 'how's your wife? Has the baby arrived?'

'Oh, yes, thank you, sir. It is a boy, a very good boy,' answered Sam.

'Congratulations. How many Naidoos does that make?'

'Six, Mr Balser. Four boys and two girls,' said Sam proudly. To possess boys was a cause for celebration in the Indian community but girls were accepted with resignation. In a few years there would be two bamboo poles in Sam's garden, topped with fluttering flags, advertising that he had two marriageable daughters.

Sam's ancestors had been brought out from India to work on the sugar-cane fields which in the time of the great Zulu monarch, Shaka, were thickly forested hills rolling beneath an unblemished azure sky. Now they were tamed and manicured with cane, and the blue was smeared with dirty fingermarks from the burning fields.

'Congratulations,' said Serge, reaching up to the cockpit to shake Sam's hand. 'With four boys you'll be able to ease up on all this overtime you've been doing.'

Sam's forehead wrinkled. 'Overtime, Mr Balser?' he questioned.

'Yes, Sam. All that work you've been doing at home. You must have clocked up a great deal of overtime to produce six youngsters.'

Sam's forehead smoothed and he shrieked with laughter, hitting his knee with his hand. 'That's a good one, sir.'

Serge grinned, slapped the door of the Beechcraft and strode towards the car park. Wonder how he supports that brood, he mused as he crossed the tarmac, soft in the searing heat. Probably grows vegetables in his back garden to sell to the hotels, he smiled to himself. With six kids he'll have no trouble keeping the crops fertilised.

His smile faded as he reached the silver-grey Mercedes sports car and flung open the door. Dropping into the soft leather of the passenger seat, he threw his bag into the back and breathed in the cool air gratefully.

Fumbling in the pocket of his blazer he found his cigarette case. Snapping it open he selected one and lit it. He inhaled. 'Right, Hans,' he snapped, 'what in the hell's so important that made you phone me at three o'clock in the morning babbling like a maniac?' Serge leaned forward and turned up the air-conditioning. 'You do, I presume, realise that I've just returned home after three weeks overseas and am still groggy with jet-lag?'

Hans Wold looked at his friend despairingly. His face was drawn, his eyes red with lack of sleep, and his blond hair was lank and matted.

Allowing him no time to answer, Serge continued. 'Toni is furious. She seldom loses her temper but when she does she is formidable.' Serge drew in angrily on his cigarette, reliving the scene at home after Hans' desperate phone call.

'You're going where?' Toni had asked icily.

'Please understand, honey. Hans needs me. He wouldn't phone at this time unless it was important,' Serge had cajoled as he replaced the receiver.

'Important! You, Serge Balser, have your priorities mixed up. You have a son who has seen you twice in the past eight weeks. He hardly knows you. Is that not important?' she'd asked. 'Do your home and family always take second place?'

She had thrown back the bed covers and was standing at the foot of the bed, knotting the belt of her peach silk dressing gown.

Serge bit back the stinging retort. He was a little unsure of Toni nowadays – she had changed. She had become more confident and he did not enjoy having his decisions queried and his moods ignored; but having returned from a holiday with Dana he wished to keep Toni happy. He did not want to have to answer any awkward questions about his business trip to London and America.

'Honey, Hans is a very old and dear friend and I'm responsible for him.'

'It's a great pity that your sense of responsibility doesn't extend to your son, your only child,' she retorted.

'If you would come back to bed, honey, we could change that, and Tim could have a playmate,' said Serge, trying to steer the conversation away from Hans.

Toni's eyes iced to a frosty blue and her soft mouth tightened. Without answering she picked up a book from her bedside table and walked out of the room.

Watching the flounce of the rich silk as Toni pulled the hem of the gown away before closing the door, Serge realised that his choice of subject had been misguided. He had a gnawing feeling in the pit of his stomach that the look he had seen in Toni's eyes had been one of revulsion, but he refused to believe that his behaviour could ever disgust his wife. Plumping up the pillows behind his head, he fell into an uneasy sleep.

The ringing of his alarm clock in the early hours of dawn released him from his fevered dreams, and he had staggered to the bathroom to prepare for the flight to Durban.

'Your story had better be good, Hans,' he said as he flicked the ash into the metal ashtray.

Hans ran his furred tongue nervously around his thin lips as he manoeuvred the car through the heavy traffic on the city's Golden Mile. He kept his eyes fixed on the road, not daring to look at Serge as he spoke. His voice, like a bluebottle trapped behind a window, droned on, rising and falling as he pleaded and explained.

Serge's composure crumbled as he listened and he ground out his cigarette, the white paper splitting, littering the carpet with shreds of tobacco.

'Let me get this straight, Hans. You took off your clothes in the hallway and added them to the pile already on the floor?'

'Yes,' mumbled Hans miserably.

'How many people did you say?' questioned Serge, a nerve twitching spasmodically in his lower jaw. 'You think twenty.'

Serge stared out of the window, his mind racing.

A colourful Zulu rickshaw boy loped along the road beside the car, giving the visitors a leisurely two-wheeled ride along the beachfront. The massive, ebony-skinned Zulus with towering headdresses constructed of yellow, red and green ostrich feathers, beads and glittering baubles, pulled the little chariots with ease, gliding with the same deceptively slow stride which their ancestors, Shaka's *impi*, had used when subjugating the neighbouring tribes.

Serge watched the rickshaw blindly.

Periodically the Zulu lifted his feet from the ground, swinging up between the arms of the carriage, causing the children to shout with excitement as the two-wheeler rocked backwards.

Hans darted furtive glances at Serge's impassive face, not daring to break the silence.

'So there were Zulu models and some Indian babes,' said Serge, flicking at his fingernails with his thumb. 'You're damn lucky that they've scrapped the Immorality Act or you'd have had another contravention to face. At least they can't get you for screwing a dark skin.'

The car sped along the coastal road bordered with tangerine and wine-coloured cannas standing crisply to attention and untidy cassia trees, their flowers clustered like scrambled eggs on the pliant branches.

The air was fresher away from the city, filled with the clean iodine scent of the sea, and the rich green cane fields undulated into the distance, polka-dotted with workers hacking at the burnt stalks beneath the grilling rays of the African sun.

'Correct me if I'm wrong,' continued Serge, as tops of the high-rise buildings, showing that the city's tentacles had reached out as far as the lovely resort of Umhlanga Rocks, rose before them. 'You couldn't find your jacket in the muddle of clothes and, throbbing to return to our company flat with the beauty you picked up at the party, you spent very little time looking for it. That jacket with your name and my flat's address is now in the hands of the police. Right?'

'That's right, yes,' replied Hans. The car took the road leading away from the Old Oyster Box Hotel with the distinctive red and white lighthouse beside it and drove up to a towering block of flats overlooking the beach. Serge made no move to get out of the car.

'Eleven,' mused Serge. 'The police arrested eleven people at the party for being in possession of *dagga*, and one of them was your girlfriend's brother?'

'Right, yes,' said Hans, his face now a sickly white mask. Serge sat very still and stared at the garden. An old man trundled a green wheelbarrow up to the car, nodded at Serge and spread out his gardening tools on the grass.

'Tell me who was at the party and what they were doing when you left,' said Serge quietly.

Hans closed his eyes and unwillingly relived the night. 'One of the men was doing a floor show in the lounge with two models,' he began in a small cracked voice. He could see the room, lit only by a large white glass ball set into a dark wooden frame in one corner. The smoke had weaved and curled around the writhing bodies, copulating like frenzied dogs in the middle of the room. The cloying smell of marijuana and the musky smell of sex excited the voyeurs and they breathed heavily as they drew deeply on their joints of 'Durban poison', the most sought-after *dagga* in the country, the plants grown and tended in the Transkei.

Serge's thoughts drifted away from what Hans was telling him. He did not really want to hear the story and become involved.

Serge knew that the Nguni tribes had grown and smoked *dagga*, the Khoikhoi name for the marijuana plant, since the early Christian era, for they had believed that it gave them great power when going into battle. On his business trips to the Transkei he had seen the old Xhosa men still playing games with the bubbles of *dagga* smoke and water, which they blew through a hollow reed on to the ground, their voices comically distorted by the effects of *dagga* in their heads and water in their mouths.

In the days when it had been illegal for black and white to be together, he had smoked many a joint of *dagga* with Hans at parties to which nubile and willing black and brown girls had been invited. The risk of the party being raided by the police, and the possibility of being arrested on the double charge of smoking *dagga* and fornicating, added spice to the evening. He had enjoyed smoking in those days, as the heightened awareness caused by the drug made a quick three-minute lovemaking session feel like a three-hour orgy. He had believed himself to be a marathon lover.

Hans' voice droned on unheeded as Serge relived his own love affair with marijuana. He remembered being in his doctor's consulting room one hot summer's afternoon when the medical man had smashed his fist down on the green leather top of his desk.

'Stop whining to me about your poor memory and inability to concentrate on complicated contracts, or your sleepless nights,' he snapped.

'But, doctor,' said Serge, stunned by his physician's display of temper, 'I swear that I've not increased my smoking. I only use half a joint and I'm stoned!'

'You're like an alcoholic,' hissed the doctor. 'Only one little drink and you're drunk.' Leaning across the mahogany partner's desk, he continued, his eyes hard and his voice crisp. 'Don't you realise what's happening to you? You've built up a reverse tolerance to *dagga*. You have so much THC stored in the fatty tissues of your body and brain that a few puffs is all you need and you're on a high.'

'THC?' he had queried, thoughts of incurable diseases racing through his brain.

'The main active ingredient in *dagga*. The better the quality, the more THC. Traces of it can still be found in your body three weeks after you've smoked a joint.' His doctor shook out a white handkerchief and blew his nose violently.

'Of course you'll not be able to concentrate. Keep it up and you'll have nothing to concentrate on. Businesses are not run successfully by stoned fools.' He pinched the skin between his eyes. He was the Balsers' doctor and his friendship with Toni had deepened over the years. He'd watched her change from a vibrant young woman into a quiet wife and had disliked the man who had wrought the change.

He opened his eyes and looked at Serge. 'You have a choice,' he said. 'Continue smoking with the inevitable deterioration in your mental capabilities and health, or stop smoking and start behaving like a respected businessman and husband.'

Serge remembered rising from his chair, but his physician had forestalled the outburst.

'The consultation is free and over, Mr Balser. Good day.' He had turned to stare out of the window at the passing traffic and only turned back to his desk when he heard the door slam.

Two days later a case of his favourite whisky had arrived with a note containing one word. 'Thanks.'

With an effort Serge concentrated on what Hans was saying. The car was heating up, and Serge rolled up the sleeves of his burgundy-striped shirt.

'*Dagga*,' said Serge, running his fingers through his hair. 'Well, I suppose it could be worse. They have your jacket which ties you in with the party, but that's all.'

Serge relaxed slightly. It would be difficult to extricate Hans from the morass but not impossible. Hans gulped convulsively, his fingers clenching and unclenching on the steering wheel. 'Serge,' he confessed, 'that's not all. I had buttons and snow in the inside pocket.'

Serge shot upright in the bucket seat as if a blunt injection needle had been inserted into his buttocks. Buttons, the street name for Mandrax, the erstwhile sleeping pill which ran a close second to *dagga* as the most popular drug in the country, was considered to be one of the original evils by the government, and retribution for possession was swift and painful. He had always scorned the users who crushed the flat white tablet, mixed it with *dagga* and smoked it either in a pipe or a broken bottle neck. The police were relentless in weeding out and prosecuting Mandrax users.

'Cocaine and Mandrax in the pocket of your coat with my address,' seethed Serge, 'and you left that coat lying on the floor. Are you mad?' He flicked angrily at the cap of his gold lighter and shakily lit a cigarette. 'I told you when you first arrived here. If you want to live in this country, learn to play by their rules. There're certain things that they feel very strongly about and they have no sense of humour when it comes to drugs. They'll take you in for *dagga*, hit you hard for buttons, and for snow they'll lock you up and forget your name.' Serge inhaled in short, angry breaths, glaring at Hans.

'I only took the coke along for her,' Hans explained, his head bowed over the steering wheel. 'She goes crazy for me after a sniff of snow, yes?'

Serge shuddered, he had never used the addictive 'yuppie drug', even at the University of Zurich where they had been students.

Although he knew that coca leaves have been chewed as stimulants by South American Indians since time immemorial, the word cocaine sent shivers up his spine. A university friend of his had died from an overdose. He had held the dying man in his arms, pulling his tongue out from the back of his throat, and struggling to calm the convulsions. The experience had horrified him.

'Coke, Hans. That's what you'll go to jail for. Cocaine, the

150

most addictive of all drugs. You idiot.' Serge opened the door of the car and swung his leg out.

Hans leaned across and grabbed him by the shirt, wadding it in his sweating palms. 'Help me, Serge. I beg you, yes? Help me,' he pleaded brokenly with his friend. 'When they see it in the newspapers . . . ' His voice broke. 'Serge, please, the newspapers are doing a big clean-up on children now and he's a big noise?'

Serge froze. 'Who's a big noise?'

'That politician. They took his name when they arrested the others at the party,' babbled Hans. 'He comes because he likes the young boys.'

Slimy strands of dread and nausea uncoiled in Serge's stomach. 'How young are these boys?' whispered Serge.

Hans bit the inside of his lip. He would have to be very careful. If Serge knew that before he left the party he had enjoyed the tightly rounded buttocks of one of the youngsters, he could expect no help.

'They looked about sixteen or seventeen,' hedged Hans.

'Don't play with me, Hans, damn you,' snarled Serge. 'I said how old?'

'The one was fourteen, maybe less,' he whispered.

Serge's lip curled in disgust. 'With children,' he said. 'Children! They should be castrated.' His thoughts tumbled over each other like horses at a water jump. The police were on the verge of cracking child abuse rings in the major cities and the newspapers were reporting every snippet they could glean.

At least the fool can't be connected with child molestation, he thought, but damn him to hell for involving me in this mess. If the papers discover that one of the members of the new right wing party was at the drug and child session, it'll be front-page news.

This ultra-Conservative party had grown like a bloated parasite on the decision of the Government to share power with all races. A smile of grim satisfaction flicked across Serge's face when he thought of the embarrassment this new disclosure would cause the party. He knew that if the new party came to power it would plunge the country into civil war, and he loved the country which had made him wealthy.

Hans watched him anxiously. 'You'll help me, yes, Serge? I beg you as a friend. Please help me. I have no one else.'

Hans' face was screwed up in despair, and Serge relented. He put his hand across Hans' shaking shoulders. 'Come,' he said, 'let's go up to the apartment and I'll see what I can do.'

Annoyed and disgusted as he was, he owed Hans a favour, many favours. He would now repay the many times Hans had provided him with alibis, convincing Toni that his meetings and weekends away from home were all connected with business. Repay him for the many times he had used his flat to entertain his passing parade of ladies.

Hans locked the car, and the two men walked out of the dazzling sun and into the cool marble hall of the building.

Serge wondered whether the few days he had told Sam he would stay would be sufficient. The thought of what lay ahead appalled him and he sighed deeply as he took out his pocket computer, punched in the code and studied the names and numbers. Heavily he moved into the apartment and lifted the telephone to start the first of many calls which would extricate his friend but place him in debt to many powerful people.

CHAPTER

10

THE traffic cop gunned his powerful white motorcycle up to the red robots and listened in amazement to the music bellowing from the car parked beside him.

'Hey!' yelled the cop as he pulled his bike up on to the pavement and prepared to monitor the traffic.

'Afternoon, officer,' grinned Nick. 'Isn't it a fantastic day?' As the lights changed he called, 'Happy Christmas, officer.'

The cop shook his head. It was only November and the man was certainly not drunk.

Nick waltzed the car into the driveway of his home, euphoric that Toni had finally agreed to leave Serge, and even the sight of Jade's car parked in front of the garage did not dispel his joy.

'Nicholas,' she called as he walked past the sitting room, 'I want to speak to you.'

Nick walked jauntily into the room and noted with disdain the cigarette smouldering in the ashtray beside her chair and the half-empty glass of whisky in her hand.

Soon this'll be over, he thought. Her taunts and rages will be forgotten and I'll have Toni at my side.

'Come and sit down, Nick. Sit down, Papa Houghton,' she sneered. 'Come and comfort your pregnant wife.'

Nick froze and stared at her in horror. She smiled, a small calculating smile. 'Wives have to be humoured when they're carrying a child, so sit down.'

Nicholas stood over her, dislike and disbelief souring his stomach.

'You may hate me, Nick, but you have to listen and you can't afford to leave me now.' She ran her tongue over her

153

lips, gloating at the expression on his face. 'You have to stay with me in case the little bastard that's distorting my belly is yours.' Her face was set into the smug expression she used when she had a good hand at bridge or when her barbed words had hurt someone deeply. Nick stared at her speechless.

'How would you feel,' she taunted, 'if it is your son, and it's born mentally retarded or physically deformed because I smoked too much, perhaps rolled a joint or two?' Seeing his hands clench with anger, she continued maliciously, 'How'd you feel if I tripped and fell down the stairs one night, and had a miscarriage because there was no one to help me, or stop me from drinking smoky apple?' She lit another slim black cheroot. 'A little blob of blood and tissue would be all that was left of your son and heir. How would you feel then, famous husband of mine?'

'You're sick and you're lying,' Nick replied.

'The report on the pregnancy tests is on the hall table,' she jeered as he turned away from her.

'Walk away from this discussion, but, Nicholas Houghton, you won't walk away from me, because even though you know you've not been man enough to make a child, you're still hoping that this brat planted in my stomach is yours.' She blew out a series of smoke rings and watched him, slit-eyed. 'I know you, Nicholas,' she taunted. 'You can't evade responsibility and this unborn brat is your responsibility.'

He felt his gorge rise, and he had an almost irresistible urge to squeeze her thin freckled neck until her breathing stopped and her vicious tongue was at last stilled.

He had to get away. The front door slammed behind him. He left the house and slid into his car, mindless as a somnambulist. As the traffic cop still on duty at the robots saw the green Jaguar he shook his head. 'There's one Christmas that didn't last very long,' he said and he studied the man's ashen face as he sat hunched over the wheel.

Nick drove aimlessly, with Jade's words 'baby' and 'responsibility' beating insistently in his skull. His love for Jade had been consumed and completely destroyed in the furnace of her abuse and jealousy. Yet over the years each time he decided to break the matrimonial ties which were strangling him, he saw

154

and heard his father as he walked out of the family home in Rhodesia, and out of their lives.

'I can't go on like this,' he had said to Nick's mother, his quiet, measured words more frightening than any shouting or swearing. 'You still blame me for our baby's death, and I can't live with your maddened rages or your hatred.'

Nicholas, a knock-kneed little boy standing in the doorway, traumatised by the enormity of what was taking place between the father he worshipped and the mother he loved, saw the flames of the camp fire in the hunting camp set deep in the African bush, and the huddled figure of his mother, crazed with grief, rocking her dead son in her arms, crooning lullabies as she fiercely resisted any attempt by the camp staff or himself to remove the cold, stiff body.

'I've tried for two years to reason with you, to explain that even if I'd returned from elephant hunt when he first showed signs of a fever, it wouldn't have helped. It would have taken five days to get back to N'dola. Our son would have died with or without me there.' His father had paused and looked at his mother, waiting for her to speak, but she stared at him in unforgiving silence.

'Children die in this God-forsaken country, don't you understand that?' he pleaded. 'They die of malaria all the time. Our son's death wasn't unique.'

'Get out,' she hissed, 'get out, you murderer.' And she scrambled up, eager to tear at his face.

'God forgive me,' whispered his father as he lifted the scuffed leather suitcase and closed the door carefully behind him, leaving his remaining son to a future of bleak boarding schools and holidays spent with a mother who became progressively more disturbed, a mother who frightened him, one he did not know. His were the feet of a child desperately trying to walk in the boots of a man. As a young boy Nick accepted the responsibility of shielding her from curious stares and as a young man he allowed others to shoulder the responsibility and protect her in an asylum.

Nick knew that again he had to accept the responsibility of looking after an unstable woman, this time his wife. And now, now that Toni had finally agreed to leave Serge, there was a baby, Jade's baby, and once again he was filled with guilt.

He reached a decision and knew that he had to talk to David Anstey and Toni before he weakened and changed his mind.

The road signs on the way to Anstey's office blurred as his thoughts circled and returned to his father.

'Look after them well, my boy,' he had said, his bush hat tilted back on his thatch of dark hair, as he had kissed them goodbye. 'Remember you're the man in the camp now and I trust you to look after the family.'

The young Nick believed that he had betrayed his father's trust, he had allowed his brother to die. He should have been able to save him from the raging fires of malaria. He believed that his mother's subsequent manic-depressiveness and his father's desertion were all his fault.

The guilt felt by the small boy and hidden in the adult man now surfaced. Nick knew that he had to protect this unborn child of Jade's. He knew he could never fully explain his feelings of guilt to David or Toni but he had to try.

Nick sat in his lawyer's office and the silence was broken only by the persistent droning of a bluebottle.

The tea had grown cold and a grey film scummed the surface. The fly, its gossamer wings folded neatly across its back, balanced delicately on the edge of one of the saucers. It carefully extended its proboscis on to the silver teaspoon and picked up a grain of sugar. Turning it round and round it lathered the sugar grain with saliva and then sucked up the sweet solution.

A large hand, the back frosted with wiry hair, flicked irritably at the fly.

'No! No! No!' David Anstey shook his head and a wave of silver hair brushed across his eyes. His voice hardened in exasperation as he spoke to the man seated in the button-backed chair opposite him. 'I will not. I will not let you do this.' He flicked the thick hair away from his eyes. 'Let me plead with you as a friend, not as your lawyer. You are a sensible, well-educated man. What you propose is madness.'

Nick rested his elbow on the arm of the chair and shielded his eyes with his hand. His head was bowed and his shoulders slumped forward in resignation.

'Nick,' pleaded David, 'look at me, Nick.'

Nicholas Houghton raised his eyes. They were expression-less.

David's heart ached for the man slouched in the armchair; he longed to take him and shake him, force him to change his mind, force him to accept the antidote for pain which he was offering.

'I beg you to reconsider your decision, Nick. From now on there are only the formalities to be completed. I can have the divorce settled within ten days. The worst is over— '

Nick broke into David's plea. 'The worst is over? No, my old friend, it's only just beginning. Hell is only just beginning.'

Stung to anger by Nick's resignation and refusal to heed his advice, David lashed out at him. 'But a hell of your own making. Principles, good intentions and a sense of duty are all very well, but not when you give them to the wrong person and for the wrong reasons. You owe her nothing. You have paid, and paid handsomely. Let her go. She'll sink to her own level which certainly isn't yours. Martyrs went out of fashion a long time ago, Nick. Why are you trying to revive the tradition?'

Nick stared at him in silence, and to break it David stabbed at the pile of papers on his desk. 'Look here, Nick, it's all in front of you, irrefutable proof, dates, times, names and photographs. I've got a list that makes the telephone directory look like a beginner's reader. Jade certainly isn't fussy. She serviced them all, from varsity students to her hairdresser. How much more do you need to be convinced?'

'Oh, I am convinced, convinced and sickened, David, but I have to remain with her, well, at least until the child is born.'

'Child?' said David. 'Whose child, Nick? Yours or one of these?' David threw the photographs across the desk and they slithered over the polished surface, and floated down on to the thick grey carpet.

'That we'll know once it's born and a blood test is done to determine paternity,' he answered softly, opening his eyes. 'Don't you understand? I have to remain in case the poor little scrap of humanity is mine. Someone has to watch that mad woman and give it a fighting chance of survival.'

'Nick,' said David placatingly, 'you know that the chances

157

of the child being yours are minimal. You have been in Zambia for the past two months doing that elephant film for TV. I also feel that you have been with Jade as seldom as possible since I saw you and Toni in my rooms. Please correct me if I'm wrong.'

At the mention of Toni, David saw the razor-toothed sharks of pain fin across Nick's eyes, and though he sat quietly waiting for Nick to speak, he fumed at his impotence to change Nick's mind. Tapping his gold pen against his teeth he sought desperately for new arguments to throw at him. They had been closeted in his room for almost two hours, endlessly thrashing over the same facts. The office staff had already left and the building was quiet.

'Nick, you never had a chance. You were snatched up fresh from varsity by a scheming woman and plunged into marriage, against, if I may remind you, parental and my advice. How long do you need to fulfil this over-developed sense of duty and responsibility that you are cursed with?' David's voice was hoarse. 'It's been seven years, Nick, seven long years. You have freedom in your hands and you are opening your fingers and letting it slip through.'

Nick swallowed a mouthful of tea but remained silent.

'Nick,' whispered David, 'what about Toni, Nick?'

Staring into his cup, Nick saw wavy hair, black as the trunk of a knobthorn tree wet with rain, a generous laughing mouth and widely spaced gentle eyes, delicate fingers smoothing his brow and ruffling his hair, and he felt a deep sickening pain.

Sensing a possible weakening, David used his next words like a rapier. 'You realise that you'll not have another chance once you've told her of this mad decision?' The words broke skin and drew blood. 'You'll have lost her for ever.'

Nick's flesh screamed in silent agony as the rapier blade drove deep into his belly. He paled and massaged his forehead viciously, trying to still the throbbing ache.

'You're denying your love, and you'll break her heart and her pride. She's very special, Nick. Don't do this to her, she doesn't deserve it,' said David softly. 'Don't lose her because of Jade's affairs.'

With a strangled groan Nick stood up, the tea slopping over the rim as he put the cup down on the tray. Resolutely he thrust the images of Toni and plans for their future down into the cellars of his mind, and locked the doors. He knew that if he allowed himself to think of her he would be lost, and the guilt of his childhood would never be assuaged. He had to remain with Jade. He had no choice.

'David, stop. Please, no more of this. Drop the divorce proceedings, and these . . . ' With a grimace of disgust, he picked up a handful of the photographs strewn across the desk. 'Burn them. I never want to see them again.'

He held out his hand in a gesture of contrition. 'Thank you, David. I know that you're right, but this is my decision.'

David ignored the outstretched hand. 'You're going to regret this, Nick. If I could have you committed until you came to your senses, believe me I would.' He watched Nick walk across the room in silence. 'You have my telephone number at home,' he said smiling at his friend sadly.

Nick raised a hand in farewell and closed the door very quietly.

'Damn you, Nicholas,' muttered David as he swung his chair around to face the large glass windows which framed the magnificent flat-topped mountain. 'Damn you for being a stubborn fool.'

He remained motionless in the chair, grieving for his friend, staring at the mountain while the late-afternoon sun painted the towering granite buttresses a golden rose and deepened the shadows in the gulleys to heliotrope and sage green.

* * *

Toni stood gazing up at Nursery Buttress for a few moments before drawing the curtains across the walls of glass in the sitting room. The great rocks stood stark and black against the dusty orange glow of the city lights. The mountain she loved dominated the skyline, powerful and menacing. She swished the silk curtains closed and turned and walked to her study, checking on her way that the doors and windows were locked.

She peeped in at Timothy who had been tucked into bed, sweet-smelling and cherubic, after his meal of fish and turnips. It had taken months to persuade him to eat turnips, until the evening she told him a tear-jerking story of poor, unwanted, unloved Tilly Turnip. Timothy was now a firm defender and devourer of Tilly Turnips, and demanded them with everything from porridge to jelly.

Chops had been quietened with a bowl of mealie-meal soaked in thick gravy and studded with chunks of meat and was padding around the garden marking his territory and growling at imaginary cats.

Her home was almost settled down for the night and she would be able to work on her article on ivory poaching.

Walking into her study she clicked her tongue irritably as she saw a white envelope stuck into the keys of her word processor. Izuba must have put it there before she went off duty. She snatched up the envelope, the thick paper crackling as she turned it over. Her name was printed in bold black letters on the front and she smiled. The writing was Nick's, the letter was from Nick. A few lines were scrawled at the bottom of the envelope. 'Izuba said you'd be back late. I have to tell you this now. It can't wait, so please forgive it being in a letter. I'll see you tomorrow.'

'Thank you, Nick,' she whispered holding the envelope to her cheek. 'Thank you for loving me.'

Like a miser she tucked the letter carefully into her pocket, hoarding it until she had locked up the house and had the time to treasure every word. She walked around, checking doors and windows in a haze of happiness, trying to imagine what the letter contained. The divorce was final. They would live together immediately. He loved her and wanted to see her tomorrow. What a lucky woman she was.

Like a liturgy, Toni chanted these happy thoughts to herself as she curled up in a leather armchair. The room glowed in the soft lights like the slipper satin lining of an oyster shell. Radiant with happiness, the glow of the reading lamp highlighting the sheen of her curls, she carefully opened the envelope, savouring every moment.

My dearest Kitten,

Before you read any further, I love you and I always will. What I have to say does not alter that. I am a fortunate and blessed man to have experienced loving you. It is without doubt the most important and most wonderful thing that has ever happened to me, but . . .

160

Toni consumed the opening words with the speed and joy of a believer eating chocolate after Lent, but as she turned the page her face drained of colour and became a death mask moulded in white clay. Her lips trembled uncontrollably, and she stared unseeing at the words.

I cannot explain it, my kitten, but I know that I must stay with her until the child is born.

No, Nick. No, she screamed in silent anguish, don't do this to me. I need you. I love you. A future without you. No, please, Nick. No.

The divorce proceedings have been stopped. I pray that you can forgive or at least understand my decision. I believe that not seeing each other will make this easier to bear, but I will love you every moment of each day that passes . . .

The hours crept by quietly. The ridgeback, alarmed by the sobs from the sitting room, left his kennel, sniffed under the glass doors and whimpered softly to Toni before curling against the cold glass, uttering the occasional low bark to comfort his mistress and to assure her that he was on guard.

The autumn evenings were cold and the thin cotton dress Toni wore afforded little protection against the chill. Goosepimples stood high on her arms and legs, but she sat cold and rigid in the chair, like a statue carved to adorn a grave.

Not to see Nick. Not to feel his arms tighten about her, to hear his voice become husky with desire, to tremble with excitement as his fingers traced the contours of her body. His voice echoed through the empty chambers of her heart. 'I never want to wake in the morning without you beside me. We're one.'

Her fingers played a mindless game, folding and unfolding the crisp white notepaper.

A baby. She refused to accept it. His wife refused to have children. She hated babies. It was a lie, it must be a lie, there could be no baby. If there was a child, then it could not be Nick's.

Her mind would not rest. Like a mighty river in full flood it rippled, swirled and overflowed with memories. Words whirled around ceaselessly.

Yet if fate reserves its malice but to break the lifted chalice,
Let me mingle with the elements where once I was a part.

The closing words of the love poem Nick had murmured to her the night they met came back to haunt her.

Then on some supernal morning which your beauty is adorning
As the dewdrop in a lily, I may nestle in your heart.

With a broken cry she slid from the chair. 'Oh my God, let it not be true,' she cried and knelt, resting her head in her folded hands on the soft seat. 'Please, God, help me. I'll make it up to you somehow. What am I to do? I don't know what to do, God. It hurts so much.' In her pain and despair Toni turned to God, her childhood refuge. 'God,' she pleaded, tears streaming down her cheeks, crying wildly and brokenly. 'Please help me, my God. I know that I have committed adultery but you do forgive that, and I love him so very much. Please don't let there be a baby. Please, God, please.'

The birds, fluffed up into downy feather balls against the cold, were heralding a new day with tentative whistles when Chops, hearing no further sounds from the sitting room, stretched himself stiffly and walked straight-legged to his kennel.

Slumped on the carpet, her head cradled on her arms, her face tear-streaked and bloated from weeping, Toni slept, quivering and moaning in her nightmare. The letter lay on the carpet beside her, fluttering in the down-draught from the chimney as if it too were racked with grief.

In a thatch-roofed house across the valley a man sat wrapped in a dark blue dressing gown, deaf to the twittering of the wakening birds in the chestnut trees. He stared into the gas flames flickering over the coals, ceaselessly painting pictures of dancing blue eyes and a tender laughing mouth.

CHAPTER

11

THE vast African sky shimmered, blue and clear as a flawless aquamarine, and the air crackled with the crispness of autumn.

Seagulls scavenging far from the seashore wheeled above the smouldering refuse dumps, their cries wild and strident on the still air.

Wisdom was standing in the sun outside the bottle store, checking the men scurrying into the building laden down with crates of beer and wine.

'Wisdom,' called Mrs Kahn, scurrying across the yard, 'you're shivering again and I'm worried about you.'

Without taking his eyes off the workers, for he had learned that a crate of beer could vanish as he turned his head, he answered, 'I am fine, madam. I— ' A fit of coughing drowned the rest of his words. Mrs Kahn's face creased into fine lines and her eyes searched his face anxiously. HIs khaki dustcoat hung as loosely on his body as a burly farmer's jacket flapping on a scarecrow.

The polished gloss of health on his skin had dulled, and despite her medications he still had a persistent cough and paid frequent bowel-wrenching visits to the toilet in the back yard.

'Wisdom, I've made an appointment for you to visit the TB clinic in town. You can have tomorrow morning off.'

'But, Mrs Kahn, tomorrow is the end of the month and I have to— '

'Yes, I know, Wisdom, but I want you to do this to please me. You've become so thin that you can't cross the road in a south-easter without being knocked over.' She smiled to lessen

163

the impact of her words. 'The appointment has been made and I want you to keep it.'

'Yes, madam,' replied Wisdom, ticking off numbers on the clipboard he held in his hand.

Wisdom had been cleared by the clinic. Still not satisfied, she had sent him to her family doctor for a check-up.

'You're a real Jewish mama, Mrs Kahn,' her doctor had remonstrated. 'Don't you have enough to do with two sons of your own and the bottle store business and the charities you support?'

'Wisdom is like a son, Doctor Cohen. He's a wonderful young man. Find out what's wrong with him. Please.'

The phone call from Doctor Cohen a few days later had left her chilled with horror and disbelief. 'Ten years ago we believed that infectious disease was no longer a threat to the developed world, Mrs Kahn. There is no cure or vaccine yet available for this new HIV virus and the epidemic is spreading.' The doctor spoke as though giving a lecture, imparting the news as unemotionally as possible.

'No, doctor. You're mistaken. I know Wisdom and his family. They're all decent, good people.'

'Mrs Kahn,' the doctor soothed, 'AIDS is passed from mother to child and by sexual intercourse. I've questioned Wisdom and he's been clean, apart from one night spent with a prostitute in a *shebeen* last year. She probably infected him.' The doctor listened to the quiet sobbing in silence.

'Have you told Wisdom?' she asked.

'No, Mrs Kahn. I reported to you first.'

She blew her nose noisily. 'Thank you, doctor. I appreciate that. I'll tell Wisdom myself.'

'I'm sorry, Mrs Kahn. We do have drugs to ease the symptoms but none which offer hope,' said her family practitioner, running his finger down the list of appointments his secretary had just placed on his desk.

'Thank you,' she said as she quietly replaced the receiver.

Her husband had quickly capitulated before her relentless demand that Wisdom be given three weeks' sick leave to visit his family in the Transkei. She had explained only that Wisdom had a chronic cough and needed to be away from the Cape for a few weeks. She had driven to Shonalanga and spoken to Izuba explaining that Wisdom needed care, and that the unpolluted air in the Transkei and the slow-paced life in the *kraal* would help to strengthen him and cure his cough.

Izuba had been ecstatic when Miss Toni had given her compassionate leave to accompany Wisdom. It meant she would have her brother with her, see her daughter Beauty, and play with her grandson. She was certain that once they were home in their village the priest diviner would smell out what was wrong with Wisdom and would cure him.

Mrs Kahn had prepared a large basket filled with cakes and pies for their journey and had driven them to the station.

'You are lucky to work for the Kahns,' said Izuba as they watched Mrs Kahn, her small dumpy body wedged tightly into the seat of the station wagon, her head barely reaching the top of the steering wheel, swing into the traffic.

'Yes, my sister,' answered Wisdom, 'she is like a mother.' Bending down to pick up his suitcase, his thin shoulders shook violently as he coughed.

'Leave that,' commanded Izuba and swung the heavy case on to her head. Balancing Mrs Kahn's basket on top of the maroon plastic case she walked regally into the station. Soze held Wisdom's hand tightly, her dark eyes wide with delight and fear. She was excited to be going to see her big sister, Beauty, the new baby and her Umakhulu, and terrified at the thought of being swallowed by the big snake which had taken Beauty and her grandmother away.

* * *

Wisps of steam rose and curled into the crisp air as the jet of warm yellow urine soaked into the earth. The velvet sky weighed down by stars hung low over the sleeping village, enfolding it like a spangled mosquito net, and the white walls of the huts crowned with coolie-hats of thatched grass gleamed like frosted glass in the pearly light of the fading moon.

Squatting low over the dusty soil Beauty bobbed on her haunches, shaking free the last warm droplets. She shivered as she stood up and wrapped the blanket tightly around her body. The bushes and trees fringing the village were unfamiliar and menacing in the darkness, and images of foul-smelling hyenas

165

and hairy *thikoloshes*, their right hips worn away by the rubbing of frequent intercourse, peopled her imagination.

Her bare feet scuffed up puffs of dust as she ran back to the village and the safety of her hut. She closed the door of rough wooden planks and gratefully breathed in the familiar stale smell of many bodies sleeping in a smoky hut. Quietly she tiptoed to her mat on the earthen floor, hardened with cowdung and mud, and taking the sleeping baby into her arms she pulled her blanket over her head and closed her eyes.

Beauty's baby son had been born a few months before in the seclusion of a little hut at the edge of the village. She had been fed bitter concoctions by the herbalist and the *Igqira* for weeks before the birth, to ensure a safe and easy delivery, and she had taken part in numerous rituals to ensure that her child would not be born feet first or with teeth, for the attending midwives would then have to kill the baby instantly.

When the baby boy had slid easily from between her thighs as she crouched on the floor and his slippery head was safely in the waiting hands of the two old midwives, gnarled fingers were run over the tiny gums and found no sharp teeth. The efficaciousness of the medicines was applauded by the tribe and the *Igqira* strutted through the village like a rooster with a new brood of hens.

The squalling wet baby had been laid on the floor and the umbilical cord had been slowly cut with a split piece of thatching grass. The child had then been smoked.

'Aaie,' coughed the chief midwife as she passed the spluttering baby through the dense smoke, pungent with herbs, to her friend on the other side of the reeking fire. 'He's a fine child. See how deeply he breathes in the smoke.'

'He will be strong as a buffalo and fierce as a lion,' replied the wizened old woman as she took the baby.

'See how angry his face is and he will not cry.' She put the near-asphyxiated child back into the fumes and wiped her streaming eyes with a corner of her orange-braided skirt.

'The wizards will not be able to harm this one,' cackled the old woman as she finally carried the baby away from the fire to where Beauty lay on the floor.

Curled up at his mother's side the smoke-cured baby had his tiny mouth forced open and a mixture of herbal medicines was poured down his throat. Beauty watched as he railed weakly against the treatment. She did not intervene as she knew the medicines were necessary to firm the baby; all babies were believed to be soft at birth and it was necessary to dose them frequently to strengthen and form them.

Beauty and her son had remained in the hut, isolated from the tribe, until the umbilical scab had dried and fallen off. The midwives had remained in attendance, pouring concoctions into and over the little body to protect it from all the black and white magic which could be used against a defenceless baby. He would spend his life drinking store-bought and herbalists' medicines to ward off real and imaginary attacks by witches posing as ordinary people.

Listening to her baby's breath burble softly as he slept cushioned by her full breasts, Beauty was thankful that many of the tribal treatments had died out, especially the old Zulu treatment of rotating the stem of a castor oil plant in the baby's anus until the blood flowed freely to prevent the itch which caused lecherousness. She held her son's warm body close to hers, and happily listened to his soft grunting.

Ikhwezi, the morning star, had just appeared when the women tiptoed from the hut to blow the grey ashes away from the coals, kindle the cooking fires and boil the fluffy mealie-meal porridge for the men.

They huddled close to the fires, warming their bare legs, their breath forming curling white tendrils in the cold morning air, their blankets tied tightly around their shoulders. Beauty hoisted her son on to her back and tied her blanket tightly around him. As she left the hut she glanced fearfully at the euphorbia trees growing outside the door.

The tree planted for Justice was holding its branches high, the green succulent stems fat and full. The tree looked like her uncle Justice, tall and strong. He had always been bigger and more powerful than her uncle Wisdom. The old midwives said the first twin to be born was always more robust, as he inhaled the strongest of the fumes from the fire and suckled first on his mother's milk.

Wisdom's tree had not recovered and her spirits fell. The stems were wrinkling like an old man's scrotum and the branch closest to the hut was wearily resting on the thatched roof.

Beauty offered up a quick prayer to her Xhosa God, Umdali, and to Baby Jesus, who they had taught her in church also had great powers, to protect Wisdom.

She loved her gentle uncle who had arrived at the *kraal* a week ago with her mother, Izuba, and she could not bear the hurt and bewilderment in his eyes when he looked at his tree and saw it dying, for he knew that it was a signpost from the spirits to lead him on his lonely road to death.

Inside the dark hut Wisdom stirred uneasily on his mat. His sleep before awakening was light, and fears and superstitions ran wild in his dreams.

He saw his beloved brother Justice standing astride a blood-red star sawing at his euphorbia tree with a sickle, gloating raucously with each sliver he sliced from the crinkled stem. At his feet sat a hyena, cackling insanely as it gobbled up the fallen pieces.

The girl he had slept with the night he and Justice had visited the *shebeen* in Shonalanga, their heads woolly with the bearded ones' brandy, appeared naked, her long red nails raking his sides, her back arching spasmodically, her heavy breasts bouncing as she reached for him. As he was about to sink his lips into her warm, open mouth, she changed into Mrs Kahn, his white mother, sitting in her office, a medicine measure in her hand, shaking her head at him sorrowfully, tears running unchecked down her cheeks. He walked to her slowly and she held him in her arms and stroked his head gently, murmuring words of love and comfort. Her sorrow was so great that Wisdom wept with her and the world watched in silence.

Wisdom was jerked into wakefulness by a soft tugging at his blanket. He uncovered his head and blinked in the dim light. A small black figure dressed only in a short ochre skirt was crouched beside his bed, and in her hand she held a grubby ball of mealie-meal.

'For you to eat,' said Soze and smiled when she saw him accept the offering and put it in his mouth.

The sand grated against his teeth but rather than cause her distress, Wisdom swallowed the gritty meal.

'More?' squeaked Soze. 'I'll fetch more.'

Hurriedly Wisdom threw aside his blanket. 'Thank you,

Soze,' he said. 'Do not fetch any more. I will come and eat outside.'

Soze ran off to join the children seated round their communal pot of mealie-meal, happy that her uncle had accepted her food and was crossing the dusty square to join the men.

Wisdom seated himself with his back to the euphorbia trees. Dipping his hand into the black pot, he scooped up a handful of meal and stuffed it into his mouth. He washed it down with a long draught of soured milk, checking first to make certain that he was drinking milk only with his clansmen, for to drink milk with another could mean that he wished to marry their daughter.

He smacked his lips in appreciation. The meal churned queasily in his belly, but he scooped up another mouthful, knowing that it made his family happy to see him eat.

'Today, our brother,' said one of the men squatting around the pot, resting his skeletal arms on his scabbed knees, 'today, the *Igqira* comes from Velelo's village to join our witchdoctor, to sniff out the witch who is causing your illness.'

'We have watched you carefully this last week, Wisdom our brother,' continued another, his head sprinkled with curls white as ash on coals. 'You have awakened each day ill and with your eyes hollow from lack of sleep. A witch has crept into the hut at night and poured blood over you.'

A murmur of superstitious fear rumbled around the circle.

'Last night the dogs barked loudly and this morning a baboon's tracks were found in the village.' His voice dropped. 'The witch was riding her baboon backwards holding tightly to its tail.'

The men huddled closer together, the bright sunshine not dispelling their fear of witches with their vast and grotesque families of familiars.

'Before the sun dies beneath the sea tonight we will have a smelling out,' said the headman, his eyes buried deep in wrinkles seamed by squinting in the harsh African sun.

Wisdom shivered, for even though he had been raised in the city, he knew how important and terrible was the smelling-out ceremony. Witchcraft took precedence over all laws, tribal as well as Western, and a man condemned of witchcraft was doomed. He had no recourse to justice or to any court. In

169

earlier times, very few wealthy men lived to enjoy old age. Envy was often the goad to the accusations, and as the riches of the family and the man executed of witchcraft went to the chief of the tribe, the chief was naturally inclined to uphold the witchdoctor's sentence.

The men were silent as they scraped the pot, peeling off the dried pieces of porridge and chewing them slowly.

Belching loudly, the headman pulled his orange blanket around his shoulders and led the men to a cleared patch of earth near the cattle *kraal*. Today the men would remain in the village, smoking and talking until Velelo's *Igqira* arrived.

The young boys, wearing only gourds or sheaths of animal skin over their genitalia to prevent the entry of evil, had already driven the cattle and goats out to pasture on the rolling grassy downs. The men smiled indulgently as they watched a four-year-old, his dusty buttocks bobbing like corks on choppy water, run shouting after some stray white goats.

While the cattle grazed the boys would practise stick fighting, the strongest herd boy choosing the best pasturage for his father's cattle and ordering the younger and weaker boys to search for birds and rats which they would roast.

'Wisdom,' said one of the men as he took his long wooden pipe and tobacco from the beaded bag slung over his shoulder, 'you have returned from the city. Tell us what the white man's papers say of the ANC. We have heard many stories and our stomachs are uneasy.'

He lit the long-stemmed pipe and exhaled deeply, the smoke obscuring the 'keeper of the heart' beaded necklace given to him by his wife which hung around his neck, the tasselled end swinging low over his chest.

'Brothers,' answered Wisdom, pleased that the headman and elders of the tribe had asked his opinion, 'every day there is talk of the ANC.' He coughed violently, wiping his mouth with the back of his hand, and drew in a deep rasping breath. The men whispered among themselves, waiting for him to continue.

Wisdom swallowed nervously. His stay in the peace and quiet of his native village, far from television and newspapers, had strengthened his doubts about the ANC and the bearded ones. He listened avidly though silently when Izuba read

170

articles in the paper written by Miss Toni. In the latest article she had written, 'The ANC must beware of the anger in their young followers, the Comrades, mainly illiterate and disenchanted. Children spawned in the darkness of bigotry and matured in the heat of violence. They look for strength in their leaders. Public posturing and talk of violence is for fools. Let the real leaders stand tall . . . '

Wisdom translated Toni's sentiments into language the tribal people would easily understand. 'Many of our children and those who have lost faith believe that to work with the white man is weak and they talk of leaving the ANC and joining the PAC who have no wish to talk.'

The men were silent. The young man who had spoken rolled his prized fighting stick beneath his foot. He stared at the stick as it rolled in the dust.

'They say that their foot must lie heavy on the neck of the Boer, as he has no place in the land,' continued Wisdom.

The headman, his curls white in the bright sunlight, cut in. 'If the voice of reason is stilled and the violent ones in the PAC and the ANC win, and the whites are driven out, what will there be for us? Will they make our land rich, our cattle fat, our daughters fruitful?' He coughed up a gob of phlegm and spat loudly into the red dust. 'I fear that they will mouth only the words they have been taught by the chiefs over the sea.'

The tall man rubbed his beaded necklace with work-hardened fingers. 'We Xhosa and our ancestors have fought the Boers for years. Many of their men died and many of ours became shades. We know these Boers. We may hate them, but, my brothers, we know them.

'What do we know of these strangers with their stories of riches? Where have you ever seen a head-chief give away his cattle and goats? Once they have defeated the Boers they will sit on the power and keep it for themselves and we will be as we are today.'

The old men nodded sadly. The headman puffed on his pipe then, squinting through the smoke, said, 'Already our brothers are coming back to the *kraals*. The work in the cities is drying up. The men who run to other countries and cackle loudly as the guineafowl have made the countries across the sea close

171

the factories here, and our brothers' families are crying for food and work.

'When the strong men have all left the country with their money, who will then give us work, who will feed us? A man does not return to a bad wife, and once they have left they will not come back.'

The chief's feelings echoed Toni's articles. 'The ANC must beware; they are in danger of being as stubborn and unyielding as the old Boer government. They still call for sanctions, demonstrations and strikes, they threaten the use of arms, all catalysts for economic and political chaos.'

He re-lit his pipe and listened for a few moments to the ringing two-syllable trumpet call of the *ihem*. The crowned cranes would bring rain and he smiled as he saw their beautiful topknots waving like golden stamens as they walked across the hillside.

An imposing old man who had been squatting quietly in the sun cleared his throat loudly. 'My brothers, I am only an old and foolish man, but I fear for our children, my brothers, I fear.'

The old man's words echoed Wisdom's feelings. The thought of all men having *indabas* and discussing a fair future for the country they loved, instead of planning death and destruction, appealed to him. But he was still strongly influenced by Justice and could never let the brother he idolised know of his doubts. He had spent his life living in his brother's shadow and it was now too late to cast his own.

'Brothers,' he said, 'the bearded ones who talk for the ANC say that when they have power we will share everything. There will be no man richer than another, no man happier than another. Our children will all go to school, there will be doctors and dentists for all and we will not have to pay. All will be free for the people. We will vote for the ones who are to govern us and our people will look after us. No longer will we be considered to be as lean, useless goats because we are black.'

The younger man in the group, rolling his fighting stick lovingly between his hands, broke in. 'The chiefs of the ANC may be clever men, but I fear that some of their followers are like the skulking hyenas. I would not walk with them at night.

I wait with clear eyes to watch their actions, and with sharp ears to hear their words.'

The men nodded in agreement and as the sun rose high in the bright blue African sky they shifted into the shade thrown by the wooden poles ringing the cattle *kraal*.

The old white-haired tribal chief listened carefully, for he was no longer answerable only to his people and the ancestors. To remain in power he had to treat the political leaders well. The old ways had changed. Even the small villages had felt the soft tremors, early warnings of major upheavals.

The old world of Africa had moved slowly, like a herd of huge elephants ponderously walking the familiar trails and migration routes, but the new Africa with its Western-style governments leapt and ran around haphazardly like a herd of alert brown impala, and the skittishness worried the chiefs and elders.

He studied the sober faces around him, faces of men living close to the earth, men struggling to accept and understand the volcanic eruptions in government policies.

'We know the ANC have suckled, through the dark years, at the teats of their faraway Mother Russia. Will they now they brothers speak their own words of wisdom, or will they be words soured by the milk? The times ahead will be unsure like a river bank after the great rains,' he said. 'It will be necessary to watch with the eyes of an eagle and walk with the step of a hunter. But let us leave knowledge of that to the days yet to come.'

The men nodded and grunted and Wisdom was silent. Each man was allowed to speak and was listened to attentively, and the propaganda of the bearded ones paled in the light of their homespun philosophy. He sat back, content to listen as the men chewed over the stories, savouring every mouthful, pulling at the facts like toothless old women chewing at dried goat's meat.

They had turned from discussing the political leaders to discussing their most important possessions, their cattle, when the shrill cries of the women alerted them. They reluctantly left the cattle-pen to face the ordeal of the smelling out.

* * *

173

Soze balanced the empty paraffin tin on her woolly head and holding her neck and shoulders rigid she toddled after the long line of women and girls, their heavily braided skirts forming a gaily patterned orange and black snake as they swayed through the green grass on their way to the river of the precipice, the Gxara.

Beauty walked proudly behind Izuba, her face and shoulders whitened with sandstone to show that she was a nursing mother. The medicinal necklaces of wood, roots and the hair from the tail of the sacred cow clicked rhythmically as she walked. She was happy and had slipped easily into the rhythm of tribal life.

Ahead of Beauty walked her grandmother. She carried no bucket on her elaborately tied purple and white headscarf, and the bracelets of wire and beads, which covered her wrinkled arms from the wrists to her armpits and hung heavily around her ankles, sparkled in the sun.

The women lowered their buckets and tins on to the muddy verge of the river. Kneeling on the bank, they chose good round stones to pound the dirt out of the skirts and blankets they had brought to wash.

The children chased tadpoles in the shallows and crafted cattle and goats from the rich red mud. The low green shrubs were soon quilted with a patchwork of white and orange skirts, multi-coloured long aprons worn by the married women, and scarves of crimson, indigo blue and shimmering green. They were like giant butterflies' wings outspread, resting on the river bank.

Their washing completed, the women moved upstream to sit in the shade near the pool of their ancestors. The pointed aloe heads were blushing with the first traces of red and the palms and ferns protected the solitude of the waters.

'Umakhulu,' said Beauty, untying the blanket which held her son pressed tightly to her back, 'please tell us the story of Nongawuse.' Carefully she eased her swollen nipple into the baby's questing mouth and smiled as he snuffled happily and pulled strongly on her breast. The women settled on the grass, their legs stretched straight in front of them, eager to hear once again the story of the girl prophet whose visions broke the strength of the Xhosa nation.

'That,' began the old lady, shaking her head, 'that was a very bad time for our people.'

She fumbled in her heavily embroidered bag and found the mouthpiece to fit into her pipe, richly encrusted with red, blue and black beadwork. She always hid her mouthpiece very carefully, for having been in the saliva of her mouth it could be magically contaminated if it was used by anyone else.

The women and girls gathered around the old crone waited respectfully until she had lit her pipe. The silence was broken only by soft sucking as the older women who had borne sufficient children to entitle them to smoke the long pipes puffed gently.

'My children, long ago a girl prophet, Nongawuse, looked deep into the waters of this pool and saw our ancestors and heard them demand the death of all our cattle and the burning of all our crops. In return they would rise and drive the white man into the sea and all the land would belong to our Xhosa people.'

The old lady paused and sucked thoughtfully at her pipe. The women stared at her in horror. To burn the crops they planted and hoed beneath the burning African sun was madness. The little ones' eyes widened. Small as they were, they knew the value of cattle to the tribe. They were so important that women were not allowed to tend them and between the showing of the first menses and the last, no woman was allowed into the sacred temple of the tribe, the cattle *kraal*. Soze shrieked and buried her face in Izuba's lap.

'What was this lovely young girl to do? The ancestors had spoken.'

The women nodded. The ancestors were powerful and had to be appeased.

'Nongawuse told her uncle who was a chief diviner to the powerful Gcaleka branch of our nation. He knew that our ancestors were angry because we were weak. The missionaries were taking over our people with no room for our spirits, and we were allowing land to be taken by the white man.'

Beauty, her eyes fixed on her umakhulu, moved her son across to her other breast, a trickle of milk dribbling down his chin.

175

'He knew that a great sacrifice was necessary. The hills echoed day and night with the moans of our dying cattle, the night skies were bright as the skies of day with the fires of our burning crops and the Gcaleka side of the Xhosa nation were happy that they were obeying their ancestors.'

The old lady wiped her eyes with the back of her hand, her bracelets clinking loudly in the deathly silence.

'Finally it was done and our people sat on the hillsides through the long dark night waiting for the spirit armies to march and regain the land and for the great wind to whirl the white men into the sea.' Umakhulu sniffed and continued.

'The promised day dawned, but my children, it was a day like all others. The ancestors were silent, the children wailed with hunger and the shades were silent.'

Izuba looked round at the women and girls listening to her mother.

My sisters, she thought, our forefathers listened to the ravings of a young girl and the might of our nation was broken. Now, once again, some of our Xhosa people listen to those who urge them to turn away from the conference table. Our nation must not again commit suicide, political suicide.

Sensing the horror and sorrow in her elders, little Soze left Izuba and curled up in her grandmother's lap, burying her face in the old lady's dangling breasts.

'In the long months that followed the great sacrifice, our people died and lay scattered across the land like black cinders from the cold cooking fire.

'Those of our people who survived the terrible hunger became like the despised tribe of beggars, the Mfengu. Aaiee,' moaned the aged woman. 'Our power was broken, our land laid waste and our young and old were gone.'

Izuba watched her mother lift Soze from her lap and climb painfully to her feet. Even Miss Toni who knows so much about our people cannot understand how our nation almost destroyed itself by listening to a young girl's story, she thought.

There was a low murmur as the women tucked their long pipes away, shook out their skirts and left the quiet pool to collect their washing, fill their pails with fresh water and return to the *kraal*.

176

Soze carefully placed a small leafy branch on top of her tin of water to prevent it splashing when the undulating walk set up a wave motion. She steadied the tin on her head with one pudgy hand and, holding a clay goat firmly in the other, she set out with the women on the long walk back to the village.

CHAPTER

12

T ONI stretched out in the sun, letting the warmth soak into her limbs, soothing her, and listened idly to the high-pitched calls of the seagulls, the crashing of the waves and the laughter of children. Without moving her head she could see the towering cliffs of Chapman's Peak to her left, with cars small as pepper ticks scurrying along the road knifed into its red rock; and to her right the deformed finger of Hangklip beckoned the fishing fleet into harbour. She knew that if she twisted her neck and looked behind she would catch a glimpse of the back of Table Mountain.

It was a beautiful day and Toni sighed as, pulling the brim of her red straw hat lower over her face, she watched Timothy and Chops race along the beach, breaking up the line of foam, creamy as freshly whipped egg whites.

Two little girls shrieked in mock terror as their father swung them over the waves. The man was tall and lean. Watching him, she ached for Nick. It had been so long since his letter followed by one brief meeting and she still longed to be with him. She did not understand his reasons for remaining with Jade, but she tried to accept his decision.

During the long hours of darkness lying in bed watching the oak leaves dance in the wind through the skylight, she relived every moment she had spent with him. She heard his warm voice murmuring endearments and felt his hard body. She wove dreams and fantasies, and fell asleep on a pillow wet with tears.

The father misjudged one of the waves and it washed over the small girl. Panic-stricken, she wrapped her arms and legs tightly around him, coughing and spluttering.

That's what Tim needs, thought Toni, a man to admire and imitate.

Serge was at home so seldom. His business trips seemed to have become more frequent and Toni knew that he was still accompanied on most of them by a changing bevy of beautiful secretaries.

Loving Nick had enabled her to study Serge dispassionately. She realised that the endless stream of women he bedded gave him confidence in his masculinity, the circle of sycophants made him feel popular, and the alcoholic rages afforded him the opportunity to say things he would not have the temerity to say when sober.

She now accepted his embraces with compassion, like a farmer rubbing the velvety noses of his calves as he loaded them into trucks bound for the butcher. Living with Serge became less demanding, but she longed for the pretence to end.

A cold, wet body suddenly pressed against her sun-baked back, like an ice-pack applied to a burn, and jerked Toni out of her reverie.

'Timothy, you little tiger, you're wet,' she shrieked, rolling over and tickling his wiggling body until he screamed for mercy. She rubbed his skin a rosy red with the coarse towel, and he cuddled close to her, absorbing her warmth gratefully.

'I love you, Mummy,' he said, twisting one of her curls around his finger.

'How much?' she asked teasingly.

'As much as all the sky,' he replied.

She kissed him gently. 'And I love you back as much as all the sky and all the sea.'

He grinned and wound his arms around her neck. 'Mummy,' he wheedled, tracing the outline of her fingers in the sand, 'Mummy, Chops wants some snoek. Let's go and buy some. Poor Chops is hungry.'

Toni stifled a chuckle. 'Darling, Chops doesn't like fish. He never eats it.'

'He does now, Mummy, 'cause he's been swimming.' The logic defeated Toni and she capitulated.

'All right. Run and fetch Chops and we'll put him under the freshwater tap before we leave.'

179

Toni sat up and watched Timothy trying to put an end to the dog's frantic attempts to catch a seagull. The large birds, nautical smart in their navy and white, were skimming over him just out of reach of his open mouth. They flew ahead and sat on the wet sand nonchalantly waiting for him to reach them; then at the last moment they soared up into the sky over his madly yapping head and led him back down the beach.

They dragged the dog up and down the sand. It was a game they never tired of playing, and eventually Chops, his tongue lolling loosely, collapsed on to the beach, barely able to turn his head as they strutted past.

Tim, ably assisted by two adults, came struggling through the hot white sand, his legs bowed under the strain of dragging Chops. As they approached Toni's face lit up with delight and she ran to meet them.

'Helen and Clive, how good to see you,' Toni said, giving them both a hug. Clipping the leash on to the dog's collar she admonished him, 'Sit, Chops, sit and behave.'

Reluctantly he pretended to obey, squatting uncomfortably with his hindquarters held high ready for a quick escape. Toni fondled his velvety ears. 'Stupid dog,' she said. 'Those seagulls have fooled you – accept it.'

Chops nuzzled her hand but his eyes were fixed longingly on the huge white birds skimming the waves.

'We're going to the boats to buy snoek for Chops,' piped Timothy.

'Isn't it a little early in the season for snoek, old man?' asked Clive. 'They're a winter fish.'

'Yes, but Mummy says we can buy some now,' said Timothy clutching Helen's hand. 'Come with us, Aunt Helen, please.'

Timothy loved Helen and was always eager to go to her farm-house set high on a hill washed pink and mauve with proteas and ericas, overlooking the picturesque fishing harbour. Her crèche for pre-school children and practice as a child therapist were both thriving. He loved being part of her large day-family, collecting warm brown eggs, feeding the ducks and moulding lopsided animals in plasticine seated at the old yellowwood table in the kitchen.

Helen bent down and picked him up, her red hair licking her face like flames. 'Oh, you're becoming a heavy boy,' she groaned. 'Yes, we'll come with you. I want to talk to Mummy.'

Timothy never tired of the boat harbour in Hout Bay. Climbing over tarry ropes between the trawlers, slipping on blood and fish scales and chatting to the fishermen was his Disneyland.

Toni and Helen perched side by side on one of the hot grey bollards on the quayside. They watched Clive swing Timothy over the side of a trawler into the arms of a fisherman who was allowing him, hysterical with delight, to choose his own fish.

'Toni,' said Helen, 'those articles you wrote for the *Daily News* and the *Look Out* were excellent.'

Toni smiled and thanked her.

'I cried when I read of the girl who was gang-raped because she refused to join the school boycott. I still shiver at your description of the ambulance guys trying to staunch the bleeding. That's exactly what we need, someone who can write a factual piece but make the reader smell the blood and feel the fear.'

'Helen,' said Toni, 'what's this leading up to?'

'We've been granted the use of the old recreation hall in Section B in Shonalanga to use as a nursery school-cum-crèche but we have to repair the damage caused during the riots. Winter is coming and we need glass for the windows, galvanised-iron sheets for the roof plus equipment.' She frowned. 'The large businesses have been milked dry with requests for aid and even the smaller private companies are funding houses in the squatter camps.'

Helen paused and flicked her hair away from her face. Her grey eyes were serious and the smudged iris shone a deep green.

'We need help from the public. We need the public to see the plight of black mothers forced to leave their children with unsuitable people in overcrowded rooms while they go to work. We need them to see the thin legs pockmarked with scabies and sores, and the heads riddled with lice.

'Toni, you know that hundreds of lice can nest on one small head. You also know that these dreadful insects eat five times a day, and keep piercing the soft scalps. We need you to sicken the public, Toni. Please, we cannot pay you, but,

181

Toni, talk to our mothers, see our children, make the public cry for them.'

Toni clasped Helen's hand in hers. 'If Stan le Roux phones this evening to say that I can use the information I've obtained from his detectives on ivory poachers, I'll be able to finish the first of the articles tonight. That means I can bring Timothy to your farm on Monday and we can drive out to Shonalanga.'

Helen's eyes sparkled with tears. 'I love you, Toni. Thank you.' She squeezed her friend's hand. 'Why don't you leave young Tim with me this evening? Then you can work undisturbed. He and Clive can barbecue the fish in the garden.'

'Tim'd love that,' said Toni. 'He needs a father figure.'

Helen watched Clive and Timothy clamber down from the boat and walk towards them. A long time ago she had tried to persuade Toni to leave Serge and start a new life for Timothy and herself. Toni had explained softly but firmly that she had lived with a stepfather she detested and would not subject her son to a step-parent. Helen had not discussed the matter again.

She had been delighted when Toni told her about Nick, and shattered when she heard about Jade's pregnancy. She could now only offer her friend hope and comfort.

'Toni,' she said tentatively, 'I know that we agreed not to talk about this again, but have you seen or heard from Nicholas recently?'

Toni smiled, a small sad smile. 'No, Helen. I won't see him.' Her large blue eyes misted. 'It's too painful.'

Helen put her arm around her friend and hugged her.

'Hey there,' shouted Clive. 'Look what Tim has.' The two women looked up distractedly and Clive turned to Timothy.

'Tim, old man, you walk on ahead to the car and I'll fetch your mum and Helen.'

Timothy walked on, happily lecturing his dog about the fish and fishermen.

'What's wrong?' said Clive.

'Nothing,' said Toni.

'Nicholas,' said Helen.

Clive stepped forward and put his arms around Toni. 'There, there,' he soothed, 'please don't cry.'

She sniffed. 'I'm sorry, Clive. I'm just being weak and silly, but I still miss him so much.'

Clive kissed the top of her head lightly. 'Nick misses you, Toni. He was very quiet and miserable before he left for Zambia. This decision is destroying him.'

Toni sniffed and smeared her tears across her cheeks with the back of her hand.

'We're always here for you, Toni. Remember that.'

A small voice called in the distance. 'Uncle Clive, come quickly. Chops is licking the fish's nose. Come.'

Toni put on her sunglasses and they ran to where Timothy was standing on tiptoe holding the fish above his head.

Toni scolded the dog and Timothy walked ahead of them, proudly holding his fish in the gills as the fisherman had shown him. Chops, still eager to help, sniffed the silver body and licked the tail tentatively.

'No, Chops,' said Timothy sternly. 'Dogs don't eat fish, 'cause the bones will stick in your tummy and you'll get sick.' He hugged the fish tightly to his chest, keeping it away from his dog's tongue.

Toni laughed and ruffled her son's hair as he climbed into Clive's car. They blew kisses to each other until the car drove out of the harbour gates.

* * *

Chops was still barking loudly, letting everyone know that he was home and on duty, when the door of Toni's study was flung open. She stopped jotting down notes on the pad balanced on top of her word processor and covered the mouthpiece of the telephone with her hand.

'Hello, Serge,' she said. 'I won't be a moment. I'm talking to Stan le Roux.'

Serge glowered and walked across to stare at the flashing green words on the screen.

'A total ban on ivory will only make it go underground,' she had written, 'making it as impossible to police as opium from the Golden Triangle, or cocaine from the forests of Latin America.'

Serge grunted and punched a button and a new page of Toni's article appeared on the screen. His lips tightened and he scanned the lines quickly. 'But there are those who feel that a total ban would make it easier to police, as illegal ivory traders would not then be able to use fake CITES certificates and shipments could not be given retrospective CITES authorisations.'

Why? he fumed silently. Why must my wife now start writing about the illegal sale of ivory and horn? Next they'll have a committee, then investigations and my whole operation'll be endangered. Damn her, he muttered to himself, glancing across at her while the screen cleared. This writing must stop. She needs to have more children. Then she'll be too sick or too busy to run around after stories.

'So I can definitely say that the warden has admitted shooting the elephant and rhino, Stan?' she queried. 'It's no longer only the game ranger's story about the warden? Good. Now what made the ranger betray his boss? Good, great,' Toni said, writing quickly. 'This time economics worked. The ranger suddenly realised that not only was the warden betraying his position of trust, but he was pocketing money which the Parks Board should have had to improve the men's standard of living.' She snapped the notebook closed and ran her fingers through her hair, still sticky with salt and spray.

'Thank you, Stan,' she said. 'I appreciate the time you've spent answering my questions. This'll make a great story. Good night and once again, thank you.'

Serge turned to her, jabbing his finger at the processor. 'You. You should be ashamed,' he hissed. 'A woman in your position behaving like an unwashed do-gooder. Are there not enough fools in the world shouting to keep the ban on ivory? Are there not enough people out of work and destitute because of the ban?' He paused to take a breath and Toni broke in.

'I'm writing about the poachers and the middlemen who are without social conscience, intent only on the money, not concerned about the animals or the future.' She spoke quickly, unwilling to start another quarrel. 'Do you realise that the number of Africa's elephants has halved in eight short years and if the poaching continues only a few thousand will be alive to greet the new century?'

'And what makes you think that the nonsense you write will have any effect on the situation?' sneered Serge. 'No one with any intelligence even reads this drivel.' He tapped a cigarette on the top of her computer, lit it and sauntered to the door.

'Give it up, Toni. Stop writing your fairy stories and making a fool of yourself. Come to bed now.' He laughed disparagingly and slammed the door.

Toni looked at the door, straightened her shoulders and sat in front of the processor.

'So no one reads this rubbish. It has no effect,' she said. 'We'll see, Serge, we'll see.'

As her fingers flew across the keys she heard a voice deep and warm, 'Your articles are excellent, Kitten.' She saw grey eyes sparkling at her in approbation from behind horn-rimmed glasses.

* * *

Izuba leaned against the door of her hut and smiled at Beauty as she shuffled her feet in the dust, humming to the child tied on to her back. Her eyes clouded as she looked at the small black head shaking on her daughter's back.

'My heart grows weak as the maize plant when the brown beetle attacks it when I think in ten days' time I must leave you and return to Shonalanga and smell the smoke of the big city,' she murmured quietly.

Her reverie was broken by Soze pulling her hand. 'Uma, Uma, look who comes. Hold me, Uma.' Her childish voice piped high with fear. Izuba gasped and called to the men.

'The *Igqirakazi* from Velelo's village is here. Come quickly.'

The men were clustered around the cattle *kraal*. It was late afternoon and they were questioning the herd boys as they placed heavy branches across the entrance to protect the beasts during the night. The men and boys ran to gather in a tight cluster, watching anxiously as the witchdoctor and her accomplice walked slowly through the soft yellow grass towards the huts.

Izuba studied the witchdoctors, as Toni had asked her to remember every detail of the ceremony. Her Child of God had wanted to witness the smelling out but it was against tribal custom.

The lack of wrinkles on the witchdoctor's round face, shining with oil, belied her age. The animal-skin headdress, made from the first animal she saw or dreamed of after she had heard the voices of her ancestors commanding her to train as a witchdoctor, stood high on her head. The fringe of white beads which hung heavily over her forehead and ears gave her heightened perception and made her spirit light, and those wound tightly around her right forearm were to guard against evil and impurity.

The hippo-hide *sjambok* and her cowtail switch with the bead-encrusted handle hung loosely in her hand. Her face was set and hard and her eyes, the whites painted a smoky brown by the drugs she used to induce visions, bored into the men and women as she passed.

An aura of power and menace surrounded the woman, and the villagers cringed against the white walls of their huts and averted their eyes. Izuba shivered but, mindful of Toni's request, did not turn away.

The diviner's accomplice, her legs held apart by the huge bracelets of intertwined tree roots which covered her calves, ran to place a low wooden stool in the front of the headman's hut. Her face was expressionless as she seated the *Igqirakazi* and handed her a bowl of freshly brewed beer to refresh her after her journey.

The witchdoctor who had tended Beauty before the birth of her son sat facing Velelo's diviner. The hem of his white skirt, heavily edged in black braid, longer than hers, lay in the dust and his eyes were hidden behind his veil of white beads.

The two fur-crowned heads bent towards each other and parted only when dried herbs were poured into their hands from containers tucked into their medicine bags. They inhaled the hallucinatory drugs eagerly. The men and women watched the macabre tableau in superstitious dread, terrified that they would be pointed out as the witch, and the cause of Wisdom's illness.

'Leave,' the *Igqirakazi's* voice echoed round the *kraal*. 'Leave the *kraal*. The spirits need the huts empty before they will talk.'

Velelo's diviner stood up quickly and pointed her long hippo-hide switch at the villagers. They fled, knocking over cooking pots and grain baskets in their panic. They milled around on the hillside like a herd of wildebeest when the rank odour of lion is strong in the air.

The obvious choice for the diviner was the headman's son. He owned the largest hut and had as many cattle as his father. He had been able to afford two wives, each of whom supplied him with a stream of children. He had accepted the capitalist's love of possessions and had lost the traditionalist's fear of envy. As he watched the figures leaping and cavorting outside his hut his spirit died, but Velelo's witchdoctor had an old score to settle, a matter which had rankled deep inside her raddled body for many years.

She had needed a girl's internal organs to brew a powerful medicine. Believing the youngster to be alone fetching water at the river, she had crept up behind her and hit her over the head with a log of wood. The *Igqirakazi*'s foot had slipped in the mud and instead of cracking the girl's cranium the blow only pulped her eye which oozed on to her cheek like a soft grape squashed underfoot. The girl had screamed and before she could cut the organs from the child's body, for to retain their magic the internal organs had to be ripped from a living victim, the other children had called from the reeds and she had fled.

Velelo's *Igqirakazi*, who was all-powerful in the tribe, had had to suffer the humiliation of having the girl accuse her. But revenge ripens with waiting.

The girl had married and come to live in this village. The old diviner cackled as she found the hut where the girl lived with her two young sons. She would not be able to demand as high a fee by choosing this girl instead of the headman's son, but she would be repaid by the despair she would see in the girl's face when she heard that she would surely die.

Chortling and stamping her feet, she hid a dried elephant's scrotum in the thatched roof, a snake's skin beneath the sleeping mat and an owl's beak in a gourd.

Satisfied, she allowed the villagers to return. She threw herself into a feverish dance, her white skirt swirling around her legs, enjoying the terror on the villagers' faces. Her accomplice and the male *Igqira* joined her and the thick red dust swirled around the twisting sinister dancers.

The huts were casting long black shadows when she finally came to rest in front of the young woman she had chosen. Swift as the strike of a mamba her hand flew out, and the switch stung the girl's neck. There was a low rumble of shock and disbelief from the villagers. The girl was well liked, she was hard-working and a good wife. Izuba strangled a wail and held Soze tightly. She had forgotten Toni and was caught up in the terror of the age-old ceremony.

Imperceptibly the villagers distanced themselves from the girl, leaving her standing in a cleared patch of earth pressing her two sturdy toddlers close to her body. The *Igqirakazi's* accomplice emerged from the girl's hut holding the objects she had found.

'See,' shrieked the witchdoctor, her eyes rolling back in her head, flecks of spittle spraying her accomplice. 'She has the animals of a witch.'

The grey and black snake's skin fluttered and the dried owl's beak hung from her fingers.

'She has taken dung from Wisdom and mixed it with magic herbs and put it in the path for him to tread underfoot.'

The girl stood transfixed with shock, silently accepting her fate while the intimidating figures screeched and pranced around her. Her husband would lose all of his goats and his cows. She would be ostracised by the villagers and would begin her living death.

In earlier times the chief would have ordered her to be killed, either by having thatching grass thrust brutally into her anus or being burnt to death, but their powers had been curtailed and the order was silence.

No one would look at her. The tribe's store of maize would not be shared with her, the *Igqira* would mix no herbal medicines when her family fell ill, the circle around the women's cooking and eating pot would be closed to her and the children would run from her sons for fear of their mother, the witch.

The young woman born into a society where the individual is only important as a member of the tribe, with its complex system of customs, rituals and beliefs, would soon fall ill. Knowing that she was damned, unable to accept the fear and silence from the villagers and the uncomprehending unhappiness of her children, her spirit would break, the flesh would melt from her body, her skin would become dry and grey and she would will herself to die.

If she lasted too long, a member of the tribe unable to live with a witch in the village would quietly kill her and hide her body. No one would remark on her disappearance and the people would sigh with relief.

Wisdom stared at the young woman as she walked to her hut. Her dulled eyes did not see her husband slumped against the side of the hut and her ears did not hear the plaintive cries of her children as they toddled after her.

The sun defiantly painted the vast expanse of pale blue sky with streaks and whorls of scarlet, purple and gold. But the splendour of her setting passed unnoticed by the villagers.

They slunk into their huts. Wisdom lay down on his mat and Izuba whispered to him before he pulled his blanket over his head.

'Wisdom, my brother, be happy. You will be well soon. The *Igqirakazi* has found the witch. Soon your tree will lift its branches, once again fat and smooth with water, to the heavens.'

Wisdom did not answer.

'Do not grieve for the witch, my young brother, for often the most evil of witches use the bodies of good hard-working people to mask their black deeds. It is done. The smelling out is over and you will be strong. Sleep, my brother, sleep and grow well.'

Izuba crawled over to her mat and drawing Soze into her arms she pulled the blanket over them and closed her eyes.

Wisdom stared into the furry cocoon of the blanket. The soft wool pressed down lightly on his face and nostrils. His mind raged. In the darkness he saw the eyes of the young woman, the terrified eyes of her sons as they held tightly to her orange skirt, and the gloating stained eyes of the *Igqirakazi* as she savoured her revenge.

He stifled a moan and shook his head. He desperately wished to believe that the young mother was evil and had cast a spell over him, but his schooling in the city no longer allowed him the joy of blind faith, and the staring eyes sickened him through the long hours of that lonely night.

The stars stared down on the sleeping village and no ray of starlight entered the dark hut where a young woman, rigid with horror, her two small sons curled beside her cold body, prepared to die.

13

A SMALL, dark, curly-haired bombshell, legs pumping wildly, exploded from the french windows opening on to the rough stone terrace, and scrambled down the steps as he recognised the sleek white car coming up the gravel drive.

'Mummy, Mummy,' he cried, almost incoherent with excitement, 'I'm going to have white shiny trousers and a black bow on my neck like Daddy and I'm going to be a boy.'

Toni breathed a sigh of relief. Timothy was so happy he had not realised that she had been away for four days. Toni was proud of having her own column in the newspaper and found the work exciting and stimulating, but she disliked spending time away from her son.

Toni swung her legs out of the low car and bent down to hug him. 'You are a boy, my love.'

'No, Mummy, Aunt Helen says I can have cake and I'm going to church and I will be her book boy.'

Toni laughed and lifted him on to her hip. He tightened his legs around her waist and patted her cheek as he tried to make her share in the excitement.

'Whew, Tim, my baby, soon you'll have to carry me,' said Toni as she reached the top of the steps. 'You're as big and heavy as an elephant.' Timothy chortled happily and slid down from her hip.

Taking her hand he pulled her into the house. 'Aunt Helen is in the bathroom because Billy is being a baby. He won't sit on the potty and Aunt Helen says he must spend a penny before he sleeps after lunch. He spitted in his bed yesterday and Aunt Helen was cross and says he mustn't spit again,' explained Timothy, leading her through the cool dim lounge.

'Don't you mean he wet his bed, sweetie?' asked Toni.

'No, Mum, he just spitted,' said Timothy, staunchly defending Billy from the ignominy of being a bed-wetter. They walked into the dormitory, a low-ceilinged room with a floor of wide yellowwood boards. It had been used originally as a barn, but was now bright with twelve gaily painted beds. Helen had turned her rambling farmhouse into a crèche and Timothy took a proprietary interest in her charges.

Helen, her lovely red curls held away from her face in a severe bun, turned away from Anna, the buxom Xhosa lady who was seated in a chair at the end of the room. Old Anna's steel crochet hook flew in and out of the intricately patterned bedspread she was making while her eyes darted along the rows of flower-patterned beds, checking that the tiny occupants slept during their hour of rest.

Most of the children had resigned themselves and lay like cherubs under the lacy pink and blue blankets. They had learned that nothing escaped Anna's eagle eyes. She foiled all attempts to tiptoe out of bed, enjoy pillow-fights or torment friends. Holding her finger to her lips Helen led them out of the room, Timothy stopping in the doorway to wave goodbye and blow a kiss to Anna.

'Aunt Helen,' squeaked Timothy, once they were out of earshot of the resting children, 'please tell Mummy that I'm going to be your boy.'

Helen laughed and linked arms with Toni. 'Come into the kitchen for tea and a sandwich and I'll tell you all about it.'

Seated at the old yellowwood table, the *riempie* gut-stringed seat imprinting a trellis on the back of her legs, a cup of steaming tea made from the wild red tea-bush and a slice of cheese and mushroom quiche spiked with fresh green herbs in front of her, Toni listened to Helen, her face breaking into a splitting smile of radiance as she ended her story.

'Helen, Helen,' exclaimed Toni, scraping back her chair and rushing to hug her friend. 'Congratulations! I'm so very happy for you.'

'Oh, Toni, I can't tell you what this means to me. I love Clive so much. I was desperate when I thought that I'd lost him after that party at your place. He was so angry. I didn't think that he'd ever forgive me. He didn't come to see me or telephone for months.' Toni kissed her friend on her soft cheek. 'He's a wonderful man, Toni, and I am going to spend the rest of my life making him happy.'

'Clive'll make a superb husband, Helen. It's wonderful news, the very best. Of course, Tim can be your page boy— ' Timothy shrieked with joy, splattering crumbs of cheese and pastry over the red checked tablecloth. 'If the excitement doesn't prostrate him,' added Toni, smiling at her son, 'and I am honoured to be asked to be matron of honour.'

The arrival of old Anna a few minutes later with her charges put an end to their animated discussion of dresses, flowers, catering and all the many details which combine to make weddings mystical.

Leaving Helen and Anna to cope with the tea plates and children, Toni bundled Timothy into the car. Whilst negotiating the twists and turns in the road as it wound up to Constantia Nek, she explained the part he would play in the marriage ceremony. He bridled a little at having to share the limelight with two small girls, but relaxed when he was assured that they would not be wearing white satin trousers and a black bow-tie.

The telephone was shrilly demanding attention as Toni parked the car. Timothy rushed to greet Chops and once the frenetic greeting of slobbery dog kisses, tail wagging and jumping was over, Timothy led the large lion-coloured ridgeback to the kitchen steps and, arms twined around the dog's neck, he told him about the shiny satin trousers, the church and the large iced wedding cake.

'You can come too, Chops,' invited Timothy and then paused uncertainly and corrected himself. 'I'll ask Aunt Helen if you can come and help me be her boy. You can have a white— ' He stared at his dog's hindquarters and frowned. 'You can have a black tie like mine,' he amended and grimaced as Chops, infected by the excitement, ran his tongue across his young master's face.

Toni, hurrying over the paved courtyard to answer the strident ringing, cautioned Timothy as she squeezed between him and the dog to open the door.

192

'Don't let him lick your face, Tim. You'll get worms.'

Toni snatched up the telephone and Helen's voice greeted her. 'Toni, I was so excited about the wedding that I forgot to tell you the most important news of all. The managing director of Timbertown read your article "Care for a Child, Create a Crèche" which was reprinted in one of the in-flight airline magazines. He contacted me and has donated all the chairs, tables and desks we need. This means that the Toni Balser Day Centre will open on Friday.'

'The Toni Balser Day Centre?' repeated Toni quietly.

'Yes,' answered Helen. 'We held a meeting with the Shonalanga town council and the parents, and the decision to name the crèche after you was passed unanimously. In fact the meeting disintegrated into a stamping singing tribal dance!'

Toni was silent. She held the telephone tightly and blinked back her tears. Taking her friend's silence to be a possible refusal, Helen quickly explained. 'We all know that if it were not for your articles highlighting the plight of the Xhosa mothers we wouldn't have received the contributions which have enabled us to complete the building. We'd like to name the first of what we hope will be many such centres in your honour.'

'Oh, Helen,' whispered Toni. 'Thank you. I'm indeed honoured.'

'The ceremony will be at ten. We'd like you to cut the ribbon and open the centre. We've decided to have a Christian priest and a tribal diviner present, both to bless the building and ask the spirits to protect it.'

Toni laughingly interjected and teased her friend. 'A priest and a local witchdoctor – won't that lead to some conflict of interest, Helen?'

'No,' answered her friend seriously. 'You know that the tribal people are Christian and these people feel that if they love Christ, it will strengthen the witchdoctors' medicine. They have a good working relationship with the Christian deities.'

'Well,' said Toni thoughtfully, 'Christianity has been called one of the greatest and most beautiful living superstitions, which is probably why the black people with their traditional magical beliefs have no difficulty in accepting it.'

'I was talking to the reverend who'll be attending the opening ceremony, and he tells me that a survey was carried out on one of the church's largest congregations, and that almost eighty per cent of the Christians believed that sacrifice to the ancestors was not sinful, and over forty per cent prayed to their ancestors as well as to Jesus.'

'Then', agreed Toni, 'your decision to have a priest and a diviner present is an inspired one.'

'Oh, I'm certain that it'll be a wonderful opening, Toni. Everyone has worked so hard and they're very excited. The local council and their families have been invited, as have the future pupils and their families. Clive has been magnificent. He has wheedled food from every bakery in the city telling them that the television cameras will almost certainly pan in on their delivery trucks and he dangled the same carrot in front of a soft drinks factory. The children will be able to eat and drink until their little bellies bulge.'

Helen continued, scarcely pausing for breath in her eagerness. 'Everyone who's contributed to the work will be there as well as the labourers. We are expecting three hundred people and when they see the television team setting up their cameras, we'll have to set up barriers to keep the aspiring young film stars away.' Helen laughed. 'Oh, Toni, you'll be expected to make a speech.'

'What!' shrieked Toni. 'In front of three hundred people? No, thank you. Writing is an intimate occupation, talking is baring your soul publicly. No, Helen, you can't do this to me.'

'Toni,' pleaded her friend, 'you can't disappoint all these people. We've worked so hard to make the centre a reality. The mothers and children want to see and hear Toni Balser, and the men who gave so generously of their time and money want to hear the woman who opened their wallets, and most of all I want my dearest friend to make a speech.'

There was a long silence.

'Please say yes. Give it to me as a wedding present. Please.'

Toni quailed at the thought of making the opening speech, but she was unable to ignore Helen's plea.

'Helen, you'll regret it. I'll stutter, leave out the most important parts and embarrass you dreadfully.'

'I love you, Toni Balser. Thank you,' said Helen.

'You're a manipulator, Helen, my friend. You set the scene, wait until I'm soft and dreamy about your wedding plans and then lasso me with your lacy wedding garter into making a speech. Dear, gentle Clive needs warning and some friendly advice. Before you lock him up with that gold band I'll have to talk to him.'

Shrieks of laughter greeted Toni's threat.

'It's taken me almost four years to wring a proposal from him,' giggled Helen. 'I suggest that you devote your energies to that little speech for Friday.'

'I'll devote my time to finding a reason not to be there,' teased Toni.

Helen laughed throatily.

'I must go now, Helen. I left Tim and Chops sitting on the kitchen steps and Timothy probably has gravel rash on his cheeks where Chops has been licking them. We'll see you on Friday at ten. Give my congratulations to Clive. You deserve each other and the happiness you've found, and I know that I'll see you both at the age of eighty, toddling along the beach still holding hands.'

Toni stared at the telephone as she replaced it on its cream cradle.

Helen's joy had once been hers. The world had once been a wonderful place filled with Nick's love for her. Now the petals had fallen and only a faint perfume lingered. The thorns of remembrance pricked her sharply and she slid the geometric black stool back beneath the glass-topped telephone table and went to rescue her son from his dog's wet kisses.

* * *

It was Friday. The dreaded day had arrived and she could not remember her speech. Toni muttered extracts to herself as she scrabbled through her cupboard looking for a new pair of stockings. She had just laddered the black Lycra ones as she ran to the car, trying unsuccessfully to reach it before Chops jumped up to greet her.

'Damn,' she whispered as she dragged out a pair of silk stockings. 'Black bows behind the ankles. I'll look like a can-can girl, not a sober matron about to open a crèche in Shonalanga.'

195

The opening ceremony was less than half an hour away and she still had to bypass the minivans hurtling between the city and the townships.

'Izuba,' she shouted, 'please see that Timothy stays in the car and don't let Chops climb in. I'll only be a few minutes.'

Her fingers, clumsy with haste, smoothed the stockings over her legs and she tightened her mouth in exasperation as the black seam zigzagged up her calf, evading all her efforts to straighten it.

Twisting around to look at the back of her legs in the mirror, she snorted. 'Ladies always have straight seams on their stockings, loose women have crooked ones.' She'd questioned the term 'loose women' when her grandmother, watching her gingerly tug on her first pair of stockings, had insisted that the seams were straight before the stockings were clipped on to the suspender-belt.

'Loose women are not ladies,' was the only explanation she had been given by the dour, raw-boned woman she adored.

'Right, Gran,' grunted Toni as, the tight skirt rucked up around her waist, she peeled off the offending stockings, shook them out and once again carefully eased them over her feet. She glanced at her watch and paled. To be in Shonalanga at ten o'clock she would need all of the three things the Indian driver who had drive her and Serge to the Taj Mahal had said were necessary to survive on the roads of that overcrowded continent – good brakes, good nerves and good luck.

* * *

Wisdom paced the long cement aisles between the shelves laden with crates of dumpy beer bottles, slender bottles of wine, round bottles filled with cane spirit from the sugar-cane fields of Natal, and the small flat bottles of brandy, easily slipped into a man's coat pocket, but his eyes, dull with anxiety, were fixed on the floor and were blind to the polished army of bottles standing in smart formation on the shelves.

He wheeled right and marched away before he reached Mrs Kahn's glass-walled office. The back of his throat was still oily with the sickly-sweet vitamin syrup she had forced him to drink, and he dreaded a second dose.

Mrs Kahn was seated at her chipped desk, her feet propped up on a wooden soda-water crate. The teetering piles of invoices and ledgers dwarfed her small figure as she laboriously juggled rows of figures, scratching her grey head with the back of her pencil as she battled to make columns balance. No flickering green screen entered her domain. She refused to work with obstinate machines which would not co-operate and blinked messages at her.

She paused in her work and watched Wisdom walk down the aisle, her motherly face puckered with compassion and worry. He had seemed happier and more relaxed when he returned from the Transkei but he was painfully thin. Since she had heard her doctor's diagnosis of Wisdom's illness she had read and studied everything she could find on AIDS, spending hours trying to understand the genetic make-up of the new virus. Its ability to use the viral RNA as a template for making DNA, and then, as a viral DNA, to insinuate itself among the host's genes, lying dormant and powerful until stimulated to make new virus particles, confused her.

When they noticed her new obsession with the disease her sons teased her unmercifully, assuring her that old Mr Kahn was unlikely to stray and that, as they had been married for over four decades, she was safe.

She knew that the disease was inexorable. Once it had chosen its victim it sucked at the defences of the body like a thirsty man sucking a sweet orange until all the juice was extracted, and then it threw the body on the garbage heap of death.

Mrs Kahn was determined that Wisdom with his sweet smile and gentleness would not die, and regularly visited the local pharmacy, adding bottles of coloured vitamin pills, ginseng extract, Devil's claw and herbal tisanes to the bulging bottom drawer in her desk.

Pulling the old crate closer to her chair, she eased off her shoes and replaced her stockinged feet on the crate. Soon she was deeply immersed in the calculating world of figures and Wisdom was, for a short while, forgotten.

Wisdom reached the end of the long aisle and stood staring at the bright red telephone resting on an index cabinet. Mrs Kahn had insisted that a payphone was installed for her workers, but like most things the Kahns possessed it had been installed where she could keep watch over it. She believed in providing amenities for her staff, but made certain that they were appreciated and correctly used.

Fear and guilt played a grim game of tug-of-war with Wisdom as he stood transfixed in front of the phone. The swaying of his emotions from one side to the other sickened and confused him. Fear jerking sharply told him that betrayal of the cause could mean death. Fear told him that his actions would be discovered and his twin brother whom he loved and admired would reject and despise him.

Guilt tugged strongly, reminding him that Miss Toni had bought the sheep to celebrate the end of their circumcision schooling, and had asked a friend to find a job for his brother Justice with the lawyers. Miss Toni was paying for Izuba's eldest son Storchman to study at university and she had given Izuba extra leave to go home with him to the Transkei. At Christmas and Easter there were always presents and parcels of food for all the family from Mr Serge and Miss Toni.

Wisdom had known Ungumtukathixo, Izuba's Child of God, since he was a skinny little boy, terrified of the large city and the school he was to attend. She had always been a part of his life. Izuba had told them many stories of Miss Toni and the man-child she adored. 'She loves her son like the green willow trees love the river, and she smiles with her heart only when her child is near.'

Wisdom could hear Izuba's low, melodious voice ringing in his ears. Guilt said that he could not allow Miss Toni's only child to be killed.

Fear said, 'Let her and the white child die. They are not important.' Guilt answered, 'Her skin may be pale and insipid but she is of your family. Her heart is with you by her actions. She is of your tribe. You cannot harm her.'

He felt the boy-child's arms around his neck and his breath soft on his cheek as he kissed them all goodbye after a visit.

Like a sleepwalker, he approached the apple-red telephone. He was alone. Mrs Kahn was absorbed in her books, the drivers had not returned from their delivery rounds and his friends were serving a clamouring crowd in the front of the liquor store.

198

He stretched out a skeletal trembling hand and picked up the receiver. The silver coins rang out sharply as they fell into the steel box. He pressed the plastic numerals gently and waited.

'Miss Toni? Is that Miss Toni?' he whispered.

* * *

The jangling of the telephone on her bedside table interrupted Toni's reminiscences of her grandmother and she lurched across the room like a contestant in a sack race, the black silk stockings hobbling her progress.

'Mrs Balser speaking,' she answered tersely, and a puzzled frown rippled above her dark eyebrows as she listened.

'Yes, I'm Miss Toni and Izuba does work for me. Who are you? What's your name?'

Her hand tightened over the plastic receiver and the powdered rouge high on her cheekbones was the only colour in her face which quickly paled to the grey-white of skimmed milk.

'No,' she gasped, 'no one could do this. You must be mistaken. How do you know? Tell me, tell me!'

'I cannot.' The voice was soft and the English words were crushed beneath the heavy African accent. 'They'll kill me if they know that I've spoken to you. I must go. Please stay away, Miss Toni, for what I tell you is true.'

'Wait. Don't put the telephone down. I need to know— ' The sharp click of a receiver being replaced cut off her anguished plea.

For a few seconds she sat frozen. Then, ripping off the stockings, she flicked frantically through the pages of the telephone directory, tearing the flimsy sheets in her haste. The Day Centre still had no telephone. It was at the bottom of a long waiting list. Helen despaired of having one installed before the end of the year. She would have to phone the police.

'Sh, Shona,' she muttered, running her finger down the index. 'Idiot,' she fumed. 'It will be listed under Police.'

She dialled the number and waited, as tense as a sprinter pushing against the starting blocks.

'Answer, damn you, answer,' she pleaded, but in the Shonalanga Police Station the shrill peals echoed around an

199

empty room. The young constable who had been left in charge had been unable to resist the excitement. The singing and dancing of the crowds as they converged on the new crèche were like iron filings to a magnet and drew him away from his office, away from his duty.

He stood on the corner of the block, a wide grin on his face as he watched the television crews setting up the lights, stumbling over huge coils of grey cable, dusting eager helpers away from the cameras. The children, crisp and neat in their freshly starched clothes, proud and very conscious of their position of importance as the new pupils, lined up behind the blue satin ribbon which would be cut to open the crèche officially once Toni had made her speech.

The wooden benches lining the pathway leading to the door of the new building, sparkling in its coat of blue and white paint, were filled with the guests of honour, men and women who had given their time and money to create the crèche. They sat shoulder to shoulder, a mosaic of black and white faces satisfied and happy with what they had created.

A throng of black bodies jostled for position behind the wooden barricades, shouting greetings to friends seated on the benches, exclaiming loudly over the tables of food and cool drinks set up for the children in the shade of the building. Eager to absorb every detail of the ceremony, they were happy to be able to watch, and hoped to receive a piece of cake or a red raspberry or green cream-soda drink from their friends who had been invited. The excitement was a living creature. It hummed and throbbed, a giant ectoplasm enfolding everyone in the area.

'It's all gone according to plan. The crowd is much larger than we expected and is still growing.' The man's small dark eyes darted restlessly over the crowd and lingered on the benches set up on the right-hand side of the door to the crèche. 'The TV cameras are well placed. They'll record the occasion in fine detail and we'll have struck another great blow for freedom. They'll see that the tiger is not toothless and that the snake still has venom.' He smiled as he ran his hand over his beard, the grey patches bristling in the bright sunshine.

'But she has not arrived. The woman reporter who is to open the building,' said the younger man. 'It's necessary that she is standing near the door with the red-haired woman and her lover. We must have her. These articles are not helping our cause. Too many are reading them and believing her nonsense.'

'Lower your voice,' admonished his partner. 'We don't wish to draw attention to ourselves. Soon we must leave. We mustn't be in the area when the police arrive. If she does not appear or comes too late, we'll make other plans. This will aid our cause, with or without her.'

He glanced at the lines of patiently waiting children, their shining faces bright with expectation, and at the benches closely packed with adults of all races, ivory and onyx links in a necklace crafted to encircle the future.

There was no sympathy in his eyes as he studied the joyful faces. He watched dispassionately as a chubby four-year-old tried to dust the red sand from the bouquet of flowers she had dropped. Her older sister left the line of youngsters standing behind the blue ribbon and ran to help her. The harsh clicking sounds as she scolded the baby and stuffed the dusty rosebuds back into the floral spray sounded like the steel caps of tap-dancing shoes. Tears flooded into the tiny girl's eyes, but she held back the sobs and clutched the flowers tightly, waiting for the most exciting moment in her young life, the time when she would hand the flowers to the lady whose name was painted on the door of her new school. Even her sister's anger could not dampen her exhilaration.

'So many, so very many children,' said the younger man, his strong features almost obscured by the beard nestling around his face like a black mink muffler.

'Children make excellent headlines. Their blood fills the pens of reporters. They'll ensure that our act is written about in all the newspapers overseas and is on all the television screens,' answered his companion glancing at his watch. 'Let's go.'

They oozed through the crowd and walked unnoticed down the road. The older man, dark glasses concealing his expressionless black eyes, drove away from the township with exaggerated care and in silence.

When they finally merged into the stream of traffic leading into the city he turned to the younger man.

'I hope that your remark about the children was not said because of weakness and misguided sympathy.' His voice was cold and the words stung like hailstones. 'Remember, the great Lenin said that the aim of terrorism is to terrorise.' He let the silence hang between them, then continued. 'He also said that a revolutionary showing sympathy is as disgusting as a soldier showing cowardice.'

'Comrade, I— '

He cut off the young man's explanation brusquely. 'There's no place for sympathy or cowardice, or for people who display these weaknesses. In our war all are guilty.'

The black-bearded man swallowed loudly but did not attempt to interrupt.

'You'd do well to remember that, and I advise you to read once again the wonderful words of Lenin.'

The great craggy point of Devil's Peak, the fire-scarred mountain separating the city from the lush green eastern suburbs, loomed large ahead of them before he dared break the silence.

'Comrade, I apologise if it seemed I had sympathy for the children. I have sympathy only for our just and honourable cause.'

The older man paused in the exploration of his nostrils and scratched his beard vigorously.

'Good,' he grunted, 'good. I'm happy to hear that.' He snorted with contempt as a white sports car, horn blaring, sped past, heading in the direction of the airport and the townships.

Capitalist, he thought, driving around in a car which cost the same as a house large enough for three families. That'll end when we take control. Only our glorious leaders will use expensive capitalist cars. You'll use trains and buses. You who've exploited the workers and grown rich and fat on their sweat and tears.

He watched in his rear-view mirror as the white car swung in and out of the traffic with scant regard for speed regulations or safety. His upper lip curled into a sneer. 'Capitalist bitch,' he cursed as the sports car vanished.

Toni's foot flew between brake and accelerator with the expertise and tempo of a xylophone player. She drove with maniacal speed, ignoring the hurtling minibuses, intent only on reaching Shonalanga before ten o'clock.

202

Her mind, calculating as a computer, evaluated the steps she had taken since the telephone call.

Izuba had been left with the telephone numbers of the Shonalanga Police Station and the local station, and was to tell whoever answered first that a bomb was set to explode at the opening of the Toni Balser Day Centre in Shonalanga. They were to be told that the time set for the opening was ten o'clock.

Timothy had been dragged from the car and left standing in the doorway to the kitchen, his face streaked with tears.

'I'll be good, Mummy, I promise,' he hiccuped as he clung to her skirt. 'Please let me go with you. I love you, Mummy.'

In her terror and haste to reach Helen and Clive, she had wrenched away from his grasp and snapped, 'You'll listen to me and stay here with Izuba.'

His eyes wide with hurt and incomprehension, he clung to the wooden doorframe, wondering what he had done to deserve this punishment. He broke into a fresh paroxysm of wailing as he watched Toni viciously push Chops away from the car with her foot, slam the door, and hurtle down the drive.

The realisation that his mother was going to Aunt Helen's party without him cracked the warm cocoon of love and faith he had nestled in since birth, and the worm of adult intransigence slithered into his child's world. It was a hard and bitter lesson, and not even Izuba's warm arms and soft Xhosa songs were able to soothe the hurt and drive away the pain of betrayal.

The enormous grey cylindrical towers, ugly as cardboard wine-bottle containers, which cooled the water for the city's electricity had receded into the distance when the white car turned off the road which continued on over the purple peaks of the Hottentots Holland mountains and away from the Peninsula.

The sports car sped recklessly down the narrow streets of Shonalanga, a streak of quicksilver scattering everything in its path. Toni's clenched hands were wet, and perspiration trickled slowly behind her ears. She prayed desperately as she flung the car around blind corners, one hand pressing down hard on the hooter.

'Dear God, don't let me hit anyone. Keep the children and animals out of the road. Please give me time to warn them. Please don't let that bomb explode. Please, God, save the children you love. They've done nothing to deserve this,' she prayed loudly, finding comfort in the words.

As Toni turned into the narrow dusty road which ran past the crèche she could hear the music and excited hum of the crowd. 'Oh, thank you, my God, thank you for allowing me to be in time. Thank you for listening to my plea.'

She felt ill with relief as she saw the children, the flowers and the benches full of people. The camera crew, alerted by the strident blaring of the hooter, swung the camera around and focused on the car as it pulled up in a whirlwind of dust and noise.

'It's Toni,' said Helen, holding on to Clive's arm to balance as she stood on tiptoe looking over the sea of black heads. 'Something's wrong,' she whispered. 'She doesn't drive like that.'

Helen and Clive watched as Toni tumbled out of the car, screaming wildly. 'Oh, Clive, it's Timothy. Something must have happened to Tim. He's not with her.' Helen pulled away from him, her long hair streaming behind her like a crimson pennant, and ran down the pathway to where Toni was pushing roughly at the noisy throng of onlookers.

She's mad, Toni's gone mad, thought Helen as she watched her friend hitting at the children and trying to push the little black bodies away from the railings. She was still too far from Toni to hear what she was shouting and the loud music and the chatter and laughter of the crowd drowned her words.

The children standing in a neat line in front of the crèche stiffened in expectation, fluffed out their skirts and wriggled their toes in excitement. The lady had arrived and the party was about to begin. They stood, incoherent with delight, eagerly waiting to catch a glimpse of the writing lady. They could not see the perplexed onlookers milling anxiously around Toni, hindering her as she tried to scatter them and force her way to the reception line. They could only hear the deeper hum of noise on the road and feel the tension.

Clive felt a tug at his trousers and, looking down, saw the chubby little girl, her white frilled dress starched to the crispness of a ballet tutu, dancing from one foot to the other, the elastic ruffles of her white lace socks digging deeply into the soft flesh below her dimpled knees. The heads of the flowers in the bouquet bobbed wildly as she stamped in agitation.

'Is the lady here, is she here?' she lisped impatiently.

'Yes,' said Clive, bending down to pick her up, 'there she is, she'll be here now. See, the lady in the bright pink suit.'

'Oh,' sighed the little one in relief, 'she's come.'

Clive smiled and hugged her tiny body as he put her down. 'You stand here and hold your flowers up and when she reaches the ribbon across the path you can give her the roses. I'm just going to help her because she can't walk quickly, there are so many people.'

Clive was worried. A prickle of unease crawled across his scalp. Toni was swamped in the crowd and more people seemed to be running to encircle her. Helen was unable to reach her and was standing helplessly in the pathway, calling to the men operating the television cameras.

The little girl smiled happily. She had seen the lady in pink and soon she would give her the flowers. She poked at the dusty apricot rosebud which her sister had thrust deep into the bunch and, satisfied that it would remain hidden, she placed one pudgy leg behind her and bobbed into a curtsey.

She had practised this for weeks and was now able to do it without losing her balance and sitting ignominiously on her bottom. She bent her knees carefully, holding the flowers away from the ground, pretending that the pretty lady in pink was watching her.

The little girl didn't have to balance as she rose. The golden gravel exploded around her and she was thrown high into the air, a soap bubble against the blue sky, her white organdie dress billowing in the blast. The hard yellow pebbles cascaded down like sparks in a firework display, and a small black arm, the hand still clutching a bunch of white and peach roses, fell upon the path. Her tiny body sank wetly into what had only moments before been a welcoming line of young children.

The television camera whirred and the black plastic strips continued to run through the machine, the cold emotionless eye faithfully recording the carnage. The camera operator, an old hand at filming death and destruction, blanched, but refused to let his mind dwell on what his eyes were seeing. This footage would add to his reputation as one of the best cameramen on the African continent and he was proud of that reputation.

He swung the camera to zoom in on the place where the benches had stood. 'Obviously where the bomb was placed,' he murmured. 'Nothing much left of that lot. They'll be lucky if they find enough to bury.'

The area was seared black and bare. In the distance he heard the distinctive wail of police sirens, and he panned in on the crèche quickly, eager to imprint as much as possible on film before they arrived and closed the area.

The new blue and white crèche had collapsed, imploded by a satanic craftsman. It was now merely a pile of building rubble waiting to be cleared. The streams of red and green liquid from the shattered soft-drink bottles mingled with crimson pools of thick blood, and slabs of flesh were coated with crumbed cakes and biscuits.

The police cars drew up in an orderly line and a wave of blue uniforms and tear-gas guns bristled like a blue coral necklace around the crèche.

The cameraman glanced up. Just time for a quick shot of Toni Balser before they get here, he decided as he focused on the woman in fuchsia pink.

Her face was white and her large eyes reflected all the dark horrors of madness. Her mouth was stretched in a scream of anguish and she was thrown around like a dry leaf in a rainwater gutter as she battled to reach the statuesque woman with a veil of flaming hair covering her face.

The crowd was panic-stricken. Those who had escaped the blast were kicking and clawing their way out of the killing area. The weak, the elderly and the children were being trampled underfoot and suffocated. The mob had become a violent demon and above the screams and cries of the wounded rose the crazed shrill sound of Africa. A sound which chilled the blood in the veins. The women were ululating, their tongues beating a tattoo on the roofs of their mouths, wild, stirring cries, a Last Post to mourn the dead.

The cameraman was zooming back to film an overall picture

when a strong hand clamped on his wrist and his nerveless fingers fell away from the red button.

'Enough of that. Pack up and get out. Report to the Wynstaat Police Station immediately. One of my men will go with you. We need to run through that film. You may have something to help us.'

The operator was about to protest but, looking into the ginger-haired man's tawny eyes, cold and merciless beneath heavily thatched eyebrows, he stifled the words and started dismantling the camera. The lights and cables had vanished in the maddened mob, and he called to his two assistants cowering over the boxes of equipment to follow the slim young policeman who was to escort them to the screening room at the station.

'And don't waste time giving them a lecture on the political aims of the ANC, PAC and all the other bloody Cs,' roared Stan le Roux as he watched Richard lead the camera crew away. 'I need you back here and bloody smartly.'

'Sir,' acknowledged the young man.

'Tough cop,' murmured the camera operator. 'Wouldn't like to work under that one.'

'He's a great guy, one of the most honourable men I've ever met,' defended Richard, and flinched as Stan's voice bellowed above the noise.

'Clear the onlookers, move the others to the sports field and make sure that the ambulance guys can get through. Move! What in the bloody hell are you waiting for? Invitations?'

The men in blue started rounding up and calming the frenzied mob. Like cowhands encircling a cattle stampede, they channelled the mob away from the crèche and into a cordoned-off area on a nearby sports field where they could be questioned.

Satisfied that the crowd was being contained, and comforted by the keening sirens of fast-approaching ambulances, Stan le Roux strode up the blood-stained gravel path towards the crèche.

'Let's hear what bloody reasons that little sod Richard gives for this butchery,' he muttered as he blew into the bull horn, clearing the mouthpiece. 'Here we have the bloody Commies drinking arm in arm with our leaders, and banned parties and political exiles all smiling and talking peace, and the sods they can't bloody control still kill and terrorise.' Stan muttered about Richard, but he had developed a grudging respect for the young policeman's knowledge of political parties.

His voice, harsh and distorted by the grey plastic bull horn held close to his lips, cleared a narrow pathway through the people and cut through the padded cell of disbelief into which Toni had retreated as she slipped and stumbled on dismembered bodies, fighting to reach Helen.

'Stan,' she choked looking up at the familiar burly figure. 'Thank God it's you. We need help desperately. I can't staunch the bleeding.'

Stan le Roux looked at Toni, hardly recognising the woman in the blood-splattered pink suit. Her hands were gloved in gore and her face was painted scarlet where she had flicked her curls away as she loosened the black velvet ribbon from her hair and tightened it around the man's thigh.

'Toni Balser,' he acknowledged and turned to bellow at a pair of nearby policemen for help.

Reluctantly Helen allowed them to lift Clive's head from her lap. 'You'll be fine, my darling,' she crooned. 'I love you, and I'll be with you all the time.' His lips, startling white and stretched thin with pain, moved hesitantly.

'My leg?'

Helen turned away, hiding her face from Clive.

'They'll have the cuts sewn up and you'll be back on the squash courts next week,' Toni answered. 'It looks worse than it is, Clive.' She forced herself to smile at him, and swallowed hard as she saw relief flood into his eyes.

'Thanks,' he whispered weakly and grimaced as the men lifted his body.

'Put the leg in one of our plastic bags and take it with you,' Stan mouthed at the policemen. 'The surgeons may be able to work a miracle.'

Looking at the remaining leg dangling from the groin like a lifeless impala held in the jaws of a leopard, Stan wondered whether the man would ever walk again.

'I'll join you later at the Lizzie,' said Toni quietly as she hugged her friend. 'Don't cry. Be brave for him, smile for him.' She bent over Clive and kissed him softly on the lips.

'Remember, you're going to be fine. I'll come up to the hospital as soon as I can.'

Stan put his hand on Toni's shoulder as they watched the ambulance crew take Clive from the men in blue.

'There's no damn justice in this world,' she agonised. 'They were to be married soon.'

Stan nodded in silence. His senses were tuned to the vibrations of the crowd, waiting to sense a change should it turn from grief and panic to raging anger.

His men were carrying out their orders efficiently and he turned his eyes away from the dispersing mob and studied the men who were filling plastic bags with limbs and pieces of flesh. He watched as their gloved hands dropped the shreds of meat and slivers of bone into the bags and tagged them.

'An unanswered telephone,' reflected Toni. 'The site could have been cleared if only someone had answered at Shonalanga.'

Stan spun around to face her. 'We received a call at Wynstaat and immediately alerted the stations in this area. What do you mean by an unanswered call at Shonalanga station?'

Toni explained about the soft African voice which had warned her and her frantic attempts to alert the police. 'I then left my maid Izuba to telephone and I drove here, hoping to be in time to warn everyone.' Her face clouded. 'Those close to me just laughed or looked puzzled, and called their friends to come and listen to my nonsense. I couldn't force my way to the crèche and the microphone.' She bit her lip. 'There was so much noise and music, my friends couldn't hear me.'

She looked up at the African sky patterned with wispy mare's tails of white clouds. Her voice broke and her shoulders started to shake. The reaction to the horror had set in. Stan held her in the crook of his arm, his blue tunic blotched with rust patches from her blood-stained arms and face. He patted her awkwardly, waiting for her sobs to quieten.

'Come,' he said. 'I'm going to the police station. You can wash there and tidy your hair and one of my men will drive you home.'

'I am quite capable of— '

'Yes, I know,' said Stan, 'but I need a statement. One of

the boys'll drive you in your car and the other will follow in a police car.'

Toni thought quickly. It was almost twelve o'clock, which meant that Timothy would soon have lunch and his afternoon rest. She could slip into the house and change and he would not see her blood-stained clothing.

'Thank you, Stan,' she acquiesced. 'That'd be kind of you.'

CHAPTER

14

A STREAM of orange icing sugar oozed steadily from the silver nozzle linking overlapping circles into an intricate design. The circular pattern was the upper half of a clown's costume, already resplendent with green and purple ruffles and bright red pompoms.

It was painstaking work and Toni straightened wearily, pressing her hand into the ache in the small of her back. She was pleased that she had decided to ice the clown weeks before Tim's birthday. It meant that she would make the cake and only have simple icing to do the day before his party. She glanced at her watch and licked a blob of orange icing from the glass face. It was eight o'clock. She should have the clown juggling his five coloured balls and Timothy's name finished by nine. She had discovered to her chagrin that small boys and icing sugar are a disastrous combination and had waited until Timothy was tucked up for the night before she completed the figure to be placed on his cake. When he woke in the morning the clown would be tucked away in a cake tin on the top shelf of the cupboard.

She ran her fingers down the white bag. Yes, she decided, just sufficient to complete the design. She ran the pattern across the clown's shoulder, down his arm and was about to end at the purple wrist-ruffle when the discordant cackle of the telephone filled the kitchen.

'Damn,' she muttered as she put down the icing bag and wiped her fingers on her flowered apron. 'If this is that dizzy Baby Botha again, I'll scream.' Baby had phoned twice during the late afternoon. First to offer to ice cakes, make fudge or whip ice-cream, all tasks which Toni knew Baby found tedious and boring. Toni had smiled to herself and refused, wondering why Baby was showing this unusual desire to be helpful.

The second call was an offer to be present at the party and help to entertain the children. Toni did not doubt that Baby was an able entertainer, but not of children. Unwilling to accept the second refusal, Baby had finally revealed why she wished to take part in the birthday celebrations. She had heard that Clive and Helen would be at the party and curiosity was riding Boots and his beery cronies cruelly. None of them had seen Clive since the explosion and they needed first-hand information.

The ringing continued and Toni lifted the receiver. Expecting to hear Baby's breathless simpering, she steeled herself to make a third polite refusal.

'Hello, my honey.' Serge's voice was indistinct.

'Good evening, Serge,' answered Toni coolly. The argument which had broken out when, three days before Timothy's birthday, Serge had come home to say that he was once again leaving on a business trip to Durban, still rankled. This time she had not dissolved into tears and left him victorious on the field of battle. She had calmly and coldly told him that he used business trips for his own pleasure and as an excuse to evade responsibilities at home. She had stated that at five years of age his son needed a father, not a stranger who called in occasionally, distributed gifts and left.

The stand she had taken had enraged him. He had reddened with anger, spat insults and stamped with impotence in the face of her intransigence. Finally he had capitulated, swung Timothy up into the air, promised to be back in time for his birthday and thundered from the house.

'Toni,' he said, 'Toni, I am truly sorry for the way I behaved. I do understand how lonely it is for you and I promise to cut down on my trips next year and spend more time with you and Timothy.'

Toni was stunned. She knew how difficult it was for him to apologise. In the ten years she had known Serge this was probably the second apology she had received.

'Thank you, Serge,' she answered softly. 'I, too, am sorry that we had the argument. Fighting only exacerbates the

212

situation. It never solves anything. Will you be back early on Friday? I'd love to go out for dinner, as Saturday will be chaotic.' She laughed. 'Timothy is almost ill with excitement at the thought of receiving twenty-four presents. He is a dreadful little financier and I'm almost ill at the prospect of having two dozen potential accidents running around the house.'

Toni chattered on happily, feeling an unusual tenderness for Serge. She was fulfilled and happy in her work for the newspaper and thoughts of Nick now lay tucked away in the camphor drawers of her memory, spilling out only when the strains of a song or the heavy perfume of roses eased the drawers open a fraction. Perhaps Serge would now be content to float in the calm harbour waters of domesticity, away from the exciting and choppy waves of all-night parties, wild friends and mistresses. Perhaps they had finally negotiated the battlefields of early marriage and now, shrapnel wounds healed, broken limbs mended and bullet holes scarred over, they would be able to live in a battle-free zone, comfortably as old comrades.

Content in her hopes for the future, she did not immediately grasp the importance of what Serge was saying. 'I know that you'll understand, Toni. I did promise to be home, but I'm locked into very important negotiations here in Durban and it'll be impossible to conclude them before late next week. Please understand, honey.'

Toni slumped on to the stool and picked listlessly at the dried bright orange icing caked on her fingernails. She was a fool. She had lost Nick and Serge would never change.

'Toni? Toni, honey, answer me,' he said sharply.

'Answer you, Serge? What is there to say? You were not here for Tim's first birthday, his second, third or fourth and now you won't be home for this one.'

'Come on, honey, don't be angry. This isn't something that I want to do, that I am doing for pleasure. It's business and I have to support our family.'

'Angry?' said Toni in a thin flat voice. 'I'm not angry, just so tired of all this pretence. Tired of having a family which consists of a married bachelor, a grass widow and a fatherless son. Good night, Serge. Oh, remember to buy a special present for Timothy. It may help to lessen the hurt when he hears that once again his daddy will not be

213

at his birthday party. Good night.' Gently she replaced the receiver.

Serge looked at the silent receiver and ran his fingers through his hair. He would have to think of something to placate Toni.

The waves boomed hollowly as they broke and pounded the beach, and the night was warm. He glanced at his watch. He had to meet his agent in an hour's time at a smallholding along the coast and he was worried. His usually reliable agent had become evasive. Serge was certain that, recently, many containers for ship and air freight handled by his firm had been cleared by customs without his knowing which ones contained illegal rhino and elephant horn from neighbouring African countries.

The middlemen in this lucrative trade had discovered the advantages of containerisation. It was logistically impossible for customs officials to open and check every container which passed through the busy airports and harbours. A gateway had been found, and the valuable horns and tusks left Africa in containers listed as containing manufactured goods.

Serge had realised that money could be bled from this trade. He had agents throughout the country seeking information as to which containers handled by Serge's import–export business held hidden cargo. Cheques were paid into Serge's foreign bank accounts to sweeten his silence.

Serge walked out on to the balcony and into the gentle blackness of the night. He was oblivious of the stars trailed across the sky like a sequinned scarf.

The morality of the issue, something which affected Toni and turned her white with frustrated rage, was of little interest to him. He had fought many a battle with her over conservation and it was one of the few subjects on which she would not yield.

'As long as unscrupulous men aid and abet the export of illegal ivory, the insane killing won't end,' she raged.

'The exporters are only doing business, honey,' Serge had explained. 'If they don't, someone else will.'

Toni's eyes had blazed. 'That is a sick justification and the scum involved in this trade should be hanged.'

Serge had backed out of the argument, convinced that the

214

conservationists were fighting a losing battle. He felt no pity for the wonderful giants of Africa who were doomed to a future padding around fenced reserves, prisoners confined to exercise yards under the watchful eyes of armed guards.

The tip of his cigarette glowed a constant crimson as he swallowed lungfuls of thick smoke to calm and anaesthetise the doubts prickling him like strands of coir in an old mattress.

The Parks Board was respected for its efficiency and commitment to conservation. It desperately needed the money gained by the sale of tusks legally culled from the stabilised herds to further conservation and combat poaching. Slowly rubbing the sleep from its eyes, the world was beginning to realise that the great armoured pachyderms which have been on earth for thirty million years, the giant, grey, tusked, wise old men of Africa were in grave danger of doing the dodo dance into extinction. When the world suddenly awakens, policies are formulated and followed regardless of consequences. Emotions rule reason; the Board needed a reasoned reaction to their culling programme. Therefore they declared war on all poachers. The tremors had been felt in neighbouring countries and informants were turning to less dangerous occupations.

Serge's overseas bank balances were fat and healthy and he wished them to remain that way. It would be necessary to adopt a firm stance with his informers.

He ground the cigarette on to the railing and flicked the stub into the garden. He punched a memo into his pocket computer to buy a gift to mollify Toni and walked back into the apartment. It was time to meet his unwilling informer.

* * *

Listlessly, Toni walked back to the kitchen, topped a clean white bag with pale icing, squeezed softly and watched as a fat pink squiggle oozed out. She iced an S followed by an E, an R and finally a GE. Quickly, she iced two strokes across the letters.

'Damn him, damn him,' she whispered and started carefully icing pink stripes down the clown's trousers. The strident call of the telephone cut into her concentration and the pink line wavered.

215

Frowning, she lifted the offending squiggle with a wet palette knife and counted the peals. At twelve they stopped.

'Good,' she muttered. 'He's given up.'

The shrill calls started again and, unable to concentrate on her icing, she capitulated on the fifteenth ring and lifted the receiver.

'Kitten.'

Toni stared at the telephone and eased herself slowly and carefully on to the leather stool. The curved chrome leg felt cool against her calf.

'Nick,' she said softly.

'Toni, I've just returned to Cape Town.' His voice cracked and he coughed gruffly. 'I have tonight's paper.' His fingers trembled as he smoothed the paper on his knee. Toni's face, smeared with blood and white with shock, stared up at him from beneath the heavy black headlines. 'Police – still no leads in crèche bombing.'

'Toni, I had no idea. I would have returned immediately.' His voice dropped to a whisper. 'You could have been killed. I would never have seen you again.'

Toni remained silent, cherishing the sound of his voice.

'Toni.' He coughed again. 'I've no right to ask you, but I need to talk to you. Please, I have to talk to you.'

* * *

The headlights cut a golden path through the dense layers of mist pressing down on the Peninsula, muting all sound and disorientating the senses. Toni had been driving fast. Her excitement at the prospect of seeing Nick made her hurtle her car through the smoky landscape, but as she drove into the avenue of chestnut trees, their bare branches thrusting at her from the thick white fog, she eased back on the accelerator. The car slowed to a crawl, hugging the pavement.

Giddy euphoria carried her into the kitchen after Nick's call, spinning her as dizzily as a toy top, as she beat the table with a wooden spoon and splattered icing across the white-tiled floor. She waltzed to her bathroom, sang under a stinging hot shower and hummed happily as she wriggled into a cherry-red cashmere sweater, the large roll-collar cuddling her wet dark curls. Finally she floated out of the house, leaving her

216

gangling neighbour's son as a willing babysitter. But suddenly, as she drove to Nick's house, the euphoria hissed away like stale air from a punctured tyre. Why was she rushing to him? Why, when she recognised his voice, had she not recited the speech she had rehearsed and perfected during the long lonely time after receiving his letter?

'It was fun, Nick. I enjoyed playing our game of love, but don't infringe the rules by continuing to serve once the set is over.'

She did not need him. She no longer desired the excitement nor the pain. She had been badly hurt and feared that if it happened again she would be destroyed.

She had a home, a husband, a wonderful son, good friends, comfort and material security. Like tiny sunbirds flitting between tangerine tecoma flowers, so Toni's thoughts and fears darted and circled.

It had taken her several months of pain and despair to accept and plan a future without Nick. Like Clive, facing a future as a cripple, she had finally accepted her loss.

It had been a long battle, lonely nights filled with memories and longing and days filled with tears and disbelief. Alone in the house, Serge overseas, she had withdrawn into total seclusion and devoted herself to her son and her writing. She emerged limp and crumpled from her cocoon of solitude.

A car hooted impatiently behind her. Guiltily Toni swung away from the centre of the road where she had allowed her car to wander. The man glared at her as he roared past, his mouth working furiously.

Toni shrugged, straightened her shoulders and glanced into the rear-view mirror, checking her appearance. The four gnarled chestnut trees which marked the entrance to Nick's gracious thatched-roof home darkened out of the swirling grey mist and Toni swung briskly through the wide gates.

She had reached a decision. She would greet Nick in a friendly manner, accept a drink and spend an hour or two discussing mutual friends. Then with dignity she would thank him for the drink, and leave. That would show him that she regarded him as a friend, and that his decision to remain with Jade had not affected her. He would realise that she

217

was immune to his charms. To reinforce her decision she whispered the words of her speech.

'We played and parted. It was fun.' Happy that she was word-perfect she switched off the ignition and listened to the deep throb of the engine bleeding into silence. She pulled up the high collar of her white cape and breathed deeply, the cold dank mist flooding into her lungs, and walked quickly towards the front door.

He stood backlit by the light cast by the brass chandelier in the hallway. Tall, thinner than she remembered, his face was soft in the warm shadows. Toni caught her breath and stood motionless. He lifted his arms, the dark green corduroy jacket pulling tight across his shoulders and his long tapering fingers stretched out to her.

'Kit— ' he said, but his voice broke and the 'ten' was lost.

For a moment Toni stared at him, frozen. Then the tightly closed drawers layered with memories fell open and with a sob she moved into the circle of his arms. He held her close, rocking her softly, stroking her silky hair, her cheek, her neck, murmuring her name. Gentling her, loving her as a mother cradles and caresses an only child. Toni buried her face in the open V of his shirtfront, and the hair cushioned her cheek and absorbed the tears which rolled soundlessly and unchecked down her cheeks.

Her firm resolutions were washed away with her tears. This was where she belonged. For long moments they stood absorbed in the wonder of each other. Then Nick held her gently away from him and tilted her face. He studied her intently and wordlessly, his fingers tracing the curve of her arched eyebrows, running across the high ridges of her cheekbones and wiping away the tears on her cheeks.

Slowly he bent over her, kissing her eyes, the long, wet eyelashes, the tip of her nose and her lips, kisses as soft as a whisper.

'Oh, my Toni, what have I done to you?' he agonised. 'How could I have ever let you go? My little one, my beloved girl.'

He buried his face in her hair, his body racked with mute sobs as the pain and desolation of the long months without her and the shock of reading how close she had been to death tore at him. Toni tightened her arms around him, trying to comfort him. She was awkward and helpless in the face of male grief.

Gradually he calmed. 'Forgive me, my love,' he whispered. 'I can't remember when last I did that. I was so afraid that you wouldn't come, that I'd lost you for ever. To be able to hold you close, rub my cheek over your hair, smell the special fragrance of your skin, these were things I tortured myself with month after endless month. My kitten, my precious one. You're here and I can't believe that I have you in my arms.'

Putting his arm around her waist, gluing her to his side, he closed the carved teak door and led her into the sitting room.

Orange tongues of flame skittered over the lumps of coal in the large fireplace built with the soft primrose and beige mountain sandstone. The deep ivory sofas flanking the fireplace looked comfortable and inviting in the warm light. Sprays of pyracantha, their blood-red berries weighing down the branches, exploded in a fountain of crimson from the jar which stood on a low oak chest.

'Oh, Nick, what a lovely room,' she exclaimed. It was the first time she had been in Nick's home and she walked across the drawing room to stand transfixed in front of a large oil painting. It was a vibrant yet lyrical work. The strokes of colour were strong and bold, but the clouds of white almond blossom covering the bowed tree were painted with a delicate touch and rested white and ethereal on the slender branches.

'Stern was such a powerful painter and strong colourist, but this is exquisite,' said Toni, turning to look at Nick as he stood in front of the fireplace watching her.

'I thought of you when I bought it. I knew you'd love it,' he answered.

He watched in silence as she inspected the room and as she ran her hand lightly over the silky grain of the library table he caught his breath. Her fingers found the jagged gash which cut deep and white into the polished wood and she paused. Gently, as if removing a stone from a cut in a child's knee, she dislodged a piece of broken crystal and it shone and twinkled in the palm of her hand.

'Jade,' he said. 'One of her parting gifts this afternoon.'

'Tell me about it,' said Toni, sensing his need to talk. As he shook his head she walked across to the fireplace and took his hand. 'Please, Nick. Please,' she insisted.

Wearily he removed his glasses and massaged his forehead. A wave of hair fell across his fingers and the firelight polished and accentuated the strands of grey. Toni studied his face as he started to speak, noting the new lines of pain etched around his mouth and fanning his eyes and her heart ached for him.

'When I returned this morning I let myself in through the back door as it was early and I didn't want to awaken Jade,' Nick said. 'I've been using one of the downstairs rooms,' he explained. Toni nodded and settled back in the chintz-covered armchair.

'I was unpacking when I heard muffled cries from upstairs. Thinking that Jade needed help— ' He paused and glanced up at the carved oak staircase. 'She's almost eight months pregnant,' he added. ' —I ran up to her room and flung open the door.'

Nick's mouth hardened and his upper lip curled in distaste. The silence deepened as he searched for words to describe Jade seated astride her lover, her belly, heavily distended, slapping sickeningly against his pale and hairless flesh as she gurgled cries of encouragement and fulfilment.

Nick swallowed. 'She was in bed with her lover. The father of her baby.'

His voice hardened. 'Jade has now left the house and the divorce will be uncontested. The man has claimed full responsibility for the child.'

'She knew,' Toni whispered. 'Jade always knew that he was the father.'

'Oh yes,' said Nick. 'She decided to get as much as possible from me before its birth, plus a settlement when she left.'

'Oh, Nick, I'm so sorry,' said Toni, her blue eyes wide with shock and her voice soft with sympathy.

'No, my kitten,' said Nick, lifting her out of the armchair, 'I'm the fool. The idiot whose extreme sense of responsibility and false values almost destroyed our future together.'

Toni kissed him lightly on the lips. 'Not destroyed, Nick,' she said. 'Definitely not destroyed.'

His arms tightened around her and he looked deep into her eyes as if searching for her soul. 'Toni, I'm almost divorced, a little bruised and battered by my innings with Jade but otherwise in good health. I have this home, a fishing cottage with one hundred and fifty acres of unspoiled flora on the east coast, and an apartment in Knightsbridge. I have an overwhelming desire and need for a certain lady and her son to share my life with me.'

His voice was low and gruff. 'Will you, Toni? Will you be my wife? I will love you, cherish you and do everything in my power to make you happy. This I swear.'

Silence swirled between them, thick as the mist outside.

Toni stared at him, her huge dark eyes mirroring her thoughts. 'Yes,' she said eventually in a small solemn voice. 'Yes, Nick.'

Nick bent down and as he kissed her the pain of the past faded and the future sparkled. 'Thank you, my kitten,' he whispered.

Toni smiled up at him and teased him gently. 'And like that cat I'm about to curl up in front of the fire and plead for a saucer of cream.'

'We can do better than that for the future Mrs Houghton. You can have cold Veuve Clicquot, with or without cream.'

'You have catered to two of my weaknesses, Nick,' she laughed. 'Champagne and a flickering fire.'

'I could cater to a third,' he answered, and Toni felt her cheeks flush.

His eyes twinkled as he handed her a fluted glass sparkling with champagne. 'Come,' he said. 'I want to show you the rest of the house or, as it will be, our home.'

'Mmm, coming,' she murmured, her nose buried in the glass, happily inhaling the tantalising bouquet of wood and dried gardenias of her favourite drink.

Suddenly he swept her up into his arms. 'Toni, Toni, to have you with me for ever,' he sang and spun her round, champagne flying from her glass and circling them like thin gold chains.

'Nick,' she shrieked, 'stop it, put me down or I'll be ill.' Still laughing and breathless they walked hand in hand down the wide passage lined with antique maps of Africa set in wide mahogany frames, to begin their inspection of the house.

'A dreamy kitchen,' said Toni, opening the white doors of the eye-level oven.

'When will you tell Serge?' asked Nick.

'I love these shiny white worktops,' she said, ignoring his question. 'I'll love cooking for you in this kitchen.' She remained standing in front of the stove with her back to him.

Finally she answered.

'I'll have to break it to him gently, Nick. I'm unhappy with him, but I don't want to hurt him. I'd like it to be an amicable divorce.'

Nick looked at the back of her curly head and ran his hand across his chin. All divorces were degrading. People hating with the intensity they had once loved with. He felt that a friendly one was as rare as the long-tailed Halley's comet. His thoughts flashed back to Jade, her narrow face blotched with anger, and her eyes slitted and venomous when she realised that her plans had collapsed. He had weathered the slurs on his manhood and the threats to leave him a pauper. He had uncovered her attempt to foster another man's child on him, and he had survived the fighting with no quarter given.

His mouth dried at the thought of Toni being placed in a similar situation. He pulled out one of the rush-seated chairs in the breakfast nook and motioned for her to sit down. Pulling up a chair opposite her, he leaned forward and cupped her hands in his. 'Darling,' he said, gently stroking her fingers. 'I don't know Serge very well, but he is a man and all men have this damn overwhelming pride and vanity.'

'Probably a sense of inadequacy because they'll never grow up to have babies like their sisters,' Toni teased and smiled weakly, unwilling to hear what Nick was going to say. He squeezed her hands.

'By leaving him you are going to hurt both his vanity and his pride, and I don't believe that his feelings towards you will be either amicable or conciliatory. It may be a long and very unhappy time for you.'

'I know,' said Toni quietly. 'I'll tell him when he returns from Durban.' She felt nauseous. Since childhood, shouting and physical violence had held the terrors of the damned for her. Her stomach muscles contracted with fear, bitter spurts of bile shot up her throat and she had to use immense self-control to keep from screaming and running away when faced with violence.

The kitchen and Nick faded as she remembered herself only too clearly, a curly-headed child of eight crying hysterically as she tried to pillow herself in front of her mother; hoping to shield her from the smashing fists of her drunk and violent stepfather. The thuds as his clenched hands smashed into the soft body and her mother's broken cries for help would haunt her for ever.

Toni curled into Nick's arms, closed her eyes and tried to blot out the immediate future which would be filled with violence and menace. She pressed closer to him, burrowing into his body, needing his strength to drive away the dark scenes which had plagued her childhood and gave her no respite in adulthood.

Nick, his face buried in the soft hollow of her neck, felt her fear and, cradling her in his arms, he carried her upstairs.

He undressed her slowly. He gloried in her body, running his lips gently over her gold-brown skin, pausing to pay homage to the firm breasts tipped with pale pink nipples, more like those of a young girl than a mother. He stopped to kiss her belly button, beautiful as it nestled in her silky brown stomach, and then moved down her firm body, making a ritual of kissing each toe tipped with cherry-red varnish, and lingering over the delicate softness of the flesh inside her thighs.

'Nick, Nick,' she whispered as she stretched out her arms and lifted his head. 'Nick, love me.'

He moved over her and their bodies joined. Their cries of fulfilment, high plaintive calls and low muted grunts, mingled like the sounds of the African bush they both loved. They lay without speaking, limbs closely entwined and beads of love dried on their skin.

CHAPTER
15

JUSTICE tightened the knot of his green and purple striped tie and checked that the top button of his light grey jacket was fastened. Satisfied, he walked quickly up Government Avenue, the rough gravel scuffing the sides of his highly polished black shoes and the leaves squelching beneath the new leather soles.

The oak-lined avenue running between the graceful old Houses of Parliament and the public gardens, set out three hundred years before, was beautiful, but Justice was blind to the beauty. He was deep in thought, perplexed as to why this meeting was necessary.

It was a clear, cool morning heralding the end of winter. The lashing north-westerly winds had lost their sting and the Cape tentatively tiptoed towards spring.

Wisdom was sitting on a wooden bench in a quiet corner of the gardens. The dappled sunlight played over his thin frame and he soaked up the warmth gratefully. When he had opened the note handed to him by one of the drivers at the liquor store the day before and had read that he was to meet the bearded ones in the gardens, a burning pain had spread across his diaphragm and the note had trembled in his fingers.

The bomb explosion had been most successful. His phone call had not prevented the crèche becoming a charnel house. The television channels had all devoted extra time to the slaughter of the innocents and it had appeared on the front pages of all the newspapers.

The bearded ones must be happy. Why should they call an urgent meeting? He had persuaded Mrs Kahn, with the greatest difficulty, not to accompany him to his mythical

224

doctor's appointment, and had reached the designated spot ahead of the others.

The burn in his stomach had become worse and he pressed his bony fingers deep into the flesh below his sternum, trying to ease the pain. Wisdom was weighed down by guilt, and the sour smell of fear was heavy in his nostrils. He looked up at the towering, flat-topped mountain which cut sharply into the pale blue sky. Without the white cloth of clouds which softened the harsh rocks, it looked powerful and intimidating as it reared over the city.

It was a good home for mighty spirits and he firmly believed that it had drawn the boats of the early Arab and Portuguese explorers on to the rocks by its great magic magnet. He also believed the white man's story that the clouds boiling up from the saddle on Devil's Peak and billowing over the mountain were the thick smoke from the pipe of Van Hunks the Dutchman and the devil as they played dice.

Wisdom was certain that there were many great spirits who lived in that mountain and he studied it with awe. He knotted his fingers together and closed his eyes, offering up a prayer for protection to the shade of his father, the baby Christ-child, and then included one to the powerful spirits of the mountain.

Justice approached the bench quietly, studying Wisdom as if seeing him for the first time. His blue shirt collar was much too large and circled his thin neck loosely. His brown checked trousers were gathered tightly into his waist with a newly notched leather belt and the folds hung in pleats around his skeletal legs. The shoulders of his jacket drooped over his shrunken frame and his clasped hands looked as brittle as twigs.

Justice loved his twin and had always taken his devotion and loyalty for granted, but looking at the wasted figure on the bench he censured himself; he had been so occupied with his studies and career that he had neglected the brother who adored him, and he determined to spend more time with him.

His prayers ended, Wisdom opened his eyes and a huge smile of joy spread across his face when he saw his twin looking down at him.

A shiver of superstitious dread shook Justice. His brother's

225

insubstantial body and emaciated triangular face drowned by his huge dark eyes looked like the stick-like praying mantis holding up its front legs as if in prayer.

Love stained with fear washed over Justice and he sat down quickly on the slatted bench beside Wisdom. 'I see you, my brother,' he said, smiling.

'Brother, why have we been called here today?' asked Wisdom. 'I feel the same unease that our cattle do when they smell thunder in the air. It is not good. The bearded ones dislike the bright light of the sun. They come always like grey shadows in the night and leave before the stars pale. Why, brother, why are we here?'

Justice shook his head slowly. 'It is strange, Wisdom. The job was well done. David Anstey did not ask why I was late. He thought that I was at the Deeds Office, checking up on title deeds. The woman with red hair did not question my presence or the box I was carrying. She thought that I was part of the team who were setting out the food on the tables in the crèche. No one saw me put the brown carton under the bench. No, the bomb was well placed. They cannot be unhappy about that.'

Justice was proud. He had been entrusted with an important assignment and had executed the task perfectly.

Wisdom listened in horror as Justice outlined the steps he had taken to plant the bomb. The streets in Shonalanga were still silent. The houses trembled to the sound of weeping. A community mourned its dead and Justice, his beloved brother, his mentor and friend, had been the killer.

'But . . . ' interrupted Wisdom, his voice quavering, 'but, Justice, my brother, the children? My heart is sick for those babies. They were the wealth of their parents. There is much grief and bitterness amongst our brothers over the death of so many of our children.'

Justice stiffened. It was treachery to the cause to speak like this and would place Wisdom in great danger if the bearded ones should hear. 'Brother,' he said, his voice low and placatory, 'we all love our children, they are our future and will revere us as ancestors, but if we do not hit hard and wound deep with our actions there will be no future here for our children. Those babies who died, they died gloriously. The

226

shades will welcome them because their deaths have driven another nail into the coffin of the ruling Boers.'

Wisdom listened in silence. 'My brother,' he whispered, 'has not the time come for us all to agree to sit at an *indaba* like our elders in the village? Should not everyone, the violent and the peace-seeking, sit and talk with the Boers and the other leaders? Cannot the killing end?'

'Do you not understand?' Justice interrupted sharply, barely containing his impatience at his brother's dove-like attitude. 'Those who talk to the Boers have to have power behind their words or like our women they will merely ululate.' He spoke earnestly, anxious to impress his brother. 'We have to continue fighting. We must impress upon the people of the world that we are seeking complete freedom for our brothers, and we must let the Boers know that though we speak, it is not from weakness. They must still fear our strength, and our followers, those who feel we have betrayed our cause by sitting with the enemy, they must know that we still have the steel claws of a leopard, and tremble. Much innocent blood has been spilled and more will feed the rich soil of Africa before we win. My brother, believe me, we, who are so many, we will win.'

Wisdom's unhappiness increased as he listened. It seemed to him that killing people only made the hard-line Boers obdurate. When they saw blacks killing blacks, they feared rule by the majority. His mother always said that children will do more for you if they are given a piece of honeycomb to chew than if they have the bitter juice of the aloe forced down their throats. His mother was a wise old woman and her words were to be heeded. He had read in the newspapers that many countries overseas were now condemning the violent killings, and they were even threatening not to contribute any money to the Party. Why, then, could not his brother and the bearded ones try to use the honeycomb and lay aside the aloe?

His spirit was no longer strong with desire to fight the whites and the blacks who did not agree with the doctrine. He was wearied by the killings. He was happy in his work, he respected old Mr and Mrs Kahn. They were good people. He considered Miss Toni to be a member of his family. She loved his people. The doctors at the hospital were kind men and looked after him well. The police were called persecutors, but they were involved in this war of terror, and war makes fornicating bedmates of brutality and violence.

He wished only to be left alone. He wished to save enough money to pay *lobola* for a good, strong wife with big breasts and broad hips. He wished to father many sons and daughters. He wished to spend his grey years sitting in the shade of the cattle pen with the men of his village. He was so weary of the anger and violence. He was a young man who wished for the peace given to the old.

The two brothers, their heads close together, did not notice the approach of the bearded men until black shadows fell across them. They looked up sharply, but the men ignored them and stood throwing peanuts to the grey squirrels darting between their feet.

Without looking at the two Xhosa men seated on the bench, the older man cracked a peanut shell between his teeth. 'The job was done well, Justice. We are pleased.'

Justice did not answer but allowed himself the liberty of a small smile. It vanished as the younger man spoke.

'But we have a traitor to our cause, Justice. He must be found.'

The young men looked up into two pairs of dark emotionless eyes. Wisdom licked his lips and swallowed nervously.

'A traitor,' he whispered.

'Read this,' commanded the younger man and threw a folded newspaper down on the bench.

An article ringed in red at the bottom of the page held their attention and the twins read carefully.

It has been learned that Mrs Toni Basler, after whom the new crèche had been named, told the police that she had received a phone call warning her of the bomb.

Wisdom's mouth dried as though he had been eating the *mobolo* plum, and the pounding of his heart drummed loudly in his ears. His hands tightened on the newspaper as he scanned the article.

Mrs Balser originally said that it was a black man who gave her the message, but later amended her statement

228

to say that it could have been someone using the accent to disguise their voice.

Wisdom, weak with relief, dropped the paper and Justice caught it before it hit the ground. You listened, ancestors, he thought. They do not know that it was me.

'The paper does not give us much help,' said Justice.

'It doesn't,' replied the older man, dusting crumbled pieces of peanut shell from his streaked beard. He turned the plastic packet inside out and the squirrels scattered as nuts and pieces of stale bread rained on to the ground. Kicking aside the turtle doves who had joined the pointed-eared squirrels and were cooing throatily as they pecked at the nuts, the young man ran his tongue around his pink and fleshy lips, and studied Wisdom.

'Not many knew of our plans. We'll find the dog, and the manner of his death will deter any other eaters of dirt from disclosing our secrets.'

The large red-eyed dove which had joined the mid-morning meal eyed the younger man warily, its carmine eyes bright with apprehension. It rose in an agitated flurry of feathers as the black-bearded man spun on his heel, turning sharply away from the twins. The older man smiled at them, but his eyes remained cold and calculating and Wisdom shivered as he watched them saunter towards the tunnel of oak trees.

The two men strolled past the ornamental ponds where the fish swam slowly in the cold water.

The older man grunted with satisfaction. 'We have him. We have the traitor.'

'I agree,' answered the younger, turning round to look at a pretty girl whose short black skirt moulded her buttocks lovingly and exposed her long slim legs. 'And if it's not him he definitely knows something about it, and that makes him guilty.'

'Choose a place and time and see that he dies in a manner which will be a lesson to all traitors. A lesson which they will not forget,' commanded the older man.

'It'll be done,' answered his younger companion. 'It may take a little time, but he will die.'

* * *

229

Silence shrouded the stone farmhouse set high on a hill overlooking the sleepy fishing harbour in Hout Bay. The children's voices were hushed and they no longer teased old Anna, the maid, or screamed with excitement as the geese waddled after them, hissing and flapping their wings. They walked on tiptoe past the library which had now been turned into a sickroom, afraid of meeting Anna or making a noise and disturbing Clive.

Helen had become as quiet as her home and when she smiled at the children it was a small, sad grimace.

She had kept Clive in virtual seclusion after the bomb blast. She had nursed him through night sweats and screaming nightmares as he relived the horror of the explosion and the shocking realisation that he would have to learn to live without his right leg. She had to convince him, in his despair, that she would love him whether he had one or three legs and that if he insisted on not making her Mrs Clive Markham she would grow old living with him in sin.

Her heart ached when she gently traced the deep lines which pain and despair had etched on his face and looked into his eyes empty of hope.

Anna had turned into a tigress after Clive returned from hospital. She guarded the farm, turning away well-wishers, journalists, friends and the curious, warning them to drive quietly as they left. She ordered telephone callers to stop ringing and, if Helen did not check up, she pulled the telephone plug from the socket, ensuring that Clive would be left in peace. Her impish charges still received the odd hug but were cowed into their best behaviour by her anger at Clive's accident.

The only people who could approach Clive without incurring her ire were Toni and Timothy.

Timothy had tiptoed into the bedroom where Clive sat slumped in his wheelchair, listlessly staring at the boats in the harbour and watching the tiny figures playing in the waves.

'Uncle Clive,' he piped, 'they said that I mustn't come and worry you because you're sick, but you're my friend and Mummy says that friends love each other all the time.'

He walked up to the chrome chair on tiptoe and tentatively

touched the man's arm, trying to attract his attention. 'I have something for you, Uncle Clive. Please read it,' he begged.

He stood unmoving until a hand stretched out and took the folded piece of paper. After a few moments of silence the man swung the wheelchair around to face the small boy.

'Oh, young Timothy,' said Clive, holding up the drawing of a laughing clown with one leg. 'With an invitation like this, how can I not come to your birthday party?'

'You will,' shrieked Tim and, climbing up the spokes of the wheel, he flung his arms around Clive's neck. 'I told them you'd come.'

Clive smiled and held the small body close. 'Sit on the arm of my chair and tell me all about this party,' he said.

Helen squeezed Toni's hand as they backed away from the half-closed bedroom door. 'Thank God,' breathed Helen. 'Thank you for little boys.'

They ran to the kitchen weak with relief, like schoolgirls having written their final examination papers, eager to see old Anna's face when she heard that Clive had agreed to go to Timothy's party.

On following visits to the farm Timothy had kept Clive up to date with the birthday arrangements and a few days before the party he had tentatively broken the news to Clive that he had promised his best friends that they could take turns to push the wheelchair.

'But no girls,' he hastened to add. 'They're sissies and this is only for boys.' Worried by Clive's silence he elaborated. 'May they, Uncle Clive? Please let them. You see, none of them is lucky enough to have an uncle with a wheelchair, so they'd never have a chance to push one.'

Timothy's easy acceptance of the wheelchair and his interest in Clive's missing leg had done much to hasten Clive's mental recuperation and he found himself looking forward to the birthday party.

Toni and Helen began planning other outings for Clive, and old Anna relaxed her vigilance slightly as they heard Clive's laughter ring out from the bedroom.

* * *

Spring had sprinkled flowers over the Cape Peninsula, heralding the return of endless blue skies and long golden days. But
the nights were still cold and Wisdom shivered and doubled
his coat around his painfully thin body as he hurried along
the dark streets, eager to be in the warmth of Izuba's home.

A fit of coughing made him pause and as he leaned against
a signpost, struggling to regain his breath, he heard again the
footfalls, soft and unfaltering, which had trailed him from the
bus stop.

He turned and stared into the gloom. His vision starred as
he strained to recognise the three dark shapes. He held his
breath, praying that they would greet him, sick with terror
that they would not.

As they neared he looked into their eyes, dead and pitiless,
and he turned and ran.

The path he chose led past a recreation hall and the ground
was soft and sandy, undermined with mole runs. He fixed his
eyes on a shining circle of blue, glowing in the distance,
lighting the legend above the door of the old brick building:
Shonalanga Police Station.

His heart hammered against his ribs, the blood pounded in
his ears and his lungs felt raw and seared as he wheezed, but
the blue light was his grail and he lurched on.

The sand deadened the pounding footsteps but he could
hear his pursuers, panting, eager and lusting as predators,
and as his foot slid into a mole-hole and he fell, he stretched
out his skeletal arms to the light which swirled blue and
beautiful through his tears until the bodies bending over him
blocked it out.

* * *

The Land-Rover picked its way carefully round the holes and
corrugated ridges in the road, like a child hopping down a
pavement, careful not to jump on any cracks.

The ginger-haired policeman fidgeting in the van, bright as
a daffodil, which had slowed down behind it, pulled angrily at
the ends of his luxuriant moustache, and his shaggy eyebrows
joined forces in a straight line. He watched in amazement as
the truck executed a complicated series of swings and turns,

dancing a madrigal across the road, and his patience snapped.

'Pull that stupid bastard over,' he growled. 'He's probably drunk or doped. Either way he's a nuisance and I hate him.'

'Yes, Stan, sir,' answered the driver and, siren shrieking, he cut across the front of the Land-Rover, forcing it to come to a shuddering halt.

'I said stop the bloody thing, not smash it,' bellowed Stan as he rolled down his window.

'Yes, sir. Sorry, sir,' said Richard.

Stan had been in a foul mood ever since he stormed out of the Wynstaat office after the phone call from Shonalanga Police Station. The Saturday-morning traffic had been very heavy and Stan had muttered and groused all the way to the township. His ill humour had not been improved by Richard's predicting that incidents of violence would continue until well after the negotiation talks had been concluded.

'It's all power play, sir. They're running for good positions, each determined to score tries and get the best possible deal. Each black political party wants to be top dog,' he explained.

'So they knock the hell out of each other, killing and burning their brothers. Determined to turn this place into another bloody African disaster.' Stan belched, the fried steak and eggs he had wolfed for breakfast refusing to be digested.

'They have different game plays, sir. One for the conference table – that's the one to watch; and another for television and newspapers – that's to keep their supporters happy and usually doesn't mean much.' Richard blanched as the stale aroma of greasy eggs filled the van.

'May not mean much to them, but it sure as hell does to the sods who watch telly. They believe it's the new Ten Commandments and they go and get rid of anyone who disagrees.' He burped again and the youngster held his breath. 'And who gets to clean up the bloody mess? We do, and get our arses kicked by the press, the right- and the left-wingers. Bloody thankless job. Should've been a preacher.'

The thought of Stan haranguing a congregation with his explicit and ear-burning language made Richard grin and he covered his mouth quickly. This was not the time to smile.

He pitied the driver of the Land-Rover and he sat quietly

233

behind the wheel, his delicate fingers beating a nervous tattoo on the plastic circle as he waited for the explosion.

'What the— ? Why, Mrs Balser. Toni. Good morning.' Stan's voice was sweet and warm as fresh honey and a wide smile lifted the corners of his hirsute upper lip.

Richard looked at his superior in surprise.

'I'm sorry if I held you up, Officer le Roux,' apologised Toni, 'but I have an idea for an article on the state of the roads in the townships. Do you know that it is impossible to drive on the correct side of the road if you wish to avoid the potholes?' She smiled. 'And if you hit one of the deep ones, both car and driver could vanish for ever. So please forgive my bad driving.'

'Quite understandable, Mrs Balser, quite understandable,' smiled Stan.

'Thank you,' said Toni. Her face was devoid of make-up, looking as clean and fresh as the patches of daisies on the road verge. 'I do hope that I haven't delayed you on any important business.'

'No, no. I was going to check on a murder in the township which they think may be ritual,' he answered. 'Good day, Mrs Balser.'

'Goodbye and thank you once again,' shouted Toni as the police car bounded and lurched away.

'A real lady that one,' said Stan. 'A real lady. Guts too. The way she behaved in that bomb explosion. Real guts.'

'Yes, sir, Stan,' agreed his driver, delighted that the cloud of black humour had lifted.

'Turn right here,' directed Stan. 'The body's in the field behind the Hall of Angels. Hell of a name for a kids' youth centre,' he grunted. 'Hall of Little Devils would be more appropriate, or even Hall of Hell, when you see some of the things these kids get up to.'

They stopped outside a small undistinguished brown-brick building, the pathway leading up to the faded red door lined with rusted tins of drooping ferns. Ignoring the path, they cut across to the field behind the building where a small knot of men in blue were huddled around a shapeless bundle on the ground.

Richard drew in a sharp breath. 'It's beautiful,' he gasped.

Stan looked at the young man and shook his head. 'How

in the hell am I going to make a cop out of you when at a murder site all you care about are flowers?' He spat noisily, and the phlegm was caught and held in the translucent celadon petals of a ground lily. 'I thought that having you with me would toughen you up. Give you balls. But you're still as soft as a bloody ballet dancer.'

Richard smiled inwardly. Working with Stan had hardened him and he now ignored all references to his failings.

'Yes, sir. Sorry, sir,' he answered automatically, his attention focused on the blinding display of flowers spread across the field. In the breeze they floated over the white sand and flowed between the clumps of fresh green grass like chiffon scarves of brilliant purple, saffron and apricot. The colours dazzled him and he squinted in the sunlight.

Awed by the scope and beauty of the wildflower garden nature had created in this sandy waste, and loath to trample the flowers underfoot, he tiptoed after Stan and found that the closely packed circle of blue uniforms which had opened to admit Stan had closed and he was thankfully unable to see the victim.

He walked quietly around the outside of the circle to stand behind Stan in case he was needed. His eyes were still fixed on the ground, marvelling at the variety of wildflowers, when the toe of his highly polished shoe dislodged a soft, dark grey object nestling in a patch of succulent-leaved mesembryanthemums. The large glowing purple flowers almost covered the fleshy object with their shiny petals and he bent down to examine it.

'The constable over there', said a burly man dressed in civilian clothes, pointing at Richard, 'is bending over the tongue.'

The group swung round and Stan strode forward. Richard froze, the words beating loudly in his skull. The bloated grey object had been identified.

The raw end, where it had been hacked from the base of the mouth, was covered with black ants delicately moving their feelers over the flesh, claiming their rich find, and the tip curled up in silent supplication.

'They cut the tongue out first to prevent the screams being heard while they slowly butchered the living body,' the man continued, his voice dispassionate.

Beads of cold perspiration broke out on Richard's forehead and the field of crisp spring flowers blurred like the reflections of city lights in pools of rainwater as he gagged and stumbled from the group.

Stan looked at the mass of grey muscle cushioned by the flowers and then glanced across the field to where Richard was crouching. No wonder he's so thin, he thought. Poor little sod still pukes at murder scenes.

'The second step', said the large man, pausing in his assessment of the murder, waiting impatiently for Stan to rejoin the group, 'is the knife in the lower back.'

One of the young policemen blanched and fixed his eyes firmly on a patch of pale mauve oxalis flowers, determined not to faint or join Richard. 'A fiendishly simple method of immobilising the victim. It severs the spinal cord, making it impossible for the victim to struggle or attempt to escape.'

'But the poor sod can still see and feel,' cursed Stan.

He shuddered, looking down at the thin black youth, the limbs twisted in the rictus of agony which had racked the body as he died.

The men were pale and quiet.

'This was not a ritual murder,' said Stan. 'None of the organs have been taken.'

The young officer wiped the cuff of his uniform across his clammy forehead, glanced unwillingly at the bloodied liver and intestines lying on the soft flowered carpet beside the body, and turned and ran to join Richard.

'No,' the big man answered. 'It's one of the must brutal murders I've ever seen. At this stage it's difficult to say when the poor creature died. It's my guess that they kept him alive as long as possible. They'd have gouged out his eyes after they emasculated him and wedged his penis into his mouth.' One of the police officers coughed and swallowed loudly. 'But the eyes were probably out when they removed the heart.'

'He couldn't have lived very long with that sort of torture, could he, sir?' asked one of the younger officers, hoping to hear that the man had died quickly.

The beefy man turned to look at him and his voice was compassionate. 'I too would like to believe that, but in England in the days when condemned criminals were ordered to be "hung, drawn and quartered", they survived for hours with their insides trailing in the dust beside them. The human body has incredible powers of endurance, gentlemen, and this man suffered agonies which we cannot begin to imagine. The swines who perpetrated this disgusting murder must be found. No man, no matter what crime he's committed, deserves to die in this way.'

The group murmured their agreement, eyes glinting with anger and revulsion, and their shoulders stiffened imperceptibly.

'How many locals have seen the body?' asked Stan, smoothing down his moustache.

'None,' answered one of the officers from the Shonalanga Police Station. 'One of my men lives nearby and took a short cut across the field on his way to work early this morning. He covered the body with his overcoat, and we've had a guard around it ever since.'

'Good,' said Stan. 'Then the message of fear and terror which this was meant to convey will not be spread. I've a feeling that this poor boy fell foul of one of the bloody gangs or political organisations which stink like gutter slime in this area. This mutilated body was meant to send a message to any backsliders, doubters or informers.' He bent over the body and rested his hand for a moment on the sunken grey cheek. 'Thank the good Lord that won't happen.'

The lips were pulled back from the teeth and the empty eye sockets stared up at Stan's face.

'We'll find your murderers,' whispered Stan as he straightened up and turned.

Plodding back to the police van he looked at Richard, a huddled figure in blue, staring sightlessly at the flowers. His head was still between his knees and the boils on his neck, aggravated by the rough serge of the collar, glowed an angry red. Stan's tawny eyes narrowed. He had become fond of the studious young man though he took great care not to show it. The kid was hardening into a good cop but still had a weak stomach.

Wonder if I should let him break the news to the family, he mused. Better not. Little swine can't hold a dead body or see a dismembered corpse without spewing up his bloody insides.

He's not ready to face the living death in the family's eyes. Filthy job. I hate it.

He eased a roll of peppermints from his pocket, peeled off the paper and offered one to Richard.

'Here, kid, have a mint. It'll help. At least, it'll taste better than that crap in your mouth.'

Richard looked up at him as a puppy does when it expects to be beaten. 'Thanks, Stan, sir,' he whispered and prised a damp white disc from the roll.

Stan tucked the roll of sweets into his pocket. 'Come on, kid,' he said. 'No sense in us waiting around. We've got work to do.'

The two men sat in the car, the silence broken only by the rhythmic sucking of mints. Stan's thoughts spun but kept returning, like moths battering against a light bulb, to the task which lay ahead. A task he had performed countless times but had never been able to accept with equanimity. Even his strong defences were unable to withstand the anguish and bewilderment of the bereaved.

Sliding his tongue into the hole in the peppermint, Stan twirled it around his mouth. He sucked it slowly, remembering a forsaken night in winter when, as a young rookie, he had gone alone to tell a woman rejoicing in the euphoria of her first pregnancy that she was widowed. The experience as she had clawed and fought him had scarred his mind and left welts, now puckered and ridged, down his neck and cheek. Running his finger lightly over his neck as the car bucketed over the gravel road, Stan reminisced and stared at the spring flowers, shimmering as richly as altar cloths in the bright sun.

'This is number twenty-four in Section NY,' said the policeman seated in the back of the yellow van. Richard slowed down and Stan, who had sat silent and morose, chin resting on his chest, lifted his head.

No, he thought. No, this cannot be the place. He stared at the Land-Rover parked in front of the neat brick house. She's been through the horror at the crèche. She cannot be involved with the victim's family.

He saw a smiling face and dark curls held back with a cornflower-blue ribbon.

'Number twenty-four?' he barked, glaring at the unfortunate constable.

'Yes, sir. This is number twenty-four.' He swallowed nervously, not wishing to experience the legendary wrath of Stan le Roux. 'This is where the victim, Wisdom Mapei, lived.'

Wearily Stan lifted himself out of the yellow van and pulled the visor of his cap low on his forehead. 'Come on,' he said to Richard. He wrinkled his nose, the peppermint hardly masking the sour smell on the young man's breath.

* * *

Izuba walked to the window as Toni's Land-Rover drew up. 'Come, come,' urged Soze, her black eyes dancing with excitement. 'It's Ungumtukathixo. It's Miss Toni.'

'Little one, it is but yet Saturday and Miss Toni is at home with Timothy,' chided Izuba. 'And we have received no message to say that our Child of God has come to fetch me or is to visit us.'

'Miss Toni,' shrieked the little girl, bouncing up and down on the bench in front of the window. Izuba leaned over Soze and peered through the pane.

'Quick, Storchman,' she called to her oldest son. 'Soze's eyes have seen well. It is Miss Toni. Open the door.'

Storchman looked at the girl seated beside him at the table and squeezed her hand, smiling at her reassuringly before walking to the door. Soze wriggled past him and was about to skip down the steps and run to open the gate when, overcome with sudden shyness, she shuffled behind Storchman and peered timidly at Toni from behind his denim-clad leg.

'Go and greet Miss Toni,' said her brother, vainly attempting to prise her loose. Her limbs stretched out and grew long as he pulled her, but her body clung to his thigh like chewing-gum to the sole of a shoe. Admitting defeat he stumbled down the stairs, his baby sister weighing down his leg.

Izuba, laughing, came to his rescue by swinging Soze on to her hip. 'You are no longer a baby,' she whispered, 'and I wish you to greet Miss Toni and lead her into the house.'

Soze uncurled her head from Izuba's shoulder and slid to the ground. Bounding up the steps she proudly held the front

239

door open. Her little chest swelled with pride as Toni dropped a kiss on her cheek.

'I was doing some work in your area, Izuba,' Toni said, 'and decided to call in on my way home. I know you wanted me to see the new bookcase you've bought.'

Toni walked into the front room. Her eyes widened and she drew in her breath when she saw the young girl seated near Joshua at the table. Her skin was as pale as the arum lilies in the jar on the table, and her short blonde hair wisped around her face and framed round, pale blue eyes which gazed at Izuba apprehensively.

Storchman went to stand behind the girl's chair, placing a hand protectively on her shoulder.

'Miss Toni,' he said, 'this is Tracy. She is at university with me. We are both attending the same classes. We arrived here just before you. I very much wanted Uma to meet Tracy.'

Izuba's mouth opened but she said nothing.

'Tracy's parents own a sugar farm near Durban,' gabbled Storchman, his eyes still pleading with Izuba to accept the young woman, but the silence lengthened. 'Tracy and I are going out together.'

'How lovely, Storchman,' said Toni, breaking in quickly to hide Izuba's discomfiture. 'I'm delighted to meet you, Tracy. I'm Toni Balser and I've known Storchman since he was a baby. You've found a fine young man.'

The blonde girl swallowed gratefully and held Toni's hand tightly. Taking Izuba's plump hand in her free one, Toni spoke to the woman she had grown to love in Xhosa.

'You love your son, Izuba, and you must find things to like in the girl he has chosen. His happiness is more important than her colour or her culture.'

For once Izuba did not laugh at Toni's misuse of the Xhosa clicks and, shaking herself as though awakening from a deep sleep, she answered, 'Thank you, Ungumtukathixo, thank you for reminding me of my love for my son.'

Dropping Toni's hand, she enfolded the girl's slim white hand in her own, the fingers lacing like black and white plaited velvet ribbons. 'You are of course welcome in my home,' she said and smiled, and as the black eyes looked deep into the blue ones a tenuous bond was formed, a bond of their love for Storchman.

Justice watched and smiled thinly. He had sat quietly in a corner of the room, interested to see his sister's reaction when she met Storchman's girlfriend.

He had watched Izuba when she snarled and threatened the bearded ones, oblivious to the danger she was courting by antagonising the disliked strangers. She was as savage in her protection of her family as a raging lioness, eyes wide and flashing, jumping stiff-legged, muscles bunched, before committing herself to the final terrible charge. He had looked forward to seeing her claw Storchman and his pale girlfriend, leaving their happiness in thin bloody shreds, but Toni had interfered.

He watched with interest as she skilfully defused the situation and realised why the bearded ones had wanted her killed in the explosion at the crèche. Toni was clever and compassionate, and was therefore their enemy. She seemed to believe that the ANC were powerful because of the funding from overseas, not because they had the faith of the people behind them. She wrote that they were power hungry and did not truly care for their own kind.

The articles she had published in the newspapers were being read and believed by the people in the townships and his sister sang her praises to whosoever would listen. Her kind were weakening their cause. His people needed to be wary of whites. They were not all concerned and caring people. His party could not afford to relax until they commanded as much power as the whites, and he believed it would have to be wrested away by force.

He knew how important it was to keep the 'armed struggle' alive. To succeed they needed the power of the people behind them. Now that they were allowed to compete in the open market it had become apparent to all that they did not hold the monopoly. There were many other vendors and they would have to sell their wares aggressively if they were to corner the market. It was not wise to advocate violence openly when all were talking of peace and negotiation, but their strong military arm had to be kept flexed and muscular, and Justice was determined that it would not weaken.

He turned his attention from Toni to his nephew. Storchman was a fine young man, good-looking and intelligent. He was sadly committed not to the ANC, but to education. He believed that education for all was more important than the power struggle.

Justice sniffed. It would be Storchman's grandchildren who benefited and took their seats in Parliament, not Storchman or his generation. The way of the ANC was unrelenting pressure until the majority ruled, and they, who had fought so long for freedom, would control the majority.

He watched with veiled eyes as Tracy followed Izuba into the kitchen to prepare fresh tea. Her flimsy blue cotton skirt hung straight over her boyish hips and her high-necked white blouse with its lacy collar and cuffs covered breasts which were only budding. Storchman had not only chosen the wrong colour, he had not even chosen good breeding stock.

'Thank you,' said Storchman turning to Toni. 'Thank you for welcoming Tracy and for asking my mother to accept her as a daughter.'

'Few women respond well to shocks and surprises,' replied Toni softly. She smiled at the serious young man. 'Izuba and thousands of others are finding it difficult to adapt to the startling changes which are flashing across the southern tip of Africa, but I hope and believe that the future will be moulded by the Storchmans and Tracys and not the radicals.'

She pulled out a chair and sat at the table opposite Storchman, eager to discuss Tracy and his course at university with him.

'Are you not being a little harsh on the young people, the so-called radicals?' broke in Justice, a slight sneer edging his question.

Toni turned around. 'Justice. Hello. I'm afraid I didn't notice you sitting quietly in the corner. I've not seen you for so long,' she said.

'Correct,' he answered. 'We last met in Mr Anstey's office when you were with Mr . . . ?'

Toni did not supply the name but a dull rose flushed her cheeks. 'David Anstey thinks highly of you, Justice. I'm so pleased,' she continued. 'Your family must be very proud. I know that I am.'

'They're proud only of the fact that I wear a suit and work with lawyers, but they do not understand.' Justice paused. He found himself warming to Toni's praise and interest and had to caution himself against divulging too much to this woman.

Toni waited expectantly, but Justice waded out of the deep water and returned to paddle in the shallows.

'The radicals you were talking to Storchman about, they are our young people. Very special people. They are tired of promises. They are weary of waiting for Christmases that don't come and stockings which remain empty. They have realised that Father Christmas spreading love and peace for all is an illusion. What of these people? Are they to be branded as reactionaries and terrorists because they are weary of watching others open presents and want their own parcels to open? What of them, Mrs Balser?'

Unwilling to witness or become involved in an argument between his uncle and Miss Toni, Joshua quietly pulled his chair away from the table and went to join his mother in the kitchen.

Like Beauty, his sister, he considered Toni to be a member of his family and refused to include her in the bearded ones' damnation of the whites.

'Iboni,' smiled Izuba as her son closed the kitchen door, 'come and tell me what you learned at school this week.' She held him close to her side and buried her lips in his frizzed halo of hair.

Joshua was losing his tense and suspicious attitude and his laughter once again filled the house. Izuba was content to see her son happy and did not enquire into the reasons. She prayed that it was because the ancestors had intervened and lessened the strangers' hold on him.

He had risen in the ranks and was now second in command to Beauty's lover. They still held meetings and paid lip service to the ANC doctrine but, influenced by the change of heart of the Government, bridling against being treated as children and dictated to by the bearded ones, and eager to sample the future riches being offered, they had turned the group's skills at evading the law into the illegal and highly profitable business of running drugs, *dagga*, from the Transkei.

Joshua now listened to his older brother Storchman as

243

intently as he had once listened to the strangers, and his goal was no longer death and destruction, but a place in the university, followed by a job in the new government.

'Uma,' he laughed, sneaking a raisin bun from the tea tray, 'I am working hard and you will be so proud of me when I go to work in the Parliament.'

Izuba cuffed him lightly behind his ear. 'It is good to dream, Iboni, but now you can help set out the tea tray and leave some buns for the others.'

The young boy smiled shyly at the pale girl who went to his brother's university, and he handed her the gaily patterned mugs.

Toni noticed Justice's deliberate use of her name, Mrs Balser instead of Toni, and prepared to answer him but, scarcely pausing for breath, he continued.

'These young people never appear in your articles as anything but hooligans, blind followers of the Communist doctrine, or dumb counters being used in a game of draughts. Do you not pity them, Mrs Balser? Do you have no tears for them? They have had nothing for so long. Can you imagine what it is like to be treated as unclean, always to be the spectator, never the participant? Do you wonder at their anger when even now they are treated as the poor child in borrowed clothes at a birthday party? You say they are brutalised and violent. They only use violence because they were denied any other form of expression.'

'My heart aches for them, Justice, please believe me, and I do understand their anger, but the violence has to be controlled,' interjected Toni. 'These groups no longer owe allegiance to any party. You cannot control them. No one can control them. They run wild.'

'They are vital people willing to die for a cause they know is just and right,' said Justice, ignoring her interjection, 'willing to sacrifice their lives for the chance to share in a brighter future.'

Stung, Toni replied. 'No, not share in the future, Justice, but control the future, and the brightness will not be for them. It will be kept for the new masters in power. They're being used – can't you see that? – and they'll be discarded, just as all the masses have been in all revolutions. Wishing to sacrifice their lives is their choice, Justice, but what gives them the right to sacrifice the innocent? A monster is being spawned and there's no place for monsters in the new future.' She stared into his eyes, willing him to understand. 'The government they hated has changed. Now there are men who are compassionate; they reject the laws of discrimination; there'll be room for all political parties. There can be a good future for these young people but they must— '

'The tea's ready.' They were interrupted by Tracy, walking into the room with a red and white striped tin tray piled with mugs. She smiled at Storchman and set the tray down on the table. Discomfited and surprised by Justice's unexpected attack, and unwilling to mar Tracy's first visit to the family by having a political argument, Toni turned from the conversation and spoke to Izuba's son.

'Have you met Tracy's parents, Storchman?'

He grinned. 'Yes, they came to the Cape for Easter and invited me to spend a few days with them.' Recognising the unspoken question in Toni's eyes, he added, 'Like my mother, they are uncertain of our relationship. They worry about the vast cultural and background differences, about any children being neither Xhosa or European, but lost in the twilight zone.'

Izuba nodded as she sipped her tea, taking comfort in the hot sweetness. Storchman put his hand over Tracy's. 'We believe that the future is for sharing and we want our families to share in our happiness.'

Storchman looked at his mother and smiled with relief when she answered, 'The happiness of our children is as important to us as silent wings are to the owl, but you will need to be strong, my children.' She swallowed. And so will I, she thought.

'Uma,' called Joshua from the kitchen, 'there is a police car stopping in front of our house.'

Justice lifted his mug high, drained the last sweet drops of tea and walked through to the kitchen. He wanted to avoid the police.

Izuba nervously picked at a piece of cotton lace in the table-cloth with her fingernail, separating the delicate threadwork and enlarging the hole. She was afraid that her man Abraham was in trouble. He had learned to drink the brown devil-water

245

which the bearded ones brought to the house and the fiery liquor made him as short-tempered as the lumbering black rhino. When his belly was burning he had no fear.

'Let them not be here because of Abraham,' she muttered. 'Or because of Justice,' she added, knowing that he occasionally slept at the *shebeen* with the unclean girls who weaned the men's wages from them when their minds were softened by brandy and their bodies relaxed by the release of their manhood.

Justice stood at the kitchen door and listened as a man, large as a red ox, greeted Miss Toni and asked for Mr and Mrs Mapei. There was a long silence, then a very low murmur of voices.

Suddenly a shriek, sharp as a screech owl, reverberated through the house, and Soze, caught up in the primaeval fear and terror of ululation, threw back her head and howled in unison.

Justice waited in the kitchen, chilled by the shrieks, until he saw Toni walking to the gate flanked by a burly ginger-haired policeman and a slim one.

'Stan, are you certain that it was a political killing? Revenge for betrayal?' she gulped, her face pale with shock. 'Do you think that I caused this? I reported that a man, probably black, had phoned to warn me of the bomb at the crèche.' She choked as she thought of Wisdom, the quiet, gentle young man. 'It could have been Wisdom who phoned.'

'No, no, Toni,' Stan said.

'Yes, Stan. It would've been easy for the planners to find out how many people knew of the proposed bomb explosion and also knew me. It was merely a process of elimination. My thoughtlessness caused a brave, considerate man's death.' Her fingers shook as they gripped the garden gate. 'How could anyone murder gentle Wisdom?'

'You cannot blame yourself, Toni,' Stan comforted. But even as he spoke he decided to run traces on Wisdom. Perhaps this murder was linked to the explosion. The case was cold, they had no leads at all.

Richard Dalton turned away. He could not look at Toni.

Heaving himself into the van, Stan looked at Toni bent over the gate as if convulsed with stomach cramps. Listening to the howling from the house, he was relieved that he had kept the gruesome details of the murder from them. They were unable to accept Wisdom's death. How could they be expected to accept his torture?

Hearing the sharp slam of the car door as the policemen climbed into their van, Justice ran into the front room, Soze trailing behind him like a crumpled shirt-tail. Tracy sat huddled at the table staring at Izuba who was rocking on her chair screaming her pain to the heavens and berating her ancestors for having failed to protect her beloved young brother.

'What is it? What has happened?' demanded Justice urgently.

Tracy was speechless in the face of such raw grief and she stared at him dumbly, her fingers fluttering like blind white moths over Storchman's arm.

Justice dug his hard fingers into her shoulder and felt the bones, soft and fragile. 'Speak to me,' he commanded. 'Speak.'

Tracy gave a low moan of pain and Storchman prised his uncle's fingers from her shoulder.

Drawing the young girl close to him, he said quietly, 'He is dead. Your twin brother Wisdom has been murdered.'

Justice stood paralysed, as frozen as he was the day he and Wisdom had run naked from their circumcision hut to plunge into the icy swamp. He heard Wisdom shrieking as the water covered his head and shoulders and saw him explode like an otter from the marsh's frigid embrace, no screams able to pass his chattering teeth.

Like a video racing out of control he saw his twin when still a toddler herding goats, bravely stoning a yellow cobra. The snake, its golden body speckled with brown and rust, had reared up in the dusty path in front of him, its neck hood expanded, ugly with rage. He had stood transfixed, mesmerised by the hissing reptile, its eyes fastened on him, reddish brown and deadly beneath the fused eyelids. It was Wisdom who had broken its back with a large grey rock, preventing it from launching itself at him. His young brother had saved him from suffocating to death as the venom paralysed his motor nerves and diaphragm, a terrifying process.

He saw the weaker boy limping home, his head bloodied and body bruised from the blows taken during a stick fight with older boys when he had leapt into the mêlée to protect

247

him. He ran his fingers lightly over the scar above his ear. A memento of that fight. It had taken three days before his sibling could join the children around the communal eating pot. The village witchdoctor had prepared the family for the youngster's probable death as he poured medicinal brews down his throat and wrapped his swollen and tender belly in steaming leaves and mud packs.

He saw Wisdom, his dustcoat imprinted with the liquor store's red logo flapping round his legs, standing proudly outside David Anstey's offices, eager to escort him home after his first day's employment with the prestigious law firm.

The mental video ran on remorselessly, flashing images of their lives together. Wisdom always smiling, always running to defend the brother he adored and admired. He had accepted Wisdom's adulation and deference but he could not accept his death.

They had curled around each other in the amniotic fluid of their mother's womb. He was his moon shadow. Their destinies were entwined and strengthened like the brown monkey vines swinging from the tall trees. The roaring of denial thundered in his ears and the clouds of pain and anger boiled in his head.

He refused to believe that it was Wisdom, but the mental pictures continued and now they included the bearded ones. Justice stiffened. He saw a bench in the gardens, Wisdom dropping the newspaper, his fingers trembling uncontrollably.

He heard the bearded one say, 'We'll find the traitor.' Storchman said Wisdom had been murdered. His mind recoiled in horror, unable to accept that the party he served loyally and believed in so religiously had ordered this murder.

Storchman, watching his uncle closely, saw the red pain in his eyes give way to the black of guilt. 'You know,' he gasped, standing up. 'You know who killed Wisdom.'

Storchman's voice hissing in his ear abruptly threw the switch on the video and he heard and saw his family.

'No,' he denied. 'I know nothing of this.'

He walked across to the window and pressed his sweating forehead against the glass. The ANC policy is right, I cannot question it. I must believe in them. Silently, desperately, he tried to justify his party's policies.

Violence had been, and, he believed, was still necessary.

The party policies were right, but murdering Wisdom was tantamount to killing a part of him. The bearded ones had murdered one of his family and a fellow member of his tribe and they must pay. His tribe and family were still the most important things in his life. The bearded ones were the ones who had ordered the death of his twin. They were the black maggots buried under the toenail of the party causing it to limp, and like maggots they must be dug out and squashed. Quickly he exonerated the party he followed and worked for so loyally and placed all the blame for his twin's death on the strangers.

He glanced up as the police car rounded the corner at the end of the road, its hooter blaring, warning dogs and children to scramble on to the pavements.

Yes, he thought. The red-haired policeman, that le Roux, the hero of the people, he would be a worthy adversary for the bearded ones.

The political parties were unbanned and their membership an open secret, but the government did not accept acts of violence perpetrated on its citizens. They would set the dogs on them. He smiled and, still watching him, Storchman shivered.

An anonymous note suggesting that he pay some attention to the two gentlemen, plus a hint of their activities and a clue to their address. His mind raced. Once they were caught, even a life sentence would not make them divulge the names of the members committed to acts of violence. They were professionals. He would be safe. No one would know of the bomb he had planted.

He rested his head against the glass again and his fine mind, honed by legal training to concentrate only on relevant details, worked out a way to avenge his twin brother's death.

Toni did not notice the face pressed hard against the window, the dark fathomless eyes staring at her as she walked up the path. Guilt was riding heavily on her narrow shoulders. Each time she tried to recall the nuances and tone of the voice on the telephone, sharp spurs of remorse dug into her sides. Every mental picture of Wisdom and each wail from the house was a whip lashed across her back. Toni was shattered and she dragged herself up the steps to arrange for the identification of the body and for Wisdom's funeral.

You are to blame as are the bearded ones, Justice muttered silently as he watched Toni mount the steps. You led the killers to my brother. Your loose tongue wrote directions which led to Wisdom, directions so clear that a blind man could have followed them.

His sickening guilt and his anger at the bearded ones and Toni coagulated and churned in his belly like a writhing tapeworm frantic to be fed.

Toni walked into the room and was caught up and spun around in a maddening vortex of sorrow. She glanced around the room quickly.

The young girl Storchman had brought home to meet his family sat slumped in a chair, stunned and silent.

'Storchman,' said Toni, putting her hand on his arm, 'let me take Tracy back to the university. You stay and comfort your mother.'

'Thank you,' he agreed with quiet dignity and led the shivering girl out of the house and down to the Land-Rover.

Putting her arm around Izuba's broad shoulders and pressing her cheek up against Izuba's wet one, Toni rocked with her, crooning to her softly. 'You must be strong for your family, Izuba. You have children who are frightened and need you.' Their tears mingled and the two women sat welded in sorrow, sobbing for Wisdom and a world gone mad. She chanted the words of comfort like a liturgy as they swayed, and gradually the screams died down to a whimper. Izuba's massive body shuddered, like death throes shivering through a dying animal, but she was quiet. Soze left Joshua and ran to curl in her mother's lap.

Leaving Izuba talking softly to her young daughter, Toni crossed to the window where Justice stood anchored in disbelief and hate.

'Justice,' she said, 'Wisdom was a wonderful man. I'm so sorry. I wish there was something I could do to help lessen the pain.'

Without turning round or looking at her he said bitterly, 'You have done enough, Mrs Balser. Your thoughtlessness gave my brother death. Can your thoughtfulness now give him life?' His words were cold and flat. 'My sister calls you Child of God. For what you have done Child of Satan would be more fitting. You meddle in things you do not begin to understand. The clearest rivers flow over mud and slime. You and your writing stir up the bottom, making the rivers filthy. You and your kind confuse my people.' He snorted. 'Lessen the pain, Mrs Balser. You cause the pain.'

He turned to face her, and deep in his dark eyes Toni saw the humiliation of centuries, the sapping battle for acceptance, the animosity and the overwhelming desire for revenge and power. She stared into a future turgid and menacing.

Justice dropped his voice and broke into Xhosa. The words slithered over Toni, evil and loathsome. She stood hypnotised, staring into his black eyes, and as he cursed her, her skin pimpled with dread.

Izuba's broken voice tore aside the sticky threads of the web of terror which Justice had spun around Toni. He straightened and as he turned to face his sister the hate and pain of Black Africa died in his eyes and they mirrored merely the concern of a young man for his sister.

'I am coming, Izuba,' he said softly. 'Miss Toni and I were discussing the future. There is much to do to honour our brother's shade.' He smiled sweetly at Toni and she felt her reason fraying, like the unhemmed edge of a silk cloth, the threads of sanity unravelling.

'Izuba,' she said shakily, 'I'll leave you now and take Tracy home. I know that Justice and Storchman will look after you until Abraham arrives.' She squeezed Izuba's hand and hugged Soze. 'If you need me I'll be at home.' Her voice cracked. 'I'm truly sorry, Izuba.' Fresh tears washed over the dried ones on her cheeks. 'Wisdom was a special man. Why is it that the best are always taken?' She bit her lip trying to control her tears.

She straightened up and left the room without looking at Justice and he smiled as he watched her leave. As she stepped outside a small hand tugged at her fingers.

'Timothy?' queried Soze tentatively.

'Izuba'll bring you to play with Timothy when she comes back to work. You can stay with her, and you and Timothy can race the toy cars every day.'

Soze's tear-streaked face lit up and she slipped back into

the house like a black wisp from a guttering candle. Oblivious to the stares of Izuba's friends and neighbours who, attracted by the shrill ululating, had gathered outside the house, Toni walked to the car. She could not rid herself of Justice's words and she shivered in superstitious dread.

With Izuba's help she had mastered sufficient Xhosa to understand that Justice had cursed her and called on the spirits, asking them to take from her someone she loved just as they had taken Wisdom, his shadow, from him.

Walking quickly to the car in the bright sunshine, she knew that Justice's tribal curses were only a sickening reaction to the shock of Wisdom's death. He was a good, intelligent man with a bright future, and the insanity of his tirade had been caused by the loss of his brother.

Yet the blood of the Celts flowed strongly in her veins and she shivered as she walked. She needed to talk to Nick. She needed his strength.

Her Celtic grandmother had peopled her childhood with gods and little people, creatures who were either good or evil. She knew that three was a sacred number to the Celts and everything was done in threes.

Helen had named the crèche after her, and Clive had been crippled and the explosion had killed and maimed dozens of innocent people. Izuba and her family had been part of Toni's life for over a decade, and Wisdom had been murdered. There would be a third tragedy associated with her.

'Mark my words, things always happen in threes, both good and bad.' Her grandmother's grey head had nodded as she wrapped Toni's pet mouse in a pink handkerchief and tucked it into a tea tin ready for burial. 'You'll cry over two other things before the fates are satisfied, my child.'

As a little girl she had trembled when her grandmother spoke of the three bloodthirsty Celtic gods: Esus who needed victims who had been stabbed or hanged; Tentates who waited beneath the cold waters of his sacred pools to receive his drowned victims; and Taranis who claimed prisoners of war who had been burnt alive in reed cages.

The early Celtic priests and Druids were steeped in prophecies and dark mysteries, and thousands of years after the sacred groves had been laid to waste and the priests slaughtered, Toni still believed that both good and evil tidings and events occurred in threes.

Turning to close the wooden gate behind her, Toni noticed that Storchman had followed her. She tucked her grand-mother's prophecies and Justice's curses away into the deep-est recesses of her mind and smiled weakly at him. 'Help your mother,' she said. 'Wisdom was her favourite brother and her big heart is slowly breaking.'

'I will, Miss Toni,' he answered.

She placed her hand on his arm, for the shoulder is the place where the shades rest and they are not to be disturbed. 'I'm very sorry, Storchman. We love your family and feel for you in your sadness.'

'We know and I thank you,' he said, his eyes glistening with unshed tears and, brushing Tracy's hand lightly with his fingers as it rested on the Land-Rover's door, he turned away. He would comfort his mother, but he wanted to question his uncle. He had not mistaken the guilt in Justice's eyes.

The Land-Rover lurched and bucketed as it climbed the bumps and slid into the potholes. Its erratic progress was followed closely by the red-haired policeman walking out of the door of the Shonalanga Police Station. He ran his meaty hand over his freckled scalp and sniffed noisily.

'Come on, kid,' he said to Richard. 'Somewhere, someone knows about this murder and if it takes a fire under every backside in the force and CID we'll find him. Filthy murdering bastards. The book'll not be closed on this one.'

The officers in the station heard with relief his mutters and curses growing faint as he trudged heavily across the fields leaving the purple flowers smeared beneath his heavy boots like blue blood on the brown soil.

CHAPTER

16

S ERGE slammed the pink door of the flat roofed cottage, cocked his finger through the loop of his navy mohair blazer and swung it over his shoulder as he ran lightly down the stairs to his car. He whistled softly to himself and there was a jaunty lilt in his step.

It had been a good idea to visit his new girlfriend on the way home from the airport, he decided. It had bolstered his ego and prepared him to face Toni when he offered Timothy his belated birthday present. He had forgotten to buy Tim a gift when he last returned from Durban, and had had to invent a story about parcels lost on the plane. But this trip he had remembered. He thought about his new beauty. She was a handful, a rare exotic flower propagated from Malay and Dutch stock. A slim yet voluptuous dusky body, deep velvet-brown eyes and a full, ripe, hungry mouth. A warm shudder thrilled down his spine and he clenched his buttocks as he recalled the hunger of her mouth and body. He silently congratulated himself on his excellent decision not to have another permanent mistress after Dana. It had taken a great deal of time and skill to weasel out of that sticky relationship and he had no wish to repeat the performance. He now firmly resisted the urge to visit her seafront apartment. Occasionally he itched for her lewd inventiveness, but was afraid that to scratch would cause a permanent rash. The Cape was renowned for its beautiful girls and he had picked some exquisite flowers recently, a colourful nosegay ranging from the tender, sweet and easily bruised woman to the more robust and hardy. He was a happy man.

His trips to the lush sub-tropical shores of Natal had been

successful. As he searched his pockets for his car key, he smiled at how cleverly he had handled the situation.

Hans' escapade had cost him dearly. It had taken many cheques and a few carefully veiled threats to quieten the tongues, and he had called for the repayment of some old favours. The newspapers had fortunately focused on the part played by the young boys at the party, the prominent party member had dominated the headlines for days until, unable to endure the publicity and the shame, he hanged himself with a necktie in his garage; but Hans Wold's name had not appeared and Serge was satisfied that the matter was safely buried.

His complacency had been momentarily shattered when Hans phoned to say that the burial site was about to be desecrated.

'Serge, Serge,' his voice had wavered, 'it was all for nothing, yes? The people from the papers, they are searching again and asking questions.'

'You've nothing to worry about, Hans, old friend,' he had soothed. 'Everything has been fixed.'

'No, Serge, no,' wailed Hans. 'It is all worse, yes? One of the men at the party, one of the men who had the young boys, has just died.' Hans dropped his voice. 'AIDS, Serge. That will make them mad for news, yes?'

Public concern exploded and mushroomed and all were affected by the fall-out. The shockwaves extended to all levels of society.

He had been unable to endure the sight of Hans' haggard face or the sound of his voice whining for help, and had sent him on an extended overseas trip. He was desperate to save himself and his friend from the contamination, and finally persuaded the reporters to take their pens and lenses to another site. Carefully and quickly he again covered the traces which led to Hans' participation in the party of drugs and child abuse. He had repaid his debt to Hans tenfold.

Whilst he was in Natal interring the information about Hans, he paid another visit to his reluctant informant and had finally convinced him that it was in his best interests to continue to supply information about illegal shipments of ivory and horn. The implied threat that his home could burn down or his wife and children be molested made him reasonable.

Finding the key and opening the car door, Serge checked that the red parcel for Tim was still firmly lodged on the back seat. He lifted a hand in farewell to the lovely face segmented by the sash window of the pink cottage.

* * *

Toni was curled up on Timothy's bed and they were deep in discussion about the possibility of Mr Plod taking the car away from Noddy because he thought it belonged to Big Ears.

'I don't like Mr Plod,' decided Timothy. 'He's bad.'

Toni hugged her son, delighting in the fresh, soapy smell of his skin.

'No, my precious. Mr Plod is doing his duty. Policemen are good people, but sometimes they have to do things which we don't like and then we think that they're bad. They're there to look after us and Mr Plod is only making sure that Noddy has not taken Big Ears' car.'

Timothy stroked the picture of the red car and Noddy, but looked suspiciously at Mr Plod's angry face. The squeaking of the nursery door startled them and Timothy watched wide-eyed as an enormous parcel wrapped in pillar-box red paper covered with tumbling yellow bears appeared through the opening.

'Happy birthday to you, Happy birthday, dear Timmy, Happy birthday to you,' sang Serge as he walked to the bed carrying the box.

Timothy scrambled out of bed, throwing aside the Noddy book, and launched himself into Serge's arms.

'Daddy, a present, my present,' he shrieked. 'Thank you, Daddy.' He flung his arms around Serge's neck and kissed him. Serge felt an unexpected rush of tenderness for his son. He hugged the child, surprised at how quickly the mewling baby had grown into a long-limbed boy. Soon he would be able to take him on some of his trips, teach him the principles of running a successful business and initiate him into the pleasures of manhood. His mind raced ahead. His business would become Balser & Balser or Balser & Son.

It had taken Serge five years to realise that he had an heir, and as he held his son he resolved to spend more time with him. He would be a father to him and mould him into a Balser man.

256

He gave the child a final squeeze and put him on the floor to open his gift.

Serge turned to Toni, including her in the sudden warmth he felt for his son. 'Hello, my honey,' he said, his voice sweet and melting as hot chocolate icing. 'I've brought something for the mother of my son.' He kissed her lightly on the cheek and handed her a small flat box. He had bought it for Dana to mark the third anniversary of their love affair, but he had ended their affair before the anniversary was celebrated.

The time Toni dreaded had arrived. As she opened the gift she watched Serge with Timothy, Serge's rounded chin rested tenderly on the small, curly head. His pale eyes were soft with warmth and pride as he hugged his son, and as she stared at the shining gold heart and chain which nestled on the blue velvet bed of the box she felt nauseous.

Perhaps this time he truly meant to change, he truly meant to spend more time with her and Timothy. Perhaps Serge was at last prepared to accept the responsibilities of a husband. But it was too late. Nick was her future.

'Do you like it, hon?' asked Serge, resting his hand on the nape of her neck as she bent over the gift. She was saved the necessity of replying by squeals of ecstasy from Timothy who had torn the wrapping off his present.

'Look, Mummy, look. It's a train.'

'Oh, isn't it lovely, Tim? You're a lucky little man. Look, it has houses, bridges, tunnels and stations,' burbled Toni. 'Tomorrow you and Daddy can set it out.'

'No, now, Mum, now,' pleaded Timothy.

'It's past your bedtime, my big boy. You can start on it early in the morning,' she said firmly.

'Let him play with it, hon,' interjected Serge, laughing. 'After all, it's his birthday present.'

'Perhaps, but it's certainly no longer his birthday and I don't want to break his routine. The two of you can spend the morning assembling it.'

Serge started to object and changed his mind.

'Into bed, Tim-Tim,' she said. 'Quickly now.'

Looking from one to the other and finding no ally in his father, Timothy capitulated and climbed into bed, but not

257

before the huge box had been placed on a chair where he could see it.

Toni pulled the fluffy blue blankets up over Timothy's shoulders, quickly covering the box which she had dropped on to the bed. She could not accept the necklace and did not want to wear it. She kissed her son softly and closed the bedroom door.

Serge was waiting for her in the sitting room. 'I'm sorry that I was late, Toni, but there was some urgent business to attend to on the way home from the airport,' he apologised. She nodded her acceptance and he put his hands on her shoulders and drew her close. 'I meant what I said on the phone, honey. I'm going to spend more time with you and Timothy. We've a great son and I'm going to be a good father and husband.' He ran his lips over her hair and down her neck.

'Where's your necklace, honey?' he asked, taking his lips away from her bare skin. 'Let me put it on for you,' he smiled at her.

Toni licked her lips and stepped away from him, certain that he could hear the pounding of her heart.

'I can't wear your gift, Serge.'

'Of course you can, honey. I want to see you wear it every day, the chain around your lovely neck and the heart resting close to yours.' He ran his hand lightly over her breasts and Toni recoiled involuntarily. Serge stared at her.

'Serge,' she stammered, 'Serge, I must . . . We have to . . . '

His pale eyes iced and narrowed and she recognised the early warnings of an approaching storm. Her carefully prepared speeches breaking the news gently and rationally vanished like birds scuttling for shelter from the rain.

'I want a divorce,' she croaked, fear breaking her voice. The silence swirled and thickened. Toni's lungs squeezed closed. She breathed in short, shallow gasps and, after a quick glance at Serge's face, the handsome lines marred with the ugly bloating of rage and disbelief, the muscles in his neck rigid and his nostrils widely flared, she kept her eyes on the ground.

The strands in the carpet spun in swirling rings and she concentrated on making them stop.

'You. You . . . want . . . a . . . divorce?' he hissed, spacing his words carefully. 'You! How dare you! How bloody dare you talk to me like this!' He dug his fingers cruelly into her shoulders, lifted and shook her.

Toni hung limp in his grasp.

'You'd make a laughing stock of me in front of my friends.' He shook her again, her toes barely skimming the carpet, and she clenched her jaws, grinding her molars to prevent herself from screaming. 'You, you bitch. Take my son from me? Never. Do you hear me? Never.' His spittle flicked her face and she blinked. 'I'll see you dead before you do this to me, you sanctimonious little bitch.'

'Serge,' she begged. 'Please, Serge.'

'Don't you talk to me,' he said. 'I don't want to hear another word. Not a word.' He pushed her viciously. 'Get out of my sight.'

She spun away and her feet caught on the step. There was a dull thud as her head hit the wall and her limp body folded like a paper fan, quickly and quietly. Serge looked down at her with all the compassion of an eagle contemplating a rabbit impaled on its sharp talons.

'Divorce,' he snorted as he stepped over her and walked arrogantly into the sitting room.

The sound of liquid gurgling and the high clink of a crystal glass filtered slowly into Toni's consciousness. Tentatively she touched her head and her slender fingers ran over the bump in her hairline. The hair around the bump was damp and matted and Toni looked at her crimson fingers in horror. She rolled on to her hands and knees and stood up painfully, leaving red fingerprints streaked across the cream rug. She gasped at her reflection in the hallway mirror.

The skin had been smeared from her cheek and the high cheekbone was already shadowed. Blood had seeped from the cut in her scalp and had run in streamers to her mouth. Nervously, like an antelope consuming all traces of blood to protect its newly born from predators, she licked away the salty trickles, afraid that the sight of blood would inflame Serge.

The sound of his heavy footsteps ringing on the tiles surrounding the fireplace galvanised her into action and she hobbled to the front door, leaving it open in her haste.

'Divorce? I'll show you,' he threatened as, fortified with a glass of brandy, he walked back to where she had fallen. He scuffed at the red fingermarks on the carpet. 'So, you've gone running to your precious son again,' he sneered and turned to walk down the passage.

A cold breeze flicked a wave of pale blond hair across his forehead and he glanced at the front door. He smiled as he slunk into the night. Toni heard him coming, cursing and stumbling over the iron stakes set into the corners of the vegetable beds. She burrowed deeper into the black hedge which separated the compost heap from the garden, disturbing the world of insects which had settled there.

Her cheek was pressed into the ground and the rasping of legs and soft scuffling of bodies and wings was magnified. In her fevered imagination it sounded as if an army was massing under her head, and only her fear of being discovered by Serge kept her immobile and silent.

'Pray, my child,' her old grandmother had advised. 'You're never alone. There is always someone up there to hear you. When you're afraid or unhappy talk to Him.'

Silently Toni followed her grandmother's instructions. Her eyes screwed up tightly, she prayed.

The footsteps stopped. A film of cold sweat blended with the dried blood on her forehead and dripped into her open mouth. She prayed desperately, prayed that he would not see her dark shape huddled in the hedge, prayed that he would not hear the whispers and scratchings of the milling insects she had disturbed and prayed above all that he would stop searching for her.

The silence was broken by the sudden crash of glass on the brick pathway. He had smashed the empty glass. Toni started and trapped the screams which were layered in her throat by biting her knuckles until the pain brought tears to her eyes.

A crimson firefly flew in a wide arc across the blackness a few feet from where she lay and her stomach churned queasily. It was the glowing tip of a cigarette. Serge had held it cupped at his side while he stood quietly listening and he was now smoking. The red glow of the cigarette moved away and Toni swallowed, gagging on the warm blood in her mouth. Serge was walking away from her. She watched the red tip become smaller and, as she was about to lift her head, the glow vanished.

He had stopped a few yards away, once again cupping the cigarette, waiting to hear the rustle of movement. Serge was stalking her with all the stealth and cunning of a wounded buffalo. He was quartering the ground, circling, listening and lying in ambush, confident that his prey would become careless.

* * *

Finally Toni's contorted limbs had ceased to scream in agony and her skin had accepted the invasion of slithering creatures. She had watched as the lights were switched off in the house but had remained silent, afraid to move, in case it was merely a ploy of Serge's to lull her into revealing her hiding place.

As she lay in the hedge waiting for dawn and the courage daylight brings, the woman became once again a young girl sitting in the dark with her mother, waiting for the bars to close and watching for the squint eyes of her stepfather's Peugeot to weave erratically into the driveway. She once again saw herself running into her bedroom, her fists clenched to stop them trembling, her eyes screwed up until purple whorls filled her vision. She heard herself praying and plea-bargaining. But Friday nights when her stepfather came home drunk and belligerent, her Baby Jesus was too busy to listen to a little girl's prayers.

Toni shuddered as the past and present fused and she clenched her teeth to stop herself whimpering.

The darkness had paled and the sliver of a pallid moon was slipping behind the mountain when Toni fearfully crawled to Izuba's rooms. She scratched on the windowpane, feeling certain that Serge's eyes were boring into her back as he stood behind the darkened windows of the house.

The door was opened and sobbing with relief she threw herself into Izuba's arms. 'Ungumtukathixo, Miss Toni,' gasped the woman, staring at Toni's bloodied and bruised face and filthy clothes. 'Who has done this terrible thing to you? Who?'

'Close the door quickly,' begged Toni. 'Lock it, Izuba, lock it.' As the key slid its oiled tongue into the groove Toni crumpled into a chair.

Izuba bustled into the kitchenette and the air was loud with clicks as she cursed everyone and anyone who could have harmed her Toni.

'Izuba,' said Toni, gratefully sipping the steaming tea sticky with sugar, 'I need to stay here for a while. I don't want to go into the house. Timothy has a new present and will play with it happily when he wakes. Unless he calls, leave him in his room until Mr Balser has gone. I'm sure that he'll leave early this morning.'

'Miss Toni, my heart is heavy as the rocks which hold back the water in the Gxara river. Child of God,' she wailed quietly, and sank to the floor at Toni's feet, her fluffy dressing gown billowing up and settling around her immense body like the winter coat of a brown bear.

'Tell me,' she urged, 'who has done this evil?'

Toni hesitated but she had been strong for too long. There had been too many nights when she had run into the garden to escape from Serge, too many nights when she had raised her hand to knock at Izuba's door and look for comfort only to turn away, her pride not allowing her to implicate her friend. Serge's reaction to her request for a divorce and the night of terror had drained her and the compassion in Izuba's voice soothed her raw and torn nerves. As Izuba took Toni's cold hand and warmed it between her own, her reserve broke and the words tumbled out.

'That, Izuba, is the story,' she ended. 'It's over.' Tears trickled unheeded down her cheeks. 'Today I'll take Timothy and go to Miss Helen in Hout Bay. I'm afraid to stay here. I'm afraid that he'll kill me.' Wearily she rubbed her smarting eyes. 'If Mr Nick phones before I can contact him, please tell him where I've gone,' she said softly.

Izuba studied Toni's face, the rings under her eyes smudged by a giant's sooty thumb, her swollen cheek dark with blood, the purple and green bruises glowing like putrescent meat and the beautiful blue eyes dead, lifeless as stagnant swamp water.

She nodded. 'Yes, Miss Toni, it is better that you take Intakumba, my little flea, and that you rest with Miss Helen.

I will tell Mr Nick. He is a good man and you have need of friends with strength.'

She climbed ponderously to her feet and took Toni's mug. 'I will stay here, so I can watch Mr Serge.' A stream of Xhosa invective followed his name.

Serge had left. Timothy, ecstatic at the unexpected holiday, was happily packing the toys he wanted to take to his beloved Uncle Clive and Aunt Helen. Toni was peering into the bathroom mirror trying to camouflage the bruises and cuts with heavy make-up when she heard Izuba shrieking. 'Ungumtukathixo, Miss Toni, come, come quickly.' Toni dropped the tube of beige cream and ran to the glass doors opening on to the patio. She tugged at the wooden frame of the sliding door and winced as her nail snapped and tore down into the flesh.

Izuba was kneeling in front of a pile of sodden clothes and Toni's childhood treasures which were lying on the lawn. Toni gave a small, stricken cry and knelt on the wet grass.

She let the white silk splashed with pink cabbage roses ripple through her fingers. Serge had been busy. The carefully pleated bodice had been slashed and the skirt hung in tatters. Toni smoothed the silk across her knees, carefully fitting the petals of the roses and the soft green leaves together.

She had worn this dress the night they celebrated their engagement. She had believed herself to be the happiest and most fortunate woman ever born. Serge loved her and she was going to be Mrs Balser. The stars had been brightly buffed, the sea burnished to a sheet of silver and her feet had twinkled in gold ballet slippers as she danced. She was young and idealistic and her world was wonderful.

With a gasp she let the dress slip off her lap and cradled the battered head of a doll. The Shirley Temple doll with its mop of golden curls and deeply dimpled cheeks had sat on a chair beside her bed as a child and on a corner of her desk at university. It had been given to her by her loved but only dimly remembered grandfather shortly before his death in a mine explosion on the Copperbelt and having the doll in her room made her feel close to him.

Serge had jeered at such fanciful nonsense and she had packed the doll away. Now the red smocked dress lay tangled

263

in the doll's broken arms and legs. Toni shuddered. Unable to vent his frustration and rage on her, he had torn the doll apart. The cold terror of the night reached out wet fingers and held her.

'Izuba,' she said, 'Izuba, please help me.' The comforting figure of her friend and maid close beside her, Toni controlled her agitation and quickly sorted through the torn clothing. She bundled a pile of tulle and net, white and frothy as lacy sea-fret, into Izuba's arms, and tossed onto the heap a Juliet cap of seeded pearls attached to a mist of fine white lace. Her wedding dress had been added to the bonfire of her dreams, and her thick cotton undergraduate gown hung in strips over Izuba's arm like black seaweed.

Timothy's christening robe, a tiny confection of exquisite handmade lace, lay on the pile, stained and torn like a dirty handkerchief.

'Izuba,' she said as she placed the robe on top of her gown, 'give these to one of the work groups in Shonalanga. I'm sure that they'll be able to use the strips for something.' She swallowed a sob as she picked up fragments of dirty paper, all that was left of her diplomas and her university degree.

Serge, the wonderful young man who had opened her eyes and ears to the beauty of art and music, had vanished. The exciting young lover whose arms had enfolded her as the haunting loveliness of Beethoven's Violin Concerto filled the room had gone. The young sophisticate who had so impressed the naïve girl from central Africa, who enriched her senses with the golden glory of Van Gogh's *Sunflowers* and the dreaming gentleness of Monet's *Waterlilies*, had changed.

He had been a dreamer encased in a pure white egg and he had hatched into the fat larva of a hedonistic young man. For a time he had spun and rested in a warm cocoon of respectability and domesticity, but now he had changed into an unstable man whose emotions dominated his actions.

Prickles of apprehension stabbed into Toni's scalp and she glanced around the room uneasily. Broad washes of sunlight carpeted the light birch floors and the deep-throated cooing of pigeons filtered in through the open windows. Everything was tranquil, yet she felt threatened.

'Listen to your feelings, child,' the quavering voice rang in

Toni's ears. 'You were born with a caul over your face and will sense trouble. Ignore your feelings and you'll regret it.'

Toni sprang to her feet holding the shredded documents. 'Quickly, Izuba, bring Timothy. We must leave.'

Toni had thrown the suitcases into the boot of her car, hugged her golden ridgeback and was tapping the steering wheel impatiently when the scarlet Ferrari swung into the yard and Serge strode across to her. Leaning into the window, he pinched her wrist cruelly between his fingers. 'So, my little honeyed bitch, you're running away.' He leaned across and switched off the ignition. 'Not so fast, Mrs Balser. We have unfinished business.'

His breath was stale and the fumes of brandy were sweet and sickening. Toni pressed back into the seat, trying to distance herself from the stubbled chin and malevolent eyes.

'Daddy, Daddy.' Timothy ran into the yard followed closely by Izuba. 'Can we play with my train today?' He threw his arms around Serge's legs and hugged hard.

'There'll be time for you,' Serge hissed as he withdrew his head from the window. His hand remained on her wrist and he twisted it as if wringing a chicken's neck. She moaned softly.

'Hello, son,' he said, bending down to kiss Timothy. 'Of course we can play with your new train. Tell Mummy to come inside and we can unpack the box.' The pleading in Toni's eyes activated Izuba and, scooping Timothy up in her strong arms, she carried him to the car.

'Come, little Intakumba. Miss Toni will be late if you don't get into the car quickly.' She clipped the seat belt around him and closed the door.

Serge stepped forward but Izuba had walked around the front of the car and was standing with her broad back to him, shielding Toni. Toni looked up into the round black face, the dark eyes wet with tears.

'Thank you,' she whispered.

Izuba fondled Chops' drooping ears. He sat against her thigh, his head hanging low. '*Salani kakuhle*. Goodbye and go well,' she called as she watched the white car drive away.

Serge looked at the large woman, impressive in her suppressed rage and dignity, and walked into the house in silence.

James Swayne, Toni's father, swung off the road in a billowing cloud of dust to avoid hitting a cockerel, gleaming in his plumage of iridescent green and black. His bright red comb bobbed importantly as he clucked and raced after a dowdy speckled hen. Dust, fine as talcum powder, coated the dark green body of the Land-Rover and he sneezed as the dry spray tickled his nostrils.

He bumped back on to the road, the wheels jarring over the ragged edges where the red soil had been washed away leaving the grey tarmac suspended like cliff ledges.

The old man loved the dry, dusty, nondescript town of Maun, the gateway to his beloved swamps and his home, which was set in the heart of the crystal-clear waterways. He braked and swerved automatically for fowls, dogs and dust-coated children rolling rusty bicycle wheels down the road. He firmly believed that the evils of civilisation outweighed the benefits, and the road, patterned with tin cans and paper, reinforced his feelings.

He grinned as he passed the peach and white buildings of the hospital, recalling the day he had brought Toni to the clinic to have a sample of blood taken and tested for sleeping sickness as she had been badly bitten by tsetse flies. Her face white with trepidation, she had struggled to release her thumb from the medical officer's iron grasp as she saw the syringe hurtle down from behind his ear. She had nursed her thumb for days, swearing that the needle had touched bone it had been plunged in so deeply, and the little hospital headed her list of places to be avoided.

The old man sighed and glanced at his daughter. The bruises had faded but her spirit had been battered and she sat silently beside him, staring blindly out of the window. Timothy, tired by the long flight from the Cape, was curled up on a mattress on the floor of the Land-Rover, snuffling softly in his sleep.

He did not attempt to talk to Toni. He knew that the beauty and silence of the swamps would wash away her fear and pain and he was content to wait.

Helen's telegram, sent without Toni's or Nick's knowledge, had shocked him deeply. In her distress and fear for Toni's safety, she had told the old man about Serge and Nick. In response he had spent an exhausting week down in the Cape.

He had decided to meet both the men in his daughter's life before letting her know that he was in the Cape. It had been a wise decision.

He had been prepared to dislike and despise Nick Houghton and to warn him away from his daughter. He believed that any man who started a liaison with a married woman was a cad and deserved to be emasculated, but to his surprise he had liked Nick immediately. He admired his forthright manner and lack of pretence. His sincerity and love for Toni were indisputable and the old man warmed to him.

After forsaking the political halls of power Jim Swayne had sat on countless boards and committees and had been chairman of some of the most powerful and prestigious companies in the land. Though he had retired and now preferred to fish in the clear waters of the great Okavango delta, instead of the murky waters of commerce, he had lost none of his flair for angling.

Serge Balser was a rock to be split and he had devoted all of his prodigious energy to the task.

He approached the job of breaking him in the age-old tradition of stonesmiths. The flames of his anger cracked Serge's composure: his anger over the treatment of his only child, his anger at Serge's demand for custody of Timothy, his anger at his refusal to open a fund for Timothy's education, and his anger at denying Toni any part of the estate or her personal possessions. The flames were fanned by the recently acquired knowledge that profit from the illicit export of poached ivory tusks was adding to Serge's wealth. Like his daughter, Jim Swayne abhorred the profiteers in the ivory trade. His heart ached for the Africa he loved and he hated Serge for the part he was playing in the possible extinction of the great mammals.

He then fractured Serge's obduracy with the cold water of threats. Pacing up and down the sitting room in the country hotel, Serge had bellowed and blustered, but the old man had been implacable. He churned out names of Serge's informants in the neighbouring black states, and the names of his own contacts in the governments of these states. He cited dates when the illegal ivory had been exported, the amounts shipped and the sources of the faked CITES certificates.

Serge crumbled, but the old man was not satisfied. He named his friends and contacts in the Internal Revenue office, spoke knowledgeably of income tax evasion and manipulation of foreign exchange, all tender subjects to a government battling to keep a healthy economy in the face of sanctions and the withdrawal of major business concerns.

The disintegration was complete. Serge capitulated. David Anstey, alerted by the old man, was asked to draw up the divorce papers and he accepted the brief with delight.

Toni's father had then driven to Hout Bay to persuade his daughter to spend a few weeks with him in Botswana. Nick urged her to accept the invitation and she tearfully left with Timothy.

As they left the dusty town of Maun behind them, he glanced again at his daughter; her head was resting on the hard back of the seat, her eyes were closed and her raven curls bounced around her cheeks as the Land-Rover jolted along the calcrete road. He stroked her cheek gently with the back of his hand and then turned his attention to the road. James had chosen to drive to his cottage, a long arduous trip on bad roads, instead of flying up in his Cessna as he needed the time to talk to Toni.

He had wanted to camp for the night at Nata, where the river mouth was smothered with millions of flamingos, floating as if without legs like rosy clouds at dawn, but it was getting late and they stopped just before the village of Tsau, a dry, characterless place which had been the capital of Ngamiland before the Tswana moved to Maun.

Toni awoke as the van left the road and jolted over dead branches and rocks and skirted spring-hare holes, driving deep into the sparse bush to find a suitable camping site. She massaged her neck and a smile flickered over her lips as she looked at her father. The stubble on his chin was coated with grey dust and his silver hair stood out in tufts over his ears. He looked like a shop-soiled cuddly toy.

Sensing her smile, he put his large hand over hers and his periwinkle-blue eyes twinkled. 'To work, my young lady,' he growled. 'We've a camp to set up.' He switched off the ignition and the Land-Rover rumbled into silence.

'Dad,' said Toni, breathing in the dry smell of the African

bush, pungent with wild thyme. 'Thank you, Dad. It's so good to be here.'

He squeezed her hand and kissed her on the cheek. 'It's wonderful to have you, Nuffy,' he answered, using a baby name which, with its connotation of smelly nappies,had embarrassed her deeply as a young teenager, but which she now accepted as a mark of his love. 'Let's wake this young sleepyhead. He can help me collect firewood.'

Timothy awoke with the instant alertness peculiar to young children and was soon banging on dead branches with a stick, like a demented drummer, to frighten any scorpions or snakes lurking under them before dragging them across the sand to where his grandfather was building a fire.

Content that the smoke-blackened kettle was hissing and that the cooking pot was standing firmly on its legs in the coals, he stirred the chicken simmering in a sauce of dried *legopo*, a delicious white truffle which grows in the desert, and nudged the potatoes and pumpkin deeper into the coals. Then, taking his grandson by the hand, he trudged with him through the sand to the river, light fishing rods over their shoulders.

Timothy stopped to untangle his fishing line from the branches of a young marula tree. He tugged impatiently and one of the branches broke with a sharp report. The old man put down his rod and came to help his grandson, deftly untangling the white nylon from the blunt-tipped twigs.

'Stupid tree,' said Timothy, smacking the pale bark.

'Not a stupid tree, Tim. This is a very clever tree,' corrected his grandfather. 'It has a fruit like a plum, and the plums can be made into beer and also into jelly.'

Timothy's eyes lit up at the mention of jelly.

'The old tusker warthogs break the stones inside and eat them, and all the wild animals gather beneath the huge marulas when the fruit is ripe, especially the old elephants. They love the fruit.'

'Just like my friends at my birthday, Grandpa,' said Timothy.

Jim reeled in the line and handed the rod to Timothy.

'That's right, son. So remember, it's a very special tree.'

Timothy put the rod over his shoulder and hugged the tree trunk. 'Sorry, tree,' he said and ran after his grandfather.

Jim plunged his hand into the pocket of his khaki pants

and brought out a handful of mangetti nuts, one of the delicious staple foods of the Bushmen. Timothy squealed with delight. He had tasted these 'Botswana peanuts' on his previous visit and was as addicted to them as were the Bushmen.

The boiling water gurgled and spluttered as Toni held the kettle over the green basin. She hefted up the jerry can of cold water and decided that she could use half of it. Testing the temperature her finger turned red instantly, and she judged the water to be perfect for a bush bath.

Knotting a thin towel around her waist she knelt over the basin, the evening air cool on her naked body, and washed away the dust and perspiration. The first mosquitoes were homing in on her warm flesh as she smoothed on baby lotion and struggled into her blue tracksuit. She scratched at the red lump on her buttock, the anti-coagulant injected by the female anopheles making it itch.

Slipping on a pair of flat-soled boots she tied a scarf around her damp curls and dabbed mosquito-repellent on her face and hands. Refilling the basin with warm water she was about to call for Timothy when her father and son arrived, empty-handed but brimming with stories of the one that got away.

Listening to her son describing he monster fish as she undressed him and stood him in the basin for a quick top and tail, she realised that a great white death shark must have found its way into the river. Nothing else could fit the description Timothy was painting and she exclaimed often and loudly, making one small boy very happy.

Later that evening, Toni scoured the cooking pots with coarse river sand and placed a pot of cocoa on the coals. She then warmed her hands around a tin mug and, inhaling the rich chocolate aroma, found it easy to talk about her life with Serge.

The old man was a good listener, grunting agreement when necessary, staring intently into the fire as the light breeze fanning the flames painted fanciful creatures on the red coals. She spoke of her husband and as her words dissolved in the night air she felt the hurt and terror melt away. A fiery-necked nightjar unable to resist the clear moonlight called, and she paused to listen, fitting in the litany 'Good Lord, deliver us' to the descending quavering rhythm of the bird's call.

It was an evocative call in the African bush on a night bright with silver light. Listening, she recalled another time when a moon had painted patterns on naked skin as it filtered through lace curtains, and another night bird had cried as she lay cradled in Nick's arms.

She continued speaking, but Nick replaced Serge, and she found that she needed to tell her father about her love. He stood up and refilled their mugs, relieved that it had not been necessary for him to raise the subject of Nick Houghton.

She paused in her recital to sip the drink, the hot enamel mug burning the soft inside of her lips, and James thought of Nick Houghton, the tall, sensitive man who had come to see him at his hotel.

Listening to his daughter talk, the old man was pleased that she was not aware that he had spent almost a week in the Mother City before he went to Hout Bay to collect her and Timothy. She was very protective of his right to enjoy his retirement, and would have been mortified to discover that he had been involved in some dirty fighting on her behalf.

A huge hunter's moon stood high over the trees, outlining them in charcoal and silvering the sand into opalescence, by the time Toni, her catharsis by confession completed, hugged her father tightly, luxuriating in his love, and snuggled into her green sleeping bag beside the fire.

He threw a fresh log on to the fire, pulled his sleeping bag up over his shoulders, and before the fountain of cadmium sparks had cooled and fallen as smutty powder his eyes had closed and he was asleep.

Toni lay on her back looking up at the heavens hung so heavily with stars that they seemed to touch the ground, closing like the spangled curtains of a four-poster around her. In the distance, the rising whoops of a pack of hyenas chilled the silence. They were often found near villages where they scavenged the offal and faeces. She loved listening to the howling of the packs at night, but their maniacal shrieking and chittering when they were in a feeding frenzy sickened her.

In the branches high above her head, a tiny, earless pearl-spotted owl called softly, the end notes slurring like a drunkard whose tongue is too heavy to form sounds. She strained her eyes trying to see the little body pressed against the bark of

271

the trunk, but the moonlight added to its camouflage and it remained hidden.

She struggled to keep awake, revelling in the sounds of the night, but she was lulled by the soft splutter of the fire and the melancholy drawn-out call of the dikkop. 'That sad bird, mourning for the dead he is, wails for the departed,' had been her grandmother's assessment of the nocturnal bird. She closed her eyes.

During the night a procession of insects marched over the sleeping bags, a black mole snake slithered past, keeping well away from the fire, and a lone spotted hyena left its spoor in the sand, the front feet supporting the massive fore-quarters splayed wide and deep, followed by the smaller spoor of the back feet. The deep silence of the bush enfolded the figures curled up around the dying fire and they slept undisturbed.

* * *

The days passed all too swiftly and they spent the last night of their journey camped near the great Tsodilo Hills. They wanted to watch the hills born in the soft light of early morning and Toni gasped in delight as the saffron fingers of daylight gently turned down the grey blankets from the great rock outcrops which rose sheer and magnificent from the sands of the Kalahari Desert. They sat in silence in the Land-Rover watching the hills as the morning star moved slowly across the sky. A lovely star, pitied by the Bushmen because it is fated to cross the sky every day before the withering sun and can never enjoy shade.

The hills formed and took shape in the silver light, and warmed from cold blues and mauves to rich red and ochre. The echoing whispers of the wind as it whistles through the masses of weathered and tumbled rock gave birth to the legend that the spirits of the hills talk to each other, but the morning was windless and the spirits were mute. The magic and wonder of dawn passed with the swiftness of a magician's sleight of hand and soon the sun was bright in the blue African heavens.

They left the Land-Rover and trudged through the sand to the little Bushman camp near the hills, but it was deserted.

'The old man will have to wait for his smoke,' said James,

tucking the orange packet of tobacco back into his pocket. 'He's probably joined the men on a hunt. He'll kill himself tracking and running after game in this heat. Old fool.'

'I was hoping to see him,' said Toni ruefully. 'I haven't spoken to him for so long.'

'And you'd like some more of his stories for your articles,' teased her father, putting his arm around her shoulders. 'We'll be back, Nuffy. Come, let's find a guide to show young Timothy the rock-paintings before we melt.'

Time passed quickly as they marvelled at the wealth of paintings which covered most of the rocky walls.

Lifting her head to look at a gemsbuck painted on the wall high above her head, its long pointed horns spiralled like a staircase, she caught her breath as she saw her son scramble along a narrow ledge of rock.

He had found a new hero, and the childlike Bushman guide had an adoring shadow. His eyes crinkled as he turned around to check that Timothy was negotiating the tricky overhang and he clicked at him in his native tongue. Timothy, not understanding Tswana or Dzuoasi, the Bushman's language, answered in Xhosa. They understood each other instinctively and Timothy faithfully copied every move made by the small man.

Toni exhaled in relief as their guide led Timothy down from the ledge, and she and her father ran to catch up with the two small figures as they disappeared into the tangled maze of rocks in search of a water seep. It was a tearful boy who a few hours later hugged his new friend and assured him that he would return to the hills very soon.

The heart-shaped face with its high cheekbones was wrinkled in concern and delving into his duiker-skin loincloth, the golden-skinned man carefully unwrapped a tortoise shell. It had been scraped clean of flesh and the open end beneath the tail plugged with a mixture of mud and grass. He tapped the shreds of tobacco on to his wrinkled hand and gave the empty snuffbox to Timothy.

The boy's tears vanished as suddenly as spring hares plunging into burrows and he ran to the Land-Rover, returning with a bright-orange glucose stick which he gave his friend. The guide licked it tentatively, his face split into a wide grin and his slanted eyes disappeared beneath the folded lids of skin. Wild honey was their great treat and this stick was as sweet as honey.

Toni looked back as the Land-Rover ground slowly through the burning sand. The small yellow figure stood motionless, dwarfed by the towering ramparts of rock which shimmered and blurred in the scorching heat.

The pale blue sky hung listlessly over the hills, but the Bushmen knew that the cornflower vastness was webbed with invisible threads, one of which touched the ground at the Tsodilo Hills allowing the Gauwasi, the spirits of the dead, to slide to earth and shoot tiny poisoned arrows into people who were to die. The legends and superstitions were what made Africa mystical and Toni felt a deep surge of love for its wildness and its people. As the figure swayed in the dancing mirage and the hills were lost in the clouds of dust towering high behind the Land-Rover, her heart ached for a world which did not begin to understand the beauty and complexities of the Dark Continent, countries which bayed like wild dogs, each running up in turn to tear pieces out of her living body with legislation and sanctions. Weakening the beautiful, strong creature with their impractical and short-sighted demands until finally bones and skin would be all that was left of a harsh and entrancing land.

Like a horse breaking into a gallop as it scents its stable, so the old man pressed down hard on the accelerator and the Land-Rover lurched and bounced along the sandy road to Sepupa. They would leave the Land-Rover in a mud and thatch garage and wind their way through the swamps by boat to James's cottage. He wanted to watch the sun set over the swamps from his verandah that night.

He loved and needed the sounds of Africa, the wild haunting cries of the regal fish eagles resplendent in glossy brown and white, and the bellows and grunts of the massive hippos as they wallowed in the muddy shallows and travelled the well-worn hippo paths on the sandy bottoms of the swamps. He revelled in the beauty of the cold pearl-grey skies before sunrise and the feathery heads of the papyrus reeds etched black against the fiery sunsets. He clung tenaciously to the small portion of Africa as yet untouched by the grasping fingers of civilisation.

Toni smoothed down the tuft of hair behind his ear only to watch it spring back. She smiled. 'It's been a wonderful trip, Dad,' she said. 'I only realise how much I miss the peace and beauty of the bush when I'm back here.'

James grinned and held the bouncing wheel with one hand as he hugged her to him. 'You were born in the wilds, Nuff, and like a bush baby you'll always be happy in the bushveld.' He glanced at his daughter and breathed a prayer of thanks. The nervous tic which had quivered the delicate skin beneath her eye had gone. The lines which had strained and tugged at her face had relaxed and her eyes, reflecting the clear blue of the skies, sparkled.

His Nuffy was back. She had replaced the bitter and frightened woman he had found in Cape Town. Soon they would be home in the swamps. He hummed tunelessly as the Land-Rover stumbled along the rutted road.

* * *

Thousands of kilometres away Serge Balser tossed restlessly in the large double bed. After his meeting with David Anstey he sought solace in the slim arms of his lover. Her skills relaxed him physically, but his mind was still tense. Toni's father had unearthed names and facts which he believed were well buried.

He knew that the old man had powerful connections, but the depth of his investigation and the speed with which he had completed it had stunned him. His whole business empire was in jeopardy. He would have to extricate himself from all existing deals, pay off his informants and bribe his helpers in official positions into silence. He might have to live overseas for a few years until he was certain that he was safe from prosecution and that the circular ripples caused by the stones Toni's father had hurled into the murky waters of his business life had faded. Then he would have to open new lines of communication and find new informants. It was a daunting task and his hatred for the old man and his daughter oozed like juice from an angry scorpion's tail.

Smoke coiled and twisted over the bed as he lay and plotted his revenge. Toni would suffer and by hurting her he would wound James Swayne. He hoped it would be a mortal wound. His brow furrowed as the smoke thickened.

David Anstey's voice resonated dully in Serge's skull. 'I have before me a list of your holdings in this country, Mr Balser, and a projected list of your holdings overseas.' His grey eyes had glinted as he looked at Serge. 'Investments which do not comply with the foreign exchange restrictions of this country. I've not made a thorough investigation, but if necessary, that can always be arranged.'

Serge had fumed silently, not deigning to look at the face in front of him, the lines set in hard concrete of dislike and disgust. Instead he had stared at the flat-topped mountain, framed by the windows of David Anstey's office.

'A trust fund set up for your son, Timothy, which will fully fund him through school and university. A substantial piece of your capital put into a private account in your wife's name. Your wife to have her choice of gifts and possessions which you have accumulated during your marriage. All her personal effects to be handed to her immediately.'

His voice had tabulated the terms of the divorce as unemotionally as a robot. 'Mrs Toni Balser is to have custody of Timothy.'

'No,' Serge shouted, turning to face Anstey. 'No, never. That bitch'll never have my son.' He felt his anger straining at the taut ropes of self-control and he struggled to prevent the ropes from breaking.

'That bitch is my client, Mr Balser, and as her lawyer I must warn you—'

'She'll not have Timothy,' Serge broke in. 'He's mine.'

David Anstey had punched a grey button on his intercom and waited for a few moments, studying Serge as intently as a chameleon watching a fly.

'Justice,' he said, 'do you have those papers I asked you to find on the foreign exchange regulations, the Internal Revenue and the board commissioned to deal with illicit ivory and tusk transactions? You have. Good. Get Forex for me. Thank you.' He put down the receiver and, still staring at Serge, stretched across his desk, picked up the ashtray and tipped the butts into his wastepaper basket.

'I respect your decision, Mr Balser, though as a lawyer I

would certainly not recommend the course you have chosen.' He stood up and walked across to the large glass windows which he winched open.

'You'll be hearing from the gentlemen in the departments I mentioned to Justice in due course. Good day.'

Serge remained seated.

'Visiting rights,' he said. 'I want visiting rights.'

'With your history of violence towards my client they'll be restricted,' Anstey had answered, swallowing a smile of satisfaction as he lifted a white receiver, cutting off the strident rings.

'If I don't have custody my rights are not to be restricted.'

'Yes? You have Forex? Would you put the call on hold for a moment?' He covered the mouthpiece with his hand. 'I beg your pardon, Mr Balser, I didn't hear what you said. Would you repeat it, please?'

Serge paled. 'I said that it would be satisfactory,' he answered between clenched teeth.

'Ah, Mr Balser,' smiled David. 'That is exactly what I thought you said.' He uncovered the mouthpiece. 'Please cancel the call. Say that I am now in conference. Send in my secretary immediately. I need papers typed and witnessed. Thank you.'

He ran his fingers through his thick grey hair. 'We'll have the terms of the divorce typed and signed now. As it is uncontested and we have agreed on the terms, I should be able to have it finalised by the end of next week.'

At the end of the long afternoon Serge had taken the gold pen from his pocket and with shaking fingers had signed the agreement. The black letters lay across the pages like leeches, sucking at his wealth and lifestyle.

Serge punched the pillows behind his head and ran his fingers over the bedside table, feeling for his cigarettes. He inhaled the drug deep into his lungs and in his mental parade of regrets he included his visit to the local pub that evening. Baby Botha had been the first to see him and had minced across the room, her tight white slacks outlining her crotch like a segmented orange. He could still hear her shrill, breathless voice echoing across the bar, alerting the drinkers.

Dozens of heads turned as one, and he saw the shades of

derision, mingled with concern, in their eyes. Their colossus no longer bestrode the world, and they no longer crept about beneath his feet. He had tumbled and some gloated as he lay at their level.

'Oh, Serge, we've been talking about you,' she lisped. She had pressed herself against him, her huge breasts pushing into his chest like over-inflated water wings. 'You poor, poor thing. We're all so sorry. What a terrible thing for Toni to have done to you.'

She had placed her arm around his shoulders and led him to the bar with all the care of a nurse for the chronically ill. Hans Wold solicitously wiped the top of a bar stool and placed it in the centre of the group for him, and Boots had shown his support by opening dozens of cans of beer and offering to take the Congo man around to Nick's house to beat him into a pulp.

'Come on, Congo man,' pleaded Boots. 'You know that the Good Book says, "Thou shall not commit adultery as the other guy will have an eye for an eye, and the wages of screwing are death." '

'Of sin,' corrected the Congo man.

'What of sin?' queried Boots.

'The Bible says wages of sin, not the wages of screwing,' answered the ex-mercenary.

'Screwing another guy's wife is a sin, especially if the other guy finds out,' insisted Boots.

Congo man sighed and dropped the subject. He seemed strangely reluctant to practise his mercenary skills on Toni's lover. He had been an admirer of Toni's for years, and he had pitied her as he sat in the bar listening to Serge boasting of his sexual exploits. He felt that she deserved better treatment and if he could not be her redeemer he was pleased that it was a man like Nick.

'Let's go, Congo,' urged Boots. 'You can clean him up without even trying.'

'Keep quiet, Boots,' chittered Baby, trying to quieten his appeals. 'I want to hear Serge.' She held a can of beer to Serge's lips and, much as he longed to swat both her and the can away, he drank deeply.

'You're not going to give her anything, are you, Serge? After all, she left you.' Her bottom lip was pink and swollen as she licked at it. 'She had an affair with a friend of yours. She's

278

to blame.' Her words stung with the fiery bite of Matabele ants, and he could feel his lips sticking to his teeth like sellotape as he kept them stretched in a huge smile.

'She'll get what she deserves. Nothing,' he said, seeing the signed pages of the divorce agreement swirling over his friends' heads. 'I'll have this divorce completed within a week and then we'll have a party which'll last for a week,' he boasted. 'Drinks are on me. Tonight I'm celebrating. Give everyone in the house a drink.'

A round of cheers rang out and glasses were hurriedly brought to the bar to be refilled.

Hans picked up the empty glasses and walked to the end of the curved wooden counter where a middle-aged woman was filling glasses and coarsely trading jokes with the men clustered round the bar for free drinks. He whistled to attract her attention and she looked up, wriggling her ill-fitting teeth closer to her gums.

'Hans,' she purred, tugging at the neck of her blouse and exposing a wrinkled cleavage. 'I haven't seen you here since Western Province rugby team lost the last match.' She leaned across the counter, her crossed arms pushing up her breasts. 'I've missed you, big boy,' she said throatily, emphasising the word big.

Hans let his eyes rest on the two mounds of flesh welling up invitingly over the round neckline and felt a stir of interest. I haven't had the old girl for weeks, he thought as he ran his fingers down the cleft between her breasts, and she sure puts her heart and soul into making one happy. He put his face close to hers, his shoulders shielding her from Baby and the men.

'Let's break the drought tonight, yes?' he grunted coarsely and rolled her nipple between his fingers. She nodded, and her eyes gleamed as she refilled the glasses he had placed on the counter. He swaggered back to Serge, eager for the long night of drinking.

Serge had staggered home when the pub closed and now ground out the cigarette roughly in the glass ashtray and squinted at the luminous green hands on his bedside clock. He sighed deeply. He had another four hours to endure before the pink smudges of dawn released him from the seemingly endless night.

As the twittering of birds greeting the new day filtered into his room Serge finalised his plans for vengeance. Timothy was the answer. He would use his son to break their hearts and ruin their lives.

* * *

The bright red face, throat and breast appeared clear and colourful through the high-powered binoculars, and the soft feathers in the broad black band across the bird's lower chest ruffled in the light breeze. It bobbed up and down excitedly, opening and closing its wings as if practising to fly as it whooped, barely giving the second black-collared barbet time to answer with a loud ringing 'dudu', before whooping again.

The binoculars moved across the tree slowly, searching for the second bird, picking up the pendulous sprays of deep wine-coloured flowers, the yellow veins running down the outside of the petals like spilled egg yolk. The unusual salami-shaped fruits weighing more than twice the weight of a new-born baby had not yet formed, and Toni was able to lie on her back under the spreading kigelia tree searching for the barbet's mate, with no danger of having her skull cracked open by a falling sausage fruit. She had just picked up a dull golden belly and a tail edged with yellow high up in the tree when, with a snarling threat note and a fast whirring of wings, the birds broke off their duet and flew away.

She clucked her tongue with annoyance and put down her binoculars as a blue and white plane circled low over the cottage. The old man left the shade of the verandah and stood in the sun waving his arms overhead. The pilot dipped a wing in acknowledgement, circled once more and headed for the grass landing strip a short distance away.

'Nuffy,' called the old man, 'won't you take the Land-Rover and fetch the pilot? My back's aching again. I must be getting old.' He rubbed his back theatrically, rolling his eyes and groaning.

Toni stood up, dusting the grass seeds and dust from her trousers, and looked at her father thoughtfully. He had exhibited no sign of pain an hour ago when he had climbed the leadwood tree, skinning his shins to rescue his blue Persian cat who, Toni was convinced, crawled on to inaccessible branches mewing piteously merely to command his attention.

Jasmine, a long silky-haired aristocrat with an impressive bloodline, had been uprooted from a life of luxury, and had been brought snarling and hissing to the old man's hideaway.

The transformation had been immediate and complete. She had shot out of the travelling basket and, ears laid flat on her round fluffy head, sky-blue eyes slit and tail twitching furiously, had snaked into the undergrowth on her short thick legs and vanished. Old James spent hours combing the bush and had finally resigned himself to the loss of his companion when Jasmine swaggered on to the verandah trailing a green grass snake. The pampered pet had become a killer. She had dropped the bloodied body at his feet, her snub nose quivering in satisfaction and had proceeded to rid her long fur of black jacks and balls of grass seed.

The old man had been speechless. His city-bred lady had become a wanton huntress.

'Right, Dad,' she answered. 'I'll take Timothy.'

'No, no. I'll look after Tim,' he said hurriedly, and seeing the look on his daughter's face he added, 'I promised him that he could drain the honeycombs which I collected this morning.'

Toni was about to pursue the subject when the sudden silence told her that the plane had landed. She ran to the Land-Rover, determined to discover the reason for her father's behaviour when she returned.

Her father's plane was taxiing along the airstrip, whipping up a whirlwind of grass and dust, as she climbed down from the cab. She stood shielding her eyes from the glare of the sun. A wide leather belt clinched in her trousers which hung loosely around her hips. The trauma of the divorce had further whittled away her curves and she stood slim and bare-headed in the hot sun waiting for the pilot. A pair of crowned plovers ran round in circles on their long red legs, squawking frantically, trying to draw the plane away from the vicinity of their nest. Then with deep wingbeats they flew up, and dive-bombed the intruder. The plane turned away and taxied into a thorn enclosure.

Victorious, the birds returned to their nest, screaming defiance at the now stationary aircraft. The pilot untangled himself from the straps and, picking up a briefcase and a tote-bag, closed the door of the plane and strode to the Land-Rover.

Toni watched the approaching figure with disbelief. She now understood why the old man had wanted her to meet the plane. She had believed that she would only see Nick when she returned to the Cape. With a shriek she hurtled across the grass to meet him. They stood moulded as one, lost in the joy of being together.

Her father had invited Nick to spend a fortnight with them. The dates coincided with the second meeting of world conservationists which was to be held in Botswana, and which Nick was to attend. The invitation was perfectly timed and Nick accepted with alacrity.

He took a buff-coloured envelope from his pocket and handed it to her. She read it and flinging the white pages into the air she pirouetted like a crazed ballet dancer. Finally she was free. The divorce was final and Timothy was hers. Nick steadied, and then stopped the spins, and holding her hands tightly in his, he went down on one knee in the dry, dusty grass. He spoke for a long time and she bent down to him and their lips met tenderly.

A troth had been plighted beneath the vast sky of Africa, witnessed by a pair of plovers.

Timothy accepted Nick with the ease and friendliness he extended to all strangers. Toni watched as hand in hand they walked down to the river's edge, deciding whether to use a red-backed spoon to entice the large-mouthed bream or worms or mealie-meal paste. She sat in the boat with them as they cast for fish between the white and mauve waterlilies which lay like drifts of mist on the water. She smiled as Nick told Timothy that the Bushmen believe that the lovely water flowers are the souls of beautiful young girls.

They watched in fascination as the jacanas trotted across the lily-pads with their chicks tucked up under their wings and they laughed as the birds flew away, trailing their long toes behind them like tangled washing lines.

She had listened as Nick painstakingly described the life cycle of the sky-blue dragonfly to Timothy as they sat on the wooden jetty watching the ethereal creatures resting on the reeds, fanning their transparent wings. She knew that Nick had won Timothy's heart when Tim offered to let him go to bed with his beloved teddy bear.

The old man and Nick soon established a ritual. Just before sunset they pulled up green wicker chairs on the verandah and set out a table with a bottle of whisky and two glasses. As the great crimson ball rolled behind the trees and the feathery papyrus heads lining the deep water channel in front of the house turned as black as broken promises, they discussed politics, ecology and world economics, and the old man told Nick scurrilous stories.

Toni usually arrived after putting Timothy to bed to find Nick clutching at his sides incoherent with laughter. James, delighted by Nick's reaction, embroidered his tales outrageously, and Toni who adored her father was hard-pressed to recognise some of the stories.

Night after night Nick and James convulsed with laughter and the big bull hippo scything the thick reeds across the river with the ease of a threshing machine grunted and snorted in response to the noise. Occasionally in the distance a lion would roar and the old man would pause. They would listen, thrilled by the call of the cat as he padded unchallenged through the night, and his panting grunts would silence their laughter for a while.

The days spent at the cottage in the swamps passed as quickly as the wingbeats of a sunbird. Then suddenly the two men had found it necessary to spend a great deal of time in Maun, and the small striped plane had bounced between the dusty village and the cottage like a ping-pong ball.

The silence of the swamps had been broken by the harsh crackling of the battery-operated radio. When Toni asked why they were spending so much time in Maun the explanation was: 'Fish owls, extra lighting, better film required.'

Toni had accepted it as part of the male reversion to small-boy excitement when involved in an interesting project. The photographing of her father's rare Pel's fishing owls and their chicks had kept James, Nick and the blue and white plane busy for days.

Toni treasured every moment spent with Nick, and she hoped that the photographic session would soon end. She wanted to spend as much time as possible with him before he left to attend the wildlife conference.

The use of pesticides such as DDT in aerial spraying was high on the agenda and Nick was one of the many men concerned with their indiscriminate use to eradicate the tsetse fly, whose stinging bite is fatal to cattle. The conservationists needed to keep the tsetse alive as it kept large areas free from cattle, protecting the grazing for the wild animals. But in African countries where a man's wealth is judged by the number of cattle he owns, they were finding it difficult to persuade the cattle owners to protect the buffalo, warthog and graceful kudu, who host the fly. Nick and James each in their separate fields had spent years trying to find a solution to the problem.

Toni had been delighted when Nick suggested that she and Timothy join him on a two-day trip with the Bushmen. He wanted to photograph the actual digging up of the *Diamphidia nigroornata*, one of the beetles whose larvae are used by the Bushmen to poison their arrows.

Now, seated on a rock beneath a green-barked poison grub commiphora tree, Toni dipped her fingers into the woody shell of a monkey apple and popped a fleshy brown segment of fruit into her mouth. She sucked at the sweet flesh and spat out the pip.

Licking her fingers, she imprinted the scene before her on her memory with the same urgency as a child who has to leave home and return to boarding school. She would be returning to the Cape in five days and even though Nick had given her the papers which finalised the divorce, she still had to collect her possessions, explain to Timothy that they were going to live with Helen for a while and that Nick would be his new daddy. She dreaded having to face Serge and clung to every smell and splash of colour in the bush with the desperation of one about to be committed to solitary confinement.

The two Bushmen were squatting on their heels, knees splayed wide, their skin loincloths tucked tightly between their legs. The holes they had dug in the soft earth with their pointed digging sticks contained them comfortably and their faces were wrinkled in concentration as they prodded the soil. Nick and Tim were kneeling side by side on the ground between the holes, watching every move the Bushmen made and conversing in whispers.

Tim had missed Nick when he and the old man flew to Maun for a few days, and on his return had followed at his heels like a well-trained pointer pup.

The nasal snort of a gemsbuck, the large desert antelope whose long straight horns gave rise to the fables about unicorns, alerted Toni and she looked up but saw no mulberry-coloured animal. It snorted again and, looking in the direction of the sound, she watched with fascination as the Bushmen blew softly through the nose and mouth each time they unearthed a round, hard flea-beetle cocoon.

She crossed to where Nick and Timothy were kneeling and gingerly touched one of the sand-encrusted cocoons.

Nick laughed. 'It's safe to touch the cocoon. It's only the body juices of the fleshy pupa in the cocoon which contain the deadly poison.'

Toni wiped her finger on her slacks.

'Why do they want the poison?' queried Tim.

'They use it to smear on their arrows when they hunt,' Nick answered, running his hand lovingly over the dark, curly head. 'They don't have guns and they have to stalk and run after the animals. As their arrows are so small it'd take days to kill anything, so they poison the arrows and then the animal dies quickly.'

Toni shivered. 'It's very poisonous, isn't it?' she asked.

'Kill a bull giraffe in thirty minutes,' he answered, 'and a man in less. They add plants to the juice from the pupae which cause local irritation and stimulate the heart. These all help the poison to move quickly through the animal's body.'

Toni nodded, keeping well away from the cocoons. 'I'm beginning to understand why you find insects so fascinating,' she said.

After a few hours' work the Bushmen checked the pile of cocoons, grunted, and stepped out of the holes and Timothy proudly held the penduline tit's nest as the Bushmen dropped the cocoons inside. They would be stored safely in the felted bird's nest until the poison was needed.

Thanking the men in Tswana, Nick said that they would eat before starting on the long journey home. The pointed faces broke into huge smiles at the prospect of roast meat. Before Toni had removed the springbuck steaks from the cold box, the older Bushman had taken out his fire sticks and twirled one rapidly between his calloused palms, starting a few wood shavings smoking.

The younger man shook out dozens of vividly coloured caterpillars which he had collected from the butterfly-leafed mopane trees and prepared to roast them, and Timothy stood close to him, ready to accept his share of the crisped mopane worms.

Watching the Bushmen and Timothy squatting in the freck-led shade of a terminalia tree, the silky leaves shimmering silver in the sun, the burgundy-winged fruits complementing the meat juices running down their forearms as they munched the steaks, listening to the delicate yet intricate melodies they plucked from their stringed *gwashis*, carved from the male mangetti tree, Toni felt the deep peace of Mother Gaia seep into her and for a short while she was able to commune with the great Mother of the Earth as easily as the Bushmen who live in such perfect harmony with her.

* * *

The wind lifted a corner of the priest's black cassock and he wriggled his bare toes in the open sandals, trying to dislodge the ants which were negotiating his toes.

'Do you, Nicholas Houghton, take this woman to be your lawful wedded wife, to have and to hold?' He intoned the beautiful marriage vows and the words rang out with the joy of church bells at Easter.

Standing close to Toni, her sun-tanned skin dappled in the shade of the kigelia trees, the port-wine flowers hanging like a canopy overhead, Nick inhaled the sweet, heavy fragrance of the waxy gardenia buds which starred her black curls and he felt such love and tenderness for the woman at his side that he choked and his words of acceptance were whispered.

He heard a soft scuffle in the sand and felt a small hand reach up and take his. Looking down, he saw his new son dressed in a white silk suit and black bow-tie standing proudly at his side.

Toni smiled, the handkerchief points of her chiffon skirt fluttering against her calves like white egret's wings, and as she curled her slim fingers around Nick's, they became a family in the eyes of God and man.

The deep rhythms of Africa floated across the swamps and the Tswana voices harmonised effortlessly in songs of joy and praise as Toni turned from the priest to face her friends.

She was still stunned by the speed and secrecy with which the wedding had been arranged. When they returned from their sojourn with the Bushmen the grass airstrip looked like an international airport. Red, yellow and green planes stood wingtip to wingtip lining the runway and as the Land-Rover jolted to a halt at the cottage, a large black figure, ruffled as a wet hen by the indignity of travelling in a machine 'which shakes the stomach like a Xhosa girl sifting meal, and which runs in the sky which is the home of spirits, not men,' came waddling to greet them. Timothy had shrieked, clambered over Toni like a soldier on an obstacle course and rushed into his beloved Izuba's arms. It had taken days to break Izuba's fear of flying and assure her that her family were capable of arranging the final details of Wisdom's funeral in her absence. Finally the thought of not being present at the wedding ceremony of her Child of God drove her to wedge her bulk into the small plane and endure the horrors of flying in the home of the ancestors.

Stunned by the appearance of Izuba, Toni had been speechless as Helen bumped Clive's wheelchair down the steps and David Anstey had enfolded her in a bear hug.

A friend of the old man's who ran a small mission near Ganzi was delighted to officiate at the wedding and had come to join the welcoming committee, a glass of port in his hand, his bald head shining in the lantern light. It had taken a great deal of talking to assure Toni that the wedding was indeed planned for the following day.

The logistics of arranging a wedding at a remote cottage in the Okavango swamps would have fazed Rommel organising supply lines for his troops in the western desert, but the old man and Nick had planned the occasion with the tactical skill of generals. James's fishing owls had provided a perfect cover for their activities.

Her friends, sworn to secrecy, had entered into the spirit of the occasion and, cancelling business appointments, had arrived in Maun laden with wedding gifts. Crates filled with champagne, salmon, pâtés and caviare arrived. An ox was roasting on the spit, carefully tended by the Tswana villagers, and all the old man's friends in Botswana had been invited to attend the wedding feast, catered for by a firm flown up from the Cape.

Like Alice in Wonderland, a bemused Toni was led through the maze of plans and details for the ceremony.

'Nick,' she had said in a small stunned voice, 'I thought that once everything had been settled with Serge, we'd slip away to the Register Office and be married very quietly.'

'My love,' he had answered, lifting her hand and stroking it gently, 'I never want you to be alone again. We'll return to the Cape and face Serge together. And . . . ' he continued, breaking into a huge smile, 'you can give your father no greater gift than to be married at the cottage. His old cronies have been lining up for invitations for weeks. He has been the most popular man in Maun, and the little town is spinning. He's having a marvellous time.'

Looking at her father, arms whirling, giving orders for crates to be unpacked and tables set up, and watching her friends running to obey, she had leaned over and kissed him. 'I don't deserve you,' she said softly.

The hours before the ceremony whipped by with the speed of a desert dust-storm and now, dazed with happiness, dressed in a mist of pale apricot chiffon, a gift from her couturier in the Cape, a diamond and pearl choker encircling her neck, a wedding gift from Nick, she squeezed her husband's hand and the gold wedding band pressed into her flesh. Her father was standing with his back to the guests, surreptitiously dabbing at his eyes with the back of his hand as she walked across to him.

'Dad,' she said softly, 'I love you and I don't know how to thank you for my wonderful wedding.'

Tears rolled down the old man's cheeks as he took her in his arms. 'You have, my Nuffy. You've brought a special man into our family and he's made you and my grandson happy. That's my thanks.' He kissed her on the tip of her nose. 'Let's join the wedding guests and make this a day to remember, my little Nuff.'

Toni laughed. 'Let's, Dad. I want to remember this day for ever.'

The day had been an enormous patchwork quilt of memories. Timothy, running to Izuba after the ceremony shouting, 'Zuba, Zuba, I've got a new daddy. Aren't I lucky? Zub, I've two daddies, a new one and an old daddy.'

'Little Intakumba, you are very lucky. Follow in the footprints of your new daddy and you will be a man.' She had forgiven Nick his lack of girth when she had seen how tender he was to her Child of God and her little flea, and when he held her plump hand in his and asked her to move to his home and continue to look after Toni and Timothy, her big heart had almost cracked with joy and he had been accepted.

Clive moving happily among the guests, his wheelchair squeaking in the sand, roaring with laughter at the old-timers' outrageous stories, slicing hunks of meat from the ox with the Tswanas, but always watching Helen, his eyes soft with love for the woman who had forced him to live.

Her father sitting on the wide wooden verandah feeding slivers of smoked salmon to Jasmine, whose snub nose quivered in anticipation as she delicately approved each slice. Old Jim earnestly explaining the words of the wedding ceremony to Timothy and then dancing a foot-thumping Xhosa war dance with Nick to the hysterical delight of Izuba and the Tswana villagers.

Nick's delight in his new son was evident. He swung Timothy squeaking high into the air, ruffled his hair and hugged the little boy, who stayed close at his side.

At the end of the magical day, she had memories, love and laughter to warm her in the coming years.

A golden moon had just crested the horizon, highlighting the leafless branches of the baobab squatting on the sand like a grotesquely fat old man, when Nick and Toni, arms entwined, walked quietly along the sandy path to the guest cottage nestling under the tree's contorted limbs. Toni made a habit of stroking the trunk when she walked past the tree, saddened by the Bushmen's legend that the trees were injured by porcupine quills when they were young and pain had distorted their limbs.

She bent to pick up one of the huge waxen flowers lying on

the silvered sand and straightened before her fingers touched the white petals. The San people believed that those who dared to pluck the flower of the baobab would be killed by lions, and so did she.

A faint smell of charred meat and smoke hung on the night air and the sobbing howl of a black-backed jackal investigating the odour rose and fell plaintively.

'Look at the moon, Nick,' she whispered, resting her hand on the swollen grey trunk and silently apologising to the tree for almost having picked up one of its flowers. 'Isn't it huge tonight?'

She stood dwarfed by the towering tree, tiny and ethereal as a watercolour of woodland fairies, her eyes dark and luminous in the moonlight.

Nick smiled. 'According to the wise old astronomer, Ptolemy of Alexandria, an object seen across filled space always appears to be further away, and any object which is further away will seem to be larger.' He kissed the top of her head, inhaling the lingering fragrance of the gardenias she had worn. 'That, my love, is why your rising moon looks enormous.'

Toni digested the 'apparent distance' theory in silence, drinking in the beauty of the night as she rested her cheek on his chest.

Tiny bats, pale as ghosts, flew over their heads and Toni instinctively covered her curls.

'Never let a bat fly near your head,' her grandmother had warned. 'Once they feel soft hair, they go mad and wind themselves into it to make a nest. Your head will have to be shaved because you can never untangle them.'

Nick smiled at her and kissed each hand in turn and they walked to the open door of the cottage. Scooping her easily into his arms, he carried her over the threshold.

The room was soft in the glow of an oil lamp and the light shone on the waxen petals of the cream frangipanis and white gardenias which were sprinkled over the sheets and lace pillows of the old wooden bed, like confetti on a bridal veil. A négligé, the ivory satin cobwebbed with delicate handmade lace, lay across the foot of the bed and Toni gasped in delight. Helen had kept the door locked all day and she had been forbidden even to peep through the windows.

'It's all so lovely, Nick.'

He bent down, drew back the voluminous folds of the mosquito net and placed her on the bed.

'Your friends made a bower of beauty for an exquisite woman,' he said huskily and sitting beside her, he eased away the wispy chiffon from her body and let it lie in a froth on the floor.

Their bodies had cried out for each other during the long nights since Nick's arrival at the cottage, but in deference to her father they had remained in their separate rooms like penitents in a monastery. Today they had been released from their celibacy and Nick was savouring the woman he desired so fiercely.

His hands caressed her silky skin and he traced the outlines of her body with his fingertips and filled them in with his lips, lingering over her slim hips and thighs. She reached down and ran her fingers softly through his hair, and as his mouth became more insistent, her thighs opened to him like the petals of a flower to the heat of the sun.

The flowers were crushed and bruised beneath their moving bodies, the perfume a heady aphrodisiac plunging them into repeated pleasure. Trembling, they lay at last in each other's arms, bodies joined, their faces close together breathing in the musk and warmth of their loving.

'I love you, Mrs Houghton,' murmured Nick, running his lips softly over her eyelids.

'I love you too,' she murmured, 'and I'll love you for ever.'

His arms tightened around her and they did not hear the high-pitched laugh of the hyena as it scavenged around the ashes of the fire with the jackal, or the enraged bellows when four thousand pounds of grey flesh exploded from the river and red jaws opened like cathedral gates as a bull hippopotamus sank its long curved tusks into the flesh of a young male who had dared to make overtures to one of his females.

Lost in the wonder of being together, they neither saw nor heard the beauty and terror of the African night.

* * *

The white hearse topped with black canvas lurched slowly past the tall eucalyptus trees, their fresh green leaves shading the crumbled gravestones and forgotten graves. It crawled down the long avenue, trailing a string of cars and double-decker buses, and at a flat open expanse of ground, devoid of trees and ridged like a mole colony with heaps of grey soil waiting to fill the empty holes, it stopped.

Wisdom's funeral had been delayed until the family in the Transkei had been officially notified of his death, until his mother, Beauty, her baby and family members had found sufficient money for the train fare, and Izuba had returned from Botswana.

But the old lady knew of her son's death long before the news reached them. His tree had been unable to hold up the drooping branches and it had collapsed in a tangled heap. She had waited in fear and silence for the news which she knew must come.

A church elder, his black suit-tails slapping his calves in the sharp wind, stood behind the hearse and, lifting his face, creased like black linen, to the heavens, he started to sing. The words and stirring melody were gathered up by the mourners as they streamed towards the open grave, and the burial ground exploded in an outpouring of longing and sorrow. The beauty and power of the voices prickled the hair on the back of Toni's neck and tears poured down her cheeks, dripping unnoticed on to her folded hands.

Justice, impassive in his dark suit, stepped out of the crowd of swaying bodies and opened the doors of the hearse, ready to lead his twin to the grave. Six men, neat in freshly pressed suits, slid the polished coffin from the car and, heads bowed and neck muscles corded with strain, they lifted the wooden box. They stumbled after Justice, down the tunnel formed by the singing mourners and over the heaps of loose sand. They placed the coffin on the white straps suspended over the oblong hole and stood back. Justice stared at Toni with dark, dead eyes as he lightly touched the coffin, and she shivered. The pathos of the soaring voices and the impassioned pleading of the prayers cradled the coffin as it lay waiting to be lowered into the suffocating darkness.

Umakuhlu and Izuba, checked blue and grey blankets

clutched around their shoulders, were crouched on the green nylon grass at the head of the coffin. Their faces were blank with despair and their bodies were doubled over with pain at their loss. They stared at the shining box with expressionless eyes, unable and unwilling to believe that their beloved Wisdom lay rigidly cushioned in the padded interior. They heard neither the prayers nor the hymns, and tears fed the floodplains of their cheeks.

Many miles away from the windswept cemetery a grey-haired woman was seated at a desk, resting her swollen ankles on an empty beer crate. She blotted at the salty drops which were blurring the ink figures on the ledger in front of her and, closing her eyes, she whispered a prayer for Wisdom and her heart ached for her black son.

The buttons of the preacher's waistcoat yielded and the seams of the long black coat were stretched as he threw his arms up to the heavens in fiery supplication. His voice was hoarse and cracked with emotion. Holding his well-thumbed bible to the skies he screamed out prayers and invocations as the coffin was taken from the sunshine and lowered slowly into the shadows.

The clear sweet singing of the women harmonised with the deep ringing voices of the men, and the singing intensified as the straps were shaken loose and pulled away from beneath the coffin and it settled heavily in the muddy water at the bottom of the pit.

Standing to the side of the grave with the singing women, Beauty peeped from beneath her lashes at a young man. He stood tall and arrogant, legs astride and arms folded, studying her, like a falcon watching a plump francolin. The young Comrade's family had been approached by Beauty's father and uncles and compensation had been demanded for the son she had borne.

The leader had come to the funeral with Joshua to show respect for Joshua's uncle and to see the girl whose face and body he only dimly remembered. There had been so many eager mouths and limbs ready to please the leader of the Shonalanga Comrades.

The young leader looked at Beauty, noting her good wide hips, the breasts thrusting against the white blouse, which had filled since motherhood, and the demurely lowered eyes, and he decided that he would pay the *lobola* for her. The Comrades had used their free time well and profitably. The young leader had proved to be an astute businessman in illegal deals, and meeting the bride price would be easy.

He glanced across at the coffin. The silver scrollwork flashed in the sun and flickered on the earthen walls of the grave as it was lowered. He then returned his gaze to Beauty. It was time to have a wife. She had produced a fine strong son and he would make certain that she continued to produce a steady flow of children, each one verifying his manhood. The decision reached, he let the ritual of interring the dead flow past him and concentrated on the physical pleasures in store when he would again impregnate Beauty.

The rhythm and words of the hymn became loud and joyous as the men, the elders and Wisdom's friends queued to wield the heavy shovels and fill the grave. Nick stood with his arm around Toni offering her silent comfort, and he marvelled once again at the ability of these people, steeped in lore and legend, to blend Christian and tribal beliefs.

Wisdom had been buried according to Christian rites; his body lay flat in a coffin, not seated in a hole in the earth. Yet the printed songs of praise had been put on top of the coffin and buried with him.

All who attended the funeral would return to Izuba's house where Wisdom had lived and ritually wash their hands, as death has a black aura and is believed to be contagious. Everyone associated with the funeral is affected and a person who does not cleanse himself is a danger to all. They would then eat the traditional cooked dry mealies and later all Wisdom's clothes and bedding would be washed and cleaned. The day after the funeral the 'waters would be drunk' by the ritual slaughter and consumption of a sheep.

Nick loved the people of Africa, and he had learned their languages and studied their many beliefs and customs as avidly as he pored over his insects. He admired the way the Xhosas used the solid traditions of the past to lead them through the maze of the present, and he felt a rush of affection for them as he watched the men beating and strengthening the sides of the grave with the backs of their spades, and the leader of the choir slapping his hymnbook against his thigh as he stamped in time to the music entrusting Wisdom to Umdali, the Creator.

Justice, heedless of the sand filtering into his shoes, twisted the heavy spade and smoothed the top of his brother's grave. He patted the soil gently with the steel blade, careful not to disturb the sand on the high sides.

'It has been done, my brother,' he whispered as the spade patterned the grave. 'The Boers who hunt the bearded ones are cunning. They are hard, skilled men.' He tapped the side of the grave as he marshalled his thoughts.

The note he had sent to the red-haired bull, le Roux, was untraceable. He had composed it of letters carefully cut from magazines and papers scrounged from wastepaper bins in police stations and law courts. The information it contained had fired Officer Stan le Roux's interest and soon he had the finest brains in the CID working on the case. Justice's inform-ant, a man in the police force to whom he had given free legal advice, told him how these men followed the meagre clues like hounds trained to detect and stay with the most ephemeral scents. They tracked the young bearded stranger to a modest township house. Then, cunning and patient as predators lying in ambush at a waterhole, they sat in surveillance, waiting for the older man.

They were certain that their quarry had masterminded many of the explosions and were responsible for the deaths of dozens of moderate men and women. Membership of a recently unbanned party would not save them from the process of the law.

The police had planned the operation with all the skill of a neurosurgeon removing a brain tumour. They were certain that their quarry were unaware of the investigation, yet the older stranger did not appear. They spent long days and sleepless nights trying to find him. Finally, tired of waiting, they apprehended the younger man as he sat at the dining-room table drafting a report which detailed the explosion of a bomb outside a municipal office.

'The younger one they have,' continued Justice. 'He will not break but will long many times for the oblivion of death.' He spoke quietly to his dead twin, certain that his shade was listening. 'The older one is clever. He has sought safety in

Botswana.' Justice paused and patted his pocket. 'But I have the ring of rope for him to wear, my brother. I have a second letter for the red-haired policeman. It will light their path to him.' He smiled coldly. 'When the strangers have ended their time with the police, I have others who will see that they do not live long. You have been avenged.' He clenched his fist in a power salute masked by the wooden handle and turned from the mound of earth.

The mourners left the graveside and like a huge wave they rolled over the desolate plain. Their full-throated singing exploded in the great surge of people.

Justice saw Joshua and called to him, but his voice was lost in the torrent of praise-giving and his nephew walked on with the young leader of the Comrades. Justice struggled to reach Joshua. There would soon be new strangers taking the place of the bearded ones and they would be as sharp-eyed as the Cape vulture after the arrest of their comrades. He did not want Joshua to be involved in anything which did not pertain to the ANC. Justice mistrusted the young leader of the Shonalanga Comrades. He had no proof, but he believed that, disillusioned by the negotiations between the ANC and the government, bored by the loss of clandestine meetings and missing the excitement of clashes with the police, the young man had turned to profiteering.

He did not want the new strangers' suspicions targeted at himself and his family because of Joshua's possible involvement with Beauty's lover and his illicit deals. He and Joshua had to be above suspicion.

He forced his way through the mourners and had almost broken free from the crowd when his foot caught on one of the splintered planks lying across an empty grave and he stumbled and fell. Pushing himself up on his hands and knees he peered into the dark hole and shuddered as he saw his face distorted and reflected in the pool of water at the bottom. As he stared into the muddy depths he saw the emaciated features of his twin, the large gentle eyes looked up at him beseechingly and he heard once again his brother's voice.

'Cannot the killing end?'

He knelt, afraid and mesmerised, until a pair of strong hands lifted him up and carefully dusted his dark suit.

'Come, Justice,' said Izuba's husband, looking into the young man's haunted eyes. 'I have brandy. It will be good for us to share the bottle.'

'Yes,' agreed Justice, abandoning his struggle to reach Joshua, 'it will be good.' And the two men stood close together as Abraham cracked the ring sealing the bottle top. They drank deeply.

Sunlight danced over the silvered plaque etched with Wisdom's name, and as Justice turned to look back at the deserted cemetery the dots of light sparkled and blinked like flashes from an Aldis lamp. A message sent by his dead twin. He stood staring at the cross, heedless of the pressure of Abraham's hand on his arm.

'Come, Justice,' hiccuped Abraham, screwing the cap on the now empty bottle. 'Let us go home.'

Justice peered at his uncle, trying to fuse the two wavering faces into one.

'First,' he answered slurring his words slightly, 'first I have an important message to deliver.'

'Justice,' cautioned Abraham, 'it is not wise for you to drive now. It is starting to rain. Come home with me.' Justice turned and walked with exaggerated care towards the grey fish-tails of his car.

'It will be done, my brother,' he muttered as he sat down heavily on the seat. 'The bearded ones will pay dearly for sending you to the land of the shades.'

Carefully he slid the envelope for Stan le Roux into the Filofax lying beside him.

Abraham watched Justice start the car, then turned and walked unsteadily to where Izuba was waiting. As the grave was blurred away by the windscreen wipers, Justice wove down the sandy road, impatient to drop the letter on the steps of Wynstaat Police Station and then seek oblivion in sleep which the brandy would bring.

17

THE short golden hair stood up straight as brush bristles on the crest running along the ridgeback's spine and soft growls rumbled from the back of his throat as he shook his head irritably, trying to dislodge the taffeta bow from his collar, but slender fingers tugged and twisted the shimmering blue ribbon and the huge bow was fixed firmly in place.

'Chops, you look beautiful. Please don't be so miserable,' said Toni, hugging the dog tightly. 'Now, lie down here and you'll be the first to greet them when they arrive.' She patted the carpet woven with leaping deer and mystical animals and persuaded the dog to lie on it.

A chocolate-brown kitten, slim as a wet weasel, stalked across the carpet, climbed up the dog's back, slid down his belly and nestled between his huge splayed front paws, purring contentedly.

Chops grunted and slurped his tongue across the kitten's face. It closed its eyes tightly, flattened its ears and crouched low, waiting for the wet caresses to end.

'Chops,' shouted Toni, 'stop it. You're making the kitten's bow wet and messy.' She knelt down to fluff out the pale pink bow tied around the Abyssinian's neck.

Nick had brought the kitten home tucked into the pocket of his tweed jacket, and it had looked like a tiny swamp rat as it nestled in the soft cashmere.

Chops had done a great deal of cautious sniffing, and the small mewing feline had been pushed around the room like a wheelbarrow, with his square black nose wedged under its hind legs, before he was convinced that the creature was a kitten and not to be killed. The kitten had soon learned to defend itself against the dog's clumsy overtures and its tiny claws ripping into his nose taught him to treat it gently.

Chops sighed and dropped his square jaw over the kitten's back, puzzled as to why he had to lie in the hallway but prepared to obey.

Toni tiptoed away, hoping that the animals would remain there until Nick arrived with Timothy. Timothy had only been with Serge for the long weekend, but it felt like a month and she was tense with excitement at the thought of seeing her son, holding him in her arms and hearing him laugh with delight as elephant kisses were blown down his neck. She glanced at her watch and ran up the carved stairway for a final peep into Timothy's room.

A small oak desk stood beneath the dormer window and his loved threadbare teddy sat in the chair pulled up in front of it. Toni leant against the door jamb and tried to visualise Timothy's face when he saw the replica of Nick's desk in his room.

They had spent a month in this gracious thatched home since their return from Botswana and every evening found Timothy perched on a cushion resting on the back of the carved wooden elephant beside Nick's desk, whilst Nick sorted through the mail. It had become a masculine time of togetherness and Toni, delighted with the bond of love and respect which had formed so swiftly between them, kept away from the study. Tim was fascinated with Nick and Nick never tired of having a curly head to ruffle at his side. The gift of a desk had been Nick's idea and Toni knew that her small boy would be ecstatic.

Helping Nick shrug his broad shoulders into the soft tweed jacket which mirrored the misty colour of his eyes, she had teased him. 'Timothy has only been away for three days and he has a new kitten and a new desk waiting for him. You're spoiling him.'

He had tugged her curls softly. 'He's my new son, the boy I've always longed for.' His eyes twinkled. 'One can't spoil gold. Only cheap metal tarnishes.' He had laughed and kissed her on the tip of her nose. 'I'm the luckiest of men, my love. Not only do I have you but I also have a son. Two for the price of one,' he teased, as he bounded down the stairs calling back over his shoulder, 'and his new father can't be late.'

He picked up his car keys from the hall table, snapped off a sprig of mauve heather from the bowl filled with proteas and ericas, and tucked it into his buttonhole. He opened the door, letting in a blustering gust of cold air. 'I love you,' he called and the door closed.

She had breathed a sigh of thanks as she walked down the stairs and rearranged the flowers. She had dreaded the thought of facing Serge when she collected Timothy. She was the catalyst to which Serge now reacted. Her presence increased his anger and damaged pride to maniacal proportions.

Nick, sensing her disquiet at the coming ordeal, had offered to fetch Timothy, and she had accepted with the alacrity of a child reaching out for a brightly wrapped present.

'A woman scorned burns with the furies of hell but a man scorned is the devil incarnate.' Her grandmother's words rang in her ears.

Her ex-husband was like the bitter aftertaste of quinine in her mouth. She could not rid herself of his face, and as she waited for Nick and Timothy she unwillingly relived her last meeting with Serge. His full upper lip had been wrinkled in a sneer as he threw the clothes she had unpacked from the cupboards into the muddy backyard. She heard again his contemptuous voice as she collected the soiled garments and bundled them into the boot of her car.

'That's right, grovel in the mud for them,' he said, lounging against the door, a half-smoked cigarette dangling in his fingers. 'It's where you belong, you whore.' And he watched with pleasure as she chased the wind-whipped dresses across the wet gravel.

His voice had followed her around the house, rasping her nerves and scraping her composure as she gathered small items she wished to keep. He followed her into Tim's bedroom and watched as she unhooked the Walt Disney figures from the wall.

'Take those,' he hissed. 'Soon they'll be all you have left to remind you of my son.' Toni's fingers whitened around the duck's plastic beak and she bit down on her lip.

Taunting and bellicose, he tried to goad her into retaliation, treading on her heels as he followed close behind her and blowing clouds of smoke into her face when she turned to

300

him, but the gold of her wedding band cut deeply into her clenched fingers, and the diamond sparkled with promises of a new life, and she had remained mute.

Determined not to brood, she shrugged off all thoughts of Serge and, restless in anticipation, she tiptoed down the stairs, careful not to disturb the dog and kitten asleep in their carefully arranged tableau in the hall. She walked into the sitting room, revelling in the honeyed smell of beeswax and the deep copper winter chrysanthemums, heaped in vases.

She plumped up the fat silk blue and lemon cushions and rearranged the folds in the heavy daffodil curtains. Pacing the beautiful room, she stopped to run her fingers gently over the petals of white camellias nestling in a bowl of dark leaves.

Then, unable to be alone, her ears straining for the low hum of Nick's green Jaguar, she sought comfort with Izuba in the kitchen.

'Miss Toni,' complained Izuba, her hands splayed across her wide hips, 'you walk around the kitchen in circles like an animal seeking a place to lie. It makes my head turn.'

Toni closed the doors of the refrigerator, licking the fresh mandarin ice-cream from her fingers.

'Izuba,' she laughed, 'I'm so happy that I should be dancing and singing and so should you.' She flung her arms around Izuba's ample waist and waltzed her around the kitchen.

'Stop, Ungumtukathixo, stop,' panted Izuba. 'I am an old woman with grandchildren and should not be hopping in the kitchen.' She smoothed her frilled apron over her sky-blue dress, breathing deeply, and her eyes sparkled like chips of black mica shot with silver. 'What would Mr Nick and Timothy think if they found me, an old woman, behaving like a young girl dancing joyously in the bridal party?'

Toni released Izuba and stood back, chuckling at her discomfiture. 'Mr Nick would say that I have to find a good sensible woman to look after the house and Timothy, not a silly young girl like you,' she teased. 'And Izuba, Tim wouldn't be fooled. He'd know that you're as happy as I am because he's coming home.'

'Miss Toni, there is a place in my heart which remains cold and empty when my little Intakumba is away. To feel the warmth of the sun I need to hear his feet on the stairs and hear his voice calling me.' Izuba smiled and Toni, unable to resist the warm wonderful grin which lit her face, hugged her hard. Together they peeped through the glass door of the oven, watching the potatoes crisp and brown and the duck turn golden.

Izuba stiffened as a car door slammed. 'They are here, Miss Toni,' she said, her white teeth flashing in an enormous smile. 'I have heard the car. My little Intakumba has come home.'

Toni whirled out of the kitchen like a woman at a summer sale, and Izuba, wiping her hands on a red-checked towel, heard her calling her son's name as she ran to the front door.

'Much joy has come to you with Mr Nick,' she said fondly, 'and you will reap more happiness for the good you have done.' And she stood in the middle of the pale wooden floor waiting for a dark-haired boy to hurtle into her arms.

'Stay, Chops,' commanded Toni, patting the dog's head, 'stay.' Reluctantly he lay on the carpet but his hind-quarters were raised and he quivered at the sound of approaching footsteps.

Toni waited until she heard the grating of shoes on the granite steps and she flung open the door with a wide smile. 'Welcome home, my— ' The words died and were whisked away by the wind.

Nick's jacket hung open and the rain glued his shirt to his body. He bounded up the steps, his eyes wild and hard.

The sleepy kitten, awakened by the cold draught from the open door, shot under the hall table and her slender body arched impossibly high as she hissed in terror.

Slamming the door he grabbed Toni's arm and swung her towards the telephone, unaware of how deeply his fingers were biting into her flesh.

'Le Roux,' he said. 'We need your friend Stan's private number. Quickly, my love, quickly.'

Seeing the fear and bewilderment in her huge dark eyes he released her arm and held her to him.

'It's Serge,' he explained. 'He's taken Timothy.'

He felt her tremble in his arms and he spoke quickly. 'They left a few hours ago with suitcases. He told his maid he'd contact her in a week's time.'

'Oh no,' whispered Toni brokenly. 'No.'

Nick stroked her soft curls.

'I used Serge's phone and called a friend of mine at the airport. The direct flight to London left an hour ago. They were booked on it.'

* * *

The cavalcade raced through the night, wet tyres splintering the streetlights reflected white and gold in the puddles.

Screaming sirens cleared a path from the Blue Route freeway to the Elizabeth Hospital, an outmoded Victorian building erected at a time when the pace of life was slower and events more predictable. The population in the surrounding suburbs had mushroomed, and as they streamed into the Lizzie she was hard pressed to cope with the thrusting, demanding horde. The staff battled desperately to repair the human flotsam which the tide of ambulances poured into their Casualty department.

A murmur of expectation, like eucalyptus leaves rubbing in the wind, swept through the crowd slouched outside the Casualty section of the Lizzie.

'Here comes one,' shouted a buxom woman, her brown face blotched and creased like a discarded paper bag. 'I told you we'd have some good ones tonight. A wet night's always a good night.'

She tugged the man's raincoat, once green, now stained and faded like a camouflage hunting jacket, over her shoulders as she strained forward to see the ambulance arrive.

'You said that last Friday and what did we get? Nothing, hey. The meat vans was as empty as your old man's pockets when you've been through them,' taunted a youth, a livid scar pegging the corner of his mouth to his cheek. The crowd chortled with laughter at this witticism, and her angry reply was lost in the roar of the ambulance as it reversed quickly towards the Casualty section, trying to reach the open doors before the crowd closed in, eager to see and comment on every bloody detail as the stretchers were rushed into the sanctuary of the hospital.

The yellow van was edged from its place in the motorcade by the crowd.

Stan le Roux's face darkened to an alarming shade of puce. 'Park right behind the ambulance,' he ordered.

'But, Stan, sir,' said Richard. 'These people.'

'Run over the bastards. Kill the bloody lot. I hate them all. Look at them hanging round the ambulance thick as ticks on a dog's backside.'

'Sir,' said Richard and, siren wailing, he closed his eyes and pressed down on the accelerator. The crowd scattered, and Stan smiled with satisfaction.

The van shuddered to a halt and he launched himself into the crowd. People moved aside, truculently muttering threats laced with obscenities as he elbowed his way through the steaming mass of bodies, the sour smell of poverty mingling with the raw rich fumes of the Cape wines.

He used his massive body to hold back the crowd as the ambumen slid the stretcher out of the ambulance and ran into the resuscitation room.

The people studied the unconscious child avidly as he was carried past, commenting on his thick dark hair and pale face.

Stan waited, arms outstretched, until a few minutes later the ambumen placed the stretcher back in the ambulance. The two men nodded their thanks to him.

'The child?' he queried.

'Don't know. The doctor's examining him now,' answered the senior man, and he turned to walk to the cab.

'Stop her,' he shouted. His partner swung his shoulder against the door of the ambulance but not quickly enough to prevent a young girl from pulling back one of the green, loosely woven blankets and scrutinising the fair-haired corpse.

'Bloody poor man's television, that's what this is,' Stan roared, licking raindrops off his moustache. He beckoned to Richard over the heads of the mob.

'Out of it,' the ambuman yelled at the girl, her face disfigured by the lack of front teeth, who was now trying to peer through the opaque windows. 'Go home. Have you nothing better to do than to gloat here?'

'No, massa, but I can do you, if you want, cheap and quick,' she retorted with a grin, her naked gums gleaming pinkly between the pointed incisors.

Many of the girls had their front teeth extracted to show the boys that they were prepared for fellatio. The custom offended him and he looked at her in disgust.

Misinterpreting the glance, the girl screeched with laughter. 'This one's hot to go.'

He turned away in embarrassment.

'It's all right, hey. The cops can't stop us any more. It's all for you,' she shouted at him as she pumped her hips suggestively.

The law preventing physical intercourse between black and white had been repealed, and once again nightclubs and street corners were throbbing market places for the sale and purchase of pleasure.

'If you're shy to do it in front of my friends, we can have one in the ambulance. Those two dead ones inside won't look.' She choked with glee at the look of repugnance on his face.

Stan looked at the ambuman and shook his head wearily. 'Load this crowd of vultures into the back of the van and dump them off on the Cape Flats,' he ordered, as Richard, panting and dishevelled, reached him. 'A two-hour walk home in the rain should dampen their enthusiasm for ogling the dead and dying.'

He wiped the back of his hand across his dripping nose. 'Find me in the waiting room when you get back. I'll get the details of the dead men and the child from the sister. Then we can break the news to the families on our way home.'

Stan watched as Richard nervously rounded up the mob. He then joined the ambuman and they walked into the hospital.

A pert, dark-haired sister, a worried frown creasing her forehead and grooving channels between her neatly plucked eyebrows, came quickly towards them. She scanned the hospital delivery voucher.

'I have two in the van who need to be certified dead, sister,' said the ambuman.

'Both doctors are busy now. But come,' she said. 'I'll have a quick look and then you can have a mug of tea whilst you wait for one of the doctors.' She turned to follow the ambuman, then paused. 'I'll have the details for you as soon as possible, officer,' she said to Stan.

Stan lounged against the long wooden counter in the waiting

room where an orderly was carefully filling in admission forms. The place could have been a macabre church; the hard benches placed at right angles to the counter were like pews, filled with a broken congregation, here to participate in a communion of blood and plasma.

The orderly looked up from his work regularly, checking that none of the penitents had collapsed, for on a busy night the less serious cases would sit in the waiting room for hours. The habitués knew this and feigned fainting spells, taxing the patience of the overworked staff.

Stan was tired. He had been up since daybreak, and now bitterly regretted the impulse which made him respond to the call for help at a car crash when he was off-duty and on his way home. He had spent over an hour in the driving rain helping the ambumeds, men who he believed could bring the dead back to life. Then he stood crucified and shivering in the middle of the freeway, halting the endless river of cars until the lights and sirens of the rescue vehicles faded.

It would be another hour or two before he could pour himself a stiff whisky and relax.

He smoothed down his wet moustache and studied the outpatients. In the front seat sat a woman who could be eighteen or eighty, a fragile collection of bones held together by a thin faded-cotton dress. Her pinched face was blotched like an old piece of purple tie-dyed silk. She was one of the walking dead. On patrol, Stan often picked up these meths drinkers. He had a sneaking sympathy for the outcast skeletons who poured methylated spirits through bread to remove the colour and then drank the white poison. Teetering between confusion and aggression until their brains and livers were destroyed, they were regular visitors to the Lizzie.

Stan picked up a paperclip, straightened it out and carefully picked at his teeth.

Suddenly he dropped the clip, fumbled in his pocket and pulled out the letter he had found in the Filofax in the old grey car at the crash. As he slit the envelope the retching sobs of a middle-aged man attracted his attention. 'What's wrong with that one?' he asked the orderly.

'He stabbed his best friend in the spinal column with a sharpened bicycle spoke – a new version of an epidural,' answered the orderly, wiping the blue blob off the tip of his pen with a sodden paper tissue. 'Now he's crying in case his friend dies. Says he loves him like a brother. Lucky for him he didn't love him like his mother or the Salt Hill mortuary would have another toe tag.'

Stan studied the man. 'Hell – a bike spoke,' he said and his flesh crawled.

'But why would he want to . . . ' The words trailed away as the doors of the waiting room were flung open and a group of five youngsters strutted in. Their black leather jackets were studded with silver stars and vividly painted sharks, and the pockets of their skin-tight jeans bulged with the killing accoutrements necessary for gang warfare. They were a menacing group haloed in evil.

'It's the Tiger Shark gang,' shrieked one of the women and, clutching her baby, tried to crawl under the bench.

Pandemonium broke out, and patients scattered. The orderly and staff fled through the swing doors into the treatment rooms. They knew that they were no match for the armed gangs, usually euphoric and fearless on White Pipe, the popular mixture of *dagga* and Mandrax.

The Tiger Sharks were hunting for a member of a rival gang who had been brought into the Lizzie earlier, virtually disembowelled. They were determined to finish a botched job.

'What in the bloody hell are you doing in this hospital?' Stan's voice cut through the screams of terror like the blade of a switch-knife. Silence was instant and deathly. The five stiffened and looked at the man in blue in consternation.

He strode towards them, his face reddening to the colour of his hair, and the group broke and ran for the door. Stan smiled as the clinking of their chains and jewellery faded in the distance.

The dark-haired sister returned as the last one pelted down the driveway. 'I wish you were here every night, Officer,' she said, handing him a sheaf of papers. 'It'd make life so much easier.'

'We'll try to have a man call in at least once a night on their rounds, sister,' he said, stepping carefully over pools of blood being mopped up by an old man. He took the papers and walked outside to wait for Richard.

He breathed in the wet night air gratefully, relieved to be away from the sour smell of pain and sickness. Folding up the letter with the papers, he decided to read them in the warmth of the car.

The police van screeched to a stop beside him, and as he eased himself into the van he watched the ambumen and a doctor climb out of the ambulance.

'Well,' he said to Richard, 'it's only two for the Salt Hill mortuary. Let's hope that bitch, death, doesn't get the kid and make it three out of three tonight.' He spat noisily out of the window. 'These bloody wet trousers are making me scratch like a hen on a compost heap,' he muttered. 'Let's read the papers and find the families.'

Stan read the letter slowly. The light was dull in the cab and he paused over the words stuck crudely on to the paper. Richard relaxed as he saw the flicker of a smile lift the edges of Stan's ginger moustache.

Stan grunted with satisfaction. The investigators would love this letter. They had believed that the younger man would succumb to their intensive questioning, but the training in Russia had been very good. Even the knowledge that he could spend a large part of his life in jail for masterminding the bombing of a government building which resulted in the death of a woman and her children had not lengthened his tongue and the information was minimal.

The instructions in this letter would lead them straight to the young man's superior in Botswana. The knowledge that his senior was in custody should breach the dam and the words would flow.

Richard coughed and Stan glanced up from the letter. Clever little bugger, he thought.

Richard had prophesied that the peace talks would not put an end to the sporadic violence. He insisted that negotiations, like a car with water in its petrol tank, would proceed in fits and starts and at times would come to a stop but, because there was no alternative transport, it would be coaxed along; and while the car was being urged to run, violence would continue, as intimidation was the African form of electioneering.

'Great stuff this,' he said to Richard as he tucked the letter back into his pocket. 'This'll make sure that they get him.

308

Now, let's see who the dead black guy is. Our letter writer.'

He smoothed the hospital papers over his knee and his smile vanished. Richard gulped and looked away, studying the raindrops playing across the windscreen.

Stan riffled quickly through the pages. He frowned and his bushy eyebrows met and quivered.

'Right,' he snapped. 'Balser's house. Wynberg Hill.'

As the van leapt forward Richard's face paled to the sickly yellow of stale cream and he stared ahead in disbelief. Stan could not possibly mean Toni Balser's home. When he had met her for the first time at the Shonalanga crèche she had reminded him of his first and only girlfriend, and he had spent long hours at the station shutting out the taunts from the men by dreaming about the day he would walk arm in arm along the mountain tops with a woman like Toni. A woman whose black curls would dance in the wind scented by the salty oceans. He was a young adult consumed by a schoolboy's crush, and as he drove he willed it to be some other Balser.

On the long drive from the Elizabeth Hospital, as the car wound through the dark forested woods of Wynberg Park, Stan's mind, like a Rubik cube, played with the names on the hospital forms and finally as they reached Serge Balser's house the facts clicked into place.

Stan wedged the dark blue cap firmly over his red hair and pulled the collar of his coat up high around his ears as he ran to the front door. Richard kept the engine running and watched Stan's arms windmill as he talked to the maid. Eventually he strode back to the van.

'Bloody hell,' he fumed as Richard backed out of the driveway. 'That made us look like a pair of idiots. Balser is away, and if we follow that fool maid's directions we'll drive round all night trying to find Toni Balser.'

Richard Dalton quailed beneath Stan's flashing eyes and his thin body shrank into his coat.

* * *

The doorbell rang loudly but Nick and Toni remained at the telephone, staring at the black receiver, willing Stan le Roux to answer their call.

309

The doorbell chimed a second time and the ridgeback growled ominously and stalked stiff-legged to stand beside his mistress. Toni put a restraining hand on his collar and the blue bow crushed beneath her fingers like the wing of a peacock's-tail butterfly.

Nicholas walked to the door, flung it open and stared at the young policeman standing dejectedly in the rain.

'Sir, I . . . ' he stuttered and suddenly his face brightened as he saw Toni. 'Mrs Balser,' he said. 'We've been looking for you for ages.' He turned and beckoned to the burly officer hunched up in the primrose van.

'Not Mrs Balser,' she answered. 'I've remarried and am now Mrs Nicholas Houghton.'

Richard scuffed his boots against the granite steps in embarrassment. 'Sorry, ma'am,' he muttered.

Toni squeezed his arm in sympathy and the blue raincoat was cold and wet beneath her fingers.

'Stan,' said Toni as she recognised the man lumbering towards her. 'I've been trying to phone you. Oh, Stan, we need your help so badly. Come inside.'

Stan licked the trickle of water which leaked from his ginger moustache like a faulty rainwater gutter and started to speak, but Nicholas interjected.

'Officer le Roux, Mr Balser has kidnapped my wife's son. We think he's trying to leave the country. He'll probably take Timothy to Switzerland. He must be stopped.'

'Please,' pleaded Toni. 'Please, Stan, help us.'

Richard gulped. Stan caught his eye and glared at him, silently commanding him not to gag, which he still did occasionally in unpleasant situations.

He coughed gruffly and the words sharp as fishbones lodged painfully in his throat. 'Mrs Houghton, Toni, there's been an accident on the Blue Route. Your husband's – ex-husband's Ferrari was involved in an accident.'

Toni stared at his mouth as it opened and closed, the wet ginger hairs lining the upper lip like the questing tentacles of a sea anemone, and her hand tightened on the ridgeback's collar. Sensing her fear, his growl deepened, and strings of saliva hung from his mouth as he curled his lips back. Stan, seeing her face pale and her blue eyes widen with realisation and pain, hurried on like a hangman eager to complete the execution. The roped words knotted in his mouth.

'Your husband . . . Mr Balser is dead.'

Looking into the hefty policeman's amber eyes Toni saw them swirl and change from yellow to the fathomless, frightening depths of black Africa and she heard again, like muffled drumbeats, Justice's voice as he invoked the ancient curses of his tribe.

'Someone you hold dear will be taken from you and you, too, will be left with only the empty darkness.'

'My son,' she whispered. 'My son.'

Toni heard Stan answer but the words were meaningless.

She closed her eyes and rested her head on Nick's shoulder, fighting hard to control the nausea and blackness which enveloped her.

'Kitten,' said Nick, frightened by her pallor and stillness. 'Kitten, we'll go to the hospital immediately.'

Stan cleared his throat. 'There is something else,' he said. 'Justice. Justice Mapei was the driver of the other car. He too is dead.'

A high, shrill wail cut across the hallway and they spun round to see Izuba slumped against the passage wall.

Tired of waiting for her little Intakumba to run into the kitchen and greet her, she had waddled out happily to find him.

'Izuba,' called Toni and ran to her maid and friend. 'I'm so sorry you had to hear of it like this.'

'Miss Toni,' she answered quietly. 'However news of death is carried it is never sweet. The stench of rot accompanies death, never the perfume of flowers.'

Nicholas joined Toni and together they seated Izuba on the old monks' bench in the hallway. Toni sat beside her friend and stroked her hand, running her fingers over the dark silky skin and smoothing the delicate pink palms.

Stan and Richard stood in silence, waiting.

'It is fitting,' said Izuba finally, as she rocked in soundless grief. 'The twins were joined at birth and are now together again in death. The shade of Wisdom will be joyful tonight when Justice is with him, once again to guide and strengthen

311

him.' She dabbed at her cheeks with her starched apron and smiled sadly at Toni and Nicholas.

'Child of God,' she said, 'it is time to go. Let us go to that big hospital and hear of little Intak— '

Her voice broke at the thought of Timothy, and helpless sobs shook her huge frame as she stumbled down the stairs behind Stan and Richard.

* * *

Toni stood in the white-tiled passage staring blindly at the nurses as they hurried past, their soft rubber-soled shoes squeaking on the ceramic floor.

She was deaf to the soft moans of the sick and dying as trolleys were wheeled from the treatment rooms and trundled to the wards.

She was oblivious of Nick standing at her side, helpless to ease either her fear or her pain.

Izuba sat stiff and upright on a chrome-legged chair, her eyes fixed unwaveringly on her Child of God. Only the shudders of suppressed sobs betrayed her agitation.

Stan twirled his blue cap round and round in his hands and stared out of the window into the rain-streaked blackness; and Richard, pale and miserable, looked down at his boots trying to bring them into focus.

The smell of disinfectant and ether was strong and the implacability of time enfolded and smothered them as they waited for the doctor.

A door, glossy in its coat of fresh white paint, creaked open in front of them and a gloved hand beckoned.

Toni felt cold sweat band her hairline and she swallowed hard to still the pounding of her heart as she followed the nurse into the room.

Timothy lay still, pale and small on the hospital bed, and as she looked at her son the sheets and pillows became the padded interior of a coffin and the doctor a white-coated undertaker.

'No,' she mouthed soundlessly. 'No.'

Nick put his arm around her waist as she moved towards the bed. She stretched out to touch her son's cold white cheek and as her fingers touched his skin she started. He was warm.

312

'Timothy,' she sobbed. 'Timothy, my baby,' and as her dark curls tickled his face he opened his eyes.

'Mummy,' he said, softly curling his finger around a lock of her hair. 'Mummy.'

'We have given your son a light sedative,' said the doctor, turning to Nick. 'He'll have a good night's sleep and will be fine tomorrow. He's a lovely little chap and certainly a very lucky one.'

Nick smiled at the medical man and turned back to the bed.

'Daddy,' said Timothy, holding Toni's collar tightly. 'Can we go home now, Daddy? Please?'

Nick looked up at the doctor who nodded. 'Yes, my son,' answered Nick, blinking back his tears. 'Yes.'

The flicker of a smile trembled on Timothy's lips as he saw Izuba and he reached up and put his arm around her neck, burying his head in her big warm bosom, and she crooned an old Xhosa lullaby to him as she cradled his head.

Toni held out her hand to Nick and pulled him close to her and Timothy. 'They chose Serge,' she whispered. 'He was the third death. The fates chose Serge and left me my son.' Her teeth still chattered with shock but she was dry-eyed.

'Justice was right,' she continued in a small flat voice. 'Serge was dear to me once and I'll always have the empty darkness of regret. Regret because I was afraid of him and regret because he died hating me.'

Nicholas knew how deeply Justice's curses had terrified her. 'It's over now, my love,' he said. 'It's all over,' and he buried his lips in her hair.

The door closed quietly. Only a faint squeak betrayed its opening.

Stan clumped down the passageway. He would tell Toni later that Justice had been a member of the ANC and had written the notes leading to the apprehension of the strangers; probably to avenge the murder of his twin. He was certain now that it was Wisdom who had warned Toni of the bomb at the crèche and he had almost certainly been killed because of the phone call.

The scene in the ward had broken through the defensive crust which shielded him from the horrors of his work. They were a wonderful family and Izuba was a dignified lady and he would make certain that the investigators treated her and her relatives well when they questioned them about Justice and Wisdom.

Richard peeped at Stan as they strode into the wind-torn darkness and he was certain that it was not only raindrops which beaded the rugged cop's eyelashes.